ELOM

E L O M

W ILLIAM H . D RINKARD

A T OM D OHERTY A SSOCIATES B OOK
N EW Y ORK

ELOM

Copyright © 2008 by William H. Drinkard

Book design by Spring Hoteling

A Tor Book
Published by Tom Doherty Associates, LLC
175 Fifth Avenue
New York, NY 10010

www.tor.com

Tor® is a registered trademark of Tom Doherty Associates, LLC.

Library of Congress Cataloging-in-Publication Data

Drinkard, William H.
  Elom / William H. Drinkard.—1st ed.
   p. cm
  "A Tom Doherty Associates Book."
  ISBN-13: 978-0-7653-1785-8
  ISBN-10: 0-7653-1785-0
 1. Prehistoric peoples—Fiction. I. Title.
  PS3604.R56E46 2008
  813'.6—dc22

                   2007047754

First Edition: March 2008

Printed in the United States of America

0   9   8   7   6   5   4   3   2   1

For my girls,
Genna, Casey, Marisa, Lil, Emmy, Sims, and Joleigh

ACKNOWLEDGMENTS

I owe more than I can ever say to my youngest daughter, Casey, who challenged me to write this book, and to my closest friend, John Ziegler, who read the first draft and pushed me to have it published. Special thanks go to Claire Eddy, my Tor editor and guiding light, who kept me on a straight and narrow path, and to her trusty assistant, Kristin Sevick. To Tom Doherty and Patrick Nielsen Hayden of Tor, who gave me advice and a chance, I am forever grateful. Thanks also go to my agent, Susan Ann Protter. Not to be forgotten is the encouragement of Charles and Sandy. And last, but not least, I thank Paula, without whose support—and collection of books on writing—this book could never have been written.

And to my childhood companions: Asimov, Heinlein, van Vogt, Bova, Clarke, Anderson, Niven, and countless others.

W.H.D.

ELOM

O N E

At first, the appearance of the blood had startled Geerna; now she smiled to herself as she thought about it. It had been the number of days spanning the time between the risings of two full moons since the crimson liquid first trickled down the inside of her leg—a signal of the onset of her womanhood. The Earth Mother had Touched her a second time with the Flowing of the Blood a moon cycle later; now, as she huddled in the Quary Hut, she felt the uncomfortable wetness of her third Flowing of the Blood.

Her mother, Zera, had assured her the great Earth Mother, Shetow, would soon give her the blessed sign. Even with her mother's promise, it still frightened Geerna when she first felt the warm, sticky liquid and lifted her deer-pelt skirt to see the bright red symbol of the Earth Mother's Touch. To her surprise, her first thought was of pride in being Touched by Shetow before Kara, her closest friend. Geerna smiled and then yelled her good news to Kara before darting off to find Zera, who was digging up fresh kasa roots with the other women of the tribe.

Geerna's boyish looks were deceiving; her body, as yet, did not divulge the curves another cycle of the seasons would bring. Zera had assured her that as a young girl she too had been "as thin as a lake-grass reed," and told her not to worry. Her mother's words comforted Geerna, for Zera's body had endured the birth of four children and her figure still rivaled that of an Earth Mother carving.

The front edge of a towering glacier filled the northern sky-line; the stories of the Teller of the Tell said it had always been so. In the summers, Geerna often looked at her own reflection in the still waters along the edges of the small pools created by the runoff from the melting ice. Her reflection revealed an elongated, ash-colored face with hollow eyes. The mangled locks of her profuse, ruddy brown hair overshadowed her thin young face. After seeing her reflection, she started pulling her hair together, allowing it to fall behind her back and spread out from a rawhide tie. As her hair cascaded down her back, it spread out as wide as her body when it reached her waist.

Geerna did not think of herself as young, even though the shape of her gangly body still betrayed the wonders of her gender. She had eagerly awaited the Earth Mother's Touch, fully aware of the perils of childbirth and the harshness of survival that often claimed the lives of girls soon after the commencement of their Flowing of the Blood. She knew her mother's longevity was un-usual. Geerna expelled a shallow breath and squeezed her eyes shut; *Blessed Shetow, Earth Mother, please grant me a life as long as my mother's.* Her eyes opened and blinked. Her life was about to change and she could not remember a time when she had not aided her mother's foraging for food to feed their family. Now she dreamed of her own children and the man who would be their father. Geerna winced; flashes of her own father's blood-splattered and battered body filled her mind. *Was it that long ago,* she thought? She realized his death, and the too frequent deaths of the tribe's hunters, exacted a levy as severe on the tribe as the toll taken by women during the ordeal of childbirth. Life was hard for the People, yet Geerna was thankful to the Earth Mother for her precarious existence. Geerna knew Shetow had cast her special; once again, the lines of her face tightened, her eyes focused, and she felt that somehow the great Earth Mother would ensure her survival.

The last two days had been the most exhilarating time of Geerna's brief life. Now she sat for a second night in the gloomy Quary Hut, where all young girls stayed for four days after they finished the first part of the Quary—the females' rite of passage ceremony. At dusk of the fourth day, and without the aid of any male, the adult females of the tribe would build a monstrous fire. Even a tiny twig added by a male toddler imitating his mother's actions would defile the ritual. Younger girls not yet Touched by Shetow were also forbidden from taking part in feeding the ceremonial flame. The ritual blaze would be lit from the tribe's Life Fire; a gift from Shetow, when She started a brush fire with a lightning bolt. Now, the tribe's Life Fire—their only source of fire—was a small, ever-burning flame nurtured and protected by the tribe's Medora. The circular stack of stones that would later restrain the Quary Fire lay a short distance from a collection of squatty domed yurts and lean-tos partly constructed from the bones and tusks of the mammoths the tribe depended on for many of its necessities.

The hastily built thin reed walls of the Quary Hut could not support the massive weight of a mammoth hide and were instead covered only by loosely woven grasses between the saplings. However, the Quary Hut was not meant to keep the biting wind from reaching its occupant; rather, it gave the young female a place to meditate and prepare herself for assuming her new role in the life of the tribe. The Quary Hut signified the Womb of Shetow, the Great Earth Mother, and time in the hut offered an opportunity for reflection and growth. In two days, Geerna would step from the Quary Hut a grown woman, and after the Ritual of the Washing, ready to pair with a male and strengthen the tribe by bearing children.

Geerna had much to think about during her forced, but welcomed, incarceration in the frigid confines of the Quary Hut. After the days of snow, the flowers would bloom and then would be her Pairing with Yugadi, a young hunter of the Black Bear Tribe. Zera said Yugadi would be a good protector and provider for Geerna's future children. After his and Geerna's Pairing Ceremony, by custom, he would leave his tribe to join hers. She had never spoken to Yugadi but she had seen him at a distance each spring when all the tribes along the Silver River gathered to celebrate the Renewal of Life and dance in the jubilation of surviving another winter. She twisted a lock of her long, tangled hair around her little finger as she remembered the last Gathering when her mother, face glowing, crept into their hastily constructed lean-to to tell Geerna she had arranged Geerna's Pairing with Yugadi. Geerna smiled at the thought of her mother's giggles and bouncing breasts as Zera recounted the haggling with Yugadi's mother before she once again drifted into the story about her own arranged Pairing with Geerna's father many Gatherings earlier. Geerna forced back a grin as she thought of the upcoming event—days and nights of dancing, the gyrating movements of tightly packed people matching the thundering rhythm from hollow-log drums seeking Shetow's blessing for the new Cycle of Life and for those Pairing at the Gathering. For a brief moment, she wondered why men danced in one group and the women in another, and then grimaced as she remembered females were chosen by Shetow to be the instruments of Her gift of life to the People; females were special. Geerna fought back leaking tears; she knew the dancing to the Mother of Life brought the power of Shetow to the People; the dancing made sure the People never forgot that only with Shetow's blessing could life continue—and then only through the wonders of the female body.

In an effort to shake off the relentless chill, Geerna concentrated on the warm memory of her mother's milky voice. She closed her tear-swollen eyes as the remembrance of Zera's hypnotic murmur brought calmness and clarity to her jumbled thoughts. Zera had instructed her eldest daughter on the wonders of Shetow's world and the cycles Shetow used to govern over Her dominion— some cycles large, others small. Zera spoke of the journey of the seasons as a large cycle—from warm to cold, then cold to warm. In this cycle was the birthing of the herding animals: first, the great white snow elk, followed by the more abundant prairie buck. Zera had noted that even the cave lion bore her cubs the same time each year. With reverence, Geerna's mother often spoke of how only the birthing of the People's children and the calves of the mammoths moved outside this seasonal cycle. This she said was proof of the lofty position in which the Earth Mother held the People and the mighty mammoths. Geerna pulled her covering tight around her shoulders as she reflected on the Cycles of Life; events, Zera told her, that were especially important to the women. To signal a coming birth, Shetow broke a woman's cycle of the Flowing of the Blood. Although being Touched by Shetow meant womanhood, suspension of the Flowing of the Blood was a sure sign of the coming of a child. Geerna lifted her Quary Mask to rub her dried lips, which resembled half-healed scars blemishing the ashen skin of her taut face. She nodded unconsciously; she knew Shetow had made her and the rest of the People special; unlike the animals, the People's young could be born any season during the Great Cycle of Seasons. Instead, Shetow had given them this special sign to let the people know when they could expect the birth of a child. With quivering lips, Geerna forced a smile. Zera had said Shetow would give her the sign soon after her Pairing with Yugadi.

Eerie shadows cast by the moonlight invaded the solitude of the hut. Geerna could hear the night sounds, which fell on her attentive ears like sweet music. Each sound generated memories of her childhood; a childhood she was now preparing to leave. She reached for an upturned tortoise shell for a drink of water; a fragile film of ice covered the liquid's surface. Her mother had carefully cleaned and then bleached the shell in the sunlight to give her daughter a container to hold the water. The water Zera brought each day to refill the tortoise shell was the only sustenance Geerna could receive during her time in the Quary Hut. The Medora told Geerna the fasting cleared both the body and mind; however, nagging hunger was a regular companion to Geerna and the other members of the tribe. She pulled her arms close to her chest and pressed her hands against her flat belly; the growl in her stomach was no stranger. She bit her lower lip and spoke a few words of praise and thanks to Shetow; it was the hard times that made the spring Gatherings and the Renewal of Life celebrations so joyful.

The Medora had placed a woolly rhinoceros hide in the Quary Hut so Geerna's naked body could endure the relentless assault of the frigid night air. Geerna began to shiver uncontrollably and buried her head under the hide to warm herself. The thick hide was stiff, having been salted down and scraped but not tanned; its pervasive odor forced her to stick her nose past its gathered edges to breathe. The ocher mud the women smeared over her body at the end of the first day of the Quary ritual dried during her first night in the hut. She ran her right hand down her left arm, feeling the scaly texture of her crusty covering, which felt like the knurly bark of the ropper tree. While giving her a sense of comfort, the unfamiliar layer also awed her. The rough casing coated her entire body; Geerna felt she possessed a second skin—an additional layer of protection against the hardness and dangers faced daily by the members of the tribe. Heavy tentacles of matted hair and mud hung from her head. A Quary Mask was her only clothing and that was purely ornamental. The headdress consisted of a rawhide string circling her head with fur-covered strips of hides from seven different female animals hanging from the portion of the rawhide covering her forehead. The strips hanging from the Quary Mask obscured her face and blended with the mud-hair ropes dangling from her scalp. She would remove her mask after her pairing but would keep her hair rolled in mud-caked ropes for all the cycles of the seasons Shetow blessed her with the Flowing of the Blood.

The mud's earthy stench again prompted Geerna to remember the chants the women of the tribe had sung during the first night of her ceremony: the Tell of Shetow—the Earth Mother, giver of life, and ultimate source of all sustenance. Geerna's astute and nimble mind raced as she watched the moisture from her breath freeze on the coarse hairs of her rhinoceros-hide blanket. Her body made a sudden, unexpected jerk; she would soon be a vessel holding a life the Earth Mother would place in her belly. A sense of belonging filled her heart and for the first time the true power and meaning of the Quary Ceremony became clear to her. The tribe's women— like their mothers before them—used the Quary to ensure the new female members joining their group understood their new place in the life of the tribe.

Her breathing slowed. Geerna knew the order of the ritual by heart. At dusk of the fourth day, five women from the tribe would come and lead her to the Quary Fire. She closed her eyes and tried to envision how she would feel when, for the first time during the ceremony, she would stand nude before all the gathered members of the tribe—male and female, young and old. The hypnotic drone of the Teller's Tell of the Quary resonated in her mind. Geerna could almost see the tribe's Medora, aided by the four oldest women in the tribe, lifting a large conch shell and pouring water from the Silver River over her shoulders. As the sheets of cold liquid flowed down her shivering body, the caked earth would once again turn into grimy mud before sliding from her body. Geerna recalled the Quary Ceremonies she had attended as a child; as the mud washed off, a slick coat of dark red blood would appear as another layer, beneath the mud, completely covering the young female's body. During the first day of the ceremony she had learned about the Taking of the Blood, blood given by each adult female in the tribe, squeezed from tiny cuts made with a ceremonial flint flake, and collected in a seashell from the distant shore of the Unending Waters at the mouth of the Silver River. Geerna drew in and let out a deep breath; washing the blood off, she knew, represented a human rebirth; washing the mud off—Shetow's own substance—would represent Geerna's birth as one of the Earth Mother's own.

Geerna began to rock her body in an effort to stave off the creeping numbness slowly spreading over her. Like countless times before this moment, she tried to blot out the growing pain by focusing on the events that would culminate in the most important moments in her life. Encircling Geerna's Ritual of the Washing, the balance of the tribe's womanhood would chant and rock side-to-side as they watched the timeless ritual. Geerna knew the chanting and dancing were as important as the washing, for it made Shetow take notice of the great event—Shetow would know Geerna had joined the ranks of Her chosen. Geerna remembered the mystery in her mother's look as she explained how each of the Medora's exaggerated movements represented an indispensable part of the rite—motions depicting the ordeal and splendor of birth and life. The washing would strip off the fusion of mud and blood leaving her naked before the tribe—people she had known all her life. Geerna blushed at the thought; it would be the last time any male, besides her Pairing Partner, would ever see her completely nude. She thought of her wifyur, the short-reed waist apron worn by all mature females, that her mother had finished crafting the day before the tribe's Medora came for her. The People wore little clothing to ward away the chill of winter, but females, after their Quary Ceremony, always wore this sign of their devotion to the Earth Mother. Geerna brushed the tips of her fingers against the tender skin along her neck and arms. At the end of the washing, the last layer, her bare skin, would display a change since the time three days earlier when the male and young female members of the tribe had seen the Medora take her by the hand and lead her to the congregation of awaiting females. Now across her face and down her shoulders were tattooed rows of black dots, a sign of her womanhood and fertility, and in the eyes of the tribe, she knew, an enhancement of her female beauty.

Geerna opened her left hand. There lay the small ivory carving of the Earth Mother given to her during the first night of the ceremony. The figurine was crude, but to Geerna it was the most beautiful thing she had ever seen. The carving plainly depicted a pregnant woman with enlarged breasts and a protruding belly out of proportion with the rest of the body; her hands and feet were small, almost indistinguishable. Geerna realized the carving had taken the Medora, using only brittle flint flakes, many days to fashion. This ivory symbol of Shetow would always be her most precious possession. All the other girls she knew received woodcarvings of Shetow. Geerna smiled; the ivory carving confirmed it. For the Medora to take such pains for Geerna's Quary Ceremony verified what many in the tribe had been whispering, that she was to become the aging Medora's apprentice. The thought of it brought as much excitement to her fluttering heart as her thoughts of Pairing with Yugadi. For the next few cycles of the seasons she would be trained in the ways of the Sisterhood of the Medoras—the guardians of the Truth of the Great Earth Mother and protectors of the tribes' Life Fires.

As the moon rose to take command of the heavens, the music of the night softened. Moonbeam shadows slowly altered as the moon crept across the star-packed sky. Geerna had never been alone, not like this. She became a little fearful. *Not the response of a girl about to become a woman*, Geerna thought to herself. She bit her lower lip as she concentrated on the events of two days ago. It was a night that would, she knew, always stay fresh in her mind—the beginning of her womanhood, the night she learned the mysteries of the Great Earth Mother. She knew she was blessed; the Earth Mother had touched her inner spirit; she could feel the change deep inside.

Without any warning, her concentration was broken. For a moment, she felt disoriented; a hint of vertigo made her place a hand on the ground to keep from falling over. Then a warm, yet somehow silent breeze blew through the hut.

No, she thought, it was not because the wind was still; there was no sound. The stillness confused her. Was this another part of the Quary? Who among the People could cause such a thing to happen? It must be a sign from Shetow, yet she had never heard of anything like this from the women of the tribe, not even a whisper. She remembered the Teller of the Tell once spoke about a time when Shetow took one of the chosen to be with Her, to help look after the People—but the Tell said that had occurred many Tellers in the past.

Suddenly, the night sky became more brilliant than the noonday sun. The unexpected change in illumination hurt her eyes. Squinting, she looked through a distortion of tears, trying to see what was happening. The hut started to shake violently. She knew the flimsy reed walls could not endure such punishment; Geerna sensed the hut was about to collapse. She fought back her rising fear and tried to control the pounding in her chest. As the hut crumbled around her, she stepped through a breach in the buckling reed wall. Instantly an even brighter light focused on her. The dazzling light brought waves of comforting warmth. She felt herself begin to float and rise from the ground as the woolly rhinoceros hide slid from her shoulders. Blinking back the tears and controlling her fear, Geerna looked into the brightest part of the light—the point to which she was being drawn. The light lost a sliver of intensity as the resonance of an oscillating hum increased.

Out of the confusion, her mind cleared. She was to join Shetow. She was truly a chosen one. With the ivory figurine tightly clutched in her fist, her crossed arms pulled tightly to her chest, Geerna disappeared into the effervescent glow.

TWO

"But if you are correct . . . that could mean the destruction of Elom . . . the end of the People," Nomee exclaimed.

"Geerna tells us in the mnemonic verses of the Shetow-ka this time would come," the old woman responded as she settled back in a rickety chair at the short side of a triangular wooden table. "The drak's announcement of the impending Second Judging is unexpected." She bit her lower lip. "We are surprised only because we became complacent; we relaxed our vigil." The old woman shook her head. "None of us thought the prophecy would be fulfilled in our lifetime."

"Berkana, what are we to do?" Ura, a younger, but still silver-haired woman asked.

"We will do." Berkana cast a stern gaze to muzzle the rumble in the room. After a few last whispers, the other women yielded to the old woman's glare. "We must make ready," she said in a softer, more deliberate tone, "for what we and our predecessors have been preparing for all this time. We must find the best among us and pray they are good enough. That their Traits are strong and their wits sharp." She brushed a strand of white hair from her face. "The fate of our people rests with our selections." The twenty-four women in the gray domed chamber found their places at the hand-hewn table that had served them and their predecessors for ages untold. The women were clothed in the same bluish gray robes they wore when not performing their ceremonial duties. One was young, many were middle-aged, a few were very old; all but three had a spark in their eyes and resolve in their voices.

"The People know nothing of Shetow's Second Judging," Bolanna, the youngest member of the group said, her voice falter-ing. "This will cause panic; Geerna was wrong to yield to the Mul-tiped's insistence on keeping it from them." Her shallow eyes added to the ghostly look of her gaunt face.

A white-haired woman to Berkana's right rose slowly. "Ma-dora Roo, may I?" The woman nodded towards Berkana, who re-turned the nod. She scanned the faces of the other Medoras but her eyes finally settled on their youngest. "Geerna's Sacred Words have guided us and the people through six Progressions, since the beginning of the Tell—the time when Shetow brought our ances-tors to this planet. To the Medoras, Geerna gave the Shetow-ka telling us of our home world, of the events that transpired after she and the others were brought to Elom, also of the Multiped and of the prophecy of the Second Judging." She placed a hand against her chest. "To us, the Medora Council, Geerna entrusted this se-cret." The woman ran the fingers of her left hand through her thin hair. "Geerna knew, with time, the Tell of our ancestors being brought to Elom would grow dim in their minds. Now, six Pro-gressions later, it's only a folktale."

"But Verna," Bolanna insisted, "Geerna and the Multiped should have included the prophecy in the Chants of the Sequa; it would make our task much easier."

Berkana rose to stand by Verna. "The burden of knowing of a coming Second Judging had to stay in the esoteric verses of the Shetow-ka, with the Medoras." She looked down a moment and unconsciously shook her head. "Sisters," she said as she lifted her face, "moments ago we discussed the fact that we thought the Second Judging would not happen in our lifetime. We twenty-four who have spent our lives reciting the Sacred Verses of the Shetow-ka, we who have—from the beginning of the Tell—been spared the force of the Mark of the Covenant's Inhibitors, have faltered and faltered badly." Again, the Medora Roo shook her head. "The People, distracted by the force of the Inhibitors and listening to the campfire stories cycle after cycle of the seasons, dismiss the story of Earth as a fable. And I fear part of that is our fault."

"Do you know who they are . . . I mean the ones who will represent the People?" Nomee asked.

"No . . . no, I do not know who we will choose. The Shetow-ka says the selection of those who will represent the People rests with us on the Medora Council; I only know we must pick our best." Her shrewd eyes narrowed. "Perhaps we should use the special gift Shetow blest the People with after the last Progression to help us choose. Surely, Shetow would not have given it to them unless She meant for us to use it."

"Berkana," said Reva, a red-haired woman whose face had lost its color. "Many of us have not recited the verses of the prophecy since we were novices." The woman searched the faces of the other women at the table, her frightened eyes begging for support. She lowered her eyes. "Why, when we least expect it?" she mumbled to herself. She lifted her waxen face, her distracted gaze finally focused on Berkana. "Why now, Medora Roo?"

"Moments of decision often happen when we least expect them. At least the Shetow-ka tells us the Multiped told Geerna the Second Judging would not occur before the People were ready." Berkana's eyes wandered for a moment before her attention returned to those at the table. Her face was drawn; her lower lip quivered. "Shetow must think us ready or She would not have demanded that the Second Judging take place now." Berkana felt an invisible pair of hands press against the top of her shoulders. *You must not show them the turmoil raging in your mind*, she thought; *you must not vacillate.* She took a deep breath.

"Four cycles of seasons ago, you elected me the leader of the council, your Medora Roo. The weight of your selection has never felt heavier, but I realize that you all feel the burden of this revelation." She took a labored breath.

"The Shetow-ka tells us the People were judged during the life of Geerna, before the First Progression, at the beginning of the Tell . . . at that Judging the People did not find favor in the eyes of Shetow. Geerna, our first Medora Roo, made a Covenant, through the Multiped, with Shetow so the People could have another chance, a Second Judging. After the conception of Geerna and Shetow's Covenant, came our Sacred Mark followed by the First Progression."

"But, Berkana," Tavanor said, "Geerna met with the Multiped, Shetow's emissary, countless cycles of the seasons ago. I thought . . ." Tavanor took a side-glance at the red-haired Reva. "Well . . . I thought the Second Judging . . ." her voice fell to a whisper ". . . was many Progressions in the future."

"You are not alone," Berkana said. "The Tell of the Medoras says our predecessors suggest that very idea. By the Second Progression, many in the Council felt the iminent danger to the people had passed, believing the Second Judging would not happen in their Progression. As the relentless cycles of the seasons went by, the fear of a Second Judging faded. Our sisters believed if the People joined them in chanting the Sequa and following the laws it gave us, then everything would be all right. However, they . . . we . . . were wrong. The Second Judging is not something in our future—we must face it now."

"The Shetow-ka does not tell us why the People did not find favor in Shetow's eyes," persisted Ura, her voice cracking as tears began streaming down her cheeks.

Berkana turned towards the troubled Medora. "No, it does not, but Geerna, through the verses of the Shetow-ka, and Geerna and the Multiped through the Chants of the Sequa, have guided us in preparing the People for a Second Judging. You . . . most of us"—Berkana moved her hands, indicating those in the room—"like many of our sisters before us, stopped worrying about the prophecy." She shifted her body to sit straighter. "But, by Shetow's Grace"—her voice grew stronger—"and even though we lost sight of the purpose for our sovereignty, the Medora Council continued to govern the people as the Shetow-ka instructed. I believe that is what matters; that we ruled by the edicts given us in the Sacred Words of the Shetow-ka. We made sure the People followed the laws Geerna and the Multiped gave us in the Chants of the Sequa; we have accomplished our charge. We kept the People's part of Geerna's Covenant with Shetow. By allowing the People a Second Judging, Shetow is now keeping Her part of the Covenant."

Verna smiled. "With the help of the Multiped, Geerna first composed the Chants of the Sequa to soothe the people; to calm them after the trauma of being plucked from Earth and then stranded on Elom. During the First Progression, when the force of the Inhibitors was the strongest, the People recited the Sequa, along with the Tell, around the campfires. At first, it held great sway with them. The need for soothing faded by the beginning of the Second Progression; now, four Progressions later only the laws in the Sequa are of any consequence to them."

Most of the women around the table nodded.

"Medora Roo, tell us again what the drak told you," Tavanor pleaded.

Berkana's eyes cleared as she refocused her attention on those around her. "Yesterday, after the Pairing, it . . . the drak, asked to speak to me. I, of course, agreed. We came here to the Council Chambers. No sooner had we entered the room, when the drak said, 'the time for the Second Judging is near, prepare your best.' I was stunned. I was only able to ask one question as the drak turned to leave the room." No one moved; their eyes fixed on her. "I asked if the Second Judging would be before the next Gathering. The drak answered no, but said it would take place soon after that." The Medoras were silent. Berkana slowly lowered herself back into her chair.

"Could you read anything in the drak's expression?" Reva asked after a short silence.

Berkana's troubled eyes darted to her inquisitor. The Medora Roo showed no emotion; then her stern face melted into her first smile of the night. "I can read the expressions of a scaly fish better than I can read the feathered face of a drak." Nervous chuckles echoed off the chamber's walls.

"As we have been discussing, sisters," Verna said after the laughter subsided, "no one outside the Council has ever known about that part of the Covenant covered by the Shetow-ka fore-telling the Second Judging, and the Inhibitors from the Mark of the Covenant have kept the People's curiosity and rebellion under control." She raised her eyebrows. "It may be prudent for us to keep this knowledge to ourselves. Geerna, through the Shetow-ka, prepared us and our predecessors for this day." Her shoulders dropped slightly. "We can only trust that Geerna and the Multiped, through the Tell and the Sequa, also prepared those who we will select as our representatives for the final judging." Verna looked towards Berkana and then made a short bow before sitting down.

The Medora Roo pursed her lips as she gripped the back of her chair and again pulled her aging body erect. "The Shetow-ka prophesized the Second Judging would occur during the days of the

Prime Progression. We are now many cycles of the seasons into the Sixth Progression, which now appears to be the Prime Progression. The Shetow-ka also tells us that in the later stages of the Prime Progression the effect of the Mark of the Covenant's Inhibitors would diminish."

"That would explain," Ura blurted, "why many of the People, especially the males, are so unsettled, almost rebellious."

"I thought," Reva said, her eyes welling with emotion, "that was a natural consequence of the cultural changes since the last Progression."

"Each Progression," Berkana said, "brought greater and greater sophistication to our culture; enormous leaps towards, it appears, the mental skills needed to face the Second Judging."

"Perhaps," Verna said, "it was Geerna and the Multiped's plan—with Shetow's blessings—for the Second Judging to take place before the order and stability provided by the laws of the Sequa totally collapsed." She moved a hand in front of her face as if shooing away an invisible insect. "Geerna and the Multiped must have foreseen the time would come when, even with the Inhibitors, the men and women would not be pacified with hunting and creating art."

"Should we contact the others?" Verna asked, after a moment of silence, her eyes questioning.

"I have already released a messenger pigeon; they should contact us before the completion of another cycle of the seasons." Then Berkana's brow furrowed as she grasped the ivory carving hanging from a rawhide strip that encircled her neck. "Geerna knew this day would come. We cannot fail her or those she left in our charge." Her eyes moved slowly around the table as she studied each woman in turn. *Brave women all, even those who show trepidation*, she thought. If she must decide those who would face the Second Judging, she knew she could not have picked a better group to help her. "We have one cycle of the seasons to select the ones who will represent us. The Council will meet every fifty days, as is customary. Before this council meeting is adjourned, we must develop a plan using our special Trait to select our representatives for the Judging; then, at the end of the next Gathering we will be ready to inform those selected." Again, she struggled to her feet. "Now, with the Grace of Shetow's Mark of the Covenant"—she lifted her left arm, revealing a purple circular mark on the inside of her wrist—"may we only choose those worthy of this vital task."

"Blessed be the Mark of the Covenant," the other women responded in unison as they raised their arms, revealing identical symbols.

THREE

Death was his only alternative. He was as prepared as anybody who had ever made the hunt, for only one in three men survived the encounter. By embarking on the hunt, Kalmar had committed to kill a cat or die in the effort. He had vowed, to himself, long ago, to one day face a cave lion. The skills learned under the Gray Beards' tutelage from the day he was pulled from his mother's nipple were about to be tested. In his excitement, he unconsciously bit his lower lip, causing blood to ooze into his mouth. With his attention focused on every movement and sound around him, the taste of the salty sweet fluid went unnoticed. What fate awaited him, only Shetow knew. Whatever his destiny, he longed for the serenity that either his death or the death of the great cat would bring him.

When Kalmar first sensed the cave lion's presence, Salune stood high in the warm noon sky. Now the sun would soon set; the coming of the twilight-of-night would force him to break off the hunt until the next morning. A bead of sweat rolled down his temple; Kalmar could sense the cat's presence. He did not realize, however, that the cave lion also sensed Kalmar's presence and was now stalking him.

The cave lion was the largest of the great cats, and with its curved daggerlike fangs and paws tipped with finger-length claws, was the deadliest predator in the valley. An adult male's weight easily equaled that of any three of the tribe's largest and strongest hunters, and as Kalmar crawled along the foot of the cliff in an effort to stay upwind of his prey, he knew he trailed a young male. That morning he found the carcass of a young doe killed and partially eaten by a lone cat. Kalmar knew that female cats always hunted in packs and provided all the meat for themselves, their cubs, and the dominant male of the pride. The cat that caught the doe, Kalmar concluded from the skills learned from the Gray Beards, must be a young nomadic male waiting his chance to challenge an aging dominant male to head a pride. Both hunter and prey were young and Kalmar's only hope of winning the life-and-death contest rested with his intuitiveness and skill with a bow. All the cat's senses, other than one, were superior to his, and those advantages multiplied if Kalmar permitted the confusion of the night's twilight to fall before he was able to take his shot.

Only the bravest hunted the cave lion alone. His Medora said it was not being brave, for only the foolish were idiotic enough to face the almost certain death of such a match. Rarely did more than one in a generation make the solo hunt for the regal creature. Killing a cave lion brought a man the highest acclaim the People could give one of its hunters, and since Kalmar was of the Cave Lion Tribe, Kalmar's prestige would even be greater among the other males in his tribe—and it would not go unnoticed by the females.

The dancing shadows cast by the flittering leaves tickled by the cool breeze kept his eyes jumping from spot to spot. The flickering sunlight creeping by the deceiving shadows looked like the flames of a partially obscured campfire. The surrounding boulders formed the walls of an imaginary Oonoc Lodge in his mind. He thought of the Cave Lion Tribe's Oonoc Lodge, with the tanned hide of the cave lion his grandfather had slain hanging above the stone hearth of the tribe's Life Fire. An anxious smile parted his lips; he realized the other males in his tribe believed he hunted the cave lion for tribal honor. However, he knew his duel with the cave lion was rooted far deeper than that; every day since a cave lion took his grandfather's life, Kalmar had known, in time, he too must face and kill one of the great cats. For eight cycles of the seasons, since the day of his grandfather's death, he had honed his hunting skills waiting for this day. He touched a fang in the necklace of cave lion teeth hanging around his neck, prized mementos from his grandfather's cat. The collar of teeth was always with him, a constant reminder of his resolve to hunt the regal beast.

A screech pierced the silence of the still afternoon air. He looked up to see a split-tailed hawk flapping its wings as it flew towards the river beyond the tree line. The sight of the hawk was a good omen. His grandfather had once said the split-tailed hawk was the noblest of creatures and a sure sign of good luck. Kalmar's grandmother responded, after kissing her partner on the cheek, by saying he spoke about everything from his youth with a bias. Urga had been a member of the Split-Tailed Hawk Tribe until he paired with Kalmar's grandmother and left his own tribe to join her family and the Cave Lion Tribe. Shetow and Geerna's Covenant decreed that females were never to choose a Pairing Partner from their own tribe; instead, they were to select a male from one of the other tribes. Kalmar smiled; in less than three months, he would leave his own tribe to join the tribe of his female partner after their Pairing. The appearance of the hawk brought memories of Urga. His eyes sparkled; his grandfather must be looking out for him.

Kalmar stood up and let the straps of his hunting pack quietly slip off his shoulders. He gently set the pack on the ground and leaned it against a jagged rust-colored rock, being careful not to damage his reed flute, which protruded past the edge of the top flap. As the Gray Beards, a select group of the tribe's older males, had taught him, he noted the landmarks surrounding the location to make sure he could retrieve the pack later. He gave mental thanks to the Gray Beards who, through their Stories of Life, not only instructed him and the other young males on how to face the dangers of the hunt, but also in the ways of manhood. As he brushed back a troublesome lock of his long hair, he remembered the chuckle of one Gray Beard, who'd told his young charges the most important lesson from the Stories of Life was how to deal with females.

The disobedient strand of hair once again fell across his face. He reached down and untied a length of rawhide cord loosely attached to one of the shoulder straps. He ran it behind his neck and under his wavy dark brown hair and crossed the ends of the rawhide, forming a knot; then, with both hands, pulled the two ends of the rawhide tight. The last thing he needed was his hair dangling in front of his eyes, obstructing his sight as he trailed his prey; being blinded for only a second could be fatal. As Salune approached the horizon, its now feeble rays allowed the temperature of the mountain air to cool; with only a single layer of soft buckskin covering him, the dropping temperature would soon chill him to a point of discomfort. He looked down at his hands as he rubbed them together, warming them as he worked out the stiffness accompanying the drop in temperature. The many cycles of the seasons of hunting under the bombarding rays of Salune had turned the color of his skin to a rich copper, which stood in stark contrast to his bright cobalt blue eyes. The cuff of his shirt hid most of the round Mark of the Covenant imprinted on the inside of his left wrist. Kalmar stretched and flexed his hands as he studied his long, strong, yet delicate fingers. His manly yet beautiful hands, his mother said, were the first thing a female would notice about him; however, it was his wide smile that he relied on to charm both sexes. His wiry body matched the slenderness of his fingers. His younger sister kidded him, saying his only flaw was his awareness of his appearance. The thought of her words sent a dull chill through his body; he did not think he was cocky. For a moment he lowered his eyes. If they only knew how bashful he really was; he felt people sometimes misread his zealous labors to overcome his shyness as brashness.

Kalmar refocused his attention when he again sensed the nearness of the cat. With only his knife, bow, and quiver of arrows, he renewed the hunt.

As he crept along the undergrowth, his sinew bowstring caught on the leafless branch of a juda bush. As he tried to back out of the snag, the branch snapped with an audible crack; the bowstring twanged as it pulled free of the broken twig. Kalmar drooped his shoulders for an instant, and then, sensing he was not in immediate danger, shut his eyes to re-fix his concentration on the cave lion and away from his careless mistake. He noticed a clump of juda berries hanging on the bush. He picked one and popped it into his mouth. After squishing the berry with his tongue, he scrunched his face and spit out the rotten pulp. He sputtered a couple of times, then licked the back of his right hand before spitting, trying to get the last traces of the rancid taste off his tongue. After a deep breath, he resumed crawling around the bush, this time more wary of its grabbing limbs. The crack of the breaking branch and the twang of the bowstring would have given the cave lion a clear bead on its tracker. Kalmar knew he could not make these types of blunders and expect to live out the day. Pursing his lips, he concentrated on the fact that he was not hunting the elusive but docile prairie buck; no, his prey was deadlier than its hunter. He eyes darted to the horizon. Salune would soon disappear; if the cave lion was going to make a move, it would wait until the twilight-of-night. *I must make the cave lion come to me now*, he thought.

He stood and pulled another three arrows from his quiver.

Then he reached in his pocket, pulled out three small pieces of coarsely woven fabric, and neatly folded each one twice. Using the arrows' sharp tips he pushed them, one after the other, through the first three layers of the cloths, but stopped when he reached the last layer, letting it lay over the points. He took a piece of string from the other pants pocket, cut it into three pieces, and tied the last layer of cloths around the head of each of the three arrows. He checked the breeze one last time; the wind was still blowing into his face. Being careful of his bow as he held the three arrows in the same hand, Kalmar pulled the front of his pants down and urinated on the cloths tied to the arrows. Satisfied with his effort, he took the first arrow, nocked it in his bow, and pulled the bowstring less than full draw and shot it in a high arc to his left. The second arrow he shot to his front and the third to his right. If he was correct, and he believed he was, the cat was between him and where the arrows landed. He would use the animal's own superior sense of smell against it. With the breeze blowing from the direction of where the arrows landed, the smell of human urine should drive the cave lion towards him.

Kalmar re-nocked the arrow he had carefully chosen that morning. The bow had been handed down in his family for many generations, from one male to the next. He looked down the length of the curved, finely polished popela wood, making sure it was not about to snag on another branch. He crept along the cliff face, straining to see in the failing light. All at once, a strange emotion flowed through his body—he was being watched. He often experienced a tingling sensation on the back of his neck that made him feel he was being watched, but this feeling was different. It was more of a feeling of being exposed; he felt naked and he shivered involuntarily.

The ragged cliff face lay to his left, close enough for him to reach out and press the palm of his hand against it. He pulled a second arrow from his quiver and gently stuck it—point first—into the soft, moss-covered ground. Then he repositioned his body, placing his back against the towering rocky surface of the cliff wall. With his rear secure, danger could only come at him head-on. Kalmar checked again to make sure his arrow was firmly nocked on the bowstring; then he squatted, resting the hams of his legs on the heels of his feet. After a quick scan of the terrain in front of him, he slowly and quietly redistributed his body weight as he placed his right knee on the ground in front of him. Once his body was set, he instinctively repositioned the second arrow stuck in the ground moss. Kalmar made a mental check of how fast he thought he would be able to reach, re-nock, and shoot the second arrow. After a moment's reflection, he pulled a third arrow from his quiver and stuck it into the ground next to the other arrow. He blinked. The chances of getting off a second shot were remote and the chances of a third shot almost nonexistent, but it still made him feel better knowing two arrows lay in easy reach.

A pair of ants climbed the first arrow, their tiny antenna waving like a hunter's blade cutting through invisible underbrush. He knew the small insects offered him no danger. An anxious smile parted his lips; only in large numbers did this fearless fighter pose a threat. Leaning over, he gently blew the unsuspecting intruders off their wooden perch. He hoped his moment with the cave lion occurred before the balance of the ants' scouting party located his pants leg.

His eyes searched the thinly wooded but rocky surroundings. He squinted, trying to see in the shadows, which had grown longer and darker as Salune neared the horizon. Eeo, Salune's smaller binary partner, sat a hand's width higher in the red- and yellow-tinted sky, but its faint glow added little, if any, illumination. Kalmar's eyes gradually adjusted to the muted light in the shadows. He sensed the presences of something or some things. To his right there was a flicker of white, like the underside of a deer's tail or flutter of a snow owl's wings, and it grabbed his attention. Then, to his left, under two abutted boulders, he detected the outline of an object not part of the rocks.

It was the cave lion. The animal had apparently been watching him for some time. The cat's amber eyes seemed to glow in the dark even shadow of the boulders. Kalmar's body tensed. His lips curled faintly, his jaw moved to the side as he ground his clenched teeth. He stayed perfectly still as he stared at the cat. After a few minutes, his sight began to go black. He blinked to clear his vision. "Nervous blindness," he said under his breath. *"Not now."* He could hear his own rapidly beating heart as the blood surged through his eardrums. His chest felt constricted as if tightly wrapped by layers of thin fabric; he struggled to fill his lungs. The cave lion rose to a crouched stance and started walking towards him, its radiant eyes set on Kalmar. The great cat moved methodically, gracefully, with its gigantic head lower than its shoulders. Other than the rhythmic pounding in his ears every time his heart beat, the cat's low growl, amplified by its echo off the surrounding rocks, was the only sound. He knew he must wait until the cave lion was close enough to have a chance of hitting it, yet not so close he would not have time for a second shot if he missed with his first arrow. The decision was made for him when the cave lion suddenly broke into a run straight at him. For an instant, the animal's eyes fixed on him—fiery coals possessing a hypnotic quality. Then reality slapped him; in the time between heartbeats and in one smooth fluid motion, he drew his bow, locked his right thumb under his jawbone, took aim, and released the arrow. The charging animal was now close enough for him to see the arrow hit the center of the cat's chest—left of his aiming point. He had missed the heart, a killing shot sure enough, but one that would take costly seconds to bring the great cat down. Without thinking, and the cave lion only a few body lengths away, Kalmar, with reflexes perfected by many cycles of the seasons of practice, snatched the second arrow, nocked it in the bowstring, and then in one smooth motion drew and shot a second time. The second arrow hit its mark as the animal sprang, but the inertia of the massive creature carried it forward. As Kalmar jumped, in an effort to avoid the cat's attack, he caught a glimpse of the cat's haunting eyes an instant before the tips of the cave lion's claws raked across his left cheek. The massive blow spun him around, knocking him against the cliff face, and slamming the right side of his head into the hard stone. The force of the impact stunned him; his head began to spin. He fought to keep from losing consciousness as he slumped to the ground at the feet of the cave lion. The blow had knocked his breath out; he strained to breathe. He felt blood oozing from his wounds, which then trickled down his neck and under his buckskin shirt. The cave lion struggled to its feet, roared, and, on shaky legs, walked towards him. The cat's chest was dark red where the blood from two arrow wounds matted its thick fur. Everything around Kalmar seemed to slow down. Kalmar detected an overpowering perfumed scent; for an instant, he wondered if the blood he smelled was his own or the cave lion's. Amber flames in the cat's eyes seemed to leap at him. He felt for his knife but found the scabbard empty. As he fought to keep conscious, his sight faded. The cat sniffed him before licking the blood from the wounds across his face. The cat's abrasive tongue felt like hot sand pressed and then pulled across his sensitive skin. The cave lion's hot, pungent breath warmed his face. A paralyzing fear gripped him. He had always known that death was the likely outcome of this venture. A feeling of acceptance brought a strange calmness. "Grandfather, I did my best—" Darkness rushed in, smothering his thoughts as he felt himself slide into blackness.

The pointed bow of the small boat was barely visible through the mist as Kalmar pushed against the weathered long pole that he was using to move the short, narrow craft across the dark lake.

Kalmar knew he was dreaming, yet the memory of the cave lion's warm breath against his skin had not lost any of its intensity. If the dream had not been the same one he had been having for the past two seasons, he thought, he would have believed the cave lion had sent him to be with Shetow.

F O U R

The croaking of the frogs interrupted Dera's concentration. Every time she seemed to have any clarity concerning her dilemma, some outside distraction caused her to fall short in her scheming. If she was ever going to deal with the situation, she must do it soon. Her puce lips quivered; the consequences of inaction were not acceptable.

She sat by a small brook that supplied water to her village. The brook flowed from a spring on the side of a hill before running down a draw, then made its way through a wooded area. She found comfort in the soft babble of the water as it tumbled over a line of smooth stones that formed a small dam across the bed of the brook. No matter how the events of her life were going, the gentle whisper of the flowing water was always the same—a sound of contentment and serenity. This was her spot, hidden from the view of anyone who did not know where to look to see her tucked away in the little clearing in the middle of the thickest part of the nutwood grove. She had sought solitude in the nutwood grove ever since she chanced upon the secluded spot as a small child. Her mother knew of her daughter's hideaway, but never broke the privacy of Dera's sanctum.

She sat on a log lying along the pool's edge, her bare feet dangling in the cold, soothing water. Tilting her head to one side, she peered through the magnifying liquid at her toes as she plunged them into the soft mud bottom of the pool. She pried her toes up through the doughy material, causing a swirling cloud of debris. The muddied water slowly floated towards the stone dam before spilling over the edge. Even though she had no purpose in stirring up the bottom of the pool, she closely followed the movement of the mud through the water. After the pool cleared, she once again scrunched her toes, causing a second swirling cloud to appear. She repeated the experiment until the twilight-of-night made it difficult for her to see the effects of her actions. In a few moments, she redirected her concentration to the echoes of a distant wolf's howling. She made a mental note of the time between the original yelp and the answering imitation. These mental exercises were a diversion against the building pressure she felt from the looming implications of her dilemma. No matter what the distraction, in a short time, her problem always wiggled its way to the front of her thoughts.

Unlike those who knew her, Dera had never thought of herself as smart or wise; she realized she had more questions than answers. Now, with her Byrrac, Choosing, and Pairing not much more than two months away, uncertainty flooded her mind. As her quandary grew, she sought more and more the security and peace of her nutwood thicket, the one place she found the tranquility that eluded her everywhere else.

An overhead illumination grabbed her attention. She looked up and saw the two largest of Elom's four moons, Boboi and Quiron, commanding the night heavens. The clarity and radiance of the spheres in the cold, nocturnal sky calmed the turbulence racing through her brain. Her eyes widened as her murky thoughts cleared. She scrunched her face as she pursed her lips. Suddenly, she jumped up, brushed off her skirt, and hurried back to the village.

His face was wet and smothered in darkness. Disoriented, Kalmar pried his eyes open. He slammed them shut as his head exploded in waves of blinding pain. After a few seconds, stabbing throbs shooting down the left side of his face joined the chorus. With apprehension, he raised his left hand to touch his cheek. He jerked his hand back as the crescendo of spasmodic agony reached its peak. His face felt like it was being pushed into the embers of a smoldering fire. His mind faded a second time.

Once again, Kalmar was on the still lake using the push-pole to propel his small boat through the water. Ahead, he discerned a dark area that appeared to be an island rising above the mist. For the first time since he had been having his recurring dream, he realized he was being drawn to the island.

Dera's brother, Isamor, sat at a table studying as she walked into their cottage. He was his mother's Second Childs and, as true with all Second Childs, almost two cycles of the seasons younger than the female First Childs. Isamor did not like his name and, since before his fifth birthday, seldom answered to anything other than his nickname, "Izzy."

"Dear sister," he said without looking up, "you are late. Have you been preparing for the Byrrac?"

"No, I was just lost in my thoughts and forgot the time—where is Mother?"

"As always, she is in the workroom," he answered, motioning with a tilted head towards the room down the hallway.

When she walked past her brother, she stopped and pulled back a lock of his hair, which had fallen across his face. His flowing hair had caught in the fingers of a branch when he jumped out of a tree as a child. The branch broke under his weight, and although the event left no physical scar, the pain and the trauma of the incident scarred his psyche enough for him to keep his ash blond hair shorter than the other young men of the tribe.

He glanced up at her. His beaming face, with its angular features and flawless complexion, never failed to meet her with a smile. *No one could ever chide him about his looks*, she thought. She reached over and mussed his hair. He laughed, knocking her hand away, then grabbed at her as she jumped back. "You will have to be faster than that," she giggled as she easily danced out of his reach before continuing down the hall. Her mind drifted to a time when they were younger: He had pounced on a much older and bigger boy who made the mistake of taunting her. She remembered the Gray Beards dragging a kicking and swinging Izzy off the dazed and battered youngster. After that, no one ever joked about her again—at least, not where Izzy could hear it. What man would ever stand up for her once her protective Izzy left the tribe after his Pairing? She lowered her eyes as she approached a partially opened door.

Dera became less spirited as she entered the workroom, where a middle-aged woman huddled over a frilly blouse, sewing on glass beads. The woman held up the sparkling, multicolored garment for Dera to see.

"See, almost done."

Forcing a smile, Dera walked over and kissed the woman on the cheek. "It is beautiful, Mother," she said, trying to show some excitement as she studied her mother's artistry, "but you shouldn't put so much effort into something I will only wear one time."

"I want it to be the most wonderful day of your life," her mother replied, lines of stress marking her face.

Dera kneeled at her mother's side and looked up into her adoring eyes. "Mother . . . it will work out fine. Don't misread my melancholy mood as anything other than my normal self. You know how I am."

"But, it is such an important event in your life; I just want to help make it as memorable for you as I can. You are the First Childs; my dearest daughter . . . let me have my moments of emotion." Her mother smiled. "It is hard for me to believe you are old enough to select a Pairing Partner . . . my child ready for The Choosing. Next year I will be a grandmother, and you . . . a mother . . . a mother with your own daughter. You love children so; you will make a wonderful mother."

Dera bit her lower lip. She could see the lines of emotion in her mother's pale face. "Mother—"

"The real challenge will come in four cycles of the seasons"—she shook her head and stopped to wipe away a tear rolling down her cheek—"when you have your boy. Shetow shows Her wisdom in waiting until the Second Childs before blessing us with a male. Raising boys is so different from raising girls . . . I do not mean to say raising girls is easy," she said, lifting her hands for emphasis. "Just different." She reached over and stroked Dera's hair. "But you will have me and your grandmother to help you—maybe your boy"—she grinned, scrunching up her face—"will be easier to raise than your *brother.*" A subdued expression crept over Dera's mother's face as she paused to look out the window, her gaze locked on an invisible memory. Then her eyes blinked and she looked back down at Dera. "You have the Traits that will make your children special . . . that is if you choose the right male to father them. You have the best of both the physical and the mental Traits from your father and me. At my Choosing, when I chose your father, I felt I needed to weigh the physical abilities with a little more importance than did most of the girls in my Byrrac, as I knew my mind was the best of my attributes." Dera had heard this story many times in her life but the occurrences increased as her own Choosing approached.

Dera wanted desperately to change the subject. "How is my father?" She knew as soon as she spoke it was not the right question to ask.

"Your father can hardly wait for the Pootash; I think he already has his eye on someone." A ripple of anguish rolled across her face. "You would think he would have the decency to be more discreet about his decision to leave me when our twenty cycles of the seasons is up." The glistening of an emerging tear punctuated the grief in her mother's voice. "I have always wondered why Shetow did not make the capacity to always love the one you are Paired with to be one of the desired Traits." She looked down, trying to hide the tear as it slowly rolled down her face. "I have also wondered why Shetow allows us to experience such pain when one or both partners in a Paired couple decide to dissolve the union after they have raised their two children." She lifted her head and wiped away the now undeniable tear with the back of her hand. After taking a deep breath, she shrugged her shoulders. "I guess Shetow believes that being forced to spend twenty cycles of the seasons with someone you do not love deserves its own reward." She grimaced. "The Pootash, the happy time, the time when one can choose the one," she smirked, "or ones you want to be with. It sounds so romantic, that is, if it is not you that is the one being rejected."

Dera loved her father, but he was distant and offered her little affection. The attention denied her by her father was made up by her mother, her best friend. Her parents were so dissimilar; it was hard for her to imagine them being close, much less intimate.

"Mother, were you and my father ever happy together?"

Her mother thought for a moment as her eyes moistened. "Yes, right after our Pairing. Since Shetow's Covenant only allows us to choose males from one of the other tribes, all we knew about our prospective male partners was what we learned about them at the Gathering. Everything was new and exciting. He was so strong and handsome, it was easy for me to pick him at The Choosing. You would not believe how shy we were. After The Choosing, we did not even speak to each other until our Pairing the next day. However, I could tell from the way he looked at me, he desired me . . . that was an intoxicant in itself. That night, after our Pairing, in the darkness and privacy of our own room, he was rough and eager in an exciting and provocative way. I had dreamed—as all young girls do—about being with a man, and after a few days, when we knew each other better, we really had fun and enjoyed each other." Her mother blushed. "From that experience I had the First Childs— you." Dera could see that muddled thoughts contorted her mother's face. "In a short time, the mysteries of my body lost their allure for your father. When we spoke, it was in stunted sentences. After your brother's birth, when our duty to Shetow to have two children was fulfilled, we drifted even further apart; I could see in his eyes that the Pootash would dissolve our union."

Dera looked at her distraught mother. Her mother had never been so explicit in her descriptions of her and her father's relationship. At first Dera blushed and became fidgety, and then she decided to take advantage of the situation. Over the past few cycles of the seasons, she had been careful to stay away from the subject of her father, but since the subject was broached, there were a few things she wanted to know. Her curiosity was more about men in general than about her father. Dera knew she was intelligent; however, on this matter, she realized her knowledge was a little skimpy. She had many questions, especially with the idea holding fast in her head.

"What causes a man to lose interest in a woman?" Dera asked. Pain distorted her mother's face. Dera had not asked the question because of her mother and father's relationship, but she could see by her mother's expression, that was what she thought.

"Do you know why women do the choosing at The Choosing?" her mother said, looking into her daughter's eyes.

"Because that's the way Shetow intended it to be done?"

"No—well, yes, but anyway, if the male were to make the choice, he would always choose his Pairing Partner based upon the female's sexual beauty; on the other hand, the female will, most of the time, take other considerations into account before she makes her choice. Women desire smart men and being smart is, perhaps, the most important Trait. Many men do not like smart women. Most men do not like the fact that we women make the choice and not the other way around. Men would like to pull as many women into their bed as they can, yet, they have no real say as to whom they will sleep with until after their Pootash. No, if men were to make the choice at The Choosing, people would be beautiful, sure enough, but not so smart."

"I guess that leaves me coming up short."

Her mother flinched at her words.

"Mother, I know and accept the way I look," Dera said.

"I am sorry. I was not thinking about you, I was just talking; you are so beautiful even if some will not open their eyes to see it. Dera, you are the most gifted young girl in the tribe. The Traits are strong in you; Shetow has blessed you. You will finish high in the rankings of your Byrrac; you will be among the first to choose a partner at the Choosing, a partner from the top finishers of the Borrac. You and your choice will certainly have the Traits Shetow desires. Shetow will surely allow your Pairing to beget children."

"Mother, I may finish high in the Byrrac rankings, but why would any man want to pull me into his bed?"

"You place too much importance on your blemish," her mother said as she reached and cupped Dera's chin, her fingers pressed against the afflicted side of Dera's face. "You have a firm and beautiful body; behind a bedroom door, in the seclusion of night, you can be the equal of any woman. Let your man judge you by your performance in his arms and not by the mark on your face."

"I *am* attracted to men; there are nights when I cannot sleep wondering how it would be to be touched, held, and caressed by a man. I know people think I do not have feelings, that I only study my Lessons or hide in the nutwood grove." She lowered her eyes, "They are wrong; my blemish may distort my face, but it does not extinguish the fire in my blood. Unfortunately," she whispered, "in this one area, I am just like the other girls in the tribe; I too am *cursed* by the affliction of desire."

Her mother sat up; her daughter's frank disclosure startled her. She had wondered if Dera had any womanly weakness toward the other sex. She did not know how to proceed; she did not want to close the door on this rare glimpse into her daughter's mind. She decided on a very simple question. "Then you do look forward to your Pairing?"

Dera hesitated, then turned towards her mother. Her eyes drifted. "No," she said in a toneless voice.

"I do not understand." Her mother's eyebrows narrowed. "You just said you have a weakness towards men."

"I am not sure I understand myself . . . but, I feel . . . no, I know I am equal to any man and I do not have the need or desire to allow any man to judge my 'performance' in or out of his arms." Their eyes met. "Also, there is something about climbing into bed with a man I do not know, having his two children, and then spending the next twenty cycles of the seasons of my life tied to him knowing at our Pootash, after our last child has left, he will abandon me." Dera clutched her mother's arm. "I am having trouble accepting it. I know it is how Shetow planned it, but something just does not feel right about this here inside." She placed the palm of her left hand against the center of her chest. After a pause she added, "or here," as she moved her hand to place the tips of her fingers against her temple. "The Choosing is not *fair.*"

"I am reconciled to the fact," her mother said softly, "that it isn't meant to be fair. . . . The Choosing is meant to pair males and females of comparable abilities so they can produce children with optimum Traits."

"But for what end?"

"The Will of Shetow."

"There has to be more to this than we grasp," Dera said, looking down.

"I do not understand. . . ."

Dera looked up. "There has to be some greater reason. One that isn't readily apparent to us," she said, but more to herself than to her mother.

"This is more than I know how to help you with."

"I know, Mother, but please don't worry. I will be all right."

"I love you my child."

"I know, Mother; I love you, too," she replied, patting her mother's arm, and then she stood up and left the room.

———

Kalmar awoke with a jerk and reluctantly opened his eyes. Pain still drummed his temples, but the intensity had receded a bit. As his sight began to clear, he remembered the jarring blow from the cave lion's paw. He struggled to raise his torso, supporting himself on his right elbow and trembling forearm. He detected movement and turned to see a blurred outline of a person mixing something in a small wooden bowl. The person appeared to be taller, but not as thickly built as he was. As his sight cleared, he analyzed the nameless visitor with a hunter's eye. The stranger's movements had the fluidity of a young, masculine person. The man's chalky white complexion mirrored the color of extreme age, the color of bleached bones. A large, floppy straw hat covered his head, the kind women often wore when gathering fruit in the orchard. Kalmar had never seen a man wear this type of hat; the brim bobbed every time the stranger moved his head. The dancing of the hat's brim produced a flood of emotion, a sense of security. He had somehow survived the cave lion's attack and the stranger must have played a part.

After a few seconds, he shook his head to clear his thoughts. He squinted in an effort to lessen the drumming at his temples. The next thing that struck him was the man's cloth clothing. Males often wore fabric clothing, but buckskin was the normal garb for a man on a hunt. Kalmar released an unintended moan as he struggled to remain conscious. The stranger turned to look at him. The stranger's irises were light gray, but the pupils were a penetrating red and he was plagued with an involuntary flickering eye movement. Kalmar recoiled; the stranger was an albino. Kalmar had seen albino animals, but he had never seen or even heard of a human one. He remembered how one of the tribe's young hunters had once caught an albino rabbit; the puffy ball of snow white fur looked cute and cuddly. Not so for his rescuer, whose white skin and hair looked wan and sickly. If the stranger had not been so stocky, thought Kalmar, he would think him malnourished. A sense of grief invaded his troubled thoughts; the stranger was someone the Trait-conscious females would shun.

"So . . . the intrepid hunter has awakened," the stranger said as he moved towards him, bent over, and began rubbing the contents of the bowl on the left side of his face.

Kalmar detected a hidden smile on the stranger's face. He knew the man would have a conquering smile if he wanted to show it. He had never really noticed another man's smile before; he felt a rare tinge of jealousy—the power of a smile was his dominion.

Kalmar flinched from the pain of the man's nursing touch but offered no resistance as he managed a weak, "Who are you?" He then noticed the inside of the stranger's left arm. "You . . . *you don't have Shetow's Mark.*"

Kalmar's nurse ignored his remarks and continued treating his wounds. "The stitches seem to be holding. I had to use line from my fishing kit—not a pretty job, but the best I could do under the circumstances. We can only hope the stitches and the salve will keep it from becoming infected; the slightest scratch from any cat is the hardest kind of wound to heal and your gash is far from being insignificant." The man's touch did not rekindle the expected stabbing pain; instead, it yielded a cool, numbing sensation.

The stranger pushed up the brim of his hat, leaned forward, and gripped Kalmar's chin with his fingers. With a firm grasp, and like a young girl inspecting her doll, the stranger moved Kalmar's head around, eyeing his face. "Even if we keep down the infection, there is little I can do to keep you from having some nasty scars."

The stranger's scrutiny allowed Kalmar a better look at him. Although the stranger's hair and skin color were those of an old man, the closer inspection confirmed Kalmar's first guess; the stranger was a young man, probably only a few cycles of the seasons older than he was.

The stranger nodded towards Kalmar's left cheek. "You will always carry a reminder of today's events etched across your face, a visual testament to your bravery. You must be *very* proud of yourself."

Confused, Kalmar's jaw sagged. What was the man talking about? He looked around and tried to raise his body further; he recoiled when he realized the warm body of the freshly slain cave lion had been propping up his head. "What is—"

"A dead cave lion must be good for something; surely you don't fault me for giving it one last purpose," the stranger said, noticing his surprise. There was a bite in the sound of his words. "That is, a last one before you skin the poor animal so you can take its coat to hang on some dusty wall and pull its teeth"—he nodded towards Kalmar's necklace—"to add to the collection around your neck."

"I do not understand." Kalmar's face exposed his confusion. "The last thing I remember was the cave lion standing over me licking the blood off my face."

"I thought the lion was going to kiss you."

"You were watching the cave lion when it was standing over me—*how?*"

The stranger shrugged his shoulders. "I was sitting on top of that small outcropping." The stranger pointed at an area to the right of where Kalmar had first spotted the cave lion.

"What were you doing there?"

"Just—" he raised, then dropped his shoulders. "Just watching."

Kalmar nodded. "Thank you for allowing me the first chance at the cave lion."

"Young hunter, you had the first and last chance at the cave lion. I was not hunting the cave lion. I wasn't hunting anything. . . . I am not a hunter."

"Not a hunter?" Kalmar asked with more than a little bit of

confusion in his voice. He studied the bleached face of the stranger, trying to glean any hint of jest. Males hunted. They might concentrate on other tasks in the workings of the tribe, but all males in the tribe, at some time in their lives had been, were, or were going to be hunters. Hunting was the role of a man; it was the essence of being male. To the People, the words male and hunter were virtually interchangeable. *It is his white color,* Kalmar thought, *and his sensitivity to sunlight that keeps the albino from being a hunter.* Kalmar felt that to ask further questions on the matter would be rude.

"If not a hunter, then what are you?" He added, "You *are* male?"

The stranger let the "male" question pass. "I am a Seeker."

A Seeker, thought Kalmar. "Seeker?" he said to make sure he had it right. The stranger nodded. There was something about that word; he would think about it again after he found out the answer to a much more baffling question. "Why am I not dead?"

"I stopped the cave lion from killing you," the stranger said with a nonchalant shrug.

"You killed the cave lion?"

"Absolutely not! I do not kill."

"I am confused. The last thing I remember before blacking out was the cave lion standing over me with its muzzle so close to my face I could feel and smell his sour breath. I awaken with my head lying against the cave lion, the only person here is you, and you say, *you didn't kill the cave lion!"*

The stranger nodded with a disinterested smile.

"You *had* to have killed the cave lion; there is no one else who could have killed it."

"I told you," the stranger said, the tone of his voice a little sharper, "I did not kill the cave lion, and there was someone else who could and did kill the cave lion."

"Who?"

"You."

"Me?"

"I did *not* kill the cave lion, you killed the cave lion; I just kept the cave lion from killing you long enough for your arrows to take their full measure and finally bleed the big cat to death."

"*How,* by the Will of Shetow, did you keep the cat from killing me?"

The pale stranger walked toward Kalmar a few steps. "I distracted it," he said, raising his arms for emphasis.

"I do not understand."

"I distracted him." The stranger seemed a little agitated. "I made him think about me and not about killing you."

"How did you do that?"

"Let's see."

Kalmar still wondered if the stranger was mocking him.

"I yelled at him, jumped around like a fool, and, oh yah"—he reached down and picked up a thick tree branch that was almost as large as Kalmar's arm—"I threw this stick at him. At first I didn't think he was going to come after me."

"You saved my life by not killing the cave lion, but by getting the cave lion to *attack you?*"

"Come after me, yes; attack me, no," the stranger said matter-of-factly. "Once I had gotten his attention, the cave lion only staggered a few steps before it collapsed and died; as I said, you killed the cave lion, not me."

Kalmar thought about what the stranger had said. "Stranger, please do not take what I am about to say the wrong way. I do thank you for saving my life, but you are either very brave or very foolish."

The solemn stranger looked at Kalmar and then sat down on a large rock before answering. "*Foolish?* I am not the one who was hunting a hungry cave lion, and bravery was not a factor. As I said, my actions presented little danger. I knew the cave lion had two arrows buried deep in its chest. One of them—it appeared—piercing its heart. The cave lion could have killed you during the last few seconds of its life, but he would never have caught surefooted Snook. You faced a cat in perfect health; I faced one just two wobbly steps from death."

The stranger's words were lost on Kalmar. "You risked your life to save me."

"If it makes you feel any better"—the stranger scrunched his face as he tilted his head—"I'm not so sure I did *save* your life."

"What do you mean?"

"Well, he may have only chewed on your face before collapsing. You might have only lost your ears, nose, and if lucky, only one of your eyes."

Kalmar looked hard at the stranger. "Snook, I take it that is your name; you do not take this very seriously, do you?"

The stranger seemed taken aback. "Yes, Snook is my name, and no, I take the death of the cave lion very seriously. I was just pointing out the cave lion might not have killed you and the loss of an ear or eye would only bring you *more* honor from the other members of your tribe."

"Snook, I am sure I would have lost more than an ear, nose, or eye if you had not, as you say, distracted the cave lion . . . and the loss of one of them is not worth one smidgen of honor. Besides, I did not hunt the cave lion for honor." Kalmar paused as he looked into Snook's eyes. "Or, at least, I don't think I did."

"That's interesting." Snook raised an eyebrow. "Then why did you make the hunt?"

"My grandfather was killed by a cave lion." Kalmar's left hand reached up and clasped some of the cave lion teeth hanging around his neck. "Ever since the day he died I have known I must also hunt the great cat." He looked down at the necklace. "My grandfather was also able to put two arrows into his cat's chest, but the cave lion was still able to get to him before it died."

"You and your grandfather were close?" Snook asked, his voice losing some of its harshness.

"Yes . . . I have had an empty spot"—Kalmar pressed his right hand against his stomach—"inside me ever since the day the cave lion killed him."

Snook slid down the side of his rock perch and sat on the ground with his back against the cold stone, his knees drawn to his chest. After a moment's reflection, he looked at Kalmar. "You loved your grandfather and hated the cave lion." He rubbed his chin. "That makes sense. You hated the cave lion for taking your grandfather; you hunted the cave lion as a matter of revenge," Snook stated, almost to himself.

Kalmar eyed Snook. "I thought I hated the cave lion—"

"It is only by love," Snook spoke with deep conviction, "that we rise above the animals, but we pay a horrible price—with the ability to love comes the ability to hate just as deeply. Love unshackles the joys of our inner spirit," he said, his expression somber. "But hate, like loneliness, tracks us like a relentless pack of hungry wolves."

Kalmar nodded. "Now, I am not sure it was hate that drove me to hunt the cave lion."

Snook tilted his head. "You said you did not make the hunt for your own acclaim; could it have been to restore any loss of honor your grandfather and family might have suffered by his being killed by the cave lion?"

"There was no dishonor to my family; the fact my grandfather did not flee when he faced the ferocious cat only added to his esteem among the tribes." Kalmar unconsciously ran his fingertips across the teeth in his necklace. "The story of Urga's hunt was added to the Tell and is now recited by the Tellers of the Tell around campfires all along the Valley of the Twin Rivers."

There was silence as the two men reflected on what had been said.

Kalmar spoke first. "I just don't know . . . what seemed so . . . so very clear to me this morning is now muddled in my mind . . . you know . . . if I could hunt and kill the cat—"

"Would it honor your grandfather's memory?"

"No." Kalmar hesitated. "I don't think . . . there was something missing in my life . . . hunting and killing the cave lion would fill that missing part," he said, almost as a question.

"Did it?"

"Did it what?"

"Did killing the cave lion fill . . . the missing . . . whatever you were missing?"

Kalmar lowered his chin, took in and let out a slow, deep breath. A dazed look covered his face. Kalmar, to his own amazement, said, "I feel . . . I feel nothing."

Snook's gaze shifted to Kalmar's somber face and after a moment's reflection the albino responded in a voice almost too low for Kalmar to hear. "And neither does the cave lion."

"What did you say?" Kalmar asked, even though he had heard Snook clear enough—he just did not understand what Snook meant by the remark.

"I said the cave lion does not feel anything either." Then he added, "You said you did not kill the cave lion for your personal or your grandfather's honor, and now, after the cave lion's death, you realize you didn't kill it for revenge . . . you feel nothing. I was just pointing out the cave lion . . . the cold, dead, cave lion . . . does not feel anything either."

Kalmar shivered as a chill rushed through his body. He felt

empty. He did not know what to think. He looked at Snook—
Kalmar was now even less sure what to make of the stranger who
had saved his life. It was obvious Snook was no coward. He'd faced
the cave lion without a weapon and acted as if it were no special
feat—an admirable Trait in any hunter. Yet, Snook was a man who
claimed he was not a hunter; he even scorned the idea. How baffling this seemed to Kalmar.

After a few moments of the two men looking at each other,
Kalmar said, "Snook."

"Yes."

"You saved my life; I am in your debt." Kalmar rose with unsure feet and then carefully walked towards the chalk-colored
stranger. The albino stood to meet him. Kalmar thrust out his right
hand and arm as he stumbled into Snook. "I am Kalmar of the
Cave Lion Tribe." Snook put out his arm and grasped the inside of
Kalmar's forearm with his right hand. As Snook's hand gripped his
arm, Kalmar grasped Snook's forearm, completing the timeless sign
of friendship and greeting among the People.

"As you already know, my name is Snook, Snook the Seeker."

"Seeker?"

Snook hesitated, looking ill at ease. "I am on what you might
call a ramble," he said, his tone sounding like a question. Snook's
eyes flitted faster than normal. "I seek knowledge by visiting the
different tribes."

Kalmar studied Snook's smooth, milk white face. *I wonder*, he
thought, *if it is because of his color that a Pairing Partner did not choose
him*. If he had a Pairing Partner, he would not be free to wander.
Kalmar smiled. "My new friend, Snook, you're a brave man. How
can I ever repay you for saving my life?"

"The saving of a life does not need any additional reward.
That a life was saved is reward enough . . . and . . . the only thing I
could wish for now is impossible."

"Impossible?"

"Yes, if I had my wish, the cave lion's life would also have been spared," Snook said in a muted tone.

Kalmar studied Snook for a long time before saying, "Snook, you are a different kind of man than I have ever met. I do not understand you, but I do honor your bravery and conviction."

Snook realized he was putting great trust in this person he had just met. The Elders had cautioned him not to interact with the People from the Twenty-Four Tribes. That is, no one besides the Medoras. It was his first mission into the lands of the Twenty-Four Tribes, a journey he thought he would never make. He sighed. He was ill prepared to deal with the complications that could arise. Of all those the Elders could have chosen for this task, he knew the least about the history and customs of the people of this strange land. When he tried to convince the Elders there was another obvious reason why he should not be the one given this task, he could not sway them. He remembered the lines of their stern faces as he made his case; if it was not for the seriousness of the circumstances, they said, they would have chosen someone who could move among the Twenty-Four Tribes with greater stealth. The Elders told him the situation demanded that they send the brightest of the possible candidates, not the one who would go unnoticed. They said it was imperative that they have someone reach the Medoras to learn the latest news concerning the Second Judging.

He rolled the events of the past few hours around in his mind. It had only been by chance that he had spotted Kalmar stalking the cave lion, forcing him to climb onto the rock outcropping to wait until the impetuous hunter moved on. When the cave lion charged Kalmar, without thinking Snook had moved from behind the treetop that was concealing him and jumped from his stone perch to run to the fallen hunter's aid. He never thought about what he would do if the cat turned on him. When he reached Kalmar and the cave lion, he only had to distract the cat a few moments until Kalmar's arrows allowed the last drops of life to flow from the doomed creature.

To meet with the Medoras as fast as possible was the Elders' charge; his actions were in direct opposition to these instructions— a serous breach of trust. Others of his kind, he realized, would have made a different choice. However, to leave an obviously injured Kalmar went against all he stood for; for him, there was no choice to be made. He could only hope this short delay would have no effect on the outcome of his quest. Time was of importance; he must see to Kalmar's injuries and then quickly resume his trek.

Snook turned to Kalmar. "I do have a request."

"Anything—anything I have in my power to grant."

"Oh, my request is certainly in your power to grant, and in reality there are two requests." Kalmar looked at Snook, waiting for him to speak. "First, promise me you will not take the life of any warm-blooded creature for thirty days."

The request caught Kalmar off guard. The idea of not hunting for thirty days surprised him. It would be hard to explain to his fellow hunters.

"And second," Snook continued, "you are to never tell anyone of my part in the death of the cave lion nor are you to tell anybody about these promises."

"But *why?*"

"I have my reasons. Do you promise?"

"How can I not tell anyone you kept the cave lion from killing me? It would not be honorable to let them think I killed the cave lion by myself."

"For the last time, *you* killed the cave lion by yourself," Snook said slowly, then added in a firm voice, "This is what I desire. Will you honor my request?"

Kalmar's lips turned white as he pressed them together. "I will honor your request, Snook, but only if you will honor a request of mine." Snook started to object, then, before he could speak, Kalmar raised his hands to grab Snook's shoulders. "Please come with me to my village and share the fellowship of my family, eat at our table, and be warmed by our Life Fire. Allow me to show you my gratitude."

Kalmar's request caught Snook by surprise. He knew he had to resume his journey as soon as possible. Then another thought entered his mind.

"Do you know a Medora?" Snook asked.

"What a strange question. Everyone knows at least one Medora. You know there is one living with every tribe." Then a slow understanding smile filled Kalmar's face. "I understand; you know the Medora of the Cave Lion Tribe is the leader of the Medora Council, the Medora Roo. Yes, I know her well. She showed me great compassion when my grandfather was killed."

"Would you show me where she lives if I go with you to your village?"

Kalmar guffawed. "It will be my honor to introduce you to her myself."

"Then I will make one additional request," Snook said after a pause. "You must never press me if I ask you not to question me on any subject."

Kalmar thought it a strange request, but everything about Snook was strange. "Agreed."

Snook smiled the first real smile since the two had met. "I could use a break from my travels. Yes, Kalmar, I will go with you to your village, but remember, you must not speak of how we met . . . if asked, just tell them I am from a neighboring tribe."

"What tribe?"

Snook's eyes grew larger as his jaw noticeably dropped. "One far beyond the western mountains," he stuttered.

"The Black Raven Tribe?" Kalmar guessed. "That is the only tribe I can think of on the far side of those mountains."

The lines of Snook's mobile face tightened. For a moment, his eyes seemed to look past Kalmar before they abruptly returned to meet the young hunter's questioning stare. "Yes, the Black Raven Tribe . . . I'm from the Black Raven Tribe."

Kalmar studied his new acquaintance, reflecting on the way Snook had stumbled when he had pressed him on the name of his tribe. Something in Snook's manner made Kalmar uneasy, yet he knew this stranger was the only reason he was still living. How could he challenge him?

"As you wish, Snook. Is it against your principles for you to help me take the body of the cave lion back to the village?"

Snook's gaze dropped to look at the body of the cave lion. "I suppose you will try to do it by yourself if I don't help."

Kalmar answered with a weak smile.

"Then I would only do you harm if I refused," Snook said, nodding that he would help.

"We must do something to cover your wrist."

"What do you mean?"

"You don't have the Mark of the Covenant on your wrist."

Snook rolled his eyes as if his mind was searching for the answer to a troublesome dilemma. The Elders told him to keep his arm covered and not to let anyone from the Twenty-Four Tribes see his wrist. Make as little contact with people as possible, they told him. He felt short of breath. Now he had broken two of his primary instructions. His mind raced. Snook looked down at his wrist. "The Mark is transparent on albinos," he said with the inflection of a question.

Snook's answer added to Kalmar's uneasy feeling, yet he knew he owed this pale stranger a debt he could not repay. He made a decision; he would not question Snook's assertions. For all he knew, they were the truth.

"Transparent or not, if you enter my village showing a wrist without a *visible* Mark of the Covenant on it, the members of my tribe will press you for an explanation." Kalmar thought for a second then leaned over and yanked open his pack and stirred around inside until he pulled out a small leather strip with rawhide lacing. "Here, use this wristband; it will cover the spot where the Mark would be until we reach my village; there I have some dye that we can use to make a suitable Mark."

"I told you, the Mark is transparent on albinos."

"Even so, I think it will lessen the attention you will cause if they can plainly see the Mark." Kalmar raised an eyebrow. "That is unless you don't mind bringing attention to yourself."

Snook snatched the wristband out of Kalmar's hand and looked at it. "It is leather; I do not wear leather."

"What about your shoes? They are leather."

"They are snakeskin, snakes are cold-blooded. I do not use anything from warm-blooded animals."

"Do you have any extra snakeskin we can use to make a wristband until we reach my village?" Kalmar said, a little flustered.

"I think I do."

Snook had to catch Kalmar, who started swaying, to keep him from collapsing.

"The loss of blood and the effect of the salve I rubbed on your wound has made you weak. You must rest; I will prepare something for you to eat. Something hot—the food will give you back your strength."

Snook helped Kalmar stumble to the base of a large nutwood tree where he slumped down and leaned against its massive trunk.

"Just give me a few moments; I'll be fine," the hunter said as he closed his heavy eyelids.

Snook nodded as a knowing smile filled his round face. He glanced at Kalmar's deforming wounds. "The events of this day will surely change your life," he said softly. Then he turned to start preparing their meal.

SIX

As Dera neared the Oonoc Lodge, she approached a cottage constructed, like all the others, from a mixture of wood and stone. The exquisite workmanship of the building was plainly evident and made possible because of the culmination of skills gained over the six Progressions of perfecting the art of woodworking—one of the few artistic skills reserved for men. The tribe's meticulous timber framers refused to use metal nails and built the frames of the buildings relying on mortises, tenons, and hardwood pegs. The builders crafted each timber with the knowledge the structure would remain as a testament to their skills for many generations. Each timber was worked by hand, with the timber's protruding tenon carved to fit perfectly into another timber's hollowed-out mortise. The stonework, a skill also reserved for men, was just as precise as the woodwork. The artisans' work blended in visual harmony with the rocks and trees of the surrounding area.

Dera knocked on the hand-hewn wooden door of the building facing the Oonoc Lodge. After a few moments, the door opened to reveal an old but spry woman who ushered Dera into the warmth of the dwelling.

The woman led Dera to two chairs positioned in front of a

blazing fire set in a massive fireplace assembled from rounded river rocks. The pleasant scent of burning nutwood permeated the room. Dera dropped into one of the heavy chairs, all of them draped in prairie buck skins. She studied her surroundings after the woman excused herself and left the room. Massive exposed timbers held up a vaulted ceiling that exposed the pegged wooden planks that lay across the beams. It did not matter how many times she sat in this room, her awe had not diminished over all the cycles of the seasons she had sought the wisdom of her closest confidant. One could plainly see this was the home of a Medora. All dwellings in the village housed a wide selection of the extraordinary art fashioned by the females of the People; however, the quality, variety, and subject matter of the many sculptures, carvings, drawings, and paintings in the room pointed to only one possible resident for this inviting yet mystical home. The Medora soon returned with two porcelain cups filled with a steaming liquid.

"Take this, you look blue with chill," the Medora said as she handed one of the ornate cups to Dera. "I brewed this from a blend of the leaves of the cisci plant and roots of the byda bush. It will warm you."

Dera took the cup with a smile and slight nod. "I am a little chilly. I had not noticed it until you mentioned it." She took a sip of the steamy liquid.

"That is not surprising . . . had your mind on other things?"

"Medora, I—"

"My child, no amount of questioning me, or for that matter anyone else, will bring you the answers you seek."

"Verna, my Medora and friend, I cannot talk to anyone but you and Mother about these feelings that haunt my mind; you know I have a hard enough problem with everybody as it is. If they knew about the things we talk about—"

Verna studied the girl's young but flawed face. "Dera, everybody has a part of themselves they do not want others to know about. A sexual, base part, a shadowy place right at the heart of our inner-spirit that tries to, and sometimes does, take control of our thoughts and actions to a point where we feel we are being split into two different persons. The one who has taken us over and the other, the helpless self who watches the actions of this stranger who has gotten loose from the bonds that normally hold our appalling inner-creature at bay." Verna shook her head. "Dera, the things that fill your head are not the thoughts that plague the rest of us. The difference between you and all the other members of the tribe, including myself, is that your head is filled with questions that most of the rest of us dare not think about because our minds cannot comprehend the depth one must go to understand the answers."

"But there are so many things I do not understand."

"You question the very reason of our existence. Your questions do not come from the murky part of our inner-spirit, the part that curses the rest of us. Your questions come from your very being." Verna sighed. "You are right; most people would not appreciate the thoughts that fill your head. It would scare them. But Dera, your thoughts and questions are pure; ours, on the other hand, come from the black abyss inside the inner-spirit in the rest of us. You feel isolated because of your superior intellect, not because of some . . . some personal imperfection."

Dera cast her eyes down. Verna frowned at Dera's reaction to her last words. Verna scrutinized Dera as the flickering firelight danced across her marked face. Like many redheads, Dera had a soft, pale, almost translucent, complexion and emerald green eyes; but she lacked the normal accompanying freckles. Her hair, though full, was not wavy, but fine and straight. The richness of her long auburn hair almost overpowered the blemish on her face. Her body was slim and strong, yet, the word beautiful had never been cast in the same sentence as her name, for across a portion of the right side of her face was a deep scarlet birthmark that ran from the hairline above her ear to the corner of her unblemished lips.

"Dera, please do not think me insensitive to your anguish over your blemish, but it does not detract from the fact that you are the finest aspirant to The Choosing I have ever seen. The blemish may cloud how others see you, but your so-called 'imperfection' is in appearance only and one we believe will not pass to your children; your blemish will not affect the status of your ranking in the sight of Shetow." Verna leaned over and placed her hands on Dera's knees and looked her hard in the face. "You will rank high in the Byrrac and be among the select women to mother children; no small facial blemish will keep you from finding great favor with Shetow. Your children will add glory to the People in their homage to Shetow." Verna smiled. "Pick the right father at The Choosing, and your children's Traits could be the closest to perfection in the history of the Pairings."

All the thoughts she had had earlier sitting in her nutwood grove filled her mind. She needed guidance; she needed reassurance concerning her decision. If she was going to be deflected from the path she had chosen, her closest confidant would be the one to do it.

"Verna . . ." Dera bit her lower lip as she turned her head until her gaze met that of her Medora. "We must talk."

SEVEN

Kalmar agreed to wait until the next morning before starting their descent to the village; however, a few hours after he regained consciousness, he struggled to his feet and, ignoring Snook's vehement protest, insisted on field dressing the cave lion. He lit two torches so he could see clearer in the dim light of the twilight-of-night. Then he rested on his knees while he cut the cat from below the center of its rib cage to its testicles. After opening the cat's stomach, he took his knife, reached in, and cut loose the internal organs, allowing him to pull them out of the cat's body cavity. The air reeked with the sweet scent of drying blood mingled with the sharp acrid stench of the urine released from the cat's bladder at its death. Large black flies, which appear at moments of death, swarmed around the bloody entrails. The popping sound heard every time one of the pests flew too close to one of the torch flames punctuated their faint buzz. The flickering light from the torches projected grotesque and exaggerated shadows against the cliff face—Kalmar working with his knife as he hunched over the cave lion's remains. Snook watched him lay the cave lion's heart, lungs, stomach, intestines, and other internal organs on the ground next to its body.

"You are quiet," Kalmar said, after noticing Snook's somber expression.

"That is what we look like inside," Snook said, his face blank, his voice flat.

"I was getting accustomed to your chattering."

"Don't you think it strange that human and cave lion anatomies are so similar?"

"Snook, does everyone where you come from ask such strange questions?"

"When their cubs whine, it sounds like a human child crying."

"A child's cry—" Kalmar's eyes flashed towards Snook.

"There is something strange, yet, in an odd way, logical about it."

"No, I don't."

"Don't what?"

"No, I do not think it strange that human and cave lion anatomies are so similar," Kalmar replied.

"Lungs, heart, stomach, intestines; if they were smaller they could be yours or mine."

Kalmar pulled his hands from inside the cave lion's chest cavity, leaned back, and sat on his calves. His hands and arms were encrusted with the animal's blood. "All animals breathe so they must all have lungs; they all have blood in their veins so they must have hearts to pump it."

"Fish don't have lungs."

"It is the Will," Kalmar said as he leaned forward and reached back inside the cave lion's carcass, "of Shetow."

"How original," Snook said, rolling his eyes. He turned away from Kalmar, pursing his lips. "There is such order to life. There has to be a reason."

———

Removing the cat's internal organs not only lessened the cave lion's considerable weight but it also allowed the animal's body to cool faster in the nippy night air. The cooling insured the cat's body would not become rancid before they reached the village. Snook's eyes followed Kalmar closely; he was concerned he might overexert himself. As Kalmar finished his task, Snook built a fire to keep them warm and give him enough light to continue treating the wounds that ravaged Kalmar's face. Snook might not be a hunter, but he did know the cat's claw marks demanded close attention. Untreated claws marks, like the bite of any predator, harbored sure death from infection; that is, if you were skillful enough to survive the animal's initial attack. Snook inspected Kalmar's stitches every hour.

The next morning they cut down two whitewood saplings and stripped them of their branches. With cuscu-fiber rope, they wove a loose web between the strong but flexible wooden poles to support the cave lion's carcass. When they were ready to travel, Snook scrunched his face after he made a final check of Kalmar's wounds. The two made one last look around their encampment then each reached down, grabbed one of the slender poles, and started down the incline toward the village, dragging their improvised sled behind them.

Kalmar's vigor had only partially returned when they began their arduous task of pulling their hefty cargo through the rugged terrain of the mountainside. The way Snook glanced at him out of the corner of his eye every time Kalmar stumbled only made Kalmar more resolute that he would not falter in front of the man who had risked his own life to save him. Rebuffing Snook's questions about his well-being, Kalmar pulled harder. Sweat poured down his brow. It was only when Snook asked if they could stop for a few moments' rest that Kalmar slumped down against a tree trunk. Glancing in the direction they had traversed, his pride almost broke as he realized they had covered less than five hundred feet. He fought to keep his eyes open as his pale companion leaned over to inspect his angry wounds.

Snook looked down at his patient; a red line radiated from Kalmar's inflamed wound. He gently pressed against one of the three rows of stitches. Kalmar winced as bloody pus oozed from one of the long scabs. Snook placed the back of his hand against Kalmar's forehead. *He is burning up*, Snook thought, pursing his lips. His worst fear for his new friend had manifested, and Snook wondered how he would treat the infection.

Kalmar could see the lines around Snook's eyes and mouth deepen as he stood up. Snook grabbed his knapsack and rummaged around in it until he found the items he was looking for.

"I think we could use some herbal tea," Snook said, forcing confident zeal into his voice. After a few minutes of inspecting the surrounding plants, he dropped to his knees as he pulled his knife from its sheath and started digging at the base of a scrawny bush. After a few seconds of sawing and hacking, Snook lifted a handful of dirt-covered roots from the soil. Kalmar tilted his head in an effort to see around Snook's body, which was blocking much of his view, to watch the antics of his new friend. First, Snook stripped off the skin and hair roots. After laying the roots on a smooth rock, he pounded the carrot-colored flesh with the butt of his knife. Once mashed, he dropped the moist pulp into a ceramic pot he pulled from his knapsack. Then he quickly built a small fire, filled the pot with water from a nearby stream, placed the pot at the edge of the fire, and sat down by Kalmar.

"Kalmar, I think your claw marks are infected. The next few

hours are very important. I may need to cut your stitches, open your wound, and wash it out and treat it again."

Kalmar watched Snook's eyes. He had experienced the jovial side of the albino and he had seen him indignant; now, he saw only concern in the chalky white face.

"It's unwise for us to go on with you like this," Snook said.

Kalmar dropped his shaking hands to the ground and tried to push himself up. *I must not quit*, he thought. *Every drop of sweat drains me of my strength.* When it became evident to him that he could not get up, he tried to hide his dilemma by acting as if he had only been shifting his sitting position. He could tell by Snook's grimace that his rescuer had not been deceived by his bungled ploy.

In a short time, a steam cloud billowed around the lid of the pot. Snook stood up and moved the pot from the graying embers to let it cool. After a few minutes, Kalmar watched Snook fill a cup, also produced from his knapsack, with a yellowish liquid. He immediately brought this to Kalmar and told him to drink the enigmatic brew. The strange infusion tasted bitter, almost gagging Kalmar.

"That's awful," Kalmar said, wrinkling his face, his eyes not focusing. "How can you drink that?" In a few seconds, his jaw sagging, Kalmar slumped forward.

"I don't drink it," Snook murmured as he caught the unconscious Kalmar before Kalmar's drooping head could hit the ground.

The sight of Kalmar's limp body brought an unexpected shiver. It took a moment for Snook to understand his reaction to this prostrate stranger. Memories of his bleeding mother's broken body flooded his mind like a breached dam. Guilt he thought he had long suppressed deflated his chest as blurry images of her slowly opening her eyes pummeled his emotions. The phantom remembrances then turned to debilitating grief. He knew his memories of that agonizing day were clouded by a small child's perspective. As he looked at Kalmar's ravaged face, he saw his mother's haunting eyes. *Why,* he thought, *did she have to die?* Tears streamed down his cheeks as he leaned against the tree propping up Kalmar. He buried his face in his hands, and sobbed. Several minutes later, he wiped his eyes with the side of his hand.

"I guess I had better see to your wounds before you wake up, fearless hunter." Snook peered down at the hapless man. Jumbled thoughts darted through his mind: *I must be quick if he is to live; for once, I can save a life.* He looked to the east. "Honorable Elders, I cannot let this man die." He turned and walked towards the campfire.

Snook had just finished cleaning and restitching Kalmar's wounds when a hunting party from Kalmar's tribe appeared. They told Snook they had seen the smoke from the campfire and had come to investigate. Then, because of Snook's insistence, the group set out with all haste for the village of the Cave Lion Tribe.

The village broke into pandemonium as the hunting party and Snook emerged into the clearing that lay between the village and the tree line, dragging the sled with an unconscious Kalmar lying across his prey. The village men swarmed around them clamoring to hear about the hunt. The commotion finally aroused the sluggish and reluctant hero. Kalmar tried to play down the feat, but the more he talked it down, the more the men wanted to build it up. It was, at first, very hard for Kalmar to accept all the praise. However, in a short time, he stopped trying to silence his admirers, and just smiled and obliged them when they slapped him on the back and asked him to tell them again how the cave lion had clawed his face as it collapsed at his feet with two of his arrows embedded in its chest.

After an initial interest in his skin color, Snook easily stepped back out of the limelight. He told the churning mass of admirers that he was from the Black Raven Tribe and was on a ramble, and that he had stumbled on the injured and bleeding Kalmar field dressing the big cat; after that, they never questioned him again about any possible role he might have played in the great deed. The exhilaration they felt from Kalmar's kill overwhelmed any other curiosity.

"You will join your grandfather in the Tell," said an old man as he pounded Kalmar's back, "and you not old enough to have been through your Borrac." Kalmar smiled weakly at his admirer.

"The more," he whispered to Snook, "I try to downplay it, the louder they praise me."

"My Toran . . . my teacher, says, 'people only push glory on someone who tries to reject it.' If you want people to leave you alone, start bragging about your feat. They will get their fill of you quick enough."

"It is hard for me to take the trappings of honor and keep your part of the adventure secret."

"Then you must learn to live with the veneration of your people."

"But you saved my life, maybe twice; to me, that's a far greater deed than my killing the cave lion."

Snook stopped walking and looked at him. "Well, there may be more to you than your boyish swagger."

Several days after returning from the hunt, and after Kalmar regained most of his vim, Snook and Kalmar sat with Yumza, Kalmar's mother, and Onora, his grandmother, around their family urk. The urk, a large metal cooking pot that normally dangled over the family's Life Fire, now sat on the table in front of the fire. Yumza stood beside the urk with a ladle in her hand. Even after bearing three children and seeing thirty-nine cycles of the seasons, Kalmar's mother, from a distance, could pass for her First Childs, Nima. Only a tinge of gray at her temples betrayed her age. Her long, dark brown hair, narrow waist, firm breasts, and lanky legs, accented by her fit body, still brought glances from the men of the village. They looked at her, but she pretended not to notice. Yumza—the ultimate mother—knew her role in life, at least the role she had until Nutan, her Third Childs, had her Choosing. Yumza had her mind set; if Nutan did not pick a good Pairing Partner at her Choosing, Yumza would refrain from allowing a man to get emotionally close to her as long as her daughter's life was in turmoil. Yumza could only hope Nutan would choose a Pairing Partner as wisely as Nima, her older sister. Nima's Pairing Partner, Raff, had joined the family two cycles of the seasons earlier after Nima chose him at their Choosing. No mother—if mothers did the Choosing—could have picked a better match for her eldest daughter. Yumza had learned to love Raff as a son and having him in the family would, she hoped, make it easier to accept the loss of Kalmar when he left for the Gathering and his new life after his Choosing. Yumza and her Pairing Partner, Seldan, had been one of the few couples Shetow blessed with a Third Childs. The Third Childs, in their case, was female—the First Childs was always female, the Second Childs was always male, but the sex of the Third Childs, at Shetow's discretion, could be either male or female.

Snook," Yumza said, "if you had not stumbled on Kalmar, the infection from the cave lion's claw marks would have surely killed him. I . . . we will always be grateful to you for what you did. There will always be a place for you at our Life Fire."

"It was only by chance that I found Kalmar. For the skill used to treat him, you must thank my Toran, my teacher."

"Then your Toran is also welcome."

Snook grinned. "I will tell him the next time I see him—at the end of my ramble."

Yumza ladled a rich vegetable stew from the urk and poured it into Snook's bowl. "You are sure you wouldn't like a slice of prairie-buck roast?"

"No thank you, I ate some spoiled meat a few days ago and I did not think I would ever recover; my stomach has yet to settle down," Snook said, not thinking it wise to tell Yumza he did not eat red meat.

"Oh," Onora spoke up, "I feel for you. I once got sick on bad meat and did not think I was ever going to get over it. I remember how I begged Urga, that's Kalmar's grandfather, to just kill me because I did not think I could stand the pain another instant." After Onora's revelation, the four of them talked about many things.

Yumza, why do you have three children when every other couple seems to have only two?" Snook asked.

"What an unusual question," Yumza said, her eyes rounding. Then her solemn expression collapsed under the weight of a large grin. "Snook, you are such a joker."

"It is the Will of Shetow," Onora said, looking at Snook out of the corner of her eye.

"Snook and I"—Kalmar stood up and motioned to Snook— "are going for a walk. Do not wait on us for supper; it will be well after dark when we come back."

"You two be careful." Then Yumza's eyes brightened. "But that is not necessary to say to a young man who has slain a cave lion singlehanded." Yumza's face glowed with pride as Kalmar and Snook started to leave the room.

"Thank you again, Yumza, for the excellent stew," Snook said. The two stepped out the door and walked a few steps.

"Why," Kalmar asked, "is it easy for you to take the praise of saving me from the infection, yet you will not let me give you the credit you deserve concerning the cave lion?"

"With your infection, I could not hide what the hunting party could plainly see, but the events surrounding the death of the cave lion must always remain between us. To me, to be thought of as a healer, is much different than being part of the Tell about you and the cave lion."

Kalmar shrugged. "Well, you need to be a little more diplomatic with your questions. Why would you ask my mother why she had three children? You're bringing a lot of attention to yourself. No one, besides me, understands your circumstances."

"My circumstances?"

Kalmar knew he had said the wrong thing. He had never told Snook he understood the albino's plight; that he had figured out that the people of the Black Raven Tribe must have shunned Snook and that is why he had not been Paired and was on a ramble. It became clear to him that if he was going to shelter Snook's feelings, he must find someone else to help him carry the burden of Snook's fanatic desire to be so secretive, someone to help him spurn unwanted questions from the other villagers. He thought a moment before his eyes opened wider. *Nutan*, he thought. *Yes, little sister, you will be the one to help.*

He decided to ignore Snook's question. "I just think it prudent to keep your questions to me and my younger sister, Nutan."

As Snook nodded, the brim of his floppy straw hat bobbed. "I will try to be more careful." They walked a few moments in silence. "Your grandmother took the death of your grandfather hard."

"She has been different ever since Urga's death. Sometimes she sits by the window and looks out for hours without moving. Her thoughts are jumbled; she has even called me by his name. His death has affected everyone in the family, each one of us in a different way."

•

"I am sorry I never had a chance to meet him."

As the two walked through the village, men, boys, and a few women stopped them to congratulate Kalmar. In time, they approached a small group of young boys shepherded by three old men. One of the men raised a wooden staff and held it at arms length over his head when he recognized Kalmar. "Kalmar," the old man shouted as Kalmar and Snook came closer. The man was dressed in buckskin, as were his two adult companions. His two companions were pudgy, but the man who had called Kalmar appeared to have no fat on his body whatsoever. All three had gray beards, though the beard of the one who had hailed Kalmar bordered on being white. His hair matched the color of his beard and hung to his shoulders; however, the top of his skull was completely bald and looked like it had never been otherwise. Although advanced in the cycles of the seasons, he stood as straight as his wooden staff; his erectness stood in sharp contrast to the stoop in the backs of the other two men. Kalmar and Snook stopped in front of the old man. The man's chiseled face cracked into a smile filled with teeth as white as his hair, and both teeth and hair appeared even whiter compared to the rich, dark copper tone of his skin.

"Got your cave lion did ya? Always thought you would." The old man tilted his head when he noticed the wounds on Kalmar's face. "Heard the cat took a piece of you." He grasped Kalmar's face and turned it to the side. "Half a step closer and the cat would have taken off your head." The old man raised his other hand and pushed against the closed wounds with his fingers. "Not puffy, no infection." The old man narrowed his eyes. "You will have scars, though." He ran the tip of his tongue between his teeth and upper lip. "But a good job anyway. Skillful." He looked closer. "As good as I have ever seen." The old man looked up. "Done by a healer?"

"Ayah." Kalmar stepped back. "This is Snook. He is the one who treated my wounds and stitched my face." Kalmar turned towards Snook. "Snook, this is Ayah, the senior Gray Beard of our tribe and the best teacher any young man could ever have."

"Kind words from a gifted student," Ayah said, moving closer to Snook. "His best teacher was Urga, his grandfather—a Gray Beard for Gray Beards, a man of many virtues and few faults. I was honored to call him my friend." He studied Snook a moment. "And Kalmar's friend Snook, where are you from?" Ayah lifted an eyebrow. "An albino are you. Heard of them; never met one."

Snook opened his mouth but Kalmar spoke first. "Snook's from beyond the western mountains, from the Black Raven Tribe. He's on a ramble."

"Ramble. Know all about rambles; made one myself some cycles of the seasons ago. Visited most of the villages; gone for many seasons." He looked away. "Best time of my life it was." He puckered his face as he rubbed his bald head. "Missed your village though; stayed on this side of those mountains." After a moment, he shrugged his shoulders and, as he turned back to Kalmar, a smile returned to his face. "Your mother and grandmother are doing well, I trust?"

"Yes, they are both fine."

Ayah placed a hand on Kalmar's shoulder. "You are a good man—a little too sure of yourself, but a good man. You have made your family and the rest of us proud." The other two Gray Beards walked up to Kalmar and he turned to talk to them. Ayah grabbed Snook's arm and pulled him aside. "It will be hard," Ayah said softly, "for his mother, grandmother, and sisters when Kalmar leaves for the Gathering. They have already lost a grandfather and a father to tragedy, men who stayed with their families after their Pootashs . . . men who loved, and were loved by, their Pairing Partners." The old man lowered his eyes. "Now the time has come for Kalmar, the son, to leave the family for the Gathering and his

Matage—his Choosing. A time that should be a moment of fulfillment is, instead, a time of sadness for their family. They will lose
their third beloved male in a handful of cycles of the seasons."
Ayah shook his head again. "Only Shetow knows why so much
grief must be borne by one family."

"The grandfather and father stayed after their Pootashs?"

"Kalmar's mother and grandmother did well at their Matage—
they chose the best of men. At the time of the grandparents'
Pootash, they chose to remain Paired and the continuation of their
union was blessed by the Medora at a Nukashe. His parents had
pledged to do the same but Seldan was killed before their Pootash."
Ayah scratched his head. "It is too bad more couples do not stay together. Most young people dream of their Pootash—they cannot
wait to warm their bed covers with a parade of unfamiliar bodies.
Lust of the flesh—it rots the heart out of our inner-spirit. I have
seen it corrupt the values of many people."

Snook's eyebrows lifted. "Do you think a couple should stay
together if there is no love?"

"Love, lust . . . what's the difference? As one grows older, the
feelings of your heart should move away from your crotch and migrate to your head . . . you know, Snook, I try to teach these boys it
is more important to like your Pairing Partner, at the time of their
Pootash, than it is to love or lust after them."

"I see some wisdom in that," Snook said, nodding his head.

"I can teach these boys how to shoot straight"—Ayah motioned towards the young boys who were now playing all around
them—"but I have never been able to figure out how to help them
make their pairings work. Most of the tribe's pairings raise their two
children only to have their union dissolve at the time of their
Pootash, twenty cycles of the seasons after it began." The old man
frowned. "The good Mother Shetow missed on that one." He

raised his left arm, exposing the dark circle on his wrist. "Blessed be Her Mark."

"Maybe She planned it that way," Snook said.

"She *did* plan it that way, because it *is* that way . . . but, I believe, she hoped more pairings would stay together out of respect for Her."

Snook nodded.

Kalmar finished his conversation with the other two Gray Beards and turned back to Snook and Ayah. "I trust you two could find something to talk about."

"I like your friend, Kalmar; he didn't pepper me with questions like you did when you were my student."

"You must have scared him, Ayah. He asks me a lot more than I ever asked you."

Ayah," Snook said as they walked away, "must have had a strong pairing."

"Why do you say that?"

"He has such strong feelings about couples staying together."

"Ayah has a skewed viewpoint on the subject."

"What he said made plenty of sense to me."

"Ayah's Pairing Partner took their children and left him before their Pootash, the only time in the last two hundred cycles of the seasons a female, who had borne children, left her Pairing Partner before their Pootash. It crushed Ayah. He left the tribe of his Pairing Partner and made the ramble he spoke of before returning to our tribe—the tribe of his mother and his youth."

"No wonder he is so—"

"Bitter?"

"Philosophical."

"Ayah is a revered Gray Beard, Snook. He knows more about being a man—a hunter—than any other Gray Beard in the tribe, but when the Lessons dealt with The Choosing or females, we learned his feel for dealing with females was as weak as his skills as a hunter were strong."

"Then I fear my own expectations of a successful relationship are in jeopardy," Snook said under his breath.

After breaking away from a small group of admiring children, Kalmar and Snook walked faster, and they made it to a dwelling across from the Oonoc Lodge without someone else stopping them. Before Kalmar could knock, the door opened to let them enter. Once inside the dwelling, it took a moment for their eyes to adjust to the dimly lit room.

Once their vision returned, they found a petite young woman no older than Snook standing in front of them. Kalmar glanced around the room and then noticed Snook staring at the young woman. The woman showed no reaction to the gaping man in front of her. She was unusually short, but her head and limbs were in a pleasing proportion to her torso; from a distance, you would not notice her slight stature unless she was standing next to someone else. The object of Snook's gaze was elfin, not only in size, but also in finely formed—almost pointed—features. Her jet black hair was pulled back and tied tightly at the back of her head, then flowed down her back past her tiny waist. Her hair and dark eyes stood in contrast to her pale complexion. Snook's reaction to the young woman was amusing to Kalmar; it was the first time he had seen Snook speechless. Finally, the young woman blushed and flashed a sweet, feminine smile full of small white teeth. "You're here to see Berkana?" she asked in a soft musical voice matching her appearance.

"Yes, Cabyl, but my friend here seems to be satisfied just to see you," Kalmar said. With Kalmar's words, Snook dropped his eyes.

Cabyl's face reddened and she quickly turned and started to walk down a hallway. "Please come this way."

With Cabyl's back to them, Snook looked up and quickly drew back his fist and punched Kalmar's arm. "Would you *shut up!*"

"Oooh, that hurt!"

"It was *meant* to hurt," Snook said through gritted teeth.

Cabyl stopped and turned around with a slight glimmer in her eyes and the hint of a smile on her lips. "Are you coming?"

Kalmar and Snook followed Cabyl into a voluminous room with a towering ceiling. She indicated they should sit down. Their chairs were in front of a large stone fireplace with a crackling fire that lit and heated the spacious area. The room bristled with paintings, sculptures, and other pieces of fine art. "Berkana's seeing to some important matters but will be with you as soon as possible." With that, she spun around and left the two alone in the room.

"Who is *that?*"

"Why did you hit me?"

"Did you call her Cabyl?"

"That really did hurt, you know."

Snook was about to say something else but stopped short with his mouth open and changed his approach. "I am sorry if I hurt you, but you embarrassed me."

"*I embarrassed you!* You stood there disrobing that poor girl with your eyes and you don't think I was embarrassed—and how do you think Cabyl felt? I thought she was going to melt under that stare of yours. You, embarrassed? That is a joke—if Cabyl were my sister, I would have hit you harder, and I guarantee, it would not have been on the arm."

"I was not doing that," Snook said, a little above a whisper.

"Not doing that? What do you mean? I watched you stare at her . . . do not tell me—"

"I mean . . . I was not disrobing her in my mind . . . do you . . . do you think that is what she thinks I was doing?"

"I think that is exactly what she thinks you were doing. . . . If you were not, then what were you doing?"

"Kalmar, Cabyl's the most stunning woman I have ever seen. I was dazed. I've never seen a woman that . . . that beguiling before." Snook rose out of his chair. "I must go tell her I meant no disrespect."

Kalmar grabbed Snook's arm. "You are going to find the girl so you can tell her you were not looking at her lustfully. Snook . . . you do have a lot to learn about females. I said you embarrassed her; I am not sure you offended her. My older sister once told me all women are aware men are sexual creatures and fantasize about them. Most of the time females just shrug off our probing glances, but you went too far. You denied her the chance to act as if she did not notice your looks. You did not just glance—you *glared*. You not only embarrassed her, you went beyond the acceptable stare. Some females might have taken offense at it, but, that is not what I saw in her eyes."

"What did you see in her eyes?" Snook said as he put his hand on Kalmar's arm.

"I think you flattered her—you embarrassed her, true enough, but you also flattered her—your stare was real, and she knew it. Come to think of it, she could use a little attention."

"What do you mean?"

"Cabyl is an unusual case; her Pairing did not produce children."

"Do all Pairings produce children?"

"No, but Cabyl was the highest ranked female in her Byrrac and she Paired with the highest-ranked male of his Borrac; the Tell and the Chronicles have no record of such a high-ranked Pairing not producing children. A few cycles of the seasons after their Pairing, her Pairing Partner declared a Yah-Pootash when Cabyl did not become pregnant with their First Childs. He returned to his tribe and she came to live and study with Berkana."

"Yah-Pootash?"

"If a pairing does not produce children the couple does not have to wait twenty cycles of the seasons for their Pootash—their happy time. Either partner can call for an early end to the pairing by declaring a Yah-Pootash; surely some of the Pairing Partners in your tribe separate when they do not have children?"

Snook gave a lethargic nod. "Cabyl must been devastated."

"For the longest time you never saw her outside Berkana's cottage. At first, many members of the tribe shunned her; they said Shetow had cursed her. If it had not been for Berkana, Cabyl would have been completely ostracized by the tribe." He looked at Snook; his words had fallen hard on his friend. Kalmar touched his friend's arm. "You are probably the first male to pay her any attention since that happened."

Snook remained in deep thought after Kalmar stop talking. Snook finally raised his eyes. "There is something about that girl I cannot put into words—mysterious yet subdued." Snook sat up straight. "She is concealing something."

"I also sensed something—a feeling of . . ." Kalmar paused; Snook and he looked at each other and said in unison. "Sorrow." The two kept looking at each other for a few moments.

"Sorrow is to be expected in her circumstances; there is more to it than that." Snook slid back into deep thought. "Cabyl, Cabyl, Cabyl, what are you hiding? What is the answer to your mystery?"

"Snook, the biggest mystery here is not Cabyl." Snook turned to look at him. "It is you," Kalmar said, grinning.

Snook's eyes locked with his. After a tense moment, Snook's familiar smile spread across his face. The two sat in the room talking as they waited for their unseen host. Snook studied the many different types of paintings, sculptures, and objects collected in the room. Snook noticed a leather-bound book lying on the table between them. Discoloration along the middle of its spine suggested heavy use; it took the oil from the hands of many readers to leave such a dark stain. Knowing the book was more than a showpiece, Snook reached over and picked it up. At first, as he turned the pages, he thought he had been wrong—it was art. Each page was covered with a fine calligraphy that barely gave away the fact a human hand had written the flowing text. The border of each page was an embossed strip of ornamental beauty.

"This is a wondrous thing."

"That is Berkana's favorite copy of the *Chants of the Sequa*. Isn't it an amazing example of the artistic Traits Shetow has given our females? After the Sixth Progression when the People refined our written language and mastered the art of papermaking, the women of the Cave Lion endeavored to transcribe the Chants of the Sequa and the Will of Shetow as close to that recited by Geerna to the People at the first Gatherings. Their current project is to do the same with every Tell told by every tribe." Kalmar shook his head. "The women's pride—I think it is vanity—has pushed them to produce the finest books to be found anywhere in the Twenty-Four Tribes."

"I've never seen such exquisite detail in a book before."

"Have you ever seen a prairie-buck skin scroll from the Fifth Progression?"

"I don't think so."

"I have only seen one and it was so fragile I was not allowed to touch it."

There was a hollow sound and both of them turned towards an opening door. Snook put the *Sequa* back on the table.

"Well, Kalmar, your name is on everyone's lips," an old woman with fine, stark white hair and a creviced face said as she carefully toddled into the room. Cabyl had accompanied her to the door of the room but did not follow her in. Kalmar noticed both Snook and Cabyl avoided looking at each other. He and Snook rose from their chairs as the old woman entered the room, and then sat back down once she settled into a large cushioned leather chair across from them. The old woman continued to smile and awaited Kalmar's introduction of his companion. She did not focus on Snook until Kalmar pointed to him.

He raised his left hand. "Berkana, this is Snook, a new acquaintance, someone I hope will become a close friend. He asked to meet you. Snook stumbled on me after my incident with the cave lion and attended to my wounds; he was also helping me drag the cat's carcass back to the village when I collapsed. Without his healing skills, I would have died from my infected claw marks." Kalmar shifted his body. "Snook, this is Berkana, the Medora of the Cave Lion Tribe and, as you know, the Medora Roo of all the tribes of the People. She is like a second grandmother to me. She is one of those I came to after the death of my grandfather; she helped me deal with the pain of his death. You're both important to me; I am glad to have you meet."

Snook and Berkana eyed each other—neither spoke. Kalmar looked at one, then the other. Neither seemed to hear what he had said; he felt ignored for the first time since his triumphant return.

Finally, Berkana turned to Kalmar. "Always remember, true friendship is based on the ability of one to lower the barriers of their excess pride. It's good you've found someone to whom you think you can humble yourself. Now Kalmar, I need you to do me a favor."

"Of course, anything."

"I need you to take a note to Yumza," Berkana said as she opened a drawer in the table by her chair and took out a piece of paper. After she finished writing, she folded the paper, sealed it with sealing wax, and then handed it to Kalmar.

"All right, I will give it to her," he said as he continued to sit in the chair.

"I need you to take it to her now."

"Now?"

The old Medora nodded.

"All right." He rose and waited for Snook to stand up.

"If Snook wanted to meet me, do you not think it would be more polite for you to leave Snook with me so we can chat while I wait for your mother's answer?"

Kalmar noticed Snook had not moved when he stood up. It was as though Snook had known the Medora was going to have him stay. He left the room with the two of them looking at each other.

May I see your left wrist?"
Snook slid up the snakeskin band covering his wrist. Berkana leaned forward to inspect his white unmarked skin. Then she settled back in her chair.

"Mookyn."

Snook nodded.

"I assume the Elders sent you because of my message?"

"Yes."

"I was told there were a number of albinos among you."

"Almost one in five."

"The Elders have never sent an albino to the lands of the Twenty-Four Tribes."

"The Elders thought our skin color would make it impossible for us to move among the Tribes without bringing attention to ourselves."

"I must agree. Then why did they send you?"

"Although there are many among us who know more about the culture of the Twenty-Four Tribes than I do, many of the Elders thought I was the brightest of the Seekers and, considering the dire circumstances, the reaction of your people to my white skin was deemed inconsequential."

Berkana's eyes softened. "Your name?"

"Olum."

"Your humility becomes you."

He was fidgety as he waited for the old woman to speak, but she just kept looking at him. "How can we help you prepare for the Second Judging?" he said, breaking the silence.

"I am not sure there is anything the Mookyn can do to help; there is not enough time for you to take the information back to your Elders before we must select our representatives to the Judging."

"I must be able to help in some way. The consequences of the Second Judging also affect my people."

The old woman's chair creaked as she leaned back to study her visitor. "Concentration of the Traits was not the task Geerna asked of your people. I only sent the message to the Elders out of respect; to let them know the time we have always dreaded has arrived."

"I realize the Mookyn have made no effort to concentrate the Traits; Geerna sent us down a different path. Nevertheless, our society is far more advanced than that of the Twenty-Four Tribes. If it was not for the rules that govern the interaction between our two groups, I would not have been forced to walk and would have arrived here a season earlier."

" 'More advanced' only from your perspective. Our society has been carefully guided through the mysteries"—she raised her arm to allow the folds of her robe to fall back, revealing the dark spot on the inside of her wrist—"of the Mark of the Covenant. Unlike yours, our society developed according to a set plan—a plan, though, that many Medoras had let slip in priority. It is true that the Twenty-Four Tribes lag far behind the Mookyn in many facets, but we do not have your diseases or many of the other maladies that plague your society."

For a moment, the old woman's eyes lost their focus as she stared past Snook. Snook did not move. Then she turned towards him again.

"Our society may be more primitive than yours, but we are the ones Geerna selected to Concentrate the Traits most desired by Shetow. It is upon the shoulders of those chosen from the Twenty-Four Tribes who will decide the fate of us all."

If there was any color in his pale face, it now disappeared. "You must allow me to play a part in the events that will decide the fate of my . . . of every person on Elom. Surely, Geerna meant for the Mookyn to play some part; otherwise, we would never have been allowed to exist."

Berkana nodded. "Olum of the Mookyn, you make a strong appeal. Geerna's People spread beyond the territory of the Twenty-Four Tribes." She paused. "Stay with Kalmar's family and let me think about a role you could play. If there is one, you have my word; I will give you your chance."

For an instant, Snook looked down at his feet. When he raised his head, he said, "That is all I can ask."

"I can see why Kalmar would like you as a friend. I hope you are given that opportunity."

Snook bowed his head. "Thank you for your kind words, Medora Roo."

"I will stay in contact with you. Now," she said with a slight wave of her hand, "go see that you and Kalmar do not get into any mischief. And remember to watch what you say; the People of the Twenty-Four Tribes know nothing of the Second Judging."

"As only a select few among mine do."

The old woman studied him a moment, her eyes moving over him. *Your skin color,* she thought, *will distract most of them from your verbal indiscretions.*

"You must mark the inside of your arm to make sure no one sees that you do not have the Mark of the Covenant."

Snook nodded, and then stood up and left the room.

EIGHT

It took a long time for Kalmar to reach his home; people forced him to stop every few paces as they continued to rush up and congratulate him. Once there, his mother looked surprised when he handed her the Medora's note. Yumza opened the note and read it. Once she finished, she looked up at Kalmar with wide eyes. "It will take a few moments for me to write an answer to this. Please wait." With that, she turned and walked down the hall to her mother's room. Onora looked up as Yumza entered. "Kalmar just brought me a note from Berkana."

"What did it say?"

Yumza's face had lost its color. "Stall Kalmar."

After an unusually long time, Yumza handed Kalmar a sealed note to take back to Berkana. As he worked his way back through the throng of well-wishers, he met Snook walking towards him.

"Your Medora is quite a person," Snook said as they stopped in front of each other. "Can we go down to the river now; maybe we can catch some fish?"

"I still have to give this note to Berkana."

"Oh, that. She told me to tell you she remembered what she needed to know and you didn't have to bring it to her."

Kalmar's cheeks flushed. "But I needed to talk to her about my dreams," he said in such a low voice Snook strained to hear him.

"Dreams?"

As he shrugged his shoulders, the corner of Kalmar's lips away from the stitched wounds of his battered face turned down. "Most of this season I have been troubled by confusing dreams. I had hoped to discuss them with Berkana."

"Berkana can interpret dreams?"

"She is the best of all the Medoras in such matters," Kalmar said, his eyes a little brighter.

"That is a great gift for someone to have," Snook said, his face solemn and his eyes attentive.

"The Medoras say," Kalmar said with great conviction, "it is one of the Traits most prized by Shetow. A Trait, they say, better understood since the last Progression."

"Maybe I should talk to her."

"You have dreams too?" Kalmar asked, the pitch of his voice higher.

Snook crinkled his face into a silly smirk. "Kalmar, everyone has dreams."

"Of course," Kalmar answered, his swollen lips now a childish smile.

Snook turned his eyes towards the river where the rays of the afternoon suns sparkled against the tops of the waves. "We can talk to Berkana later; the smells of the river are calling us. I will show you how to fish."

"I *know* how to fish," Kalmar said, acting taken aback by Snook's accusation.

"We will see," Snook said in a flat tone as he turned and started walking towards the river.

Kalmar threw his hands up as he watched Snook walk away. He glanced back towards Berkana's cottage, and then turned and hurried after Snook.

They sat on the riverbank with their backs against a towering duta tree, its gigantic limbs and scattered foliage spread above them like a doting mother holding out her apron to shelter her small children. Fallen leaves, shed during the colder seasons, covered the ground around the base of the giant tree. Each man gripped a fishing pole.

"I still do not see how you can say there is a difference between killing a prairie buck or a cave lion and fishing," Kalmar said as he flipped the hook end of his fishing line a little farther away from the bank.

"I do not kill and eat animals whose blood is as warm as my own. I believe the creatures of the waters are here for us to eat and the creatures of the land are here to keep us company."

"You have an answer for everything, Snook."

"No," Snook said grinning, "that is not true; there is much I have yet to learn."

"Like what?"

"Well," Snook hesitated. "About . . . the Matage."

"The Choosing? You must know the answers to the questions you ask. Why ask them?" After he said it, Kalmar winced. He remembered that might not be the case and regretted having said it; if he was correct and members of Snook's own tribe had ostracized him, he would know little about such things.

Snook raised his hand. "Kalmar, two people can watch something happen, standing side-by-side, yet describe the event so differently one would think they had seen two entirely different things. I know what I know; I just want to know how you understand it." Snook scrunched his nose. "Asking dumb questions is one of the things we Seekers do. Humor me." Frowning, Snook diverted his eyes to a point halfway down his hastily fashioned pole where his fishing line had snagged on a branch stub.

Kalmar listened to his distracted friend as he grumbled and fiddled with one of the fishing poles, which were made from two saplings, and the hooks and line Snook carried in his fishing kit. As Snook's straw hat bobbed with his every move, Kalmar reflected on this obviously courageous but equally mysterious man. He trusted Snook; few had friends, much less unarmed strangers, who would risk their own lives for them. Kalmar knew he was fortunate to have survived his encounters with the cave lion and then later with the infection, but his unfailing gratitude did not extinguish his active curiosity about his rescuer. It was obvious to Kalmar that Snook did not have and, from Snook's questions, had never had a Pairing Partner. A feeling of sadness filled his heart as he realized that Snook, with his red eyes and pale skin, must have lived a life of rejection. Kalmar's mind raced as the pain of enlightenment jolted his inner-spirit; the full force of Snook's situation finally hit him. The reason Snook was not a hunter and did not have a Pairing Partner was that Snook had removed himself from being with those who might tease or ostracize him. Kalmar's eyes grew large and round, his breathing shallow. Snook did not think of himself as one in unison with other people.

A shiver racked Kalmar's body; Snook's parents must have been so ashamed of him that they did not take him to his Koo Toc Biren. The reason he did not have the Mark of the Covenant was—he was never given one. Now Snook roamed the lands of the Twenty-Four Tribes searching for those experiences denied him. Kalmar nodded to himself. That was why Snook was slow to claim the Black Raven Tribe; as a child, they must not have rejoiced over his birth. To reject hunting was Snook's response to the hunters of his tribe's rejection of him. Deep lines crossed Kalmar's brow. Snook now sought those unknown memories that other men shared. Kalmar wondered if he was the first person ever to befriend Snook. He pursed his lips. Would he have befriended Snook if Snook had not saved his life? Kalmar's breathing was shallow and slow. Snook was thirsty to understand all the things he had missed in his life. Snook's description of himself now made perfect sense to Kalmar. Snook was a "Seeker."

Kalmar kept his mouth open for a second but didn't say anything. He closed it. "Okay, ask away."

"Tell me about the Matage, the Choosing."

"It's where males find out with which female they are going to be Paired."

"Paired? Like as in 'Pairing Partner?'"

"Snook, please—"

Snook raised his hand and shook his head.

Kalmar's eyes narrowed. Then he lifted the end of his fishing pole to check his bait. "The way *we* make sure"—he lowered the hook back into the river—"there are going to be children to take our places when we grow old and die is for men and women to have sex—"

"Sarcasm," Snook dropped his chin and glared at him, "does not befit you."

Kalmar picked up a small stone and started to throw it into the river, but he hesitated and then tossed it behind them into the trees. "After their eighteenth birthday men and women are matched in pairs to produce children, thus honoring Shetow. The Matage, also called the Choosing, is the ceremony where the females choose their male partner. The order in which the females make their selections is based upon the female's finishing rank in the Byrrac—the female games."

"The male has nothing to do with it?"

"The higher a male finishes in the Borrac—or male games—improves the odds of him being picked by a high-finishing female."

"Why does his ranking have anything to do with it?"

"It improves her chances to have children."

"Chances?"

"Only the pairings in the top ninety percent or so in the rankings will have children. Both the male and female know the higher the rank of their Pairing Partner, the better chance they have of becoming a parent."

"Why only the top ninety percent?"

"It's the Will of Shetow," he said, shrugging his shoulders. "It's like you said, some things are universal."

"I am beginning to understand why the upcoming Borrac is so important to you. You call it a game?"

"It is more of a contest. The Borrac and the Byrrac are composed of similar but different types of contests held during the middle six days of the ten days of the Gathering. Some of the contests are ones that call for skills requiring quickness and strength; other contests deal with the skills and quickness of the mind. A few of the contests challenge both the mind and the body." Kalmar frowned. "Now I would like to ask you a question."

"What is that?"

"Some of the contests deal with things we learn in our Lessons, things that we never use in our daily lives. Why is understanding advanced concepts, knowledge that has no practical use, as important as my ability to shoot my bow?" He scratched the unscarred side of this face. "Now, Snook, that's a real question."

"I wish I knew the answer, but I don't." Snook pulled his knees to his chest. "I will make note of it and let you know if I figure it out. Now, tell me about the Matage."

Kalmar considered Snook's question and thought it an opening to ask a question that would confirm his suspicions. "Snook, you're older than I am, you've already been through your Borrac and Choosing. I should be learning from you, not you asking me questions about things you know the answers to better than I do."

Snook took in a deep breath and slowly let it out. "Kalmar, do you trust me?"

"Of course, I owe you my life; I'll always be in your debt. How could I not trust you?"

"I didn't go through a Borrac or a Choosing. I know it is hard for you to understand. You must trust me; I will explain everything to you when I can. And Kalmar, this must stay between us."

The increased batting of his eyelids was Kalmar's only reaction before he gave a slight nod. So, his suspicions were true; Snook had been ostracized by the members of the Black Raven Tribe.

Kalmar noticed Snook looking at him out of the corner of his eye, searching for a response to his revelation. He frowned at Kalmar's seeming indifference.

There was a long silence.

Kalmar finally said, "Berkana . . . what did you and she talk about?"

Snook tilted his head as he thought a moment. "She wanted to hear about my travels."

Kalmar strained not to show a reaction to Snook's answer. Berkana must have heard the stories of the dejected albino; she would have been incensed at the way his own tribe had treated this noble man. He could not hold back a grin; it must have been a shock to Berkana when he walked in with the famed white wanderer.

"As I said, females make their choices in the order they finish in the Byrrac. Usually, the top eighty-five to ninety percent will choose the highest ranked remaining male. The top ten percent or so might choose a male they find more physically desirable as long as he is also in the top percentages in the ranking."

"And those in the lower echelons of finishers?"

"The females who rank in the bottom ten percent of their Byrrac realize there's little hope of them having children. They'll choose their Pairing Partners for whatever reason they may feel important."

"Such as?"

"Sexual attraction the female has for the male or for some skill he possesses. She might choose a partner who is a good woodworker because her mother's cottage needs repair." Kalmar shrugged his shoulders. "Who knows the mind of a woman?"

"Got it," Snook said, jerking the tip of his fishing pole up. "That little pest has been hitting my bait for the last few minutes." Snook's pole arched as he fought his struggling catch to the shoreline. "Nibble on my bait, will you?" He grinned as a forearm-long silhouette just below the water's surface became visible in the starlight. "Thought you could outfox Snook?" As he lifted his catch out of the water the pole snapped straight as the fish wiggled free of the hook, dropped to the ground, and started flopping around in the grass. Snook dove headlong trying to catch the evasive fish. He got his hands around it only to have the fish squirt free. The fish bounced once on the riverbank as a frantic Snook grasped for the scaly creature. The equally excited fish squirmed until it reached the slippery mud on the riverbank where it slid down the incline into the safety of the murky water. Snook had fallen on his stomach in his futile effort to retrieve his catch and lay with his legs stretched behind him and his hands and arms up to his elbows in the river.

Kalmar rolled over laughing. "Guess our fish are smarter than the ones you are used to." Snook turned towards Kalmar with a humiliated look on his face, shook his head, and then joined Kalmar in his uncontrolled laughter.

————

The two talked as they fished. One would catch a fish, then the other. Kalmar knew little about Snook, and today he found he knew even less than he thought, yet he felt at ease in this unusual man's company. It was odd, but he had not felt so comfortable around anyone since the death of his grandfather Urga.

Later, as the two lay on the riverbank, they looked up at the dazzling swath of stars spread across the sky. It was a night of a Jara Oow, one of those rare occasions when neither of Elom's two suns nor any of its four moons were visible. The orbit of the brown dwarf Eeo—the dark companion—was so close to Salune it never set more than an hour after the primary sun. However, the three larger moons—Boboi, Quiron, and Menstur—had such varying orbits, that only on this, the rarest of occasions, would one of the three not be visible. Mystery, the fourth and smallest moon, shot across the sky nine times a day, although its reflected light was feeble and did not take away from the majesty of the stars. However, a true Jara Oow only occurred when the tiny moon was also absent from the sky.

People considered a Jara Oow on a cloudless night the most inspiring events in their lives. Elom, unlike the People's mother world, lay in a tightly packed star cluster near the center of the galaxy. With the two suns and four moons absent, over a hundred thousand stars crowded Elom's nighttime sky—more than twenty times the number visible from Geerna's Quary Hut. Not only was the number of stars overwhelming, but also their proximity to Elom rendered a deluge of celestial hues not visible from a planet on the outer fringe of the galaxy.

Kalmar and Snook knew from the evening positioning of the moons that there was going to be a Jara Oow during the early hours before dawn. The earliness of the event did not really disturb anyone; most people would just go to bed a little earlier and plan to rise in time to see the last moon set. The two decided, however, to remain at the river and make a night of it; they aimed to stay up and watch the setting of all four moons. Hunger soon overcame them, so after gutting and scaling the fish, they cooked and ate them.

Snook was the chef. First, as Kalmar looked on, he rustled around the lush foliage that lined the edge of the river and came back with four large yuma tubers and an armful of leaves from an assortment of plants that Kalmar, for the most part, did not recognize. He washed the fish, yuma tubers, and leaves in a meandering stream that flowed into the river close to where they had been fishing. After cleaning, Snook took each fish and filled its emptied body cavity with a mixture of the leaves that he had crushed between the palms of his hands, and then he wrapped each fish in layers of the largest of the assortment of leaves. Kalmar watched with great interest as Snook encased the leaf-covered bundles in a clay-based mud he scooped up from along the river's edge.

While Snook prepared the fish, he had Kalmar build a fire using hardwood no larger than his forearm. Once the fire had burned down to glowing embers, Snook gently laid the bundles among the coals and covered them with small dry sticks, which quickly caught fire. Lastly, he took the yuma tubers and placed them directly on the coals with no other preparation than washing; every few minutes he would roll them over with a green stick he stripped from a nearby bush.

After several minutes, vents releasing whistling steam erupted along the sides of the clay bundles. Kalmar noted the different aroma of the cooking fish compared to the prairie buck to which he was accustomed. The mild scent of fish mingled with the fragrance of the leafy filling produced a tantalizing smell. After the clay dried and the thick skin of the yuma tubers had shriveled and blackened, Snook used the forked part of his stick to lift the clay-covered bundles and tubers from the smoldering ashes. Snook showed Kalmar how to flake away the dried clay to expose the green leaves covering the fish.

"The Gray Beards never showed us how to do this," Kalmar said as he used his knife to slice open the leaves, revealing the steaming fish. They sat around the crackling fire and ate the fish and yuma tubers using only their fingers and knives. The tubers boasted a sweet, stringy pulp; Kalmar had eaten baked yuma before but it never tasted this good. He had to agree with Snook; the taste of the freshly caught fish was as good as any red meat he had ever eaten. Really, it was the best meal he could remember.

Kalmar glanced at his new friend and wondered how he could be so amiable after the dejected life he must have had. Everyone else may have rejected Snook, but Kalmar made a silent pledge at that moment that anyone who rejected Snook in the future, also rejected him.

NINE

Later, the intense conversation yielded to silence as both men felt the dulling effects of their earlier gluttony. The fire flickered out; the hot coals hissed and crackled as the embers glowed a faint burgundy. The two kept their eyes fixed on the sky and the kaleidoscope of colors only fully seen in the absence of moonlight. Even without moonlight, the river of stars illuminated the nighttime landscape enough to make it easy to move about without the aid of any additional light. Only heavy cloud cover could subdue the twilight-of-night.

"Kalmar."

"Hmm."

"May I ask you a question?"

"You will end up prying it out of me no matter how I answer," Kalmar said with a good-hearted laugh.

"I'm not very tactful, am I?"

"Snook, when you want to know something you are like a bear after honey—you will not be denied. Now, what was it that you wanted to ask me?"

"Yesterday, after we left Berkana's, you said you needed to talk to her about your dreams. If it is not too personal, would you tell me about them?" Snook said in a soft tone Kalmar could not re-member his new friend ever using before.

He knew instinctively that Snook would not press him if he told Snook he did not want to talk about the dreams. His respect for Snook increased. If Snook had asked him in any other manner, he would have resisted his new friend's probe.

"All right."

Snook gave a slight nod. "Just tell me what you can remember about them."

"I have had dreams all my life. I know, as you said, everyone has dreams, but recently mine are often-recurring dreams. I have had the same dream night after night for the last few seasons."

"The same dream?"

"It will be exactly the same for a handful of days, then one night the dream will last a little longer and add a little more detail. Sort of like a book, it is as if I were reading a story and reading the same pages over each night, then one night, I am able to read an additional page. The next few nights the dream stays the same. This goes on until another page is revealed and the cycle starts over."

"My Toran," Snook said, moving his hands in a circular mo-tion, "believes dreams are a window to our inner-spirit." He leaned closer. "And your dream?"

"The dream always starts the same—I am alone, in a small boat on a large ripple-free body of water, a lake I guess. The boat is really more of a canoe—a dugout canoe so black I can't make out the texture of its surface. The canoe is no longer than two body lengths, has short sides, and is so narrow two people could not sit in it side by side—but I am not sitting. I am standing in the canoe with a long pole in my hands, which I am using to push against the lake bottom to move the canoe across the tranquil expanse of water."

"What time of day is it?"

"I am not sure." He thought a moment. "It has the dull illumination of the twilight-of-night, yet, even though the sky is cloudless, I do not remember any stars." He blinked as a set of wrinkles crossed his forehead. "Skimming the water's surface is a rolling mist covering much of the lake." Kalmar stopped talking as he scratched his arm, and then he looked down and slapped at a bug.

"What are you thinking as you cross the lake?"

"I remember my feelings clearly; they are not ones of fear but of wonder and anticipation. It is important I get to the shore—something is waiting for me, something is calling me—something . . ." He rocked his head side to side. "Something"—he looked at Snook—"I am not sure I am ready to face."

"And you do not have any idea what that is?"

"No."

"You said you were alone on the lake?"

"Yes—well. I am not sure," Kalmar said, dragging out the words.

"What gives you doubt?"

"In the last few dreams"—Kalmar moved his left hand behind him as if he were signaling someone to pass him—"I glimpsed something to my left just coming into my field of vision—something dark, something I cannot see well enough to recognize."

"Kalmar, I can see why you are reluctant to talk about your dreams; they would make anyone feel uneasy."

He nodded. "Snook, do you know of anyone else who has such dreams?"

"As I said before, everybody has dreams, Kalmar."

"You know what I mean—dreams like mine?" Kalmar said,

more as a statement than a question. His attention moved to the horizon as Mystery rose to start its dart across the sky.

I am aware of only one other, Snook thought, as he followed Kalmar's lead and looked to the starry heavens, *who has dreams like yours.*

TEN

The two men lay on their backs looking at the host of stars. Suddenly, Kalmar rolled over, propped himself up on his elbow while supporting his head in his hand, and looked at Snook. "Is your tribe very different from mine? You are different from anyone I know. Where you come from must be different than here—" Kalmar stopped and shook his head. "I'm not making any sense." He was broaching an area Snook had avoided, telling him he would explain everything in time. Would Snook brush off this inquiry as he had all the others?

"Kalmar," Snook said as he placed his hands, fingers interlaced, behind his head, using them as a pillow as he kept looking up at the wonders of the sky. "You told me it is unimaginable for a man in your tribe to not take part in the hunt."

"That is right."

"Why?"

"That is what men *do!*"

"But, *why?*"

"Snook, I . . . I do not know how to explain something I can't imagine being different. Why don't fish fly and birds swim in the cold waters at the bottom of the rivers? I do not know, and it's never entered my mind that birds and fish should swap their roles in life—just as it hadn't, before I met you, entered my mind there could be men who did not hunt."

Snook turned his face towards Kalmar, the back of his head still resting in the palms of his hands. "I know hunters; however, before I met you, none of my friends were hunters. If you had told me a few weeks ago I could relate to—much less be friends with—a hunter, it would have been, well, unimaginable for me." He paused, and then rose to a sitting position, pulling his knees almost to his chest as he locked his arms around his shins. "Yes, our tribes are different." He tilted his head. "And not necessarily in a bad way."

"Snook," Kalmar said slowly, ". . . all of this hurts my head." He put his fingertips to his temples. "I don't know what to think."

"Then don't."

Kalmar dropped his hands as he turned towards Snook.

"Don't think about it," Snook said. "I'm not saying you should not be aware I am different from what you believe, or at least expect, a man's role to be. It's important, however, that you give me time to learn as much about your society as I can. Then, when the time's right, I will share with you what I have learned about the differences between the two."

"But, if you would tell me about—"

"That wouldn't work."

"Why?" Kalmar's face tightened.

"For me to understand you"—Snook's features and voice softened—"and your tribe's way of thinking, it's crucial that I not influence you." He frowned. "However, it appears, I have already tainted your thinking."

"Tainted?"

"Before I came, you never wondered why fish didn't fly or birds didn't swim at the bottom of the rivers. Now you do. You are thinking about things that you would never have thought about if

I hadn't forced myself into your life. I have contaminated your mind with ideas that make it impossible for you to be the same person you were before I met you. I may have only changed your viewpoint a little"—Snook held up his right hand with the tips of his thumb and index finger almost touching—"but, never the less, I have changed it."

"Oh." Kalmar looked down a moment; his eyes were larger when he looked up. "There is one thing you haven't taken into consideration."

Snook's squinted eyes looked at him.

"Without you forcing yourself into my life . . ." He pressed his hand against his chest. "Without being 'tainted,' I would have died from the claws of the cave lion."

"Kalmar, I have told you—"

"You saved my life and nothing you say will change that."

Snook concealed his grin. "I lose either way."

"What . . . how?"

"If the cave lion had killed you," Snook said nonchalantly, "I would have no one to study, but by becoming involved in your duel with the great cat"—he could not hold back his smile any longer—"I contaminated my specimen."

"Specimen, am I?" Kalmar mocked with a half-suppressed grin.

Snook shook his head. He wasn't agreeing to having saved Kalmar from the cave lion's charge; only acknowledging he was never going to change Kalmar's opinion on the matter. He smiled. If he had in fact saved Kalmar's life, it was better to have "tainted" him than to have watched him die.

"Now that we're in agreement," Kalmar said, misreading Snook's gesture, "ask your questions. Just remember, at some point in this friendship, you must be the one who does the answering."

"Fair enough." Snook nodded. They both stood and grasped the inside of the other's forearm with their right hands. They then sat down again and continued their conversation.

"Are you ready for your Choosing?"

"Oh yes, I'm quite ready," Kalmar said, his face becoming animated.

"Being chosen by a woman as her partner for the next twenty cycles of the seasons would make me nervous," Snook said, his eyes narrowing as he studied Kalmar's effervescent face.

Kalmar grinned as he picked up a small flat stone and threw it towards the river. In the starlight of the twilight-of-night the stone was plainly visible as it skipped across the surface several times before sinking into the dark waters. "It should . . . if you don't know who your Pairing Partner is going to be."

"You know which female is going to choose you? How's that possible?"

"Well, for once I know more than my friend Snook," Kalmar said, his grin widening.

Snook's left eyebrow rose as he returned Kalmar's stare.

"Well . . . yes, and when you see her, you'll understand why I smile so when I talk about her."

"I take it she's attractive," Snook said, a little condescending.

"Attractive?" Kalmar smirked. "She's incredible. In all your travels, I'll bet you've never met her match." He began to move his arms wildly. "She has the softest brown hair and the purest, blue eyes that look right into your inner-spirit, and what a bottom." He used his right hand to outline the curve of her posterior. Then Kalmar held his hands up as if he were holding something, "And her breasts, what breasts—"

"All right!" Snook said, lifting his right hand. "Enough of the imaginative description, I think I understand what you're trying to tell me. But even with all these attributes, why would you want a woman with such flawed vision and defective judgment?" he said, shaking his head.

Kalmar's mouth dropped open.

"Okay, maybe it's something else," Snook said with a straight face. "I have heard the vanity of a beautiful woman often compels her to pick a plain-looking man so he wouldn't draw attention from her."

"Aaaah," Kalmar sputtered.

"What makes you think," Snook said, jabbing a finger at him, "she is going to choose you?"

"Her promise."

"Promise? You have a promise from this girl?"

"Arasima—her name is Arasima, and she is from the Red Fox Tribe. We met two cycles of the seasons ago at the Gathering of our first pre-games. We only eyed each other at first, but at last year's Gathering, we spent every minute we could together—on the last night of the Gathering, we promised each other we would Pair this coming Gathering." He bristled with excitement. "I know we're going to Pair because of that vow." Kalmar dipped his chin in a half nod. "It is as sure as Salune rising in a few hours."

"Even if this girl—"

"Arasima."

"Arasima—even if this Arasima has promised to choose you, another female could choose you before Arasima has her turn. What makes you so sure it is going to work out?"

"It's not as hard as it seems. Everybody knows I will win the Borrac."

"So you say, my overly confident friend. But, from what you tell me, isn't it more important how the females' game—"

"The Byrrac."

Snook closed his eyes for a second before continuing. "Isn't it more important how the Byrrac turns out?"

"Well, yes, but—"

"It seems to me if you are going to win the Borrac—"

"Which *I* will."

"Let me *finish!*" Snook said with a piercing look. "I'll ask you about that in a minute." He took a deep breath. "I don't understand. It seems to me, the higher your ranking in the Borrac, the more likely another female will choose you before Arasima has her chance to pick you."

"Normally, that would be correct. When I win the Borrac," Kalmar held up his index finger, "I will be the most advantageous Pairing Partner a female could choose. All females know Pairing with the highest-ranked male maximizes their chances of having children with the most favored Traits—it assures their chances of Shetow's Blessings."

"So why am I not correct?"

"Arasima should finish," Kalmar said, his face flushed with a mischievous grin, "in the top two or three of the Byrrac. Before the Choosing I'll let it be known that I want Arasima to choose me, and the other one or two girls who could finish higher in the ranking than Arasima will just choose the top males who come in the ranking after me."

"Is it customary for matches to be decided by the couples before the games and the Pairing?"

"Not customary, but it happens more than the Medoras and draks want to admit."

"Good plan—but not infallible," Snook said with an air of misgiving.

"How do you mean?"

"What do you do if one of the females that finishes higher in the Byrrac than Arasima won't play along with your plan and chooses you anyway? Your plan falls apart."

"I'll just reject her," Kalmar said, raising his right hand making a fist.

"You can reject the female choosing you! You didn't tell me that." Snook clapped his hands together. "Well, that changes everything. You can reject the females until it's Arasima's choice. Now, I understand your optimism. You're all set," Snook said, smiling and chuckling.

"Yes, well . . . that's not entirely correct; I can only reject one time. I can reject a choosing and still be chosen by another female. If I rejected a second female's choosing, I would be removed from the Choosing, as would she, and we both would lose any chance of a Pairing."

"Oh," Snook said in a deflated tone.

"But that won't happen; if I reject the first female the other girls will realize I am serious and they'll leave me alone. No female will risk being the second rejection and chance being removed from the Choosing completely."

"Okay, I trust you know what you're talking about—as to you winning the Borrac. How can you be so sure you're going to win?"

"Snook, that is the easiest question to answer. I have won the last two pre-Borracs."

"Pre-Borracs, I guess that is—"

"Practice Borracs and Byrracs are held mirroring the real games during the middle six days of a Gathering. Most young people are anxious to hone their skills and participate during the two Gatherings prior to their Pairing."

"And you won them both?"

"Yes," Kalmar said, the ends of his lips turning up. "About seventy-five out of a hundred of the winners of the pre-Borrac at the Gathering the year before their Pairing win the Borrac at their Pairing Gathering." He lifted his chin. "It has been hundreds of cycles of the season since the man who won both of his pre-Borrac didn't win his Borrac. And like I said, I won them both."

"Well, you won't win your Borrac."

"What?"

"The sheer weight of your swollen head will slow you down so much there's no way you can win."

"*Snook.*" He playfully hit Snook's arm. The two laughed.

"I also take it Arasima did well in her pre-Byrracs."

"Third in her first pre-Byrrac and second at the last Gathering, as a matter of fact," Kalmar said, sticking his chest out. "The memory of her naked body makes me tremble."

Kalmar's attitude made Snook wonder if Kalmar was more proud of his conquest than he was proud for her.

"Wait—you've seen her naked?"

"Every little bit of her," Kalmar said, a cavernous smile across his face.

Snook just stared at Kalmar, not knowing what to say.

"After I won last year's pre-Borrac, Arasima took my hand and led me into the forest and told me she had a special prize for me—her."

"Kalmar, is this something you need to tell me?"

"Snook, you are the only one I feel I can talk to about something so personal. I have never told anyone about Arasima, not even my little sister. I don't know why, but I feel the need to tell somebody about her. And Snook, I know you won't tell anyone."

"My Toran says 'to talk about your intimacies betrays your lover's honor.'"

"You misinterpret my intent; this is the woman I love, not a vessel I use to extinguish my sexual desires. Surely it isn't wrong for a person to speak about the woman he loves to the man who saved his life. The words I say to you I would never utter to another."

"Forgive my thoughtless words," Snook said after a moment's hesitation. "You honor me"—he made a slight bow—"by taking me into your confidence."

"Snook, you honored me with my life." Kalmar put out his arm and grasped Snook's left shoulder.

Snook nodded; he had stopped trying to talk Kalmar out of the idea that he had not saved his life.

"As I was saying, after we were away from everyone else, she set me down on an old log and stood in front of me and gradually took off her clothes as she looked at me—I mean she stared right into my eyes." He mimicked her movements. "It was as if she knew my every thought. I could see her chest move as she took fast, shallow breaths. When she had finished taking off her clothes she stood before me; the moonlight on her pale skin made her look like a polished statue. My heart was pounding; I thought it would explode. She walked to me, had me stand, and pulled at my clothes." Kalmar didn't notice Snook squirming. "I tried to help her but she wouldn't let me. Once my clothes were off, she took my hands and slowly drew them across her stomach and breast. I have never felt anything so soft." Kalmar paused a moment as he looked away. "After a few moments, she reached over and touched me. Snook"—he looked into Snook's eyes—"the feelings that surged through my body were more intense than I had ever imagined possible. I began to tremble; my knees buckled. She smiled and lay down on our discarded clothes and dragged me down on her." Kalmar's face looked wistful. "It was the best sex I have ever had."

"You've also had *sex* with other women?"

"Well . . . no," he said softly, and then added with enthusiasm, "but I have thought about it a lot."

"You *are* hopeless."

Kalmar looked away, lost in thought. He wrapped his arms around his body and his eyes refocused. "Later, as she lay in my arms, we promised ourselves to each other." Kalmar lay back on the ground and gazed at the stars. "Snook, I'm so lucky," he said, smiling again. "I love and am loved by the woman with whom I'm going to Pair. Some couples learn to love each other after their Pairing, most don't. But me, I love my Pairing Partner before our Pairing."

"*Kalmar*, how can you love someone you hardly know?"

"If you knew how it felt to have her flesh against yours, the passion of her touch and her lovemaking, you wouldn't ask me that question. I know her, and I plan to know her more—as much as I can."

"Kalmar, my Toran told me to be wary of such feelings, that 'sex can get in the way of love.' "

"By Shetow's Mark, what in the world does that mean?" Kalmar regretted his comment, this being a subject Snook may have wanted to avoid.

Snook was slow to answer, and just looked at Kalmar with a bewildered smirk on his face. "You know Kalmar, I haven't the vaguest idea."

"I wonder if you'll be spouting your Toran's words after some seductress gets her hands on you," Kalmar said, trying to make light of the matter.

"Oh . . ." Snook tilted his head as his expression became very serious. "I do not think any female wants to get her hands on me." After a moment, he forced a grin. "Guess your rambunctious stories will have to be my excitement for now."

How could I have said something so thoughtless, Kalmar thought. He shook his head. "I think we both have much to learn."

Without another word, the two gathered their things and started the walk back to Kalmar's cottage.

Like all of her endeavors, Dera excelled at her art. She toiled each day putting her artistic touch on that week's project. Although gifted at poetry and painting, her passion was sculpture. She could look at a lump of clay or block of marble and see the finished figurine imprisoned in the raw material begging to be liberated. It baffled her that others could not envision what she was about to free from the confines of an unworked mass.

The women of the tribe—in fact, all women of the People—were artists. The artistic skill shown by a woman's use of a paintbrush, writing quills, modeling clay, or sculpture's chisel constituted an extension of her femininity. Just as being a hunter was tantamount to being male, being an artist was synonymous with being female. In Shetow's world, all men were hunters, all women artists. Only in music was a barrier absent.

Dera stepped back to take a critical look at the flowing statuette of two majestic birds fixed in a soaring masquerade of a divine sky dance.

"You've outdone yourself; it's really beautiful," Izzy said as he strolled into the room.

"And what does a male know about the quality of a piece of art," Dera said with a teasing scoff.

"The fact that men don't produce art doesn't keep us from admiring it," he responded in a tone more serious than she was accustomed to. "I may act like an uncouth hunter to you but I recognize beauty when I see it." The hard lines of his expression softened. "I marvel at the wondrous beauty Shetow reveals to me every day on the grassy plains or as I'm walking through the nutwood forest. Even you, my gifted sister, can't match the beauty of the almond sky at the beginning of twilight as Salune sets over the Blue Hills."

"You know, brother," she said raising an eyebrow, "there's a little of the rhyme master in you; I think you"—she placed her right palm on her chest—"may be a better poet than me."

"Don't joke about such a thing; I swear by Shetow's Mark I will strangle you if you ever taunt me in front of my friends." She laughed as he playfully formed his hands in a strangler's hold. After a few moments, he scrunched his face as he started to say something and then stopped short.

"What is it?"

"Nothing."

"No, come on . . . what were you going to say?"

"Well . . ."

Dera grabbed his arm.

"Promise not to tell mother?"

Dera frowned; her brother's seriousness was out of character. "Izzy, what is it? You know"—she forced a stern scowl to match her melodramatic tone—"I could never betray my only protector."

He hesitated, abandoning his normal joviality. His thoughts seem to drift; his eyes appeared unfocused. Dera knew her brother well; he was trying to make up his mind whether he was going to tell her. She also knew that, eventually, he would tell her; he always did. Few secrets stood between them, only those intimate thoughts everyone tries to suppress, secret thoughts pushed to the back corners of one's consciousness. However, there was one secret constantly on her mind. A secret she had not revealed to her brother, fearing if she did, her resolve might falter.

"I have often wondered what it would be like to work the clay with my own hands," he said, turning towards his sister. "I envy the joy you must feel at being able to produce such beauty." He raised his hands, gazed at them, and then flexed his fingers. "The ecstasy that must flow through you as Shetow uses you as a conduit to express Her love of the People." His pursed lips turned white. "It would have been nice if She had saved one of the creative Traits for the males." He walked over to the worktable and picked up one of Dera's smaller sculptures. "To be an artist . . . to have the gift of fashioning such exquisiteness from a handful of river clay is beyond my ability to describe."

Dera's jaw hung loose as she stared at him. What other aspect of his personality had he concealed from her, or had she just misread all the signals? She was accustomed to a funny, playful Izzy; here was a somber Izzy, an Izzy in touch with his inner-spirit. Her brother was showing the Traits of a female, yet, she knew he was very much the male. The young females of the village infatuated him—he turned red-faced when one of the pretty ones smiled at him. On impulse, she reached into a large terra-cotta vat that stood at the end of the worktable, lifted out a glob of moist clay, and plopped it down on the table in front of Izzy. "Here, let's see what you can do with this."

Izzy's face contorted. *"I can't work the clay!"*

"Why?"

"I'm not female."

"You will not lose your manliness by working . . . playing with the clay. You won't free some demon locked in your body;

you'll not transform into a female." She suppressed a chuckle. "Dear brother, there is no doubt of your manhood." He didn't move. She had never seen his face so flushed. "Trust me, I won't tell a soul if you work the clay." She rolled her eyes. "We played in the mud as children and nothing happened to you then. Besides, it's not like you are going to try to become a sculptor."

Izzy cut his eyes to Dera. She could read the indecision in his face; he longed to try his hand at the clay but caution pulled at him. A strange sensation flowed over her. All of a sudden, it was important to Dera that Izzy work the clay. "I *dare you* to shape the clay," she said, using an old childhood ploy.

He jerked around to face her, his eyes wild. Izzy never backed down from a dare. She had given him the excuse he needed to "make it all right" to shape the clay. He gave her that "I'll show you" look he had when he was about to do something to show her up. Izzy walked over to the worktable and mounted the stool in front of the unformed clay. With no hesitation and without saying a word, his hands grasped the slippery mass in front of him. At first Izzy's face retained the smirk generated by Dera's dare, but that quickly melted away as his concentration now centered on molding the pliable material—in minutes his look of wonder changed to one of joy. Izzy had often watched her work the clay; now, she saw him try to mimic many of her techniques as his untrained hands shaped the dark gray mass. Trying to draw as little attention to herself as possible, Dera crept towards the door; she knew from personal experience that when you're trying to release your inner-spirit through the passion of shaping the clay, solitude is an artist's best companion. As she ducked out of the room, she could see the tips of his fingers kneading the moist clay.

Later she returned to find Izzy still hard at work, his full attention given to the clay. It was obvious; Izzy was molding a female's head. Her eyes opened wide as she sucked in her breath; the bust was of her. She watched in silence until Izzy grew frustrated when he could not mold the features to his satisfaction.

"By the *Will of Shetow*, it's true; men aren't meant to be artists." He slapped the table with his open palm. "I should have known better." He slid off the stool and stumbled back from his work.

Dera leaned over and studied the product of his labors. Her eyebrows raised; it was not that bad. Crude yes, lacking value as a piece of art, yet, anyone would recognize the molded mass as her. Izzy's efforts flattered her; she did not know how to respond. As her eyes moved over her clay likeness, she felt there was something not right. Of course, the gray clay did not show her blemish. The face looking back at her possessed a beauty she had never felt; she blinked back sudden tears. The sculpture revealed how Izzy saw her—without her facial flaw. If only she could block out her imperfection as easily as those who loved her did.

He has an innate skill, she thought to herself. "No. You're wrong; there's promise in your work," she murmured as she continued to look at the sculpture.

"For a male *sculptor?*" He shook his head. "Thank you, Sister, for trying to spare my feelings, but bovors crap dung piles with more artistic flair than that," he said, pointing to the molded clay, a condescending smirk on his face.

Dera could not help giggling.

"The sum of my artistic labors." He turned and gave her a toothy grin; Izzy had regained his humor. "However, I know how to improve it." He picked up a thumb-sized piece of clay from the worktable, reached over, and reshaped part of the molded head. When he stepped back, it now sported a long pointed nose. "There, what do you think of that? Real improvement, wouldn't you say?" He moved back from the worktable, making exaggerated motions as if he were a judge judging the clay head. "You know, that's not a bad look for you," he said. Dera faked a slap to his face and then they both laughed and gave each other a hug.

"My face has enough distraction without your help."

"Dera, Sister." He winced. "I wasn't—"

"Oh Izzy!" She grabbed his arm. "I didn't think you were making fun of me. Please forgive me; it's just my dogged pessimism."

"I know, Sister." He turned and started to walk away. "I think I will go wash this gunk off my hands." A film of dried clay covered his arms; they were gray up to his elbows. It looked as if he had stuck his arms in a vat of gray dye. "How strange," he said in drawn-out words. He stopped walking and stared at his clay-covered arms.

"What do you mean?" Dera questioned, a puzzled look on her face.

"The dried clay . . ." Izzy's words trailed off as he continued to examine his hands and arms.

"What, Izzy? The dried clay . . . what do you mean?"

"The dried clay . . . it feels like . . ." His eyes narrowed, ". . . like dried blood. It's the same feeling . . ." He lifted his encrusted hands higher, ". . . my hands, they feel just like they do when I finish field dressing a freshly slain prairie buck. After I skin and gut a deer, a thin layer of dried blood covers my hands . . . the dried clay feels just like dried blood." He closed his eyes as he lifted his chin. "If you took away the smell, I wouldn't know the difference between the two." He opened his eyes, then stared at the back of his hands as he turned them over. "What an odd coincidence." He continued his scrutiny another moment and then suddenly his eyes shifted as he straightened his back. He motioned towards the clay bust. "Sister, please get rid of this abomination."

"I will."

Izzy stopped at the doorway. "Is the cistern full? I wouldn't want to be half bathed and have the water run out."

"Almost . . . I filled it this morning. Remember to replenish the water in the heating pot after you are through."

"Of course," he said, giving her one of his impish grins as he turned and walked out the door.

"It will be one of the few times," she mumbled, hearing him whistling as he walked down the hall. She shook her head as she returned her attention to the clay bust sitting on the worktable. She should destroy it; it was not prudent to leave any evidence that Izzy had worked the clay. True, if discovered, he would not be formally punished; however, he would be ostracized by the other members of their tribe—a severe punishment just the same. Dera hesitated, thinking about what to do; for some reason Izzy's crude sculpture—even with a bird beak for a nose—touched her heart. She picked up the sculpture and carefully carried it to the kiln, opened the squeaky metal door and, using brass tongs, gently placed the clay head on a firebrick stand. She added hardwood charcoal to the kiln's fire and started pumping the bellows. The scent of nutwood drifted across the room. The heat radiating from the ceramic surface of the kiln warmed her face.

Five hours later, she took the hot hardened clay from the kiln and placed it in a cooling oven so it would cool slowly, preventing it from cracking. Later that night, she held the lifesize ceramic head in the palm of her left hand as she gently traced the outline of its lips with the fingertips of her other hand. She lifted her chin. "If I dropped you, you would shatter into a thousand pieces." She scrunched her lips, then sighed. "But you're no more fragile than I am." She heard footsteps in the hallway, looked side-to-side and then quickly, but gently, placed the sculpture in a wicker basket and covered it with boodo straw.

The next morning, Dera, not knowing where to hide Izzy's artwork so their mother would not find it, took it along with two of her own figurines to meet the drak traders who came to the village one day each month to trade with the women of the village. She planned to hide Izzy's creation at her spot in the nutwood grove once she left the traders. Everyone in the village knew of her spot and respected her privacy. Once there, she knew, Izzy's art would be safe.

Dera left at first light so she could conduct her business early and get on her way to the nutwood grove. A morning fog obscured the pathway as she hurried through the village. As smoke poured from every chimney, the aroma of breakfast cooking snaked its way between the houses. There were only a few other women at the trading house when she arrived.

Three leather-belted traders stood in the large front room of the trading house ready to barter with the women. The draks traded medicines, metals, precision tools, and anything else the humans could not manufacture for themselves. In exchange, the women traded their prized art. The draks' sense of a woman's artistic talent appeared to run closely to the value of the woman's ranking given by the villagers themselves. Each year the women's peers judged their art, not as a contest against each other, but a judging of the quality of a woman's work. Often ten or more of the women in a village were ranked superior.

The draks, reptilian bipeds, stood over six feet tall. A mixture of greenish gray scales and feathers covered their epic frames and a muzzle of teeth any cave lion would envy crowded their mouths.

Although the giants were fierce-looking, the women of the village did not fear them, for they played an integral part in the humans' complex culture. The draks had been trading with and performing the Koo Toc Biren ceremony for the members of the Twenty-Four Tribes for as long as the Telling of the Tell. To the People, a world without the draks was as unimaginable as a sky devoid of the river of uncountable stars spreading from horizon to horizon. Shetow sent the draks to look after them. Shetow, through the draks, furnished them all the things they could not supply for themselves; in return, the members of the Twenty-Four Tribes honored Shetow through the beauty of the women's art.

Dera walked over to one of the massive trading tables and carefully deposited the woven basket she used to transport her sculptures. The basket was fashioned from thin wooden strips from the bona tree, light yet very strong. Twice as long as it was wide, the basket also had a leather strap that fit over Dera's shoulder to support the weight of its contents as she walked. Layers of boodo straw separated and cushioned the sculptures from bumping against each other and chipping. Dera hastily pulled straw over Izzy's sculpture after carefully lifting out the two sculptures she planned on trading and gently placing them on the padded table. One of the draks ambled over and picked up one of her sculptures.

"Dera, I see your work is up to your normal superior standard," the drak said in a high-pitched voice not matching the size and ferocity of the gigantic lizard. Humans seldom recognized individual draks; however, draks always seemed to know to which human they were talking. Draks wore no clothing, just different colored leather straps and belts that crossed over their shoulders and encircled their waists forming a harness with a number of pouches and tools hanging from it. They walked upright and their hind legs were considerably larger than their slender, out of proportion, arms. Extending behind them were massive tails that acted as a counterbalance to their forward-leaning torsos.

"Thank you, trader. Your high evaluation of my work," Dera responded out of habit, "gives honor to me and my family." She made a slight bow to the drak trader. "But more so to the blessing of the artistic talent granted me by Shetow." The trader and Dera came to a quick agreement on a trading value of her two pieces of art, which she could use in exchange for the goods her family needed.

"How about this piece?" piped a drak voice from behind her. She turned to see a second drak holding and studying Izzy's creation. She froze.

"I had not planned on trading it," she said as her face turned deathly pale. The drak who had been trading with her waddled over to the second drak and took Izzy's piece from him.

"Is this one of your creations?" the drak asked in its chirpy voice.

Her mouth opened but she could not speak. Invisible bands of tightness encircled her chest; her breathing became shallow. The room blurred, becoming surreal. What had she done? She should have destroyed the sculpture as she had promised Izzy; really, it was something she should have never allowed to be created in the first place. For her mother to find Izzy's atrocity was one thing; for the draks to discover it was another. They would denounce it as sacrilege to the Glory of Shetow. She vacillated a moment and then did the only thing she knew to do; it was the only way to protect her brother.

"Yes, it is one of mine." She fought back panic. "It is a new style I've been working on. I was taking it to show a friend and get her advice," she chattered, like a small child, knowing her words only drew more attention to her blunder. It was her own fault; she was determined no blame should fall on Izzy.

"I see your new work," the drak said as it continued to inspect Izzy's creation, "is up to your normal high standards."

"Whaaat," Dera stuttered. The lines of the reptile's loathsome face had not changed; as far as she knew, the draks did not have facial expressions. Was he kidding her? Maybe he was trying to trick or trap her. Before she could decide, the drak spoke again.

"I will give you the same trading value," the drak said as it gently placed the piece back on the table, "for this piece as for the other two pieces."

Her jaw dropped as she stared at the drak. The lizard made no reaction to her amazement; apparently, it was just as incapable of reading her expression as she was at reading the drak's unchanging features. She looked down at Izzy's creation and then back at the drak who appeared to be waiting for an answer. The drak was serious; the trader was giving Izzy's work the same value it gave hers. She reached over and retrieved Izzy's sculpture. "I think I need to perfect this new style," she said as she began to repack the piece in the straw in the basket, "before I let others have a look at it."

Without comment, the two draks moved to a different table and started talking to another woman.

Once she finished packing the things the family needed as their part of the exchange, she rushed out of the trading house and headed to her spot in the nutwood grove. Before she reached her haven, she stopped, thought a moment, turned, and headed home to see Izzy.

When she walked in the front room of her family's dwelling, she found Izzy studying his lessons. "Izzy, I must talk to you, it is important."

"By Shetow's Mark, what have I done now?" he said as he looked up and pushed himself back from his study table.

"You haven't done anything—it is I who has done something and I need your help. . . . I need to understand what just happened to me."

Izzy lifted an eyebrow at his sister's solemn expression. "Sit down and tell me what you are talking about," he said in a rare moment of seriousness. Dera sat down and told her brother of the events of the morning. At first, he was upset upon learning she had not destroyed his creation as promised, but her tale soon deflected his anger. After she finished, they sat in silence.

"You're absolutely sure," Izzy finally blurted out, "the value the draks allocate each woman's work follows the ranking given to them in the judging?"

"Yes—I never thought about it before, but I cannot remember the draks ever giving a female's painting or sculpture—no matter how good it was—a value higher than the worst piece of art produced by a different female artist ranked higher than her in the judging." Dera stood up and began to pace. "Then today, when the drak trader gave your sculpture, believing it was my work, a superior rating, it became clear—the draks do not evaluate our art." Dera stopped and looked at Izzy, her pupils were small, the skin of her face taut against her jaw. "The draks can't tell the difference between the art produced by a superior-ranked artist who has spent many cycles of the seasons perfecting her skill and that produced by a man whose creation was, at best, no better than that of a six-year-old female."

Izzy flinched at his sister's remark, but let it pass. "This is—I don't know what to think. You're sure the drak trader wasn't just joking with you?"

"Izzy," she replied, giving him a stern look, "we are talking about a drak. Draks have no humor, they do not joke, they do not even smile, they . . ." She stopped and shook her head.

"What?"

"I don't know," she chuckled, "just a crazy thought."

"And?"

"I had a vision of a drak smiling." She scrunched her face. "It was terrible." They both laughed. He was no longer angry with her. She put a hand on his knee. "I'm telling you, the draks are using our evaluations of a woman's art to fix its value for their trading."

"But that doesn't make sense," he said. "Why would the drak trade for art when they don't have a real understanding of its value? Why would Shetow have beings represent Her that can't appreciate our females' art? How can that give Her honor?"

"This is confusing," Dera said, pressing the fingertips of her right hand against her temple. She started pacing again. "The draks trade goods and materials for our women's artwork . . . with the value of the exchange based on the value placed on the women's art by the draks."

Izzy raised an eyebrow.

"Yet, now we learn the draks have no sense of art value and are, instead, using our own art judging as their scale in placing value on the art they're trading for."

"So it seems."

"Which means"—Dera paused—"the value of our art—to Shetow—is really based on the value we place on it." Dera pushed her hands up the sides of her face and ran her fingers through the hair above her temples. "Or"—she lifted her head, her eyes wide open—"Shetow puts no value on our art at all and is using the drak traders simply as a way to supply us with needed goods."

"Letting us trade for the goods, thereby allowing us to keep our honor," Izzy said, nodding.

"I don't know about honor, but there's something amiss with our thinking—we're overlooking something."

"How do you mean?"

"I'm not quite sure. Something just doesn't make sense. But I do know one thing."

"What's that?" Izzy answered.

"We need to keep this revelation to ourselves."

He was soon lost in deep thought as she walked out of the room.

TWELVE

Inseparable since their ordeal with the cave lion, it came as no surprise to anyone when Snook accompanied Kalmar to the Oonoc Lodge. Tribal members gathered for an Oonoc the night before the young aspirants departed for the Gathering and their fate in the Choosing—the Matage. For Kalmar and the other young men who would participate in the Borrac, this night—the Night of Tears—was the last Oonoc they would attend as members of the tribe. If chosen by a female from a distant tribe, it might be many cycles of the seasons before they had a chance to visit the tribe of their birth. Yumza came, like the mothers of the other young men in Kalmar's age group, hoping to find comfort and an answer to why her son had to leave the tribe. The mothers of the departing young men huddled together, many crying in each other's arms. For many, this was the most difficult night of their lives, a moment they had dreaded since their sons' births.

When they entered the Oonoc Lodge, Snook marveled at the women's art that filled countless displays along the walls. The meeting chamber was wedge-shaped, with the ceiling and rows of seats rising in height the further you were from the narrow front of the room. A pictorial tapestry depicting eighteen stories from the

Tell hung along the expanse of the taller back wall. Exhibited in chronological order, the scenes portrayed selected events from the First to the middle of the Fifth Progression. The first recounted Geerna and Shetow's Covenant. Woven into the fine fabric was a life-size picture of a solemn young girl with her face and extended arms lifted toward a hovering black cloud. Black dots peppered her face and exposed shoulders. Even though the Tell proclaimed Geerna was a young woman at the time of the great event, the dots disguised that fact. Snook shook his head; he was glad the practice of facial tattooing was confined to the Medoras. The last scene depicted the Grand Oonoc where the Medoras stopped the hunting of the long tusked mammoths. The tapestry had occupied this place of reverence since the beginning of the Sixth Progression; it had taken the artistic skill and deft fingers of forty of the tribe's best weavers three generations to complete. Countless art treasures filled the Oonoc Lodge; each, like the tapestry, venerated Shetow.

Nutan, Nima, and Raff joined Snook on the highest of the stair-stepped rows of pews that were arranged in semicircles around the hearth of the tribe's Life Fire. Their elevated position gave them a clear view of the speaker's dais and those seated below them. As Snook had predicted when he first met Kalmar, above the hearth hung the hide of a male cave lion. Nima, accompanied by Raff, came to support her younger brother and to console her mother when the meeting ended. Now, as Yumza faced the certainty of losing her male Second Childs to the Choosing, she looked to her female First Childs for comfort. Nima and Raff also attended because they were taking their infant, young Targo, to her Koo Toc ceremony where she would receive Shetow's Mark. Nutan came in support of her revered older brother, but her attendance was also mandatory since this was the last Oonoc before her first pre-Byrrac.

Yielding to his Seeker nature, Snook craned his neck as he

resumed surveying his surroundings. He wrinkled his nose as he sniffed the air; the faint odor of old wood lingered in the room—a delicate, almost musty scent exuding timelessness and constancy. The lodge's construction exhibited the same skills evident in the villager's homes. Since the beginning of the Sixth Progression, the current Oonoc Lodge and most of the village's dwellings had welcomed each new generation of occupants. The men of the village took great pride in this limited chance to express their artisanship; they fitted each stone and timber together with the utmost care and precision. The quarried stone fit so tightly it was impossible to see the mortar; also invisible were the tenons and mortises binding the wooden timbers. The structure's walls were stone to the height of a man and cured red nutwood timbers above that. Granite keystones capped the arched stone doorways and window casings. Inside the lodge, the ceiling angled up from the front of the room to where it was twice as high where Snook sat as it was above the dais. The slope of the ceiling enhanced the room's acoustics; a person speaking from the dais could be heard anywhere in the audience.

Kalmar and the other Second Childs sat in the first two rows of the section to the right of the Life Fire hearth—all male. Directly in front of the Life Fire hearth sat a handful of Third Childs—an equal amount of males and females. The First Childs sat in the first two rows of the section to the left of the Life Fire hearth—all female. Other tribe members filled the remaining seats, mostly parents, grandparents, and the young males and females going to the Gathering for their pre-Borrac and pre-Byrrac events. Even though there was only seating for about seven hundred, there were usually empty seats at an Oonoc. If more people attended, the Oonoc was moved outside.

Once the crowd had settled, Cabyl and Berkana entered through a side door, Berkana with an Ooroc—a long engraved wooden staff—in her hand. The old woman faltered on the stone stairway that led to the top of the Life Fire hearth. Cabyl rushed to Berkana's side and helped her climb the last few steps. The stone hearth extended out into the semicircle of seats and served as a stage, allowing a person standing at the head of the extension to have people on three sides of them. The rumble from the crowd dropped to a whisper when the Medora Roo stepped upon the hearth; then a hush spread over the room, like ripples on a pond, when she raised the Ooroc and started to speak.

"In the name of Shetow, the Giver of Life, and the blessings She has placed on the People and on each of us, I call this Oonoc to order." She paused for a moment. "As you know this is the last Oonoc before the Gathering." Berkana turned towards Kalmar and the rows of Second Childs and continued. "It is the last time many of you will ever see some of our Second Childs and it will be the last time they will ever gather as a group before they leave for the Gathering." She looked directly at the Second Childs. "You young men have grown up in our midst; we love you and will miss you. Your mothers will cry as they long for the sound of your voice and the sight of your smile, but the memory of the time you spent with us will forever fill our minds and rest gently in your mothers' hearts. At the Gathering, you'll compete in the Borrac and then be chosen at the Matage by a young female to Pair." She raised the Ooroc slightly and gave it a shake. "Give your maximum effort in the Borrac; in so doing, the Will of Shetow will Pair you with the right female." She lowered the Ooroc; a dull thud sounded as the tip of the staff struck the stone hearth. "When you escort your new Paired Partner back to the house of her mother, don't forget, you show honor or dishonor to your own mother by your actions toward your new family and their tribe. Your actions are also a reflection on all of us that helped raise you. Let the stories we hear of you at future Gatherings bring pride and not shame to the tribe of your birth. Lastly, remember your new Paired Partner will be as confused and anxious as you; it will be much easier on you both if you try to build love in your heart for this young female. She will feel the full weight of her decision; the decision to put all her hope and faith in the one she's chosen—*you*. She will learn to love you if you just open yourself to her. Be sweet to her, do not try to intimidate her; in dealing with women, the size of a man's ego causes more problems than the size of his manhood can solve." Snook glimpsed a twinkle in the old woman's eyes at the laughter from the older members of the audience.

Berkana slowly turned her aging body around to look into the faces of the young female First Childs looking up at her. "Shetow has placed a different, but also difficult, task on you. In Her infinite wisdom, She has caused the First Childs to always be female. Many think this is so your mothers will have help raising her more rambunctious male Second Childs. Others believe it is because you will come back, after your Pairing, bringing your new male partner into your mother's home before she loses your brother two cycles of the seasons later at his own Matage." Berkana stopped, slowly studied each female's upturned face. Her eyes worked their way down each row before she started again. "There is a little truth in both those reasons, but I think the main reason She had females born first was to prepare you for motherhood and the raising of your own children.

"The difficult task you confront, however, has nothing to do with the order of your birth or with your brother's." Berkana stopped again, took in a deep breath. "You must go to the Gathering with the daunting task of choosing the father of your children. If you choose the correct partner, Shetow will bless your children with the enhanced Traits needed to enrich the People. Your chosen partner will return with you to live among us as a member of the Tribe, but more importantly, he will live in the home of your mother. The Pootash may come between your father and your

mother; your Pairing Partner may be—once your brother leaves—
the only male in your home. Your brothers, the Second Childs, are
responsible only for themselves; you, on the other hand, will affect
all the members of your mother's household by the choice you
make. Your choice, through the Traits of your children, will affect
the future of the People. Shetow has given you, the First Childs—
the female child—the responsibility to be the one to choose your
male Pairing Partner, rather than the male choosing you. Shetow
knows if the man were to do The Choosing, he would choose a
partner for her physical attributes; a female, Shetow trusts, will consider the greater good and make her choice for rational reasons. As
a test of your worthiness, Shetow will tempt you with lust. She will
use the physical attraction of the males from whom you must
choose"—Berkana raised her right arm and pointed her finger
while shaking her hand for emphasis—"against you, but you must
only yield to lustful temptation if your choice's other attributes are
equal to or greater than all your other possible choices."

The old woman stopped talking and motioned to a person
who had followed her into the chamber. Berkana's pale-faced apprentice stepped from the shadow. In contrast to the Medora Roo's
scarlet robe and mustard yellow sash, Cabyl was shrouded, head to
toe, in the powder blue habit of a novice. Only Cabyl's radiant
black hair could be distinguished as the young woman's other features were obscured by the habit's partially lifted hood, which was
bunched up on her shoulders. At the Medora's beckoning, the
youthful novice quickly climbed the stone stairs, stepped up on the
hearth, and walked towards Berkana. When she reached the old
woman, Cabyl raised her left hand, revealing a ceramic flagon that
had been concealed in the folds of her robe, and gave it to the
Medora. Without saying a word, Berkana raised the container to
her lips and took a long swig of the unknown liquid. After what
seemed to Snook an unusually long time, Berkana lowered the flask

and handed it back to Cabyl. Berkana patted Cabyl's hand as the young woman retrieved the container. Cabyl smiled back at Berkana; everyone knew their Medora had a special affinity for her young apprentice, who she treated more like a daughter than an understudy.

As Cabyl turned to leave the hearth, she glanced into the audience, giving a clear view of her radiant face with its pale skin contrasting her dark hair. Snook could tell she spotted him leaning forward and peering at her from the edge of his seat. Their eyes locked; they held eye contact until she reached the stairs leading down from the hearth. Cabyl's facial expression did not change, yet Snook felt the extended eye contact was an expression of something in itself. Lightheaded, his stomach began to churn, and then he realized he had not breathed since they had first made eye contact. He gasped a deep breath and slowly slid back in his seat.

Berkana returned her attention to the First Childs. "Shetow has given you the tools"—she stared down a snicker from a few of the older males in the audience—"that will allow you—in the beginning—to lead your sexually-driven male partner wherever you like. However"—she furrowed her brow—"it's in how he looks at you, late at night, when his hunger for you is spent, that the signs of his true feelings will be visible. Only when he gives you his heart will he stay past the Pootash. For those of you who choose your Pairing Partner poorly, the Pootash will not come soon enough. The nights of wonder and passion will yield to dark, sleepless times floated by endless tears."

Her gaze lingered on the wide-eyed females a few moments. Then Berkana shuffled around to face the smallest group—the Third Childs. "You're the bonus that comes to Pairings Shetow finds most pleasing. Shetow chose your gender to meet Her needs." The Medora leaned the Ooroc against her body as she held out her hands, palms up, like two pans of a balancing scale. "Sometimes a male," she lowered a hand, "sometimes a female." She lowered the second as she raised the other hand. "You're the ultimate components in Her quest for Order. To reinforce in the People the Traits Shetow finds desirable in your brother and sister, She bestowed on your parents a great honor—the birth of a Third Childs. You are not superior to your siblings, but a testimony to their exceptional blend of Traits. Many of you will fall short of Shetow's expectations, but some of you will Pair and parent three children as have your parents. The honor of being a Third Childs will always be with you and your parents. As for you male Third Childs, what I said to the Second Childs also applies to you and what I said to the First Childs applies to you female Third Childs."

After finishing her speech to the First, Second, and Third Childs, Berkana looked higher in the audience. "Many of you will be taking your children to their Koo Toc Biren. What greater accolade can you have than to have your child Marked by Shetow as one of Her own? You have prepared your whole life for this event: the cycles of the seasons you studied your Lessons readying yourselves for the Byrrac or Borrac; the trial of the games themselves; then the Matage, and the ordeal of Pairing and being coupled with a stranger. The Koo Toc Biren is Shetow's recognition of your trauma."

Berkana spoke for another hour, covering their upcoming trip to the Gathering, and then raised her right arm. "Blessed be the Mark of the Covenant." She indicated for everyone in the audience to stand up. "As it has always been—"

"Let it always be," everyone said in unison.

———

As Berkana left the hearth, Targo the Teller came forward. "There has been a new episode added to the Tell of the People, the Tell of the Hunt of Kalmar of the Cave Lion Tribe"—a ripple of applause crossed the audience—"and of the Scars of Courage that now adorn Kalmar's face."

Unconsciously, as the Teller spoke, Kalmar reached up and ran his fingertips down the tender wounds.

"A face that is a testimony to the courage a hunter from our own tribe showed at his moment of truth." The room fell quiet as Targo found his rhythm. "It was the forty-first day of the second season of the four hundred and fifty-seventh cycles of the seasons after the Sixth Progression . . ." As the Teller spoke, Kalmar's face flushed; he looked over his shoulder to see Snook raise his hand and clutch his fist—the symbol of support. *How could anyone ever deserve such a friend*, Kalmar thought to himself.

The Teller first told the Tell of Kalmar's exploits, then he told the Tell of Urga and his cave lion. At first, Kalmar's embarrassment swelled into a cocky pride as he heard the whispering of people in the audience and saw them point him out. A few of the young females blushed when his eyes met theirs. Later, his pride deflated into sorrow when the Tell of Urga began; his sorrow plunged into shame as the Tell of Urga ended. Kalmar rushed out when the Teller was finished. In a few minutes, Snook joined him.

"Why did Urga die and I live? How could Shetow choose me over him?"

"I don't think it's about a choice being made between the two of you. Would you have made the hunt if your grandfather had lived?"

"No . . ." Kalmar answered after a long pause. "No, I do not think I would have made the hunt if Urga hadn't been killed; there would not have been a reason for me to make the hunt."

"Well then, you surviving or not surviving had no effect on

determining if Urga survived his hunt since you wouldn't have gone on your hunt for the cave lion if he hadn't been killed. I do not believe there was a choice made by Shetow or any higher power between you and Urga—maybe there was a decision made as to if you were to live or die but not that Urga would die so you would live. It was Urga's death that caused you to risk your life on a cave lion hunt; the only cause and effect was that Urga's death almost caused your death," Snook said. The skin on his chin tightened as deep lines crossed his brow.

"I guess you are right," Kalmar said as he grudgingly nodded his head. "I just don't understand why he made the hunt."

"And you will never know and maybe you are not meant to know." Snook lifted his head. "Remember, you have never been able to explain why *you* made your hunt." His attention visibly shifted at the sight of a small figure clad in a powder blue robe walking towards them. The hooded intruder headed towards Snook.

They both knew it had to be Cabyl since she was the only person in the village who dressed in the unmistakable garb of a novice. She stopped in front of Snook, reached up with both hands, and pulled the hood back off her head. She had never looked more enchanting. Kalmar studied the two as they looked at each other. A moment passed before Cabyl reached into a large pocket in the side of her habit to retrieve a folded brown envelope. She thrust the envelope towards Snook, who vacillated a second before reaching and cautiously taking the mysterious package from her outstretched hand. Their fingers brushed as Snook withdrew his hand with the envelope in his grasp. Cabyl hesitated, cast her eyes down, lowered her head, and then turned on her heels and briskly walked away.

"Trying to fool me, were you?" Kalmar said as he drew closer to gain a better view of the contents of the puzzling envelope. "I could tell she had her eye on you too."

"I—I don't . . ." Snook stammered.

"Just open the envelope and read the note, will you."

Snook tore open the envelope and carefully unfolded the crisp brown paper and read the note to Kalmar. "I think it best you accompany us on our journey to the Gathering.—Berkana."

Kalmar looked at Snook. "You know"—he wrinkled his brow—"it never occurred to me that you might not go to the Gathering."

Snook shrugged his shoulders. "It does not matter now." He sighed, and then closed his eyes for a moment and nodded to himself. ". . . I'm going."

THIRTEEN

A few days later Kalmar, Snook, and Nutan walked down a long row of waist-high granite cylinders with circumferences of a strong man's thigh. The row was one of many such rows running parallel to each other. They stopped in front of one of the stones. Nutan turned to Snook. "This is my father's grave. He died when I was very young; I barely remember him. My mother, Kalmar, and Nima tell me he was a good father—to me he's just a hazy memory. I'm not sure, but what I remember about him may not be real; it could be I've heard the stories so many times they seem real. As time passes, it gets harder and harder for me to tell the difference between my memory and their stories." Snook moved up against her left side and reached his arm around her shoulder.

Nutan closed her eyes as she tried to dampen a wave of emotion that threatened to capsize her stoic reverence. Kalmar had told her he had concluded that Snook's own tribe, because of him being an albino, must have rejected him. There could be no other explanation for Snook's lack of sophistication, he said. She thought this strange, since, in many ways, she found Kalmar's friend to be charming. Despite the color of his skin, she also found Snook to be the most sensitive male she had ever met. Whatever Trait Snook was missing, she found too abundant in the other males she knew. Whoever decided Snook should not undergo the Matage had denied the People a truly special Trait.

When Nutan felt Snook's arm go around her, she leaned against him and laid her head against his chest. She looked up into his eyes. "We children were lucky that Urga and Onora had stayed together past their Pootash. Urga was there for us, more like a father than a grandfather. When he was killed by the cave lion the grief was magnified because it was the second time the family had to cope with the loss of its male part of the Equilibrium."

"How did your father die?"

"He was killed when a timber fell on him when he was helping rebuild the roof on one of our neighbor's homes."

"I am sorry," he said with a sympathetic frown.

She looked up. "Thank you, Snook, you are very kind. Kalmar is lucky that you are his friend."

Snook looked at Nutan and thought of his mother and the day she died. He empathized with Kalmar's bewilderment in not understanding why his grandfather had hunted the cave lion; his own desire to understand why his mother fell from the cliffs above his village and his dark thoughts about the reason brought the taste of bile to his mouth. Did he know the reason and just would not admit it? No, there had to be another explanation. He forced the horrible idea from his mind.

Kalmar had not interrupted Snook and Nutan's conversation; he just listened. *Nutan*, Kalmar thought to himself, *really does have the best Traits of the three of us children.* In a way, he had a father's pride in his younger sister. After all, he had been the Male Equilibrium of the family until Raff Paired with Nima two cycles of the seasons earlier.

Kalmar glanced at his younger sister standing next to Snook.

He could tell Nutan relished the responsibility of helping him look after his albino friend. The horror Kalmar saw in her face when he told her about his belief that Snook was an outcast among his own tribe soon brought a sympathetic softness to her usually bright brown eyes. He pursed his lips. Snook's secret was as safe with his sister as it was with him.

After the three left Seldan's grave, they stopped at Urga's grave. Kalmar could feel the pounding of his heart. After a few minutes of silence, Nutan kneeled down and gently brushed her fingertips along the chiseled letters of his name on the top of his headstone. Kalmar and Snook stood looking down at the solemn face of the young girl. In a few moments, without saying a word or looking at either of them, she stood up and started walking home. They both watched her walk away—head bent, deep in thought.

"I think I have figured out why I made the hunt for the cave lion," Kalmar said, while keeping his gaze fixed on his sister.

Snook's eyes opened wider. "And?"

"Something inside me felt," Kalmar said as they continued to watch his sister, "that if I made the hunt I would unlock the mystery of why Urga made his hunt—why he felt he had to risk his life." Kalmar stopped talking, took in and let out a long breath. "You see, I had to understand why someone who had everything to live for deemed it so important to chance death." Kalmar turned towards Snook. "In the last few weeks before my grandfather died—he changed."

"How?"

"I don't mean he became a different person—I mean he became . . . well, he became distant and preoccupied."

Snook waited, his eyes fixed on Kalmar.

"It's hard to put in words. He—he became anxious."

"About what?" Snook said, tilting his head.

Kalmar looked hard at Snook; his eyes opened wider than normal. "*I don't know*. I do think whatever changed Urga is what caused him to make the hunt." Kalmar flexed his jaw muscles each time he paused. "As I think about it"—he talked faster and louder—"I made the hunt to see if I could find out what changed Urga—why it was important enough to chance a high probability of death." Kalmar paced and moved his arms around wildly as he spoke.

After Kalmar finished his discourse, Snook waited a moment before responding. "But your hunt did not help you understand the reasoning behind your grandfather's hunt."

Kalmar lowered his unfocused eyes as emotional pain contorted his face. "No, it did not—in fact, I am more confused now than I was before my hunt."

Snook nodded, his white lips pressed tightly together. They turned and started home to join Nima, Raff, and Nutan in preparing for the journey to the Gathering.

FOURTEEN

The Gathering was the fulcrum of Elom's cultural structure. Each spring of the cycles of the seasons, during the ten days between the third and fourth months—Saytar and Durgo—when the days were warmer and the fragrance of new grass permeated the air like the perfume of a new bride before her Koo Toc ceremony, members of each tribe would travel to the Plains of Baylibor in the shadow of Mount Alar.

Unlike most mountains, Alar was not encircled by foothills, as one of its sides rose from the lush flat grasslands at a near vertical angle. The adolescent mountain was the result of a recent shift in the planet's mantle that forced a smooth slice of the fractured edge of Elom's crust to jut from the fertile soil of the surrounding plain at a perpendicular angle. Because of its young age and the hardness of the igneous rock, there were few signs of erosion to mar the flat plane of the mountain's surface, which soared above the Gathering's compound. The face of Alar was an immense sheer wall of stone you could walk up to and press the palm of your hand against. The towering expanse of rock never failed to humble the vainest of men or still the chatter of the most strident of women.

The morning air is calm at the junction of the grasslands and the mountain, but as the day progresses and the warm rays of Salune heat the rock faster than the grasslands, the air flows like a mighty river across the cooler plains and ascends the warmer surface of the mountain face. The breeze generated by the uneven heating of the mountain and grasslands reverses at night when the mountain—which cools faster than the grassland—cools the surrounding air, making it heavier than the air above the grasslands. The cooled heavier air then rushes down the mountain, causing the breeze to flow down the rock face and out onto the plains. The breeze blows all day and night except for the short time twice a day when the temperature of the mountain and the grasslands is in balance as the temperature of one rises and the other falls. The sustained breeze made the grounds of the Gathering not only cool but also, for the most part, free of flying insects.

Another benefit of the perpetual winds were the sights and sounds it triggered. The vegetation inside the perimeter of the Gathering compound and the tribal encampments were kept trimmed and groomed, but outside of this well-defined area was a sea of chest-high boodo grass. The relentless breeze danced across the top of the towering grass, generating continuous waves and ripples of greens, browns, and gold among the twisting, ripening stalks. Often, mesmerized individuals would stand for hours and stare at the hypnotic movements of the oscillating reeds. The breeze's visual impact on the grass complemented the whooshing sound of the ever-moving stalks. The melodic sound of the breeze moving through the grass had a calming effect on all those who attended the Gathering; even the parents of fretting infants found their children soon lulled into an easy sleep by the whispering of the relentless winds.

Painted on and chiseled in Alar's hard surface was graffiti of the People's history. The oldest inscriptions were only handprints and crude pictograms of stick people and animals, and most of the initial drawings were of hunting scenes roughly scratched on the rock surface. Later inscriptions, chiseled right into the hard stone, were, at first, hieroglyphic in structure; however, by the middle of the Fifth Progression the hieroglyphs gave way to a crude alphabet. By the early cycles of the seasons of the Sixth Progression, the alphabet was fully developed. The inscriptions moved from right to left in a chronological sequence, thus allowing a person to walk along the Promenade in front of the rock face and view the aeonic evolution of the People's written language and the shepherded development of their intellect. Moving along the mountain face, people would trace the chiseled inscriptions with their fingertips to gain an extra sense of those who, over the cycles of the seasons, had chiseled the history of the People into Alar's surface; the feel of the grooves in the chiseled letters seemed to bring to life the words etched into the stone. At the end of each Gathering, since the middle of the Fifth Progression, scriveners would etch the major events since the last Gathering, along with a list of the Pairings of that Gathering, on the stone surface. Also added was a list of the Koo Toc Biren children and their parentage.

Even with six Progressions of the Chronicles of the People covering the rock face, the mountain would still yield many thousands of cycles of the seasons of easily accessible stone surface before the scriveners would need scaffolding to reach higher up the mountainside. Relying on the recited Tell and the stone as the sole mediums to keep the record of the People had ended in the Fifth Progression. At the beginning of the Sixth Progression, Shetow, by way of the draks, had introduced the art of papermaking. By that time, however, the custom of using the mountain face to keep the Chronicles was as ingrained into the customs of the People as the Gathering itself. To walk along the Promenade at the base of Mount Alar and read the history of hundreds of cycles of the seasons was one of the wonders afforded the first-time participants of a Gathering. For those who stood at the foot of Alar, the Chronicles confirmed their reason for being. The Chronicles of Alar was one of the bindings that held the culture together; it gave the People a sense of their place in the Order of Shetow's world.

Snook, Kalmar, and the other members of the Cave Lion Tribe made camp together near a small clear brook that ran close to the Chronicles of Alar, the same location the members of the Cave Lion Tribe had been using at the Gathering since the beginning of the Tell. Each tribe had an assigned campsite. Although not identical, the layout of each campsite was similar, with each tribe responsible for their area. The tribes sent teams of workers each spring to maintain the grounds. Over the cycles of the seasons, the tribes had constructed a number of permanent buildings on their assigned locations; the dwellings were small wood and stone replicas of the dwellings the tribe members used in their villages. The Medoras' larger dwelling and a dining hall stood in the middle of the camp, the hub of activity for the tribes' attendees. The other dwellings encircled the two structures in ever-larger rings, each ring spreading out like ripples from a stone splash on a still pond. Quarters were assigned to tribe members based upon the number of times a person had attended the Gatherings; the more times you had attended, the closer you were housed to the Medora and the dining hall. Radiating like spokes of a wheel from the Medoras' dwelling were eight pathways allowing easy access for members to move about their tribe's compound. Locating someone in a tribe's campsite was a matter of knowing his or her assigned ring, quadrant, and building number.

The Cave Lion Tribe arrived at the foot of Mount Alar midmorning the day before the Gathering was to begin. It took the rest of the day to unpack and secure the food stocks the tribe had brought with them to feed their group at the Gathering and for the return journey. Once their campsite was secure, the tribe's contingent was encouraged to explore the rest of the Gathering's grounds.

Snook sensed Kalmar was anxious; his scar-faced friend became more and more distracted as they neared the Baylibor Plains, which ran to the foot of Mount Alar—the location of the Gathering. Snook did not think Kalmar was worried about the games; he knew of Kalmar's confidence in his chances in the Borrac. In fact Snook believed Kalmar was too sure of himself. After they unpacked and had their supplies arranged, Kalmar motioned for Snook to follow him away from the camp and led him towards Alar and the Chronicles that adorned the cliff's face. At first, Snook believed Kalmar's actions were to show him the spectacular writings covering the rock surface; it quickly became obvious that the ageless story of the People did not hold Kalmar's full attention.

"Kalmar, you remembered," purred a silky feminine voice behind them.

Both turned to see a young woman walking towards them. Kalmar did not have to tell Snook who she was. She could only be . . .

"Arasima," Kalmar said as he rushed to meet her.

Kalmar's descriptions of Arasima had been sketchy: long light brown hair, beautiful blue eyes, rounded posterior, full breasts. The verbal portrayal fell short of picturing the beauty standing before them. Her hair was brown, but it had a rich, wispy texture few women possessed that formed a perfect backdrop for the flawless lines of her face. Her delicate features and sulky full lips could sway any man's heart. Her eyes were not a deep blue as Kalmar had reported, or at least they did not appear so in the waning light of the afternoon, but a softer hue. Clearly, Kalmar's skimpy description was an injustice to the exquisite female—what description would not be? No wonder Kalmar had been anxious; it was obvious the two had arranged this meeting a year earlier.

Snook had tried to be an objective, detached person ever since becoming a Seeker, but he could feel his heart soften and legs weaken as he stood before this radiant creature. After a moment, he experienced a new feeling, a feeling different from when he met Cabyl; baser, more sexual—territorial. He blushed with shame as he looked at and desired this young woman. His urges were carnal, but also ones of possessing her, to have her all for himself, to just lose himself in her nearness. Kalmar was lucky if this creature had promised to choose him. Snook fought back mounting waves of jealousy; Kalmar had already slept with her. For an instant, rage blinded him; then he forced a smile.

Arasima, I told you I'd be here," Kalmar said grabbing her hands. He had resisted taking her in his arms in this public place. The world around them dissolved as they caressed each other with their eyes—on his face, a dreamy, almost foolish look; on hers, one of fulfillment.

She reached and placed her hand on the scarred side of Kalmar's face. "I heard that you faced and killed a cave lion." Tilting her head, her eyes inspected Kalmar's wounds. "Your scars are a testament to your bravery. Kalmar, your name is mentioned in every conversation at the Gathering." Kalmar seemed not to hear her words as his eyes danced over her body.

The intensity of the moment subsided when another group inspecting the Chronicles walked past. With their concentration on each other broken, they became aware of their surroundings. With a glowing, almost comical look on his face—and trying not to take his eyes off Arasima—Kalmar turned towards Snook. "Arasima, this is my new friend, Snook." He turned back to Arasima as he squeezed her hands. "Snook," he said with great pride, "this is Arasima."

For the first time Arasima's gaze moved to Snook. She studied him for a moment. Her unblinking eyes scanned his features. The intensity of her unexpected scrutiny made him uneasy. She was measuring him, judging to see if he was worthy of being Kalmar's friend. As she appraised the self-conscious Snook, it gave him an opportunity to observe her closer. She had a fair complexion, high cheekbones, and thick eyebrows that intensified the piercing effect of her majestic eyes. A second inspection confirmed that her eyes were not blue but a greenish gray, almost hazel in color. They were clear and bright, probably the reason Kalmar thought them blue. Arasima's eyes were also intense, far too knowing for a girl of only eighteen cycles of the seasons, eyes that gave no quarter—eyes that knew and got what they wanted. Kalmar had not exaggerated Arasima's other physical charms; she had a compact, yet slim body with all the hills and valleys in the right places in the proper proportions. However, Arasima's bewitching beauty was not in her hair, eyes, lips, or shape; she was not beautiful because of the beauty of any of her parts—the sum of her parts is what gave her such an overpowering presence. Her arms were slight and led to long, slender fingers that would be the pride of any artist, yet from a distance, they didn't look strong enough to endure the trials and many cycles of the seasons of exertion females bore in their efforts to create their art. The women of Elom were self-reliant and accustomed to the rigors demanded by an agrarian society; Arasima seemed too fragile to have been produced by a system in which the men were dedicated to spending most of their time hunting and the women entangled in an unquenchable spiral of artistic creation. Arasima appeared fragile but not frail; it was not so much that she looked breakable, but that she looked out of place. The females of the People, by custom, were the creators of fine art; Arasima was an anomaly, she *was* a piece of fine art—an artistic creation a man was helpless to resist once under the spell of her allure.

There are moments in a person's life when time and all about them slows while the working of the brain accelerates; for Snook, this was one of those moments. The fog of uncertainty cleared. Arasima was an unknown factor tossed into his world without warning. Arasima was not going to be a part of his life—at least not an intimate part—but her entry into his life was going to have consequences that were, as yet, unclear. She may never be more than the Pairing Partner of his new friend, but, he knew, she would be a female who would always make his heart beat faster. Arasima was a stabbing pain in his chest, and the sickly feeling she caused in the pit of his stomach was, for some strange reason, a dishonor to the feeling Cabyl gave him. When Snook's mind refocused, Arasima had finished her evaluation of him and had already turned her attention back to Kalmar, with whom she was now speaking in her soft voice, which was accentuated by the graceful movements of her hands and body. It was obvious from the way they were talking that he had missed part of their conversation.

"Snook," Kalmar said with a goofy grin, "isn't she everything I told you she was?"

Arasima looked Snook straight in the eye and gave him the slightest of smiles. She knew she was in command.

"Kalmar," Snook heard himself whisper, "she is all you said . . . and more."

With Snook's answer, Arasima's smile grew, revealing more of her teeth and exposing her only imperfection. She had a small but very noticeable space between her top two middle teeth. The shock of this imperfection did not diminish Snook's anguish; it fueled it. The flaw made her real, it made her human, and seeing the gap in her teeth unleashed a baseness Snook had never experienced before. His feelings abruptly changed from one of possessing and protecting to pure lust. Snook sensed Arasima used her imperfection as an arrow in her quiver of feminine weaponry; a bolt of sensuality she kept ready to shoot into the desires of any unexpecting male. A shiver ran through his body; this woman exposed a part of him that reviled his paltry sense of gallantry. Snook glimpsed a dark, damnable corruptness in himself that, until now, had remained hidden.

Arasima had not used one of her many bolts on him but had just shown him she had a full quiver. She had no interest in him; he was no more than an insect flying around an open flame. If he flew too close, he would only singe his wings and fall to his own demise. The only way he could control his madly beating heart was to stay as far from her as he could.

She motioned for Kalmar to bend down so she could whisper in his ear. When she was through, he smiled and raised a hand. "Our secret's safe with Snook. Besides, it won't be a secret much longer, and Arasima, there's nothing I wouldn't trust Snook with—including my life." He gave Snook a knowing wink.

Snook lowered his eyes at Kalmar's unexpected words. Arasima glanced at Snook and raised an eyebrow. Snook quickly dropped his hands and clasped them in front of him. He hoped neither Kalmar nor Arasima saw the front of his pants. As Kalmar turned away, Arasima gave Snook a sultry smile, letting him know his swollen manhood had not escaped her notice.

Arasima grabbed Kalmar's arm and pulled him down so she could again whisper in his ear. Kalmar then turned to Snook. "Arasima and I are going for a walk," he said with a pleading look. "You don't mind going back by yourself, do you?"

"No, that's fine. I'll study the Chronicles a little more, then head back to camp."

"Great, I won't be long, lots to do tomorrow," Kalmar said as he and Arasima started to walk off arm in arm. As Snook watched them walk away, Arasima turned her head and gave him one last look. She pouted her lips and gave him an impish smile. This woman not only had Kalmar in her spell but she was working on him. Then he recognized she was not giving him any special treatment;

she had all the female weapons at her disposal and derived pleasure in keeping them honed.

Arasima led Kalmar deep into the woods that bordered the Baylibor Plains and ran perpendicular to the Chronicles' end of the cliff facing. When they were out of sight, Arasima stopped, turned, and faced him. "You've not forgotten our pledge have you?" she said as she leaned against him. Kalmar could feel her firm breast press against him.

"No, how could I forget? I will reject any female until it is your turn to choose," he said, breathing harder.

"You will win the Borrac, just as you won your two pre-Borracs. All the females will want to Pair with you," Arasima said as she laid her head and placed the palm of her open right hand on his chest. "Kalmar, I have fallen in love with you these past two Gatherings; I don't know what I would do if you are chosen before I have had my chance." All of a sudden, she jumped back. "It's your fault," she said as she hit him high on his chest with clenched fists. She then buried her face in her hands and started crying.

"What did I do?" Kalmar said, his mouth open, his eyes round. He stepped forward and tried to put his arms around her. She pulled away again and turned her back on him.

"You have always known you were going to be the top-ranked male at our Matage. You planned it this way; you set out to make me fall in love with you." She looked back over her shoulder with tears in her eyes.

Kalmar could only stutter.

"You have been playing me," she continued, "using me; you're going to let yourself be chosen by a higher-ranked female." She buried her face in her hands again. "How could I have been so foolish?"

There had been promises made by couples at their pre-games

since the beginning of the Gatherings. Most of the promises were kept, but some had been made, usually by males, only to win sexual favors before the final Pairings. Sex by itself did not bring children; only sex blessed by Shetow after a Koo Toc ceremony produced pregnancy. Sex before Pairing was discouraged but not forbidden. There was, however, a strong custom against having sex with someone born from the same tribe, which meant that only during the twenty days of a person's pre-games was pre-Pairing sex possible.

Arasima's words caught Kalmar off guard. He had lived through the death of a father and a grandfather, both deeply loved by the women in his life. The only tears he had ever seen were the tears of great pain; tears caused by something he had no ability to control. When he realized what Arasima was crying about, he knew, at last, he could help a woman he loved deal with her pain. Kalmar grabbed Arasima by her shoulders and held her fast. If there had been even the smallest doubt he would wait for Arasima's turn at the Choosing, it was now gone forever. He put his hand under her chin and raised her face. She opened her tear-soaked eyes to look at him.

"I swear on the grave of my grandfather Urga that I will reject the first female, other than you, that chooses me. I'll let it be known, I will only Pair with you," he said, his jaw set, his voice firm.

Arasima threw her arms around Kalmar's neck and pulled him close to her. "Do you really mean it—you will keep your promise to me?"

"I promise," he said softly. She looked up at him and opened her lips as he bent down to give her a long, passionate kiss.

After a time, she pulled partly free from his embrace. "I may be the third or fourth to choose, but if you will wait for me, *I promise you*, you will never be sorry."

"I told you," he said with a hint of a cocky smile, "I *will* wait."

Arasima leaned against him again and started kissing him on

his neck and chest where she had unbuttoned his shirt. As he closed his eyes, concentrating on the softness of her lips, she smiled to herself; *this was so easy, men are so malleable.* She reached down and gently massaged the bulge in the front of his pants as she slowly kissed around his nipples. She grinned as he began to sway and almost fall. She stepped back and looked him in the eye as she opened the front of her woven dress and let it slide down her body to gather around her feet. Then she slowly walked around him, keeping her body at a slight angle to the direction of his view, accentuating the swell of her breast and the flatness of her stomach. Her long hair danced against her bare shoulders at every step.

She walked completely around him as he stood in place, rotating his body, never losing eye contact with the splendor before him. His heart pounded. *She knows what I want before I do; how,* he thought, *could any man desire more?* Again anticipating his cravings, she reached over and pulled his head down to her chest. His open mouth found the softness of her breast and the hardness of her nipples. After a few moments, he stepped back to marvel at her naked body. Then, he frantically finished removing his own clothing. Arasima puckered the moist lips of her slightly opened mouth. He could see her chest swell with each rapid breath. Her arms reached for his body, her sensuous smile tore at his desires. They kneeled down together and made a bed of their crumpled clothing.

A much earlier time filled Arasima's mind. "Bird legs," the other young girls sneered. Taunted because of her sinewy figure and gapped teeth, the females her own age had shunned her. *See who is bedding the killer of the cave lion,* she thought. When she took Kalmar back to her village as her Pairing Partner, they would see she had bested them all. Her spite was to be rewarded. The very ends of her tightly pressed lips turned up.

———

Much later, Snook heard the sheets rustle as Kalmar slid under his bed covers. "Snook," Kalmar whispered, as Snook knew he would. Snook did not answer, lay still, and kept his eyes tightly shut. He did not want to hear about Kalmar's night with Arasima—it would be more than he could endure.

Believing Snook asleep, Kalmar settled down in his bedding, hoping slumber would come quickly. It did not. He could not get Arasima out of his mind and stared at the multitude of stars in the twilight-of-night sky just visible through the open window.

Later, after Kalmar eventually fell asleep, Snook quietly crept out of the confines of the building and went to sit by the brook separating the tribe's campsite from the vast Baylibor Plains. Snook watched the waves of changing reflections as the breeze played with the tall boodo grass. The rustling stalks sounded like a melodic ocean surf. In a short time, its calming effect caused his heavy eyelids to close. His body slumped over.

Kalmar was on a mist-covered lake. The black water was perfectly still; not a ripple marred its mirror-flat surface. He stood alone in a slender boat, slowly gliding over the tranquil plane of the featureless expanse. The boat moved through the water by his pushing against a long pole. With his arms extended behind him, he would pull the pole from the lake bottom, move it towards the front of the boat, let the submerged tip sink back to the bottom of the lake, and continue pushing. His working the pole and the moving boat made no sound as it glided through the velvet water. The lake's only blemish appeared to be a distant island in front of him. Something on the island was drawing him to it. He pushed harder; it was important he get there. There was movement to his left; he tried to turn his head, but for some reason his head would not turn far enough for him to distinguish what had caught his attention. After a time, he quit trying to see what had made the movement and returned to pushing the boat—it was more important that he reach the island.

Snook flinched as he awoke; his head had slipped off his knees, and a sensation of falling startled him. He shivered from the cold; beside him was the sound of running water. He remembered where he was, stood up, and returned to the room. When he crawled into his bed, he looked over at Kalmar and could tell he was dreaming by his fidgeting. Snook was careful not to wake Kalmar. Soon after his head touched his pillow, he was again asleep.

FIFTEEN

Dera and the other members of her delegation approached Mount Alar from the direction of the Blue Hills, which lay three day's travel from the grassy plain. The trip was not difficult for any of the tribes' representatives to the Gathering since the majority were young and healthy contestants of the games and pre-games and the not-much-older parents of the children who were to go through their Koo Toc Biren ceremony. The Paired Partners would take turns carrying their one-cycle-of-the-seasons-old toddlers, who found the excursion to be great fun. The only persons who had any difficulty with the physical demands of the expedition were the older Medoras, who could only make the journey by riding in modified wheelons.

Shetow had hard and fast rules concerning how people were to travel. She limited them to walking, small boats, and, on rare occasions, riding in wheelons. Wheelons, used to transport supplies and materials, were constructed of wood with metal fittings. On each side of the wheelon was a single large wooden-spoked wheel with a diameter the height of a tall man. All wheelons were of similar size: roughly as wide as the diameter of one of their wheels and half again longer than they were wide. Harnessed to large castrated male bovors, the wheelons moved at a slow but steady pace. The animals' sexual loss ensured their staying docile as they pulled the heavy wagons. The bovor were the only domesticated animals, besides dogs, kept by the people—the steers as draft animals and the cows for their milk. The bovor were never a source of meat; hunters provided the meat through their skill, not the slaughter of slow, submissive animals.

Shetow, in Her infinite wisdom, allowed older Medoras incapable of making long journeys on foot to ride in wheelons, but only to and from the Gatherings. Everyone else walked. People did not mock Shetow by not using the strength She had given their legs. The People had good health and long lives, something so fleeting to their ancestors so long ago. The Tell said their ancestors had lived short, hard lives before Shetow made Her Covenant with them, now people often lived long robust ones. The People, as their part of the agreement, followed the Will of Shetow; a set of laws perpetuated by the Chants of the Sequa, the Tell, the Medoras, and, only rarely, new ones handed down through the draks. The Order of Shetow's world ran smoothly; everyone knew who they were and their place in the workings of the world—almost everyone.

Verna, with the assistance of a few helpers, set out for the Gathering three days before the balance of the main body of the Gray Wolf Tribe's delegation. The aging Medora asked Dera to accompany her and walk beside her wheelon so they could talk as the two-wheeled wagon made the slow trip to the foot of Alar. Dera obtained Verna's permission for Izzy to join the select group.

The Will of Shetow had the People walk so their legs would stay strong—along with the rest of their bodies. Verna told Dera walking also helped clear the mind. The Medora figured Dera needed a mental rest before her Byrrac. Although walking made the legs and body strong, Verna knew the slower pace would give

Dera's lower limbs a better chance to recuperate from the lengthy journey and be fresh for the ordeal she faced. Dera, for her part, was just happy to travel at a leisurely pace, taking in the beauty of Elom in the waning spring days leading up to the Gathering. The tempered pace also allowed her time with Izzy; more importantly, it gave her time to reconsider her plan and the consequences of its resulting calamity.

It was Dera's third time to make the journey; however, the Medora had covered the distance ninety-four times before and was far more familiar with the things they discovered along the way. Verna told them about new wonders at every turn of the trail. It being Izzy's first trip to the Gathering, he stayed big-eyed from the many unusual things they encountered. Verna gave a running travelogue as the little band made its way along the dusty path; the humor and wisdom of the grand old woman kept everyone entertained. It surprised Dera to see things she had missed on her two previous trips, things clearly visible by just looking with open eyes.

On the fifth day after leaving their village, the group emerged from a forest they had been traveling through for the last day and a half. Before them was a large lush meadow that would take several hours to cross. They continued out into the wide green expanse for a few minutes before they saw the great beasts.

"Long tusk," Izzy said in a tone of admiration. After a moment's hesitation, the group started moving again. The herd of gigantic animals seemed to become aware of their visitors at the same time.

"They've caught our scent," Izzy said with caution in his voice.

"They will leave us alone if we just keep moving and do not stop," Verna said. The males in the group all looked at the Medora. The reading of an animal's intention lay in the domain of males. Verna being a Medora prevented any sarcastic assertions from the otherwise brash younger males about a female telling hunters how to deal with wild animals. The males held their tongues, knowing the Medoras had a special relationship with the long tusks. The Tell told of how, in an earlier Progression, the Medoras had stopped the hunters from hunting the long-tusked mammoths to extinction. The Medoras had saved the long tusks; now the long tusks were a reminder to the males of their prowess as hunters.

As the group made its way across the meadow, the long tusks stood their ground and watched them, their steady white eyes in stark contrast to the rich russet hues of their mountainous bodies. The group of humans left the tree line within two hundred paces of where the great beasts were standing. The herd consisted of eighteen adults plus half that many calves. Dera had never been this close to a long tusk. As she walked through the short grass along the trail, she could not help but stare at the majestic animals. A layer of long coarse hair covered their bodies and the shoulders of the adults stood at the height of two men; at the beginning of their necks was a large hump. Supporting their substantial bodies were four legs, each thicker than the trunks of hundred-cycles-of-the-seasons-old nutwood trees. Their oversized heads were in proportion to their huge bodies, but their ears were much larger in relation to their heads than Dera thought looked right. On the front of the animals' heads, however, were the three things Dera could not stop looking at: a long flexible trunk and two tree-sized ivory tusks. Their trunks would have dragged the ground if the animals had not curled the tips of their elongated noses. The ivory tusks were as long as the animals were tall and each would, Dera believed, weigh more than the combined weight of several men. *What magnificent creatures*, Dera thought, as her eyes moved from one animal to another. The calves stood next to what must have been their mothers. She noticed the herd stood in some sort of formation; after closer analysis, she determined they were standing in a circle.

"*Stop,*" Verna said, as she scanned the surrounding area. The Medora leaned forward and braced herself against the side railing as she pulled herself to a near-standing position. Since the bed of the wheelon was chest high, her new vantage point was much better than that of anyone else in the group. She studied the herd a moment; her head turned as she surveyed the area around the vast clearing. "Isamor, go back to the tree line and shimmy up one of the taller trees at the wood's edge and see what's moving around in the tall grass four or five hundred paces on the other side of the herd," she said pointing towards an area of high grass. Izzy did not respond to the Medora using his hated name, but turned and quickly moved back to the tree line. Once there, Izzy skillfully climbed up a stout tree that stood, by itself, a little ways out in the open grassland. After a few moments of scrutinizing the view, he slid down the tree and ran back to report.

"There are twenty to thirty wolves, cave lions, and hyenas moving in a number of small packs around the tall grass beyond the herd," he said, a little excited, "And—"

"I know, there's a long tusk lying down in the center of the circle of long tusks," Verna said as she started to move to the back of the wheelon. "Please, I need for you to help me down." Izzy and two others stepped forward to aid the Medora's climb down from her perch in the wheelon. After she was safely on the ground, she turned to the young men and women. "Remain here, and no matter what happens none of you are to come to me or try to help me unless I give you a signal to do so. Is that understood?" They all nodded. Verna patted Dera's hand. "Don't worry my child, everything is all right. Now hand me my staff." Dera reached into the wheelon and picked up Verna's walking staff, lying on the bed of the wagon, and handed it to her. Verna reached over and took Dera by the arm. "Walk with me a few steps. I am not as steady as I once was," Verna said loud enough for all in the group to hear her; she often tried to hide her partiality to Dera. Dera held the Medora's arm as they started walking towards the herd of long tusks.

The long tusks had not moved since the small band of humans emerged from the forest. The mammoths on the side of the circle facing the humans just continued to stare at their unexpected visitors as they made muted trumpet sounds. Dera wondered if the animals' bellowing was a challenge. She walked with Verna almost halfway to the herd. Dera had not asked the Medora what she was doing, knowing Verna would tell her what she felt Dera needed to know. She also sensed Verna's tenseness and did not want to say the wrong thing. Verna turned to look at Dera and once again patted her hand. "Don't worry, but if anything should happen, it's your responsibility to keep the group safe. If something goes wrong or I signal you to back off, take the group and retreat into the trees. Don't let the others try to come and help me." She squeezed Dera's hand. "Do I have your word?"

Dera looked at her mentor. A tear formed in the corner of her left eye. "I understand, Verna." The old Medora did not take her eyes off Dera nor did she change her expression; she just continued to look at Dera. Dera bowed her head. "You have my word, my Medora." Verna nodded. Verna knew Dera better than Dera knew herself; she might break her promise to her beloved friend Verna, but she would never break her word to her Medora. They both knew she would keep her word to the Medora, not because of any honor Dera held for the revered position, but because of Verna's reverence for it. For Dera to break her word to Verna—her Medora—was to disgrace the essence of Verna's very existence; being the tribe's Medora was an honor Verna held above all others.

"Now go back my child, I will go the rest of the way by myself; I must walk this trail alone." The old Medora gave Dera a reassuring smile then resumed her walk to the herd. After a hesitation,

Dera turned and walked back towards the wheelon, Izzy, and the other waiting youths.

When she reached the group, she turned to find Verna had only covered a third of the remaining distance to the herd. For the first time, Dera noticed movement in the sky above them; she looked up to find winged specks floating, almost stationary, in the still air far above them. *Scavengers*, she thought to herself. Salune and its much dimmer partner Eeo also hung high in the afternoon sky. She lowered her gaze and focused on Verna as the old woman carefully made her way toward the herd. Dera felt the old woman's pain as she watched Verna hobble along on her arthritic legs. Izzy moved closer to Dera and held her left hand as they watched in silence as Verna continued her slow but steady trek to the herd of long tusks.

The long tusks took no action, other than some snorting, as Verna approached the hairy mountains of animal flesh. As Verna drew near the herd, Dera heard the low rhythmic tones of her chanting. Verna walked between two of the long tusks and disappeared behind the wall of their bodies. After a snort and low trumpet sound from of one of the largest long tusks, it and three others turned inward so their backsides faced out from the circle. For a time nothing happened, then Verna walked out, pointed at Dera, and raised four fingers. The signal was clear; Verna was indicating she wanted Dera and four others to join her at the herd. Dera quickly turned and pointed to Izzy and three others: Coot, Uyan, and Gylor—a male and two females. No sooner had Dera picked out the ones to accompany her than Verna motioned for them to hurry.

The five moved briskly towards the herd, resisting the impulse to run. As they neared the huge beasts, they slowed their pace to a forced walk. Dera tried not to make eye contact with any of the animals as they breached the wall of circled long tusks. They were even bigger than she had thought. The slight wind shifted, causing a breeze saturated with the pungent, almost suffocating, stench of the beasts to blow in their faces. Her heart pounded as she came so close to the nearest animal she could see beneath the forest of coarse hair enveloping its gigantic ears. So close, she could see the blood surging through a spiderweb of veins with each beat of the animal's massive heart. Out of the corner of her eye, she glimpsed the look on Izzy's face as he marveled at the size of the tusks of the animal to their right. It seemed impossible that any living thing could be so large.

Lying in the middle of the herd was one of the largest mammoths they had seen. Verna motioned for them to gather around her. "The matriarch, the head female of the herd, is dying. The other females are standing guard to keep the packs of animals waiting in the tall grass from killing and eating her. It appears their vigil has been a long one. I am hoping with us here, they will take turns and go water themselves. Without water soon, the mother cows' milk will dry up and they will not be able to feed the calves; within a day the calves will start to drop; in another, they will begin to die. We are going to stand vigil with them and chant the Jaqukyn, as their leader goes to be with Shetow."

The People believed in an afterlife, but were not sure if the animals of Elom joined them with Shetow after death. If any animal was special to Shetow, it was the long-tusked mammoth. The Jaqukyn was a chant to let Shetow know one of Her faithful was about to join Her. Verna's command seemed strange to Dera and the others, but none would ever question a Medora's decisions, especially one dealing with a long tusk. Verna positioned Dera and three of the others at specific spots around the fallen animal and sent Izzy to retrieve water flasks and pemmican for the chanters, plus her personal leather bag. When Izzy returned, Verna opened her bag and removed some incense, which she lit with a fire starter and placed at the head of the fallen animal.

As soon as Dera and the other three were set in their spots, Verna started to chant and motioned for them to join her. The Jaqukyn, along with the Koo Toc Biren, Dera felt, were the most inspiring chants of the People. The Jaqukyn started as a low set of long, deep tones, which slowly increased in volume until the tones were replaced with words. It was important that the rhythm and pitch be faultless. After five rounds, the first of the four chanters would change pitch and they would continue in harmony. On the seventh round, the second chanter would change to a third pitch. This would continue until all four chanted at different pitches. At the same time the four young people chanted, Verna sang a slightly different chant—the Medora chant, a part of the Jaqukyn reserved for a tribe's Medora. As they chanted, the long tusks did not make a sound. After the four young singers made a complete round of all the different pitches, the fifth person would take one of their places so that each of the four would rotate out of the group for one round then, once refreshed, they would replace the next person scheduled to rotate out. Verna was never relieved, but only sipped water from one of the flasks. After the group had been chanting for some time, one of the larger long tusk females snorted, then lifted her trunk and trumpeted. With this signal, the mother cows turned and led the calves away.

As the group of long tusks slowly withdrew, Verna motioned for Dera and Izzy to take a break in the chanting. Verna also stopped to take a swig from her water flask and chew on some pemmican—a mixture of dried meat, dried fruit and berries, and suet pounded into a paste then formed into cakes and dried. Pemmican was what sustained hunters on the move and travelers who could not stop to cook and, as now, eaten in cases of emergency. Dera and Izzy also took the opportunity to drink from their flasks and dine on the hunters' staple.

"The mothers are going for water," Verna said as she nodded towards the retreating mammoths. "I am afraid the old lady will not last until they return." Verna was obviously tired; her exhaustion exacerbated her stagger as she moved around the dying matriarch. The breathing of the prostrated animal had grown shallower as Salune set and a trio of Elom's moons began their trek across the star-packed sky.

The short break, water, and food rejuvenated Verna. "Dera, you and Izzy go and replace two others so they can have some water and eat some of this"—Verna looked down at a pemmican cake, shaking her head—*"food."*

"I am glad I don't have to live on this stuff," Dera said, biting into the last of her cake as they walked over to relieve two other chanters.

"You females don't know what you're talking about," Izzy said as he held up the last of his cake. "After a couple of days on the hunt, this stuff can taste really good."

"My intrepid brother, as the hunter in our family it would be hard for me to question you on this matter," Dera replied, as she tilted her head in a condescending manner, "but I must say that I have overheard the Gray Beards say that after five or six days of a steady diet of this stuff it begins to taste pretty rancid."

"I must admit you are right," he said with a sheepish grin, "after a few days it can get a little rank." Izzy and Dera took the places of two other chanters and started to chant as Verna resumed her part in the ritual.

The group chanted deep into the night. The cows and their calves returned and all the other females but the apparent new leader of the herd made a dash for water. In the twilight-of-night, the multitude of stars and the bright moonlight reflected off the eyes of the many scavengers moving around in the tall grass a few hundred paces from the herd—opportunistically looking for an easy meal after the old matriarch died.

The last of the long tusks returned a little past midnight, just in time to be present at the end. Verna and the new leader of the herd seemed to know the moment the old matriarch died. Vera changed her chant to a high-pitched shrill. The new matriarch lifted her trunk high up and gave a long, wailing trumpet.

At dawn, the long tusks began to move around. Earlier Verna and the others had sat down around the body of the long tusk; exhausted, they had leaned against each other and had fallen fast asleep. The stirring of the herd awoke them.

"Time to face another day, my children," Verna said, struggling to her feet. She and Dera had slept with their heads propped up by Verna's leather bag. "Dera, go and tell the rest of our group to start gathering wood."

"Wood?"

"Yes, we are going to give the matriarch the farewell she deserves; we're going to cremate her in the manner of a Medora."

"But Verna, it will take half the forest to turn so much flesh to ashes," Dera protested.

"Then you had better start gathering the wood and stop complaining. We need to be ready to leave by the time the other members of our tribe catch up with us. That gives us at best, one, possibly one and a half days to gather the wood and perform the cremation and ceremony." Verna turned and started walking among the long tusks as Dera left to organize the gathering of the vast amount of wood it was going to take to cremate the body of the long tusk. Verna sang a simple soothing chant as she weaved randomly between the members of the herd.

As Dera started to walk back towards the balance of their group, who had slept on and around the wheelon, she motioned for Izzy to follow her. As he caught up and matched her stride, they saw the eyes of the wolves, cave lions, and hyenas still watching from the tall grass. "They can't wait for us to leave so they can have their feast," Izzy said, "and with that much food they might not even follow their normal feeding order."

"Feeding order?"

"Yeah, the scavengers have an order of how they feed on a carcass." Izzy hesitated when Dera looked at him out of the corners of her eyes. "Well"—he shrugged his shoulders—"you know, the strongest eat first, then the next strongest." Dera was still looking at him with a frown on her face. "Okay, it's like this. Basic Gray Beard training for a five-year-old boy—"

"*Izzy*, just tell me what you're trying to tell me."

"Scavengers eat a carcass in an order based on their strength. First, the cave lions will have their fill, then the wolves will gorge themselves, and if there's any of the body remaining, the hyenas have a portion. But here the order doesn't matter."

"Why?"

"Because, the long tusk is so large there is more food than they can all eat in the next few days. The cave lion won't be as vigilant when the other scavengers try to take a portion of the carcass."

"Well, they have a surprise coming," Dera said as they reached the wheelon.

"A surprise—what do you mean?"

Dera gave her brother a smirky smile. "'Cause we're going to cremate the long tusk."

"*We're going to what?*"

"We are going to cremate the long tusk and Verna's going to perform the Medora ritual while we do it."

"That's the craziest thing I've ever heard. It will take forever to cremate an animal that large."

Dera smiled. "I have seen that expression on Verna's face before; it does not matter how crazy you or I think it is, we are going to do it. I suggest we gather the others and get to it."

Izzy nodded; he was not familiar with Verna's expressions, but he was with Dera's—there was no sense in arguing.

Dera, Izzy, and the others gathered fallen tree limbs, carried them back, and stacked them next to the carcass. They emptied the wheelon to use as a cart for the heavier timbers. After collecting all the dead wood, they cut down trees and used the bovor to drag them back to the pile for the cremation. As Salune rose to a noon place in the sky, Dera walked over to take a water break and talk to Verna. The Medora had spent much of the morning petting and singing softly to the skittish calves that were very playful after they finished nursing.

"I think we will have enough wood for the fire by late afternoon."

"Dera, you and the others have done a fine job, and I haven't heard them complain."

"Oh," Dera said grinning, "they all know the rule—when you complain about the Medora, you make sure you don't talk loud enough for her to hear you." They both laughed. Dera drank deeply from a water flask and chewed on a pemmican cake. When she finished, she smiled at Verna. "Guess I'd better get back to work."

Verna put out her hand to Dera. "No, stay. I feel the need to talk." She noticed Dera's eyes dart to the others still working. "They'll be fine, besides I must get you ready to perform the ceremony." Dera had wondered how the Medora was going to follow the rite of the cremation of a Medora all by herself. Verna sat under a tarpaulin stretched out from the side of the wheelon, which was not being used while the bovor dragged logs from the forest. Verna motioned for Dera to sit in the shade with her. Dera hesitated before sitting down beside her mentor; she felt guilty leaving Izzy and the others to finish the backbreaking work.

"I saw all of this," Verna said, moving her hands in a circular motion. Dera leaned forward so she could understand the Medora's soft voice. "I saw the cremation in my dreams."

"You saw the death of the long tusk matriarch in your dreams?"

"Not exactly; Shetow only showed me the cremation in my dreams. She had me prepare to perform the Medora Cremation Rite. Shetow showed me what was going to happen; I brought all the accoutrements needed for the rite." She raised her leather bag.

"I have dreams too."

"I know my child; you told me."

"Verna, I wish I could understand my dreams . . . like you can understand yours."

"Dera . . ." Verna closed her eyes for a moment. "I don't understand what Shetow's trying to tell me in most of my dreams. This dream, though, was so clear—I was performing a cremation ceremony, a Medora cremation." She looked into Dera's eyes. "And you're in the dream helping me."

"I am?" She cast her gaze down. "Verna, my dreams usually make no sense at all."

"Dera . . . to be honest, this is the first one in a long time to make any sense and it only started doing that when we came upon the dying matriarch. The dream was so real—if it hadn't been, I wouldn't have brought this." She patted her bag.

"Why would Shetow want you to perform a Medora Cremation Rite for a long tusk? Is this done often?"

"I will perform the rite—" she leaned over and touched Dera's leg "—with your help, because that is what Shetow has indicated to me, by the dreams, that I am supposed to do . . . and as far as I know, this will be the first time the ceremony has ever been performed for any non-Medora, much less a long tusk."

"But Verna, does it not seem strange to you that Shetow would have you do this?"

"I would doubt my dreams if we had come upon a herd of bovors; but we didn't, we came upon a herd of long tusks at the death of their matriarch. My child, a long-tusked mammoth lives as long as we do and there are far fewer of them than there are of us. For a human to be at the side of one of the great creatures' matriarch at her death is something I have never heard of." Verna leaned back against a spoke of one of the wheelon's wheels. "No, I do not think it strange that Shetow is instructing me to perform the rite." Her voice dropped to a whisper. "No, not strange at all." She turned to Dera. "Shetow is giving me a great honor. She is, I think, giving me a message to carry to the People."

"Message?"

"That the long tusks are still very important in the Order of Shetow's world. She is telling us the long tusks' survival is important to Her and also to the People." Verna looked off, lost in thought. Her eyes refocused and she looked back at Dera. "That's it. The survival of the long tusks is important to the survival of the People."

"How can that be?"

"I am not . . . sure . . . that part is still unclear to me. . . ." Verna's eyes opened wider. "Dera, there is something important about to happen . . . something important to the future of the People, something that will change the People forever."

"Verna—"

"My dreams . . . they are a message from Shetow. The meaning of the dream . . . the dream about the cremation rite for the long tusk, is just one of many signs that are now becoming clear to me."

"I am also trying to understand my own dreams," Dera said to Verna, now lost in her own thoughts. Dera opened her mouth to speak, but closed it, choosing not to interrupt her mentor. Verna spoke of change; this was exciting to Dera; change was something the Tell and the other Medoras spoke against. There had been changes in the way the People lived their lives over the Progressions, but they were few and were usually handed down from Shetow by way of the draks at the Gatherings. Verna had always been a Medora who adhered to the strict doctrine of the Sequa; her words of change were totally out of character, which, in itself, was change. Dera sat up straight. "Oh, Verna . . . you must prepare me for the cremation."

Verna's blank expression faded as she turned to Dera. "Yes . . . yes, I must prepare you . . . we haven't much time." Verna gave her head a little shake, as if she were trying to clear her mind. "It's not that hard. I will read the sacred text and chants for the rite from the *Sequa*; you'll read the answers and chant the chants designated for the second performer of the rite when I give you the sign." As Verna was speaking to Dera, she reached into her personal bag and took out a second copy of the *Chants of the Sequa*. "As I said, I came prepared." She handed a tattered hand-copied book to Dera. "I have marked where the ceremony begins." Verna ran through the pages of the *Sequa* covering the ceremony until they both felt Dera understood her part. Dera then stood up and walked away from the shade of the tarp to stretch her legs.

"Well sister, did you enjoy your nap?"

Dera looked up to see a sweaty Izzy walking towards her. "Yes," she faked a yawn, "but I'm still sleepy. It woke me up every time one of you inconsiderate people dropped logs on the pile. You know, not a one of you showed any respect for someone trying to get a few hours sleep." Dera tilted her head to the side and raised her eyebrows, daring him to make another wise remark.

Izzy nodded. "Point made. I saw you with the Medora. What's going on?"

"I'm to assist the Medora in the ceremony. She was preparing me."

"Dera, that's . . . good . . . isn't it? I mean that is a big honor . . . to assist a Medora . . . how do you feel about it?"

"I . . . I'm not sure—"

"You don't think it is an honor?"

"*Yes, Izzy,* I know it is an honor. That is not why I hesitated. It's just . . . there has never been, Verna thinks, a cremation ceremony for a long tusk and here we are about to perform one, and the one we are going to perform is one reserved for Medoras."

Deep lines crossed Izzy's brow. "I see what you mean."

"For the first time in the Tell of the People, we are about to perform a ceremony reserved for a tribe's most revered member . . . a Medora, and we're performing it for a long-tusked mammoth, an animal, and I'm going to be helping do it. I don't know, it doesn't seem wrong, but it does seem strange. . . ."

"I agree; it is strange to think we are going to have a cremation ceremony for a long tusk." Izzy looked at his sister, and then tilted his head. "But I don't think it is strange that you are the one doing it; you have done a lot of strange things, my crazy sister."

Dera made a playful swing at her brother; she knew he spoke in jest—at least she hoped he did. "Thanks, your understanding is reassuring," she said with a deadpan expression.

"That's what younger brothers are for," Izzy said grinning.

"Be serious for a moment. What do you really think?"

It was not in Izzy's nature to be serious. Except for the time he jumped the boy who made fun of her birthmark, Izzy always displayed a toothy grin. For a second time the ever present grin left his face. "I don't know what to think, but I do know this might be the biggest event in our lives. We have talked about the need for changes in our lives; after the ceremony for the long tusk, things will be changed forever. We have discussed things we dared not tell anyone else about. Now, to be unexpectedly part of an event that could bring the wrath of the other Medoras is a little scary. In the past, we have plotted our little schemes, little jokes to break the monotony of our lives. However, this . . . this isn't something we have planned. This is no prank on our mother or friends—"

"You're saying we shouldn't do it?"

"Do you think we . . . you should do it?"

"Yes," she said after a hesitation, "I think I should do it. Even if I didn't, I would do it because Verna asked me to."

"Guess you are right." Izzy nodded. "You must do what our Medora asks."

"Izzy, I am not doing it for our Medora; I am doing it for Verna—the only friend I have besides you and mother." The lines of her face hardened. "Now, let us see that everything is ready." Dera looked around at the young men and women as they continued to bring wood and add it to the pile. She glimpsed Verna walking among the mammoths singing to the rambunctious baby long tusks. The death of the matriarch broke the veil of silence that had fallen on the mammoths ever since the herd encircled their leader as her aged heart failed her. The calves played hide-and-seek among the legs of the adults. Their mothers and the other herd members abandoned their silence, filling the air with a flood of deep throat grunts. The resonance of their communications echoed off the nearby tree line. The older long tusks, during their wake for their fallen leader, seemed oblivious to the young men and women moving in their midst.

"Izzy, I think we have enough wood," Dera said as she surveyed the mountainous pile of logs and branches lying next to the body of the long tusk. "It's time we start stacking the wood around the body."

"It would have been much easier if we had stacked it around the body as we brought it in," Coot said as he wiped sweat off his face with the back of his hand.

"Yeah, next time we build a cremation pile for a long tusk we'll know better," Izzy said as he gave Coot an ugly look.

"Izzy, Coot was only saying what we all were thinking," Dera said.

"Yeah," Coot said, "I was only—"

"It's all right, Coot," Dera said. "We know. Now, let's start restacking the wood around the matriarch. We need to be finished, fed, and rested before morning so we can continue our journey. You two, go round up the rest of the group to help us stack the pile."

As Coot and Izzy turned to do Dera's bidding, a scream pierced the low guttural rumble of the long tusks' grunts. Dera's head jerked up as the chilling sound was cut short. The sound had come from the area where Dera had last seen Verna playing with the long tusks' calves. Dera sprinted in the direction of the scream. She had only taken a few strides when she detected movement in the high grass right past the edge of the herd. A baby long tusk, its trunk pointed up, shrieked as it scurried from the spot of the commotion. Dera ran faster, then screamed, *"Noooo!"* As she drew near, she could see her worst fears were borne out. A pack of wolves waiting to devour the fallen long tusk had attacked Verna.

Verna stopped moving as the three animals looked up at the fast-approaching shrieking woman. The wolves, their muzzles red with blood, did not back away from their helpless prey but casually turned towards Dera, intending on adding another victim to their meal. Without slowing down, Dera pulled her knife from the scabbard on her belt, dove into the snarling collection of flashing teeth and bristled fur. The fury of Dera's unexpected assault stifled Verna's attackers for the few seconds it took Izzy and Coot to reach the blur of feminine wrath and canine voracity. Now, with three humans confronting them, the hesitant wolves broke away and began to slowly back away from Verna's blood-soaked body. Scratched and blood-splattered, Dera rose to her knees as Izzy and Coot, knives in hand, began to spread out and confront the snarling wolves. They had only taken a few steps when a handful of young men and women with knives drawn ran up to join them. The hungry wolves had been looking for an easy meal, not a fight; the frustrated animals turned to withdraw. The wolves' attention focused on their retreat; they stopped abruptly. Behind them stood, shoulder-to-shoulder, eleven highly agitated mammoths; the confused wolves found their escape route blocked by a gauntlet of eleven trunks, twenty-two dingy white tusks, and forty-four massive feet. The surrounded wolves dropped their ears and started to whimper. The wolves' plight brought no sympathy from those whose only thoughts were of their destruction.

The end came quickly. An arrow, shot by one of the last males to reach the group, brought a loud wail from one of the wolves as it thrashed around in a tight circle. The screams of pain from the mortally wounded wolf panicked the other two, who then, foolishly, chose to run through the long tusks and not the humans. An agile wolf should have had no trouble running through a herd of lumbering mammoths. That would have been true if the long tusks needed to move their feet to stop the fleeing canines. That was not the case.

The mammoths had aligned themselves so that there was not a single place, from one end along their collected front to the other, which was not in reach of one of their powerful trunks. As the second wolf reached the line of vengeful mountains, the nearest long tusk swung the end of her trunk and hit the fleeing wolf in its side, knocking it in a high arc back towards the humans. The last wolf stopped when it saw the fate of its companion, doubled back, and ran straight at Dera and Verna. There was the twang of a bowstring and a precisely aimed second arrow stopped its charge. With an arrow penetrating its neck, its tongue hanging out of its open mouth, the last wolf lay quivering, surrounded by an expanding moat of blood.

The wolf the long tusk had knocked down was trying to rise

on its front legs; with its back broken, its hind legs were useless. One of the long tusks broke rank, walked over to the struggling wolf, and snorted. Then, in one fluid motion, the great beast lifted a front leg and slammed a massive foot down on the head of the whining canine. The two other wolves now also lay still as the arrows had drained the life out of them. The new matriarch walked over and sniffed each of their carcasses before lifting her trunk, and for the second time since Dera and the others' arrival, trumpeted a long, piercing blast. The regal creature then turned and walked back with the ten other long tusks towards the seven remaining members of the herd, who were standing guard over their calves.

With the wolves vanquished, Dera dropped down beside her old friend and put her lips to Verna's ear. "Verna, Verna, can you hear me?"

Izzy and Uyan joined Dera at Verna's side. "Is she alive?" Uyan asked.

"She's alive. Her pulse is weak—but she's alive," Dera answered. "We must stop the bleeding . . . she has lost so much blood, she has no chance if we don't stop the bleeding quickly."

"Dera, shouldn't we move her to the wheelon?" Uyan said.

"No. That would surely kill her. Izzy, you and Coot bring the wheelon over here and rig the tarp above her. Uyan, go search everyone's packs and bring back as much clean cloth as you can. Gylor, run and get the medical kit and some water flasks out of the wheelon before Izzy and Coot start moving. . . ." Dera thought a moment. "No, Izzy, let Coot get the wheelon, you stay here and help me stop the bleeding." Coot, Uyan, and Gylor bolted towards the wheelon.

Izzy dropped to his knees, probed Verna's blood-drenched clothing to locate the wounds, and then, with both hands, pressed against her deepest gashes. "Her face is white; we must raise her legs to get more blood to her brain."

Dera nodded and looked around. "Drag the body of that wolf," she said to the remaining members of their group, pointing with her head towards the body of the nearest wolf, "over here."

The movement of her legs caused Verna to regain consciousness. "Dera," said a barely audible voice.

She had not seen Verna open her eyes, but at the sound of her name, she turned to look into Verna's face. "Verna, I'm right here." Dera leaned down, placing her right ear above Verna's lips.

"The baby long tusk, they're so precious. One wandered . . ." Verna breathed a gurgling breath, little red bubbles formed at the corners of her mouth ". . . too far from its mother . . . I tried to—"

"We know, it's okay. The calf is safe."

"I didn't see the wolves . . ." she wheezed, "until it was too late. It was gray wolves, wasn't it?"

"Yes Verna . . . gray wolves."

"How ironic." A faint smile crossed her face. "Come closer. I don't have much strength left." Dera again lowered her head, placing her ear next to Verna's lips. "I dreamed right; I am to take part in a Medora Cremation Rite on this trip . . ." Verna chuckled; blood gushed from between her lips. "I just didn't realize it was going to be my own." She coughed; the blood flow increased.

"Verna, you're going—"

Verna's head made a slight side-to-side movement. "I don't have time to waste on what you and I both know isn't true. Now listen to me."

Dera nodded. "Yes, Verna."

"You must perform the ceremony—you sing the elegy. Have Uyan be your second. Cover the matriarch with the wood as we had planned, and then place my body on top of the pile. The matriarch and I will meet Shetow together. Before you light the fire, remove the matriarch's tusks and take them to the Medoras at the

Gathering . . ." Verna took a shallow breath. "It isn't a desecration of the matriarch; the tusks will be used to honor Shetow. Dera . . ."

"I'm right here, Verna."

"The changes I told you about . . . they are bigger and more important than I thought. I don't know how, but some of the changes will come through you." There was a gurgling sound deep in Verna's chest. She spoke again in a soft but forced voice. "My child, your Traits are the most complete of anyone I have ever met. Whatever place you will have in the Tell . . . will be because of the purity of your inner-spirit. I didn't tell you, but I also had a dream about you. I dreamed . . ." Verna's voice trailed off.

"Verna, what did you dream?"

Verna slowly raised a trembling hand and gently touched the birthmark on Dera's face. "Dera, be true to your inner-spirit, you . . ." Verna's lips curled into a contented smile as her eyes glazed, and then all expression vanished from her face as her hand dropped to her chest; her head gently rolled to the side.

Dera screamed as she rolled forward to place her tear-streaked face on Verna's still bosom. Izzy wrapped his arms around his sobbing sister.

The dancing flames grew as the fire spread over the towering pile of wood. The luminous inferno fought back the night as crackling cinders rose in the glowing vortex of hot gases. Dera, Izzy, and the other young people watched in silence as the flame's fingers reached the shrouded body of their beloved Medora.

SIXTEEN

Kalmar, Snook, and the other members of their group walked along a path that followed a brook that ran next to the tribe's campsite. Near the edge of their encampment, a stone bridge built during the Fifth Progression crossed over the brook. The stone structure was in excellent repair, yet seemed ageless because of its moss-covered masonry. Once over the bridge, the path headed straight for the Grand Oonoc Chamber located at the left end of the base of Alar's towering rock surface.

Like orderly lines of ants, people from the Twenty-Four Tribes, following their designated paths, made their way towards the Grand Oonoc that would officially start the Gathering. The paths, like their campsites, were the same ones used by members of their respective tribes for the last three Progressions. The eons of use had left their mark; the well-worn paths were free of grass and stones, and the powdery fawn-colored dust covering them appeared as a pale ribbon contrasted against an emerald-colored background easily followed even during the twilight-of-night. The paths were filled with members of each tribe, walking slowly, wearing multicolored clothing dyed with patterns in variations unique to that tribe. The flowery tunics worn by the men and the matching chemises worn by the women would be mementos they would cherish the rest of their lives.

"I had no idea it would be like this," Snook said, as he craned his head around and almost stumbled. "The colors, the people, it's overwhelming."

"The first time I saw it, I couldn't believe it either, but Snook, do not talk so loud," Kalmar whispered. "At your age, you don't want anyone to know this is your first Gathering." Snook nodded and refrained from his gawking.

"Kalmar, isn't that Nutan?" Snook asked, pointing at a figure jogging back down the path towards them.

"I don't think . . . no, you are right. It *is* Nutan."

Kalmar and Snook kept walking as Nutan reached them and turned to fall in step. "Have you heard what happened?"

"No, little sister. Tell us," Kalmar said, a little melodramatic.

"The Medora from the Gray Wolf tribe was killed on her way to the Gathering."

"Killed!" Kalmar and Snook exclaimed simultaneously. They both stopped walking to look at Nutan. "How, where, when?" Kalmar demanded in rapid order, before Snook could pose a single question.

"Well, I don't know everything, it just happened this morning—"

"She was killed this morning?"

"No, brother, let me explain. Her tribe's delegation arrived early this morning and we learned what happened."

"But—"

"Let me finish telling you what little I know before you pester me with more questions."

Kalmar nodded. The three stepped off the path to keep from blocking the flow of people moving towards the Grand Oonoc Chamber.

"The Medora from the Gray Wolf Tribe was attacked by three wolves while she and a small advance group stopped to help a herd of long tusks—" Nutan lifted her hand. "Let me *finish*! I don't know what they were doing with the long tusks, but I do know they brought two huge tusks strapped to a wheelon with them. The story is they stopped to help a long tusk herd keep their dying matriarch from being attacked and eaten by scavengers. After the mammoth died, the Medora had her group build a cremation pile, and she told them she was going to perform the Jaqukyn—the Medora Jaqukyn—for the dead matriarch. While her group was gathering wood, the wolves attacked her and she died soon after that. She did live long enough to instruct them to remove the matriarch's tusks. The Medora also told them to cremate her body along with the fallen long tusk." Nutan raised her eyebrows. "Now, won't that be an addition to the Tell."

Kalmar raised a finger. "May I ask a question now?"

"Yes, but that is all I know."

"How did wolves get so close, and who performed the Medora Jaqukyn?"

"Well, the group was small, about ten. The Medora was too old to walk, so she had to ride in a converted wheelon. She and the smaller group started a few days before the rest of their tribe's delegation."

"But who performed the Medora Jaqukyn?" Kalmar pressed.

"A young girl in the group who was coming to her Byrrac. The last instruction of their dying Medora was that they not bring her body to the Gathering, but to have her Medora Jaqukyn performed by the girl. The group cremated their Medora and the long tusk matriarch together while the young girl chanted the Medora's Jaqukyn."

"I don't remember anything in the Tell like that ever happening before," Kalmar said, as he first looked at Nutan, then at Snook.

"I wonder what the other Medoras think. Let us get to the meeting, we will learn more there." The three stepped back on the pathway and hurried towards the Grand Oonoc Chamber.

The three moved at their quickened pace until they neared the chamber. The paths from the twenty-four campsites converged at the promenade that stretched from the Grand Chamber along the base of Mount Alar to the starting point of the Chronicles.

The crowd in front of them slowed as they neared the promenade—this was odd, thought Kalmar. "The crowd should be speeding up not slowing down as we reach the promenade. I don't understand."

As they got closer, they approached a knot of people moving slowly past a wheelon with two massive ivory tusks, tied down at each end, lying across it. More of the tusks extended out the front and rear of the wheelon than were resting on the wheelon itself.

"I did not realize a mammoth's tusks were *so big*," Nutan said.

"Yeah," Snook inflated his voice, "and think about the size of the animal it took to carry them."

"We need to hurry," Kalmar said, "the Gathering will be starting at any moment."

The promenade led them to the three entrances of the Grand Oonoc Chamber. The outside of the chamber was the flat mountain face, which was marred only by the arched openings that served as entrances. Each portal was wide enough for fifteen people to walk through at one time and stood one and a half times as high as it was wide.

They followed the crowd through the middle entrance, and walked down a short tunnel before the Grand Oonoc Chamber mushroomed before them. Snook was not prepared for what awaited him. He stood speechless, stunned at the size and design of the great hall. Inside the mountain was a gigantic towering cavern. The cavernous wedge-shaped chamber's seating started at the rear wall, which arched for a third of a circle. The aisles leading from the three entrances to the podium area were a set of steps, with a semicircle row of stone bleachers on every other step. Because each row of seats was higher than the row in front of it, there was not a place in the chamber without a full view of the podium.

"This is not natural; this was made," Snook said as he arched his back to look at the ceiling hundreds of feet above him.

"The Tell says," Nutan whispered in his ear, "it was carved out of the mountain by the draks during the Third Progression. The People left a Gathering and there was no Grand Chamber; when they came back after a cycle of the seasons, it was here."

"The draks built it in *one cycle of the seasons?*"

"Well, that's not completely correct. They expanded it after the Great Split."

"Great Split?"

Nutan shushed him. She pressed an index finger against her lips and said, "At the beginning, when Shetow made the Covenant with Geerna, during the First Progression, the People consisted of only three tribes. Those three split into six tribes several hundred cycles of the seasons later. At the beginning of the Second Progression, the six tribes split into twelve tribes. During the Third Progression, the tribes split for the last time and for the last three Progressions there have been twenty-four tribes."

"Why so long without any more splits?" Snook asked, a questioning scowl distorting his pallid face.

"Well," Nutan answered, "the population stabilized and there hasn't been the need to increase the number of tribes."

"Three Progressions, thousands of cycles of the seasons, and no increase in population," Snook said in a hollow tone, more to himself than to his two companions. *I tried to tell the Elders I was not the one for this task,* he thought, *I know so little about these people. Nutan must think I'm brainless.*

The three walked into the chamber and took seats assigned to their tribe. "These aren't the best seats," Snook said, after they sat down a third of the way from the back of the two-hundred-meter-deep chamber.

"They will be better next year," Kalmar replied.

"What do you mean?"

"Seating is assigned to the tribes based on the ranking of their contestants from the previous Gathering. After I win the Borrac," he said with complete assurance, "next year the Cave Lion Tribe will be assigned seating at the front." He pointed to the seats at the front right of the chamber.

Snook rolled his eyes, then scanned the chamber. The dreary gray of the rock enclosure contrasted sharply with the participants' bright garb—a random patchwork of colors spreading across the great hall like a field of vibrant wildflowers. The domed ceiling sloped down the sides of the chamber like the inside of an over-turned bowl. The crown of the dome emitted a soft yellow glow that permeated the spacious chamber. Rumbling from muffled whispering choked the air.

Snook stiffened when he saw Cabyl at Berkana's arm. The old woman limped onto the stage after entering from an obscure open-ing in the rock wall at the front of the chamber that had escaped his notice. As she had at the Oonoc Lodge in the village, Cabyl assisted Berkana all the way to the podium. With her Medora situated at the podium, Cabyl quickly retreated from the stage. The sight of the an-gelic Cabyl sparked a contracting pressure in his chest, and for a rea-son he did not fully understand, a wave of remorse flowed over him—a feeling of guilt, regret, and betrayal as he compared the admi-ration he felt for Cabyl with the primordial lust Arasima unleashed.

———

Berkana stood at the podium, looked around the chamber, and then lowered her eyes to the group seated directly in front of her. Nutan leaned towards her brother. "Who is Berkana looking at?"

"The Council of Medoras."

"The what?" Snook said leaning towards the other two.

Kalmar shifted his weight so he faced Snook. "The Council of Medoras . . . the twenty-four Medoras, from the Twenty-Four Tribes. In this case, there are only twenty-three in the chamber: the twenty-two seated in the audience and Berkana—the Medora Roo—at the podium makes twenty-three. Remember, the twenty-fourth was the Medora killed by wolves—" He was interrupted by the cracking sound of wood hitting stone. They looked to the front of the chamber to see Berkana striking the rock floor with the butt-end of an Ooroc. The wooden staff hitting the hard rock sent a dull, reverberating sound echoing throughout the chamber. Silence gripped the people in the chamber as the Medora Roo's actions signaled the beginning of the opening session of the Gathering.

"Blessed be the Mark of the Covenant," Berkana said as she lifted and extended her left arm from the folds of her robe, exposing the dark spot on the inside of her forearm.

Everyone in the audience raised their left arm and answered in unison, "Blessed be the Mark of the Covenant."

Snook noticed there did not seem to be any one way to do it; some of the people made a fist as they extended their arms, others had open hands. He did notice, however, most males used fists and females more often used open hands. Snook only raised his arm and half-cupped hand enough to not be conspicuous.

"In the name of Shetow, the Giver of Life, and the blessings She has placed on the People and on each of us, I call this Gathering to order. We gather to remember Geerna, the first Medora Roo, and the Covenant she made with Shetow for the People. Shetow has kept Her Covenant with the People. We gather, as we have once every cycle of the seasons since the first Gathering, to reconfirm our commitment to Shetow and the Covenant that has guided us since the beginning of the Tell." The old woman grabbed the podium with one hand while still clutching the Ooroc with the other. "We convene overwhelmed with sorrow for the loss of one of our Medoras and the void her absence will leave in the lives of so many people. Verna was beloved by all, especially members of her tribe and those of us blessed by the unerring wisdom of her council. As we mourn her loss, we mustn't forget she's in a better place . . . a place . . ." Berkana faltered and lowered her head for a moment before looking back into the audience. "A place where she'll bask in the Shadow of Shetow."

When Berkana hesitated, Snook quickly glanced at those around them. All eyes stayed on the Medora Roo, their faces not betraying their reaction to Berkana's hesitation. Was he the only one who sensed something askew in the tone of Berkana's words? Snook knew Berkana to be a sincere person; one of the most pious people he had ever met. He must talk to her again—soon. The rhythm of her words drew his attention.

". . . tonight we dance. We dance in remembrance of Verna." She looked down at the members of the Medora Council, nodded, and gave them a reassuring smile. Then she again lifted her face to the crowd. "We dance as a tribute to Geerna, the first Medora Roo, the one who led us out of the darkness of ignorance, the one who turned back our fears, the one who taught us the Holy Chants. Geerna, first to recite the Sequa." Berkana held up a copy of the sacred book, first transcribed only several hundred cycles of the seasons earlier. "The one Chosen by Shetow to instruct the People on Her Order for the World."

"And, most importantly, we dance to honor Shetow, the Earth Mother, the one who gives us life, the One who controls our future as She controlled our past; Shetow, the One who causes Salune and

Eeo to rise and the gentle rains to fall; Shetow, the One who rules the complexities of the heavenly bodies"—Berkana spread out her arms still holding the Ooroc in her right hand—"as effortlessly as our females work a potter's wheel."

As if by a prearranged sign, Cabyl walked out to Berkana as the old woman lowered her arms. Cabyl helped the Medora Roo to a chair behind the podium. As Berkana lowered herself into her seat, Cabyl started to turn and leave the dais, but Berkana caught her arm and motioned for her to sit down. Snook watched Cabyl glance around before kneeling at Berkana's side, as there was no other place for her to sit. As Cabyl knelt, another Medora rose from the front row and made her way to the podium.

"Tonight," the younger Medora said, "we will observe the Celebration of Life around three great Life Fires on the promenade, a custom timeless before the baby Geerna first suckled milk from her mother's breast. The Celebration of Life keeps us mindful of the quality of our lives . . . a fullness our Covenant with Shetow has bestowed upon us. The celebration reminds us there was a time, before the Covenant, when winters were brutal, existence hard, and the cycles of the seasons of our lives few. A celebration so we would never forget. . . ." The Medora, at that point, started to chant. She chanted a complete round. For the second round, the twenty-two other Medoras joined her. For the third, and final round, a combined chorus of the balance of the audience overpowered the soft feminine voices of the revered women. Snook was dismayed by the force and power of the hundreds of voices chanting in unison, a swelling, methodical sound that could control the actions of men, a resonance, Snook thought, that could surely shatter mountains—a reverberation to command the attention of Shetow.

At the end of the chant, the young Medora addressed them once again. "At the close of this meeting, you are encouraged to mingle and talk to those from other tribes. Shetow has divided the

People into twenty-four small tribes, thereby allowing us to have a personal relationship with everyone in our own village. Yet, we must never forget the People cover a vast area; some of you walked for twenty days to reach the Gathering. Except for the young males who joined your tribe after the Matage, you've spent your whole lives surrounded by the same people. It is the Will of Shetow that we live our lives this way. You may never see many of the people gathered here ever again. Take this opportunity to share with them your thoughts and feelings, explore your similarities as well as your differences. Remember, it's the similarities Shetow has given us that make us strong; it's the differences—one from another—that She has blessed us with that make us unique in Her sight." The young Medora scanned the upturned faces. "Take the time to walk along the promenade and read the Chronicles of the People chiseled in the rock face of Mount Alar. It'll heighten your sense of who you are and Shetow's Plan for us." Her face lost all expression. "To comprehend your own existence is Shetow's ultimate gift."

The young Medora waited several moments before continuing. "Tomorrow—the second day—will be the Koo Toc Biren for the one-cycle-of-the-seasons-olds and also a time of rest and preparation for the participants of the games and pre-games beginning on the third day. They'll continue until they finish on the eighth day. On the ninth day will be the Matage—the Choosing. On the tenth day is the Koo Toc—the Pairing Ceremony—for the young couples matched the day before at the Matage. On that, the last night, we will have a final gathering around the three Life Fires where we will chant and dance in honor of the new Pairings and their place in the Order of Shetow's World." A few other topics were covered, then the young Medora sat down and Berkana stood up, and with Cabyl's aid, tottered back to the podium.

"We, the members of the Medora Council, who trace our line back six Progressions to the first Medora Roo—to Geerna, the

Maker of the Covenant with Shetow, the first Chanter of the Chants of the Sequa, the Protector of the People—honor you. Every Gathering is important to the People, but none has ever been more important than this one."

Kalmar cut his eyes to Snook.

"The Shadow of Shetow has fallen heavy on those of us here today." Then the old woman started a chant, a chant very simple in form, but one with a haunting, almost sad, tone. The chant seemed to catch the other Medoras by surprise. After a moment's confusion, the remaining twenty-two Medoras stood and chanted with their Medora Roo.

"I don't understand," Kalmar said under his breath.

"What?"

"Snook, this is my third Gathering. Berkana has never talked like this before, nor did she use this chant at either of the last two Gatherings."

Before Snook could respond, Berkana stopped chanting. "Blessed be the Mark of the Covenant." She exposed the purple marking on the inside of her left arm and indicated for everyone to rise. "And as it has always been—"

"Let it always be," the audience responded in unison. Berkana's final words ended the meeting. Kalmar, Snook, and Nutan made their way out of the chamber and to the promenade.

"Kalmar!" The group turned to see an attractive female approaching.

"Arasima," Kalmar said, stepping forward to meet her. He grabbed her hands and smiled.

"Who is *that?*" Nutan asked Snook, her eyebrows narrowing.

"She is a friend of your brother's," Snook said, looking at the two of them together. Kalmar had not spoken of Arasima that day and Snook had refrained from asking about her.

Nutan did not hesitate and walked up to Arasima. "Hello, I am Nutan, Kalmar's sister."

Arasima, her eyebrows almost touching, turned to face Nutan. "Kalmar's sister? . . . Oh, you must be a Third Childs," a somewhat cool Arasima replied. "Kalmar did not tell me he had *two* sisters."

"Well, that is all right," Nutan shot back, "he did not tell me about you either."

Kalmar's discomfort was obvious. He gave Snook a pleading look.

"Nutan, I am going for a stroll down the promenade to look at the Chronicles; would you like to come with me?" Snook knew Kalmar's fiery younger sister was infatuated with him. Kalmar had told him it was common for romance to develop at a Gathering. He felt Nutan would welcome an advance from him, but that feeling made him uncomfortable. He had done nothing to encourage this bewitching young woman, yet he saw no other way to remove Nutan from Kalmar and Arasima than by playing with Nutan's emotions. Another, more dubious reason lurked in the background; Snook wanted to distance himself from Arasima before anyone heard the thunder from his pounding heart. Kalmar's look for help had given him the excuse to use Nutan as an instrument to that end.

Nutan's dark eyes flashed up at Snook. "I will go with you," she replied. Her precocious look told him she knew what was happening, but played along because she was more interested in being with him than sparring with the self-assured intruder. Arasima was many things: a tear in his heart, the most sensual woman he had ever met, the future Pairing Partner of his new friend, but the one thing she was not was a match for Nutan's feisty intellect. Nutan had one of the nimblest minds he had ever met—witty, yet intrepid. Nutan's intelligence, in tandem with her looks, made Kalmar's younger sister quite provocative in her own right.

As Nutan and Snook walked away from Kalmar and Arasima, Snook looked back over his shoulder. Arasima was watching them go with a victorious grin covering her face. Nutan noticed Snook looking back; she also turned and caught a glimpse of Arasima's smirk.

"What does my brother see in that?"

"I don't know . . . I guess it's because she's beautiful."

"Beautiful, just because she has long hair, a turned-up nose, and large breasts you think she is beautiful . . . wait, she has you under her spell *too*."

"*Me!* I just said she was beautiful . . . I am not under any spell—"

"Men are as dumb as a pile of rocks," she said, a scowl distorting her perky face. She walked ahead and did not speak to Snook for a long time. They strolled along the rock face of Alar reading the inscriptions, jumping from one time period to another. Snook was careful not to get in Nutan's way. It was impossible to read all the Chronicles; they were so vast it would have taken weeks to traverse the five Progressions of drawings plus the one of script. After a few hours, Nutan bumped against Snook and slipped her hand into his.

"Snook."

"Yes, Nutan?"

"Would you walk me to the Celebration of Life tonight?"

Nutan's request caught Snook by surprise. For a moment, he did not know how to respond; his eyes rounded, his mouth felt dry. "I would be honored," he answered, barely above a whisper.

She tightened her grip. Gone was the vixen he had seen earlier. Nutan was even more mature than he had first thought. In a few cycles of the seasons, thought Snook, she might be Arasima's match in more ways than just wit; these women learn our weaknesses much too quickly. He smiled as they walked hand in hand.

Unexpectedly, a tang of sadness dampened his euphoria; his mother had been the last female to hold his hand. The painful memory of his childhood drove a hot poker behind his eyes. He almost released Nutan's hand, but found in the firmness of her grip his only sense of constancy.

". . . and we feel there are powerful forces against you, forces that, for some reason, want you to fail." The women in the room, their faces lined by the intensity of the moment, stared in silence at the drak as it spoke. Two draks had appeared at the chamber door saying they needed to speak with the group. One drak, noticeably smaller than the other, had thus far done all the talking, which it did in a stilted, yet clear voice. It was late afternoon, only a few hours before the Celebration of Life ceremony, and all the Medoras were gathered round the triangular table in the Council Chambers.

"What forces and why are they against us? Can you not tell us of what is to happen?" Berkana pleaded.

"Draks are not players in the fate of your race; we are only surrogates. We do not know what fate awaits you." The giant lizard shifted its massive feet. "We've talked among ourselves and come to this conclusion . . . we do not understand why the forces might be against you or why they were against our ancestors, but as I have said, we are only messengers."

Berkana scanned the room full of troubled faces and then turned to the reptilian intruders. "We do not understand what you are trying to tell us. Surely Shetow wants Her people to be Judged worthy."

"We can only—" the smaller drak stopped when the larger drak stepped forward and touched it on the shoulder.

"We have said more than we should." The larger drak's granular voice was much harder to understand. "We will return after you have chosen those who will represent you at the Judging and speak with you again." Both draks turned to leave the room.

"When do we need to have our choices made?" Berkana said in a loud firm voice to the backs of the retreating reptiles.

The draks stopped and turned to face them. The smallest said, "Soon. We haven't been informed when to collect them, but we know it'll be very soon." They again turned to leave.

"How many should we choose?"

The draks stopped a second time and hesitated. "You can choose however many you like."

There was silence, the draks waiting to see if there were more questions and the Medoras not knowing what to ask. "How many would you choose?" piped a voice from the end of the right side of the table, a seat reserved for the youngest member of the council. The other members nodded their approval of their newest member's question. The draks stood perfectly still, the flickering of their eyelids the only movement.

"You can choose too many, but you need to choose enough to have a balance." The draks turned and left the room. Once again, the room was silent.

"We must increase our efforts. We will assemble again after the Celebration of Life ceremony," Berkana said.

Sitting in the anteroom, Cabyl heard most of what the Medoras said. Usually the thick wooden anteroom door would have sealed the chamber from uninvited ears, but inadvertently, Cabyl failed to pull the heavy door completely shut. The draks used the outside entrance to the Council Chamber; the change in the chamber's air pressure caused by the door closing behind them when they entered had forced open the unsecured door to the anteroom where Cabyl waited. She was horrified to see the door open a hand's width as she sat on a nutwood bench located just inside the doorway. Cabyl considered shutting the door, but decided against it, fearing the noise would bring notice of her failure to shut it correctly the first time. The words of the draks and Medoras numbed her; what were they talking about—judging . . . what judging? She thought serving Berkana would give her a sanctuary away from the difficulties of life; now she was more troubled than ever before. She was reconciled to spending the rest of her life alone, but she had never felt this kind of loneliness. A glint of moisture trickled down her pale face. Berkana must not know she had overheard what had been said in the chamber. If Berkana wanted her to know, she would tell her.

She felt trapped, a feeling she had faced twice in her life. Thoughts of her father sneaking into her bedroom when she was a young girl made her body rigid. The feel of his cold hands was as real as if it were happening at that moment. One hand tightly covered her mouth as the other first cupped her immature breast before snaking down her quivering stomach. The harder she squirmed, the tighter his grip. Once again, the thoughts of death beckoned her. Her face as still as stone, Cabyl sat in the small room staring at the wall until Berkana summoned her.

s it not the most amazing thing you've ever seen? I mean how the drak carved out the mountain like that," Nutan said as she and Snook walked from their encampment along the path to the Celebration of Life ceremony. The two had not talked about nor seen Kalmar since Nutan snapped at Snook hours earlier. He was thankful Nutan had not pressed her onslaught against Arasima. He had learned in the last few hours that Nutan's fervor could be as overwhelming as Arasima's allure.

The night was cloudless and the evening breeze moving down the mountain face was beginning to be noticeable. The mounting sound of the wind stirring across the boodo grass reminded Snook of walking along the ocean shore. The heady aroma of cut hay filled the air. Salune and Eeo had set, leaving Quiron as the largest celestial body in the twilight sky. Quiron's dominance was to be short-lived, however, as the larger Boboi could be seen peeking over the horizon.

When Nutan was not so mischievous, she could be quite delightful. Snook did not think she was trying to be so beguiling; rather, she was just being herself. "Nu," Snook said, using Kalmar's nickname for his sister, "the Celebration of Life ceremony doesn't make much sense to me."

It seemed peculiar to Snook that Nutan never questioned his ignorance about so many things. Kalmar told him it was either because Nutan thought Snook was dumb or she found him handsome. On second thought, Kalmar said, he cast his vote with Nutan thinking Snook was handsome and just overlooking the fact that he was also dumb. Kalmar had also joked that Nutan loved to hear herself talk. For whatever reason, Nutan seemed flattered that he sought her opinion on so many things. There was a sad gladness in his heart; Nutan was the first female since the death of his mother to whom he felt he could talk.

"Before the Tell and the Covenant," Nutan said, her head erect, her voice serious, "men and women lived an aimless existence. The Chants of the Sequa reveals little of the time before Geerna's Covenant with Shetow, but it is clear Geerna had experienced many of the hardships the Covenant lifted from the People. We know Geerna realized how futile the People's lives were before the Will of Shetow guided them. The Tell speaks of very cold winters; the People had to continually look for food and illness took the lives of most of them before they were thirty cycles of the seasons old. Once Geerna made her Covenant with Shetow, the lives of the People changed forever—"

"And the celebration commemorates Shetow's Covenant with Geerna."

"No," she said, shaking her head. "The Celebration of Life

ceremony is a remnant of our past that predates the Covenant. The Covenant with Shetow does not speak of this ceremony; it is the only ritual, besides the rites of passage ceremonies and Life Fires, that comes to us by the wish of Geerna and not, like all the others, by the Will of Shetow. The Celebration of Life, our most festive ceremony, celebrates our surviving another winter. The Tell tells us, as I said before, that winters before the Covenant were much harsher than they are today; many people would die from the bitter cold. To survive the winter and see the spring was cause for great jubilation—literally, the ceremony is to celebrate life."

The two continued walking towards the promenade. Even from a distance, the glare from the three gigantic Life Fires held back the night and dimmed the splendor of the star-filled sky. As they drew nearer to the celebration area, Snook could see the crowd churning, like schooling fish, in anticipation of the start of the ceremony. They had just arrived when Berkana, with the aid of Cabyl and two of the youngest Medoras, climbed a flight of stairs leading to the pinnacle of a rock platform. The platform was a gigantic boulder reshaped by stonemasons; steps cut into the side of the stone formed a spiral stairway encircling it twice before it reached the top. The boulder was so massive it was hard for Snook to imagine the draks, even with their incomprehensible power, having positioned such a large object on the promenade precisely in line with the middle entrance to the Grand Chamber.

The rock hearths for the Life Fires stood along an arc at equal intervals on the front side of the platform away from the Grand Chamber's entrances. From her position atop the boulder, Berkana commanded a full view of all those who had gathered below her.

"Tonight we celebrate the memory of Geerna, the first Medora Roo. We also celebrate the memory of Verna, the Medora of the Gray Wolf Tribe. As you know, Verna was killed on her way to the Gathering. The matching tusks of the mammoth she was trying to protect now rest on the wheelon you passed on the promenade. The tusks will be cut into hundreds of thumb-sized sections, then carved into small Earth Mother statuettes like the one Geerna always kept with her."

"The carving of ivory Earth Mother statuettes has not been done for thousands of cycles of the seasons," Nutan whispered to Snook. "Not since the Second Progression when the Medoras stopped the hunters from killing the mammoths."

"The long-tusked mammoths have always held a special place in Shetow's World," the Medora Roo said. "The long tusks' matriarch, through the gift of her ivory for the carvings, will honor Shetow— the Earth Mother—in this special way. The Medora Council has concluded that Verna's unusual death, and the visions she had, are signs from Shetow. We, as yet, do not understand the meaning of the signs, but we do believe they are only a few of the many signs Shetow is now giving us." An uneasy rumbling rippled through the crowd. Berkana lifted her hand to quiet them. "To remember Verna and her vision, and the mammoths and their special place in the Tell, the Medora Council has changed the name of the Gray Wolf Tribe to the Long Tusk Tribe, the tribe of the mammoths." Berkana paused and motioned for Cabyl to hand her a water flask.

Berkana's announcement surprised Dera and Izzy, who were standing near the back of the crowd. Dera nodded. The Council had honored her mentor. The Medoras had not informed Dera of their intentions when she met with the Council earlier that day. She could tell the Medoras thought the events surrounding Verna's death extraordinary, but they had not given her any reason to expect the changing of her tribe's name.

"Has this ever been done before?"

"No, little brother," she said. A smile brightened her face. "I am sure the Tell has no record of a tribe having its name changed."

N|ow, *let us dance,*" Berkana said, in a voice amplified by some un-
known means. A cheer rose from the throng of people as the
sound of beating drums boomed from the edge of the crowd.

The drums were of two sizes, all constructed in a similar manner.
The sides were wooden staves held together by metal hoops with each
end of the drums covered by tightly stretched prairie-buck skin. The
four larger drums, with drumhead diameters equal to wheelon wheels,
lay on their sides. Their eight drummers—a man on one end and a
woman on the other—stood next to the stretched hide and beat out
the deeper tones; the balance of the sexes denoted the Equilibrium.
The other thirty drums were only a tenth the size of the larger ones
and were played by only one drummer each; fifteen of the drummers
were females and a like number male. The smaller drums rested on
cradles with curved runners fashioned from strips of nutwood lashed
to the sides of the drums with rawhide lacing. This sturdy framework
permitted the drummers to wrap their legs around their drums and
lock their feet in leather stirrups attached to the drums' sides. Once
mounted, the drums' center of gravity shifted, causing the symbiotic
partnership to teeter to one side like a top-heavy cork. From this rocking platform, the drummers, straddling their instruments, pounded out
a faster, less reverberating beat than the larger drums.

All thirty-eight drummers struck their drumheads with the
tips of their curved drumsticks in perfect cadence. The concussion
of the pounding drums was the most gripping sound Snook had
ever heard; his whole body could feel the reverberation of each
collision between the drumsticks and drumheads. Those in the
crowd had experienced the lure of the rhythmical beat of the
drums many times—for Snook, it was his first time.

T|he thought of Snook made Nutan feel alive. She glanced at him
when he looked away. How could his tribe not have revered this

special person, even if he was wrapped in his blanket of white skin? If Snook were not so serious, she thought, she would wonder if he was taking them for fools. The floppy straw hat, which she found humorous the first time she met him, now, strangely, gave him an air of cleverness. Her jaw tightened. No matter what his own tribe thought about him, she found him alluring.

Snook had never danced, and had not planned on dancing now, but he found the unconscious swaying of his body matching the tempo of the drums. Nutan grabbed his hands and pulled him into the pulsating mass. The tempestuous young female started to move her limber body in ways Snook thought impossible; she snaked her narrow hips and budding bosom in a gradual gyration accentuating her feminine attributes. At first, Snook thought Nutan's dance was for him, but her eyes never met his. He soon began to think her attention was not focused on him, and the provocative display merely a release of excess energy. He felt himself yielding to the intoxication of the hypnotic sound; he stopped worrying about how foolish he might look and lost himself in the frenzy of the moment.

The dancers were between the climbing flames of the Life Fires and the ageless mountain. The light from the fires cast exaggerated shadows of the rejoicing people against the mountain face. Accenting the jumble of moving shapes was the amplified beating of the drums as their echo rebounded from the towering rock surface. The echoing sound of the drums made the shadows seem alive. As Snook moved with the beat of the drums and the flow of the crowd, he could not help but stare at the fluid movement of Nutan's sinuous body.

The nonstop dancing went long into the night. Even though the breeze rolling off the mountain was now brisk and steady, Snook was soaked with sweat. Many of the men started pulling off their tunics, wrapping the sleeves around their waist and tying the ends together. As sweat poured down his face, in one motion Snook pulled his tunic over his head and tied it as the other men had. For the first time since they started dancing, he noticed Nutan's gaze was fixed on him. She danced closer, eyeing the lines of his lanky body. She reached down, grabbed the hem of her chemise, and gradually pulled it over her head as she moved to the beat of the drums. Under her chemise, she was wearing a halter that matched her short skirt. Snook now noticed that many of the girls were taking off their chemises revealing similar clothing; he realized the girls came to the celebration knowing they would shed part of their clothing as they grew hot from the prolonged physical exertion.

The fine layer of sweat covering Nutan's body shined in the flickering light of the Life Fires. Snook fixated on the movement of her petite but perfectly formed and partially exposed bosom. Sweat trickled down her neck and chest until it was diverted by the swell of her breasts, where it glistened as it collected between them. Snook's stare seemed to intensify her efforts to feed his desires. After a time, Nutan stopped and motioned for him to lean over so she could whisper in her ear.

"I really need a drink of water. Can we go and try to find some?"

Snook nodded and they made their way to the edge of the dance area next to the small drums. There, Snook asked a woman walking by if she knew where they could find something to drink. The woman pointed to a place behind Berkana's stone platform. As Snook and Nutan walked to the back of the platform, they could see a cluster of wheelons, each filled with a cistern-sized water urn. Men and women were quenching their thirst by filling terra-cotta mugs with water from spigots in the sides of the urns. Once satisfied, they would hand the mugs to the next person waiting in line. Snook and Nutan waited their turn; when they were handed two of the mugs, they quickly filled them, raised the mugs, and guzzled their contents so fast water sloshed down the sides of their faces. Once emptied, they refilled the mugs; Snook started to drink again, but Nutan raised her mug and poured the water over her head and sweaty body. The wet fabric of her clothes revealed even more of her womanly properties. He gaped at her unexpected and hedonistic exhibition. Yes, he had really underestimated this young woman. They handed their empty mugs to those next in line.

"That felt wonderful," Nutan laughed as she rung out her hair. "Can we wait just a little bit to cool off?"

"Sure, I am a little hot, myself." The two strolled leisurely away from the crowd walking along the promenade near the cliff face. As they approached the middle entrance to the Grand Chamber, Nutan paused and took Snook's left hand in both of hers. Snook stopped and turned to face his companion. He had never felt so alive, he thought, as he looked down at the bright, effervescent young woman. There was a light dusting of salt on her naked arms and shoulders where the sweat had dried, but he still detected moisture in her stringy hair and the valley between her scantily covered breasts.

Her feminine intuition told her Snook was attracted to her by the way his eyes lingered on her when he thought she would not notice. Besides the Pairing Partners the females of her village brought home from the Gatherings, she had known all the males of her tribe her entire life. This man was different, exciting, and most intoxicating of all, infatuated by her.

Nutan reached up and softly ran the tip of her index finger over his bare chest. Without thinking, Snook bent over and gently kissed her neck. Her dried sweat tasted salty and sweet. After a moment, as he rose up, Nutan placed her left palm on the middle of his death-white chest, reached behind his neck with her right hand, and pulled his head and lips down to hers. The kiss was long and full of passion. Snook did not want the feeling to end and, he could tell, neither did she. In time, the kiss did end, and as Snook lifted his head, Nutan laid hers on his chest. They did not speak; it was not a time for words.

Snook felt the presence of someone else. He turned to look; it was Cabyl. She stood next to the mountain face watching them. He stared back at her forgetting, for a moment, that Nutan's head was resting on his chest. He could not tell how long Cabyl had been standing there, but he was sure it had been a few minutes.

Cabyl seemed confused. She finally took a step forward. "Berkana sent me to find you," she stammered. "She asked that you come see her when the Celebration of Life ceremony is over." She hesitated, dropped her gaze, turned and darted off.

Snook had not said a word. Nutan though, had lifted her head off his chest at the sound of Cabyl's voice and glared at Snook while he had his eyes locked on Cabyl's retreat. Nutan put both her palms on Snook's chest and pushed him away with all the strength she could muster.

"You are no better than my brother; an attractive woman looks at you and you go into a trance. Snook, I really thought you were different from all the other men I know . . . but . . . but you are not," she said, shaking with anger. She continued to glare at him for a few moments and then she stomped her foot, turned, and stormed off. Snook had not moved, still stunned by Cabyl's dejected look.

Snook was slow to adjust to the sudden change in his situation. How could things change so much, so fast? A few moments ago, he felt the best he had ever felt in his entire life; now, only moments later, he felt the worst. A sickening hollowness churned in his stomach. An emotional vise squeezed his chest; no matter how much air he sucked into his lungs, his body felt starved for oxygen. The pain robbed him of his breath and brought a pounding to his temples. Lightheaded, everything seemed surreal. His mentor had told him caring about a woman would open his heart to pain, and he did care about these two women. He knew he had not known them long or well enough to love either of them; for that he was glad. He did not think he could stand the greater pain that must come from hurting someone you loved. He had seen anger and disappointment in Nutan's eyes, while a mask of torment had covered Cabyl's face. He was upset Nutan was not beside him, touching him and kissing him, as she had earlier. It had been a new and wonderful experience for him. Beautiful and vivacious women had never paid him such attention. Just as he had adjusted to the idea there might have been a sexual future with Nutan, it soared out of reach.

Then there was Cabyl; the first time he had ever seen her, he embarrassed her by the way he had stared at her. Later, Kalmar convinced him that, although embarrassed by his stare, she could tell his looks were real and was honored by his homage. He knew any honor she had felt was now discarded, replaced by the belief that he was just another man out to get what he wanted. The pain intensified; if Cabyl had not appeared, he would have been—just another man getting what he wanted. He shut his eyes and shook his head; he was just as base as any other man. He had fallen in the eyes of the two women about whom he cared the most. He had fallen even further in his own prideful self-esteem.

Snook relived the night's events as he walked in the twilight along the promenade, waiting for the Celebration of Life to end so he could go talk to Berkana. He wrapped his arms across his chest and leaned over. He had freely chosen the life of a Seeker, pledging to forgo relationships with females until later in life, after his Illumination. Females had always made him uncomfortable; now he wondered if he had used his preoccupation with trying to understanding the mysteries of the world and his quest for truth as a shield against emotional attachments. Snook winced at the memory of his father's devastation when Snook's mother deserted them when Snook was still a young child. His father blamed his mate's abandonment on the vast difference in their ages. Snook unconsciously shook his head; differences in age could not have been the only problem between his parents—partners in the land of the Twenty-Four Tribes left their mates even when they were the same age. What made some partners stay together and others separate?

He again thought of his mother and the painful whispers that she had jumped from the cliff. Two seasons after she left him and his father, she lay dead at the bottom of the cliff. He pressed his eyes shut, trying to stave off the memories. Were Nutan and Cabyl's feelings similar to the ones he and his father felt after his mother's rejection? How could he have ever let things get so out of control?

He closed his eyes, ravaged by confusion. "You let yourself become too close to these women; you are ill-prepared to deal with matters of the heart," he whispered.

SEVENTEEN

Kalmar and Arasima arrived at the celebration early and were some of the first to start dancing. They had agreed to sneak away early but thought it best to make an appearance. The evening was only beginning when Kalmar excused himself and told Arasima he would be right back. While Arasima was waiting for Kalmar, she recognized someone at the edge of the crowd.

"Dera, Dera."

Dera and Izzy stopped and looked around, trying to find who was calling Dera's name. It was almost impossible for them to determine the origin of the shouts because of the pounding drumbeats.

"Dera, Dera, over here."

Dera finally saw Arasima waving her arms over her head and she motioned for Izzy to follow her as she walked over to speak to the young woman.

"Dera, I thought that was you," Arasima said as she grabbed and hugged Dera.

"Arasima . . . it is good to see you," Dera said, as loud as she could, to be heard over the booming drums.

zzy could not tell if his sister was uneasy or just did not know what to say to the breathtaking woman.

"And who's this handsome young man?" Arasima asked, as she noticed Izzy.

"My brother Izzy."

"What a cute name," Arasima said, giving Izzy her brightest smile.

Izzy studied the woman closely; she was stunning, as close to feminine perfection as he had ever seen. He knew he was staring, but he could not help himself. He watched the females talk for a few moments before Arasima gave Dera another hug. Dera then turned and walked towards him. As she turned, Arasima gave Izzy a sultry look; then she parted her lips before finishing the torrid smile with a slight pout. The earthy look in her eyes sent a shiver through his body. No woman had ever read his mind so easily. As Dera turned and left Arasima, a young man with a scar across his face walked up to fill her spot. As Dera approached, Izzy turned and got in step with his sister and they walked away from the mass of dancing bodies.

"Okay, what was that all about?" Izzy asked, as the sound of the drums faded behind them.

"That's Arasima, one of the other contestants in the Byrrac with me," Dera said, not volunteering anything else.

"And?"

"*And what?*" Dera stopped walking and turned to look at her brother with a deadpan expression.

"Why are you so sensitive? What's going on between you two?" he said. Dera stood there slowly shaking her head. Izzy threw his hands up. "It's not important. It's just—"

"*Just what?*"

"I have never seen you react to someone like that before. It doesn't suit you."

zzy's words, like a slap across her face, made her draw back. After a few moments, the hard lines around her mouth and eyes softened. "I'm sorry Izzy, it's just . . . that woman just makes me fly apart," she said, shaking her head again. He did not respond, but puzzlement clouded his face.

"Arasima plays by her own rules." Dera started to pace back and forth. "She has never been good enough to win the pregames—third or fourth at best—but the way she acts . . . she would smile at you right before she pushed you off a cliff. She doesn't care how she wins, but only that she wins. I don't understand how someone can be like that."

"The Gray Beards speak of such people. Dera, you compete in the Byrrac because it is a requirement that the young compete; the Borrac and the Byrrac are part of Geerna's Covenant with Shetow. We compete for the honor of Shetow and for the improvement of the Traits. Your opponent, I feel, competes for her own glory, her own gain, not the People's."

"I think you are right about Arasima. She has always told the other women in our pre-Byrrac group that she was going to win."

"But she can't beat you . . . can she?"

"No, I don't think so; however, the rumor is that is not where she is planning on prevailing."

"What do you mean?"

"She boasts, I'm told, that she will do the best at the Matage—"

"But, how—"

"By having the male she wants reject any woman who might choose him before it is her time to choose."

"Oh . . . I see . . . but . . . but how would she be able to do that? I mean, how can she be so sure the man she wants as a Pairing

Partner will reject a higher-ranked female and wait for her to choose him?"

"Brother, you are smarter than that. How does any female get something from a man if she is willing to use any means? What would make you wait?"

Izzy looked back in the direction they had left Arasima. "Well, if any woman could make a man reject a woman ranked higher in the Byrrac, it would be Arasima." He turned back to see Dera eyeing him, a broad grin on her face. "I don't mean that . . . it wouldn't work on me, but you should have seen how she looked at me . . . someone in whom she has no interest . . . she put a . . . if she wanted to use all her charms on a man and he thought they were reserved for him alone . . . well, it would take . . ." He looked down. "Most men would fall into her trap." Izzy looked at his sister, who was nodding her head, the grin still on her face. Izzy regained his composure. "Sister, no matter what you think, you are as beautiful as any woman here, but you *do not* or *will not* recognize it. I may be a young man, but I *am* a man. It is more than just a woman's looks that grabs a man's loins . . . and his heart; it is also how she uses her looks . . . how she uses her femininity on him."

"That's what mother says."

"Well, for once, *she's right*."

Dera looked in the direction they had left Arasima. "Izzy, there's something else." He looked at his sister with a blank face. "I wonder if this thing that Arasima is using—I don't mean her overt sexual appeal, but her overwhelming drive to prevail—is something in itself. Maybe there is a Trait for manipulation, for wanting to win at any cost. A Trait that drives you to get what you want no matter what means you have to use. If Shetow is looking for that, Arasima is the answer." Dera rubbed her face. "I have a new respect for

Arasima; she may be the ultimate Concentration of that Trait the People have ever produced, a Trait that will not let her give up."

"You may be right." He became animated. "But her allure only affects men."

"That is because the Trait can only pass to her children with the help of her male Pairing Partner. I will bet the Trait isn't gender selective and both her female and male children will prossess it."

"Did you see who joined her as we were leaving?" Izzy said.

Dera shook her head.

"I believe it was the lone hunter who killed the cave lion, the one everyone's talking about. I could see the scars on his face that the cave lion gave him right before the great cat collapsed at his feet."

"Kalmar," Dera said softly. "He won the two pre-Borracs the same cycles of the seasons I won the pre-Byrracs. He must be the one she has her sights on . . . that makes sense; I remember seeing them together at last year's Gathering."

"Ha," Izzy chuckled. "She will leave scars on him a lot worse than the cave lion did." He shook his head. "Sister, I think you can cross that one off your list. If she has her claws in him, he will reject you and any other female who tries to choose him."

She turned and watched Arasima and Kalmar until the mass of squirming bodies engulfed them. "Little brother, I believe you are right," she mumbled as she brushed an auburn lock away from her eyes.

Kalmar walked up to Arasima as Dera and Izzy walked off. "Who's that?"

"One of my competitors," Arasima said, with no expression.

"She looks familiar."

"That's Dera, the woman who won the pre-Byrrac the two times you won the pre-Borrac." She scanned his face for a reaction.

"Dera . . . I remember her; she's the one who has that birth-mark on her face. . . ."

Arasima nodded.

"Too bad." He winced. "She would be attractive if she didn't have it." His face rounded before his eyes narrowed and then he reached up and felt the deep furrows across his cheek.

"Yes, it's too bad about her face," Arasima said, a gleam in her eye, a half smile on her lips. She noticed Kalmar touching his face. "Kalmar, dear . . . your scars don't detract from your looks—they add to it, they give you distinction. Everyone at the Gathering knows how you killed the cave lion. Your scars, they say, are marks of courage. You're the most talked about person at the Gathering."

His face grew solemn as he looked away.

With Berkana's words still raging in his mind, Snook's head reeled as he walked back along the path to the tribe's compound. As he left Berkana, the other Medoras started gathering in the Council Chamber. Cabyl had kept her distance and he had not gotten a clear look at her; actually, he had hoped he would be spared the humiliation of having to face her. As he stepped out of the chamber door, he looked back and saw all twenty-three Medoras join hands and start to chant. When he reached the cabin, he found it empty; Kalmar was still with Arasima. He climbed into his bed, pulled the covers over his head, squeezed his eyes shut, and tried to will himself to sleep. However, slumber escaped him as the events of the last few hours kept rolling over in his mind, forcing him to relive every painful moment. Other than the one after his mother's death, this had been the worst night of his life. Images of Nutan's agitation and disappointment flashed in his brain; he realized that image and the rejection he had seen in Cabyl's delicate face would not soon leave him.

———

Kalmar and Arasima lay in the small woods at the end of the promenade, beyond the beginning of the Chronicles. The trees formed a border between the sea of boodo grass and the highlands that started at the far end of the cliff face away from the Grand Chambers. The draks lived, people said, on the other side of the highlands, a place of mystery, and a place where humans did not go.

Arasima slept with her head resting on Kalmar's bare chest, their intertwined bodies partially covered with their hastily shed garments. Kalmar's eyelids flickered as he dreamed about being in the boat on the tranquil lake; no matter how hard he tried, he still couldn't make out what was to his left. It stayed just out of his view. The urgency to reach the island ahead was the strongest it had ever been.

EIGHTEEN

The second day of the Gathering was when all the children born during the year before the last Gathering underwent the Koo Toc Biren ceremony. Snook, Kalmar, and Nutan joined Nima and Raff as they took their daughter, Targo, to the ceremony. The five of them walked along the path from the tribe's compound to the Grand Chamber while Nima and Raff took turns carrying the fretting child. The second day was, to many, the most important day of a Gathering; it was the day when the toddlers took their places in the ranks of the People, the day they would fulfill part of Geerna's—and the People's—Covenant with Shetow, the day they would be Marked by Shetow.

The morning air smelled fresh and invigorating; a trace of perfumed scent coming off the miniature yellow blooms of the boodo grass mingled with the gentle breeze just starting to flow from the flat grasslands towards the mountain. The sky was cloudless and the two larger moons were well above the horizon, looking like whitish gray saucers sitting on a light-blue tablecloth. As the day progressed, the bright rays of the rising Salune would eventually overwhelm the reflected light from the moons, making them gradually disappear. The feeble illumination of Eeo, Salune's constant companion, narrowly escaped a similar fate.

Kalmar and Snook had not talked much when they had gotten up that morning; Snook was emotionally drained from the events of the night before, and Kalmar was listless from his nocturnal exploits with Arasima. Arasima had allowed him little rest, and what sleep he had had was never sound as his recurring dream about the boat on the tranquil lake invaded his mind every time he drifted into slumber.

Nutan had not spoken to Snook since she stomped off the night before. She was having an ongoing mêlée in her mind. Her night, like Snook's, had been uneasy; she had gone over the events of the previous night and wondered if she had been too hasty in how she reacted to Snook staring at that woman. Maybe he'd been startled, or just embarrassed. *He is a man, and a man will always look at a beautiful woman.* Snook was bright, funny, and, until she stormed off, in her arms. She had set out to see if her feminine charm would have any effect on Snook. It had. The more she thought about her actions, the more she became convinced she had made a mistake; she should have stayed. She convinced herself he was hers until she criticized him for staring at Berkana's helper. *Dumb, dumb, dumb*, she thought to herself. She had always been rambunctious; in this case, the consequences of her tempestuous behavior left her mad at herself and a little embarrassed. She had been more than enough of a woman to get Snook's attention; now she realized, she needed to work on the finer art of dealing with a man who had succumbed to her charms. She was at a loss as to how to undo the damage she had done to her relationship with Snook. To hide her feelings of discomfort, she avoided having direct eye contact with Snook and stayed near her sister, Raff, and the baby.

The pathways were full of Pairing Partners and their one-year-olds as they walked to the ceremony. Unlike the dusty secondary paths, the primary path to the Grand Chamber was paved with a mixture of sand and river rocks; the small stones crunched in the sand as the group walked on them. When they approached the promenade, it was crowded with mothers and fathers walking around with their young children in their arms.

"What are they doing?" Nutan asked.

"The walking soothes the toddlers," Nima said. "The parents didn't want them to start crying so they walk with them as long as they can. . . . they will wait until the last minute to enter the chamber and find their seats. Nutan, take a good look; in four cycles of the seasons you will be walking around the promenade with your First Childs in your arms; watch and learn as much as you can."

"Nima, four cycles of the seasons . . . that's forever. I have a lot of other things I need to learn before then."

Nima and Raff laughed and then looked at each other with knowing eyes and smiled. Nima looked back at her younger sister. "Four cycles of the seasons will go by as fast as Mystery crosses the twilight-of-night sky. It is never too soon to learn about things you know you'll have to deal with someday."

The group reached the promenade in front of the Grand Chamber.

"Little Targo is fast asleep," Nima said. "But I think I'll walk her a little longer. Nutan—you, Kalmar, and Snook go on ahead into the chamber and save us some seats. Raff and I will bring Targo inside in a little bit."

Nutan, Kalmar, and Snook followed Nima's instructions and went to find seats in the Cave Lion Tribe section of the chamber. Only a few words were spoken between the three of them until they spotted five empty seats.

"You two sit in the first couple of seats and I will sit in the last seat so we can save the two seats between us for Nima and Raff," Kalmar said as he entered the row of seats before Nutan and Snook could react. As stated, he skipped the first four seats before settling in the fifth seat. Nutan and Snook were startled at Kalmar's sudden move; both had assumed Kalmar would sit between them. They stood motionless for a moment, and then Snook stepped back and indicated for Nutan to go in.

"Beauty first," Snook said without thinking. With his words, Nutan looked up into his eyes as she moved to the second seat. The look on Nutan's face was one that he had not seen in the few months he had known her. Looking down at Nutan, Snook felt like he was looking into the face of a child; her eyes were wide and full of innocence. His spontaneous words had eased the tension between them; Nutan was, once again, the younger sister of his close friend, and not the fiery temptress of the previous night. For the second time, Snook did something on impulse. As he lowered himself into his seat, he leaned over and gently kissed Nutan on the forehead. Nutan jerked her head around and looked at him a second time; after a moment, she lowered her eyes. Snook heard Nutan sniffle and felt the weight of her head as she nestled against his shoulder. He was not sure of what had happened, and, for sure, did not understand why, but the tightness in his chest released a bit of its grip.

Three couples carrying their toddlers interrupted Snook's thoughts as they slid in to fill some of the seats on the other side of Kalmar. Right after that, Nima and Raff came to claim their seats. The soft cooing of the mothers and fathers comforting their children was the only sound in the chamber.

Nutan's head rested on Snook's shoulder. Her earlier anguish had eased; once again, she was happy. When she'd first met Snook she realized he was different; his questions were those of a five-year-old, yet his mind was as sharp as a Medora's. She had asked Kalmar about his unusual friend and her brother answered, in a hushed voice, " 'Snook is a servant of Shetow and shouldn't be questioned.' " Taken aback by what Kalmar had told her, she retreated until she saw the grin on her brother's face. It was then, after Kalmar told her of what he believed about Snook being rejected by his own tribe, that her heart went out to the vulnerable young albino.

She liked Snook from the moment she first met him; he was new and different, yet he was like Elom's smallest moon—a mystery. It became a game for Nutan, an exciting game she did not want to end. She wondered if there was more to Snook's story than implied by her brother's simplistic analysis. If his own tribe had shunned Snook, why was he so at ease around the members of her tribe? Why had he not avoided members of the Black Raven Tribe? Not pressing Snook about his peculiar behavior, she believed, was the best way to keep Snook a mystery; to understand Snook's actions would be to uncover the answer to the mystery—and end the game.

Her eyes widened. *He does not care what they think about him,* she thought, *they rejected him, and now he has wiped them from his mind.* She pursed her lips as she slowly nodded her head.

Berkana and Cabyl entered from the hallway door that led to the Medora's Chamber. At the same time, a second door opened on the other side of the dais and two draks walked out draped in wide mustard yellow sashes. The sight of the draks' habiliments caught Snook off guard; he had never seen draks garbed in anything other than the scant leather straps and belts they always wore. They were identical, except one drak was a good head taller than the other.

For the first time, Snook noticed a large shiny metal container near the front edge of the dais. The object was unlike anything he had ever seen; it was the size of a small covered boat. Its curved sides were polished and reflected light like mirrors. Its metallic construction stood in sharp contrast to the wood, stone, and ceramic composition of most of the People's possessions.

"What's that?" he whispered to Nutan. She raised her head to look.

"It must be the Ewer-Biren."

Snook arched an eyebrow and waited for her to give him more information.

"The Ewer-Biren, the Vessel of Shetow . . . it is the means by which Shetow places the Mark of the Covenant on the children."

"How does it work?"

"Snook, how would I know? How would anybody know? All I know is the draks place the toddlers in the Ewer-Biren, the top is closed, and Shetow puts the Mark of the Covenant on the child. It is a vessel to hold the toddlers while Shetow connects with the child's inner-self. The Ewer-Biren also protects us from seeing Shetow. No one, but Geerna, has ever seen Shetow, and when Geerna saw Her . . . well she didn't really see Her; Geerna only saw Shetow's shadow, not Her physical body."

"Her shadow—"

"Shetow told Geerna not to look at Her, so Geerna averted her eyes and only saw Her shadow. It is where we get the expression the 'Shadow of Shetow.' "

Snook could not detect any hint of Nutan's earlier tension; she touched his arm and spoke to him just as she had before the incident the previous night. Snook was thankful for the reprieve from Nutan's scorn; he wondered if she would return to her previous pursuit of him. He hoped she would not—at the same time praying she would.

Berkana, Cabyl, and the two draks met at the Ewer-Biren, the two humans standing on one side and the two draks on the other. Berkana raised her left arm. The sleeve of her robe fell back down on her shoulder; the purple spot on the inside of her forearm plainly visible. "By the Mark of the Covenant." Everyone in the chamber, except the two draks, stood and raised their left arm and repeated the Medora Roo's call. After everyone lowered their arms, Berkana continued. "As prescribed by the Covenant between Geerna and Shetow, as now recorded in the Chronicles, as now written in the *Chants of the Sequa*, and as told in the Tell, the People come to the Gathering, as we have for the countless cycles of the seasons, for six Progressions, to present their children to Shetow for Her approval . . . and Her Mark—"

Berkana's words escaped Snook as he watched Cabyl moving around the dais. The tightness in his chest increased. He could not understand nor control the feelings this woman brought out in him; they were just like the ones Nutan made him have, yet completely different. The confusion he grappled with was intensifying. It was hopeless, he thought to himself.

The Medoras still sitting in front of the dais rose from their seats and moved to join the four already on the platform. As the Medoras took their places, Nima and Ruff, and the other Pairing Partners, stood up with their children and formed a line beginning at a small set of steps at the edge of the dais on the right side of the chamber. Snook noticed no one giving directions or signals.

He leaned over to whisper in Nutan's ear. "How do they know when and where to go?"

"They have all seen this ceremony at least three times before being participants," she whispered back. "Those at the front of the line are carrying their Second or maybe Third Childs . . . when they moved to form the line, the Pairing Partners with their First Childs knew to join them."

". . . by the Mark, the People show their faithfulness to the Covenant . . . it's also a sign of the People's love and commitment to Shetow," Berkana continued, again raising her left arm. The audience once again stood and repeated Berkana's call. When those in the audience retook their seats, the first set of Pairing Partners stepped upon the dais and walked over to Berkana. Berkana leaned over to let the female Partner say something to her. After a moment, the old Medora nodded, reached over, and took the toddler from its mother. Berkana cradled the small child in her arms as she looked down at it. She tickled the attentive youngster under its chin. Snook could not understand how the muted sounds made by the child and the soft words spoken by those on the dais could be heard so clearly even in the back of the chamber. *This must be another wonder provided by the draks*, Snook thought, as he looked and listened to the proceedings at the front of the chamber.

"The People present the Second Childs of Resa of the Prairie Buck Tribe and Ual born of the Wood Owl Tribe," Berkana said, turning her body perpendicular to the front edge of the platform. She tilted her cradled arms so the toddler could be seen by those in the audience. After slowly rotating her body to allow the child to be seen by everyone, she turned and handed the toddler to the smaller of the two draks. The grayish reptile was very careful as it carried the child to the back side of the Ewer-Biren where the second drak was standing. The humans on the platform stayed on the front perimeter of the dais as the larger drak placed a clawed hand on the side of the metallic container. There was a low hissing sound, like steam venting from a green log on a campfire. The top half of the glistening container slowly swung open. With the open part of the container away from them, it was impossible for Snook to see inside the enclosure. A pulsating purple glow emanated from inside the strange container, casting a lilac tint on the ceiling, the wall behind the container, and the top halves of the two draks. The drak carrying the child gently laid the strangely tranquil bundle inside the enclosure and then stepped back. The larger drak touched the side of the container a second time and the top half of the container, making the same hissing sound, lowered to its original position. As the top started to close, the Medoras and the members of the audience started to chant. Snook looked around the chamber; everyone was swaying as they chanted. He noticed there had been no reaction from the child's parents when Berkana surrendered the child to the giant lizard; thousands of cycles of the seasons of the same ritual must have removed any anxiety the couples had of the draks holding their young.

After a short time, the container opened on its own. As the top rose, the hissing sound and the purple light were once again present. With the top fully extended, the smaller drak walked over, picked up the child from inside the container, and then walked over and handed the child back to Berkana. The old Medora, holding the child close to her chest, turned to face the audience.

"The People rejoice! By the Mark of the Covenant, we have gained a new member, Eurl, Second Childs of Resa and Ual." Berkana turned towards the toddler's parents. "Do you, Resa and Ual, make a vow, before Shetow and all those who are gathered here today, to raise this child by the Truth as handed down to us by Geerna through the Sequa; will you love and nurture him; will you keep him from harm?"

"We will," the young couple answered.

"As the child is not old enough to answer for himself, I ask you, his parents to answer for him until the time he comes of age. Do you vow for this child that he will follow the Will of Shetow as revealed to us by the Sequa and honor Geerna's Covenant with Shetow?"

"We do."

Berkana turned from the child's parents to look towards the section of the audience where the members of the Prairie Buck Tribe were seated. "Do you, the members of the Prairie Buck Tribe, vow to raise this child by the Laws given to the People by Geerna through the Sequa and to teach him to honor and be faithful to the Covenant?"

The members of the Prairie Buck Tribe had stood when Berkana faced them and now answered Berkana's charge in unison. "We will."

"Will you watch over the child and his parents, protect them from harm, and supply them sustenance should they ever have that need?" Again, the members of the tribe answered in the affirmative. "And lastly, do you reaffirm the vows made for you by your parents at your own Koo Toc Biren, to follow the Will of Shetow as revealed to us by the Sequa and honor the Covenant?"

"We do."

Berkana, with Cabyl's aid, shuffled back to where the child's parents stood and handed the child back to his mother. "I relinquish this child back to the care of you, his parents, where he will live as a member of the Prairie Buck Tribe until his Matage." Cabyl handed Berkana the Ooroc, which the old woman raised, with shaking arms, over her head. "By the authority granted me by the Medora Council, and in the Name of Shetow, Giver of Life, Sovereign of all that was, all that is, and all that will be, I welcome Eurl as one of the People—one carrying the Mark of the Covenant—and remand him to the care of his parents and the members of the Prairie Buck Tribe until his Matage eighteen cycles of the seasons hence."

It took hours for all the children to take their turn in the Ewer-Biren. Towards the end of the ceremony, Nima and Raff, carrying baby Targo, climbed the steps to the dais. Snook watched Nutan and Kalmar strain to see every detail of what was happening to their sister, brother-in-law, and niece. Once Targo's Koo Toc Biren was over, Nima and Raff brought the baby back to the two seats next to Nutan. Kalmar had moved to sit next to his younger sister when the couple had gotten up, but he returned to his previous seat when they returned.

"Oh, let me hold her," Nutan said as she held out her arms to Nima. Nima smiled and handed Targo to her younger sister.

Nutan pushed up Targo's left sleeve, exposing a bright purple spot on the inside of the child's left forearm. "See, isn't it beautiful?"

"Can you touch it?"

"There is no pain to the baby."

Snook reached over and ran the tips of his fingers over the spot. "There is a slight swelling of the skin."

"It will be gone before we head back to our village; after that you will only be able to see it, not feel it—the same as ours."

Snook nodded and thought it best to change the subject. "I wonder why Targo didn't—or for that matter, why none of the babies cried when they were in the Ewer-Biren?"

"You know . . . I don't know, but I have been told that the children never cry when they are in or when they first come out of the Ewer-Biren. It is one of the wonders of the ceremony." They stayed, as did everyone else, until the end of the Koo Toc Biren.

Salune and Eeo hung low in the sky as they strolled back to the tribe's compound in the still of the late afternoon as the crickets in the boodo grass began their nightly serenade. The heavy scent of coming rain saturated the air. Nutan, at first, stayed close to Nima and the baby but in time dropped back to fall in step with Snook and Kalmar. Nutan would occasionally bump against Snook as they walked.

As they entered the compound, Nima stopped and turned to face Kalmar and Nutan. "Remember what Berkana said: it's important that you both get a good night's sleep. Tomorrow you will start the Borrac"—her eyes shifted to Nutan—"and you the pre-Byrrac. If you are like Raff and me, you will need clear and rested brains and your bodies will require the strength only a full night of sleep can bring. Two cycles of the seasons ago, we were so tired by our Matage that we could hardly stay awake. . . ." Raff nodded as Nima spoke ". . . and we slept like hibernating bears each night. It was only the excitement of being Paired with Raff that kept me going that last day."

Raff smiled and bent down to give Nima a quick kiss on the top of her head.

Nima glanced at Raff, who smiled back at his adoring partner. "I hope you two are as fortunate as I am in being matched with the right Partner." She moved Targo to her left arm and grabbed Raff's hand as they walked off towards their cabin. Snook, Nutan, and Kalmar walked to the dining hall, where they ate and talked, reliving the events of the day.

When they finished, they walked outside. Salune and Eeo had already fallen below the horizon but the nighttime sky was darker than usual. Overcast, dark clouds blocked most of the light from the moons and stars. Only occasionally was the menacing canopy breached by a fleeting glimpse of the luminous spectacle above them. A gusty crosswind shepherding the cloud front along battled the breeze coming off the mountain. The turbulent air over the expanse of boodo grass produced a new sound with every turn in the wind's direction; the moving reeds sounded like a driving rainstorm, yet no water was falling. The three stood in front of the dining hall listening to the whooshing sound.

"It looks like it is going to rain," Snook said. He lifted his head and sniffed. "And I can smell it coming."

Kalmar lifted his head. "I smell it too, but it is still the dry season; we shouldn't get any rain for another few weeks." He glanced at the dark clouds. "But the clouds should keep the heat down tomorrow."

Snook glanced up and nodded.

"Guess Nima's right, I think I will turn in," Nutan said. She walked over and gave her brother a hug, and did the same to Snook. The embrace Nutan gave Snook was longer than the one she gave Kalmar; she also finished it with a wet kiss on Snook's cheek. The two men watched Nutan as she walked off.

"I think my sister likes you."

"She's a good child and she will make some man a fine Pairing Partner someday," Snook said, hoping Kalmar would not press the issue.

"Yeah, she will. . . ." His expression hardened. "Guess I need to get some sleep myself. Are you going back to our cabin with me?"

"No, think I will take a stroll down by the brook."

"Okay, see you in the morning," Kalmar said, as he headed towards their cabin.

Snook walked along the small brook and stopped at the spot where he had fallen asleep the night before. He sat down and watched flashes in the distance, lightning so far off he could not hear its thunder over the sound of the wind in the boodo grass. The jagged illuminations reminded him of his meeting with Berkana. A heavy weight pressed against his shoulders; like Berkana's words, the lightning flashes foretold an approaching storm. The storm had not arrived, but it was coming—it was just a matter of time.

Snook felt himself falling over and, by reflex, put out his hand to keep from hitting the ground. A quick shake of his head and he was wide awake but disoriented. The sound of running water made him remember where he was. After his mind cleared, he stood up and made his way back to the cabin. Not wanting to disturb Kalmar, he tiptoed into the bedroom and then slid under his bedcovers as quietly as possible. The clouds blocked starlight from entering through the windows and lighting the darkened room. Snook lay in his bed staring into the blackness; the room was strangely quiet. Cocking his head, he listened. The only sounds were coming from beyond the windows; the wind would blow, then there would be a moment or two of quiet stillness. He slowly rolled out of his bed and crept towards Kalmar's bed. For a moment he doubted his senses: there were no breathing sounds. For a brief moment, there was a break in the clouds and starlight shone through the windows and lit the room. Kalmar's bed was empty; the sheets were as taut as they had been when they left that morning. Snook stared at the empty bed. "That woman," he said through his teeth. His shoulders slumped as he dragged himself back to his own bed and collapsed.

Izzy was full of questions. This was his first Gathering and everything he saw was exciting. He stopped to study anything unusual and was forever gawking at every pretty girl that walked by. Nevertheless, even in his excitement, he noticed a difference in his sister.

"Dera, I don't remember you ever being calmer. You're about to begin the Byrrac, and then choose a Pairing Partner. The next eight days are the most important days in your life . . . well, at least the most important up until you have your own children . . . yet you seem to be freer and more at ease than I've ever seen you." He twisted his hands in front of his chest. "How can you be so calm?"

"Little brother, I realized I control my own future—"

"Sure! You win the Byrrac and you get to choose the Pairing Partner you want . . . that's control of a sort," he said in a tone gushing with pride. "Everyone knows that you are going to win the Byrrac. . . ." He cocked his head, smiling. "Guess you have reason to be calm." He chuckled. "Verna told me you had the highest Concentration of the Traits of anyone she had ever heard of."

Sadness swept over Dera at the sound of her old friend's name. For a moment doubt flooded her mind; then she remembered what Verna told her as she lay dying: "Some of the changes will come through you." Dera did not know what fate lay in her future, but she did know the events of the next few days offered her best chance to influence the outcome. Verna spoke of change, yet she admitted she did not know what those changes were going to be. Dera had no idea what to think about Verna's words or the changes she predicted. Verna had said the coming changes "are bigger and more important than I thought." The only thing Dera knew to do was to proceed with her own plans and trust her actions were reconcilable with Verna's prognostications.

"Little brother," she said as she looked into his eyes, "don't worry about your big sister. You won't have to come to her rescue this time." Izzy had always been there for her. The love between them was the great light in her life, but she felt it best to keep her plans to herself. He would only try to talk her out of them. She winked at him. "I am tired; we should try to get some sleep."

"I know you will make us all proud." He grasped her right shoulder. "Remember, you are the best of the best."

They hugged and parted; each walked towards their own cabin. Izzy disappeared behind a row of cabins. "Dear brother," Dera muttered under her breath as she looked over her shoulder in the direction he had disappeared, "I hope you do not think less of me when this is over and done with."

NINETEEN

Bright morning sunlight saturated the room. Snook jerked awake, sat up, and looked around. Kalmar's half-dressed body lay sprawled across the other bed. Snook peered out the window as realization flushed his face. Frantic, he jumped out of bed. "*Kalmar, wake up, wake up.*" Kalmar did not move. Snook shook him to no avail. He grabbed a ceramic pitcher full of water off the table and threw its contents into Kalmar's face.

"*What the . . . why in the name of Shetow's Shadow did you do that?*" Kalmar sputtered as he sprang to a sitting position and forced his eyes open. He swung his legs around to sit on the side of his bed. He wiped the water from his face. "Snook, I should break your neck."

"Kalmar, we overslept; you're going to be late for the beginning of the Borrac if you don't get moving."

"*Blessed Shetow!*" Kalmar jumped up and stumbled over his moccasins as he tried to find the rest of his clothes. He stood still for a moment, his face a contortion of confusion; then he grabbed a towel and made for the door.

"There is no time for a bath; you will just have to compete dressed as you are."

"I . . . guess you are right." He sat down on his bed and fumbled around, trying to put on his moccasins. Snook noticed Kalmar's trembling hands.

Once dressed, they ran out of the cabin and headed towards the promenade. Snook was not in the physical condition needed to make such a long run, but the energy gained from an adrenaline surge gave him the extra stamina needed to stay relatively close to the already exhausted Kalmar as they raced towards the foot of Mount Alar. They had to weave between couples carrying their children on their way to watch the games. Running behind Kalmar, Snook had a clear view of his friend. Normally a creature of quickness and grace, Kalmar now struggled against his rebelling body to put one foot after the other. He stumbled once and plunged face-first into the graveled pathway. Snook, a hundred steps behind, rushed to help. Fresh abrasions bloodied an already scarred face; bits of gravel clung to the fresh wounds. Kalmar lay stunned for a moment before he jumped up and started running again.

They ran for fifteen minutes before they spotted the group of young men gathered outside the Grand Chamber's left entrance. Snook, gasping for breath and falling farther behind, stopped running, bent over, and placed his hands on his knees—for a moment his head spun and he almost blacked out. He looked up to see Kalmar stop running short of the group, walk the last few hundred steps, and casually approach the other contestants, trying to draw as little attention to himself as possible.

As he tried to blend with the group, Kalmar saw that he was noticed by the Medora, who was already talking to her attentive audience; she gave him a stern look but did not change the cadence of her talk ". . . will be expected to make your best effort in all the varied contests that comprise the Borrac. All of you have competed twice in the pre-games; there'll be no surprises as to how they will be set up." Her eyes flashed from one young man to another as she scrutinized her wards. "Some of you think"—she gave Kalmar another piercing stare—"the outcome of the Borrac is preordained. Trust me; it is not. There have been many who came to their Borrac, after doing well in the pre-Borrac, only to fall short of where they thought they would be in the final rankings. They found their potential Pairing Partners at the Matage weren't interested in how well they'd done a cycle of the seasons earlier, but only how they performed at that Gathering." She redirected her attention to the others in the group. "Those of you who didn't do as well in the pre-Borracs . . . you mustn't lose sight of the fact that there's often a big change in a young man's abilities between his seventeenth and eighteenth cycles of the seasons. If your fates were already decided, Shetow wouldn't have you go through the games a third and final time. The Borrac is Shetow's method of putting Her finger on those of you where the blending of your parents' Traits has produced superior males, males who'll father children with even greater Concentrations of those Traits."

She studied the group of young men another moment and then smiled as the lines around her eyes softened. "For six Progressions," she said in a more pleasant tone, "the People have waited for the ultimate male and female; a man and woman with all the Concentrations of the Traits Shetow finds desirable. Pairing Partners who will parent children who'll fill the Tell with their exploits. If this man and woman exist, they're at this Gathering." She paused to let her words sink in. "You must do your best in the games . . . it is one of the ways we know who you are."

Kalmar looked around, wondering if anyone else understood what the old woman meant; the Medora had changed the direction of her speech. One moment she had talked about their future children, and then suddenly she was talking about them.

"You will now divide into four groups, as you did for your last pre-Borrac. Those of you who finished in the top fourth of the last pre-Borrac will be in the Blue Rotation, the second fourth in the Red Rotation"—she unconsciously raised the tip of her walking cane and gestured toward different points on the Promenade—"the next fourth in the Green, and the bottom fourth in the Yellow. Each rotation will compete in the same events as the other three but at different times during the day. As you know, the rotation placements will change each day based on your overall ranking after scores from the previous day are added to your individual running total. The higher your running total; the higher your ranking. Scoring of the written competitions and the times or judging for the physical competitions is based on your performance compared to all the other contestants. For most events, your rotation placement will not have an effect on your score. There are a few events—such as running—where you might do better pitted against someone who is as fast as or faster than you are. Just keep in mind you are racing for the best possible time. The draks' timing devices do the scoring for those events, and not how you finish against those you're racing against in that particular heat."

A second, younger Medora stepped forward. "The secret to a high ranking is not in winning a few contests, but in scoring near the top in a number of events." She shook her finger. "The Tell speaks of many winners of the Borrac who did not win a single event; contestants who never placed in the top three of any event have been the top-ranked male because of their combined totals when it came to the Matage"—she raised her right hand and made a chopping motion as she spoke—"contestants who excelled in many events although they weren't the best in any single one of them."

"The rankings will be posted," the older Medora spoke up, "for each day's performance, along with your overall ranking, on a Borrac Board in front of your tribe's dining hall after the evening meal. It's crucial that you check the chart daily for your running total and ranking; it is your responsibility to know which rotation you will be competing in the next day." She scanned the group. "Are there any questions?" No hands appeared.

"Good. Now form into groups. Blue Rotation, there." Again, this time intentionally, she pointed with her walking cane to a spot on the Promenade. "And Red, Green, and Yellow, in that order, form up in groups to their right."

Once each group was assembled, guides escorted them to different parts of the Gathering compound to begin their first event. Kalmar's group, the Blue Rotation, filed into one of sixteen testing buildings shared by all the contestants of the Borrac, Byrrac, and the pre-games. The testing halls, minus the lofty ceilings, were built much like an Oonoc Lodge: chest-high stone walls with the top portion of the walls and the rafters constructed from timbers using mortises, tenons, and nutwood pegs. The Borrac contestants competed in four events on the first day.

At the end of the last event, an exhausted Kalmar found Snook waiting for him.

"I don't think I've ever been so tired. I must go back to our cabin and lay down," Kalmar said as he stumbled past Snook. Snook dropped in beside him and they headed towards the compound.

"How'd you do?"

"All right . . . I guess, but it was harder than any day I had during the pre-Borracs. It was all I could do to keep from falling asleep."

Snook had followed the Blue Rotation around all day. He knew what tests Kalmar had faced, but did not interrupt Kalmar's monologue.

"That first test . . . it was the hardest. I don't mean it was hard—it was easy—it's just that my mind kept wandering . . . no matter how hard I tried I could not concentrate. When that was over, I went to the washroom and stuck my head under a water tap to wake myself up. The next test was the first of the four archery contests."

Snook had watched Kalmar shooting the bow during the late morning and could tell he was off.

"I couldn't stop my hands from quivering . . . a couple of shots went wide of the mark. The last three tests . . . I really don't know . . . I just got through them."

They did not talk again until they neared the cabin. "I'm famished," Kalmar mumbled.

"Go to our cabin; I'll go to the dining hall and bring you something to eat." Snook darted off. When Snook returned to their cabin, a bleary-eyed Kalmar attacked his food. After inhaling a few bites, he slumped over in his bunk.

Snook walked along the path heading back to the dining hall. "Snook . . . Snook."

He turned as Nutan ran up. "Well, if it isn't the prettiest girl I know," he said with a sheepish grin.

She responded with a flirtatious smile, but it soon faded into seriousness. "What happened to my brother?"

"Oh, he's back in the cabin asleep."

"Not where is he; what happened to him? He's ranked fifteenth. He has never ranked lower than third for a single day's events in the pre-Borracs. Is he sick?"

"No . . . no, just tired."

"*Tired!* Kalmar's in the best shape of his life, why . . ." Her eyes grew large; her mouth dropped open. "It's that girl isn't it?"

"That . . . that woman kept him out all night; she knew better; she may have cost him his first place ranking in the games. I—I'll show her," Nutan sputtered as she paced wildly, swinging her arms and jabbing her hands like exclamation points to her rage. Snook thought Nutan had been angry the previous night; it was a ripple compared to the tidal wave of fury distorting her face.

Her tirade continued until she finally sat down on a bench under one of the nutwood trees. There were benches positioned every few hundred feet along the pathways and Promenade. She leaned over, resting her elbows on her knees, and buried her face in her hands.

Snook wondered how she had deduced Arasima's role in Kalmar's poor showing so quickly. Nutan was revealing more of her clever mind. This girl was smart, and he *liked* smart. "Nutan, how did you do today in your pre-Byrrac?"

She looked up. "What?"

"How did you fare today?"

"Oh . . . first . . . I think." The lines of her face betrayed her effort to refocus her thoughts. "Some women should be disqualified. They set traps for men. . . ." Her eyes glazed. He could see her eyelids flutter as her face became rigid. She sat up abruptly. "It must be part of the Borrac; it's a final test. Shetow's allowing those women to influence the men. Shetow is seeing if a high-ranked male will reject high-ranked females because of his sexual desire for a lower-ranked female." Her eyes rounded. "It's Shetow's way of weeding out the males who pay more attention to the head in their pants than they do to the head on their shoulders." She nodded. "This leaves the thinking males to be chosen by the higher-ranked females." Her face was alive with speculation. "Surely I'm not the first person to figure this out," she said without expression.

"You're wrong, you know."

"Why do you say that?" she said, putting her face closer to his after jumping up to stand beside him.

"Oh, you have made some good points, but there are a few things that make me think you are wrong." He reached down, picked up a small stone on the pathway, and threw it into the restless sea of boodo grass.

"Name *one,*" she said as she plopped down again on the wooden bench.

He reached down, picked up a second rock, and threw it after the first one. "You," he said as he sat down besides her.

"Me? What is *that* supposed to mean?"

"You are leading in the ranking in your pre-Byrrac—"

"So?"

"You are the sexiest female I've seen at the Gathering, maybe the sexiest female I have *ever* seen."

She scrunched her face and blushed.

"It's not only because of your provocative body, but because you know how to use it to captivate a male. The way you danced for me at the Celebration of Life ceremony would render any male helpless."

She blinked; her breathing quickened.

"But the thing that makes you irresistible," he reached over and gently tapped her on her temple, "is what is up here." He stood up. "Your brain . . . how you use it . . . along with your wit, is as sexy as . . ." He gestured towards the unlaced opening at the top of her chemise ". . . as the swell of your half-exposed breast."

Nutan looked down to see that her lacing had come undone; she averted her eyes as she pulled the laces tight and retied them. She continued to look down when she had finished.

"Nutan."

She slowly lifted her head and looked at him; her eyes were moist.

"You are as near perfection as any female could be; no man could desire more." He shook his head. "Shetow didn't give you your looks and feminine charms to test some male—at least not in the way you're thinking. Shetow isn't weeding out males because they have a hard time resisting beautiful women. Any process whereby females use sex as a way to get the male they desire . . . in the end, favors the smarter females. I believe the test, if Shetow is testing males using feminine charm, is all in the favor of you smart and sexy females over those females that have only their sexuality." He looked to the hills beyond the open grassland, the direction he had seen the lightning two nights earlier. "If sexy females were a test to weed out the weaker males, then females would be dumb and beautiful." He leaned towards her. "Or smart and plain," he whispered.

Nutan now sat erect, her hands resting in her lap, her eyes fixed on him.

"No, Nutan, if your idea had merit, you would not exist. You are as smart as they come." He reached over and brushed a lock of hair off her face, "Beautiful and sensual. You are the evidence that destroys your own theory."

zzy!"

Izzy turned to see his sister walking towards him.

"Hello. I saw on the board where you crushed them as usual."

"It was a good day."

"Good day," he said rolling his eyes. "I heard one of the Medoras telling someone that your lead's unprecedented. She said if you keep this pace up, you'll set a new record for the largest point spread between the females ranked first and second."

Dera scrunched her mouth and nodded to her brother.

"Don't you understand? The Tellers of the Tell will spin a story about you. I can hear them now, 'Dera the Undefeated, Dera the—' "

"The Insane and how she strangled her brother. That's what the Tellers of the Tell are going to say."

He grinned. "I'm proud of you. You had me worried."

"Worried. *Why?*"

"I wasn't sure you were looking forward to your Byrrac. You have been acting a little stranger than normal the last few weeks; then, when Verna was killed, well . . . I wasn't sure you had your heart in the competition."

"Don't worry about me and the Byrrac. I have every intention of being first in the competition. . . . I want to be the first to choose at the Matage."

"Sister, you will make some fortunate male a great Pairing Partner. I hope I will be as lucky as he is when I'm chosen."

Her humorous smile faded as she lowered her chin. "There are few things I know for sure, but one of them is that you will be luckier than any male I choose."

"What do you mean by *that* comment?"

It was a few moments before her face gave way to a broad grin. "Do you think there is any other female as stubborn as I am? How lucky could any male be who has to put up with your, as you say, 'strange sister'?"

"Since you put it that way, maybe you are right . . . anyone you choose might not be lucky after all." They both laughed.

"I saw on the boards you did pretty well yourself; even won one of the events. Not bad."

"Thanks, but coming from the person who won three of her events and placed second in the other, you sound patronizing."

"You are right, your performance wasn't worth a pile of mammoth dung," she said, poking him in the ribs. They laughed again. "I think I will turn in early."

"Another long day tomorrow."

They hugged and then each started walking towards their separate cabins.

————

After Izzy had walked only a few steps, he stopped and turned to watch Dera as she walked away. *You are keeping something from me,* he thought. He and Dera were closer than close; what could she be thinking about that she did not feel comfortable sharing with him? As close as they were, they still used discretion in what they told each other. She had always been the serious one, he the joker. He knew she would be slow to tell him about something he could use to tease her. A shudder ran through his body; he had a feeling that whatever was on Dera's mind was not something he would find funny. He watched her until she was out of sight. He turned and continued walking towards his own cabin.

The light from Boboi shone through the cabin's opened windows. As Elom's largest moon set, its beams slowly but methodically crept across the room's planked floor. Snook had come to bed late and found Kalmar still sleeping. He had been careful not to disturb his friend as he undressed and climbed into his bed. He soon fell asleep but later awoke covered in sweat. It was obvious he had been asleep for at least an hour since the moonbeams had moved from the middle of the floor and were now shining on Kalmar's face. Something had awoken Snook, but he wasn't sure what. Kalmar's face, now awash in Boboi's glow, caught his attention. Kalmar's eyelids were fluttering just as they had the last time he had seen Kalmar asleep. Every few seconds Kalmar would rock his head back and forth on his pillow. He watched Kalmar, wondering if he should wake his friend or let him continue his fretful sleep. As he watched, Kalmar stopped moving his head and appeared to drift back into a deep sleep. Snook lay back, turned away from the moonlight, and pulled his bedcovers over his shoulder as he closed his eyes.

I think we should stop now and get some sleep," Berkana said as she released the hands of the Medoras to her right and left. The other

Medoras who sat around the triangular table also released the hands of the Medoras on each side of them. The Medoras shuffled towards the outside doorway. The older and more feeble women moved the slowest and were met outside the Medora's Chamber by waiting members of their tribes who would aid them in getting back to their tribe's compound. Petra, a Medora of considerable age but one who could still move about without the help of others, lingered to talk to Berkana by herself.

"I'm concerned; shouldn't we have had a response by now?"

"Old friend, don't lose faith, our efforts will produce results soon enough," Berkana answered as she forced the most sincere smile she could on her face; she must not allow her fellow Medora to see her own concern. "If you will remember, we've always thought the response would take time." She reached over, took Petra's left hand and patted it. "Geerna said Shetow is just. Surely Shetow wouldn't help us through six Progressions to only abandon us now, at the time of our greatest need."

"I guess . . . I know you are right, it is only . . ." a weak grimace shaped Petra's lips ". . . the fate of the People is at stake."

"It will be all right." Berkana closed her eyes for a second before reopening them. "We've had countless cycles of the seasons to prepare. I trust the People are ready for the Judging. Do not worry so."

Petra nodded tepidly. She patted Berkana's hand in return, and then started towards the doorway to the promenade.

Berkana watched her walk away. *Petra, if you only knew how unsure I am about what to do,* Berkana thought. She kept watching until Petra walked out the door then turned to see Cabyl standing inside the corridor that led to the Grand Chamber. Cabyl's face was whiter than its normal pale complexion; she had the look of perplexed fear. It was obvious to Berkana what had happened—realizing the meeting was over, Cabyl had entered the Medora's Chambers and had overheard her conversation with Petra. Cabyl kept her thoughts to herself, although in the last few days, Berkana could tell the intuitive young woman sensed the tension among the Medoras. Berkana motioned for Cabyl to come to her. Cabyl refocused her attention and rushed forward, sliding her arm around the old woman's waist.

"My child, please sit down; there is much I need to tell you."

T W E N T Y

The seventh day of the games was over, only the eighth day—the final day—remained. The contestants' previous day's results and running totals were posted on the bulletin boards outside the tribes' dining halls. The games and pre-games were turning out to be ones that would give great honor to the leading participants; there would be many accolades chiseled into the stone wall of the Chronicles at the end of this Gathering. Dera was far ahead in her point score; the other contestants had conceded to her the first-place ranking and for the last few days concentrated on the lesser spots. Dera was proud of Izzy's high ranking in his group's pre-Borrac. Nutan's scores in her pre-Byrrac rivaled those of Dera in the Byrrac; their scores were the two highest ever achieved at the same Gathering. Many speculated that Nutan might even beat Dera's record breaking score in two cycles of the seasons at her own Byrrac.

The talk of the Gathering, though, was not Dera or Nutan, but Kalmar. The account of his climb up the rankings in the last seven days captivated everyone; it was a feat unmatched by any of the names inscribed on the face of Alar. After his pathetic fifteenth place ranking at the end of the first day of the Borrac, his daily totals for the next six days were phenomenal: highest for four of the days and next to the highest for the other two. Now, his running total was only a few points out of ranking him first. If his first day's scores had not been in the totals, he would be far ahead and setting records like Dera and Nutan.

Gwyther was ranked first; all Kalmar had to do was to top Gwyther's score for the last day—something he had done soundly the last six days—and Kalmar would be first in the final ranking of the Borrac. Everyone knew Kalmar was going to prevail; his efforts were a testament to the power of will over pain and distraction. Kalmar's perseverance added to his fame as the cave lion killer; it also gave the spectators an underdog to cheer.

Snook, Nutan, and Kalmar walked along the promenade reading the Chronicles. A steady breeze blew across the grasslands before climbing the mountain face. The night was clear of clouds and the three larger moons, along with a wealth of stars, lit the nighttime sky to the fullness of a twilight night. The minuscule Mystery, the fourth moon, streaked across the middle of the sky, its path bisecting the heavenly canopy into near equal halves. The three friends were as loose and cheerful as they had been in weeks, and Kalmar had declared tomorrow was going to be a "special day." The three were bending over reading an inscription near the base of the stone surface when they heard footsteps behind them.

"Kalmar . . . Kalmar, is that you?" The three stood up, turned, and saw Arasima walking towards them accompanied by two girls. All three women wore colorful clothing that denoted they were from different tribes. Arasima had been absent ever since Kalmar's poor showing on the first day of the Borrac. Kalmar hadn't spoken of her, and Snook and Nutan thought it best not to mention her either.

"Hello Arasima," Kalmar said in a guarded tone. Arasima leaned over and whispered something to her companions. The two girls looked Kalmar up and down, smiled, and then walked on without Arasima. Arasima kept her distance, and motioned for Kalmar to come closer.

"Kalmar," Nutan said under her breath as Kalmar started to walk towards Arasima.

Kalmar hesitated for a moment, squared his shoulders, and then started walking again. When Kalmar had covered the few steps that separated them, Arasima skillfully moved her body between Kalmar and his two companions. Nutan and Snook could only see her back and the outline of Kalmar's larger frame not eclipsed by her compact body.

"I cannot believe he's talking to that woman," Nutan said scowling. "She cost him an early first place ranking; now that he is within grasp of his rightful standing, she pops up again like an adolescent's pimple."

"I think your brother understands her game, Nutan. He will be all right." Snook hoped Kalmar would have more willpower than he felt he could have mustered if Arasima had summoned him. She looked as radiant as ever; the gentle glow of the twilight-of-night made her delicate features seem even softer, a softness he could almost feel. Unconsciously, he rubbed his thumb across the tips of his fingers. "He will be just fine," he said with forced conviction.

Nutan nodded grimly, crossed her arms, and cocked her head.

Right after Snook finished talking, Kalmar walked back over to them. "I'm going to talk with Arasima for a few minutes. Go on with out me; I'll catch up."

"Kalmar, *that* woman," Nutan sputtered, "is out to bed you so she can control you. Your indiscretion . . . this loss of concentration, could knock you out of a first ranking in the Borrac." The protruding lines of her set jaw and the white knuckles of her clenched fists contrasted with the smoothness of her tanned skin.

"Sister, believe me, I know what I'm doing," Kalmar said, raising his hand as if trying to deflect her rage.

"You stupid pile of bovor dung, that . . . that woman will get her claws in you and not let go until you do what she wants you to do, she—"

"Snook"—he turned towards his friend—"take care of my sister. I won't be late," Kalmar said with his old air of self-assurance; then he spun around, walked back, grabbed Arasima's hand, and led her down the promenade.

"Men . . . dumb as a pile of rocks," Nutan said through compressed lips as she watched her brother and Arasima hurry away.

Snook's eyes followed Kalmar and Arasima. The unexpected sight of Arasima filled his mind; how could seeing a woman cause so much pain? The tightness returned to his chest; his heart pounded. "Kalmar's a grown man. He can take care of himself."

"I do not see how he can be so *stupid,*" Nutan said, slowly shaking her head.

"Maybe he has learned his lesson. You don't—"

"Learned his lesson? I say. Don't you see Snook, when it comes to *that woman,* my brother is inept. He is going to put all his efforts into controlling the head between his legs, but a smart woman— and she is smart—will change her attack. She will work on this head—" She pointed to her temple. "Once she has his brain under her control, his defenses against her sexual assault will evaporate." She shook her head again. "She will have Kalmar willing to believe whatever excuse she tells him. He will convince himself that she can do no wrong. She will grab his manhood and lead him wherever she wants." She sighed. "That woman's going to be my brother's Pairing Partner, and if she does succeed, she has him"— she held out her open palm—"right here." She glanced in the direction Kalmar and Arasima had disappeared. When she looked back at Snook, he was staring at her with a perplexed expression on his face. "What?" She turned to look behind her. Seeing nothing she said, "What are you looking at?"

"You."

"*Me.* Why?"

"How do you know so much about people? No man has a chance against you. You understand everybody's weaknesses."

"Snook, you knock me in the head with a big, round river-rock if I ever use any ability I might have to the detriment of someone else . . . especially a male."

"Just promise me you won't play with some man's heart. Choose the male you think best before you unleash your charms . . . for once you do, he will be powerless to resist you."

"What," she said with an impish smile, "if I chose to run away with you and forgo the Matage?"

"Why would you want to do that?" Snook said laughing. "You have already conquered my heart. It would be wiser to find the best man, not the easiest," he said, tapping his chest with his finger. Her forehead wrinkled for a moment before they both laughed again.

"Snook, you're the *best* man I know."

"Well then, in two cycles of the seasons—after your Byrrac— if you still feel that way, I *will* run away with you."

She grinned, then jumped up, threw her arms around his neck, and hugged him. "Now, don't go and let some woman run off with your heart before that time," she said, flashing him another toothy smile, while unconsciously tilting her head in a way that accented her brown eyes.

He gazed at her. *What a beautiful and vibrant flower,* he thought.

I must be careful; I have only one chance to regain control of the situation, thought Arasima. She thought of Kalmar telling her of his time of apprehension. The time after his grandfather's death and the cycles of the seasons when, as an adolescent, fate thrust him to become the male factor in his family's Equilibrium, to hunt to feed them and have the male input for family decisions, had given him a sense of responsibility not often borne by a male so young. She smiled to herself. Kalmar was a man dedicated to those who relied on him.

"I was so worried about you. I felt responsible for your first day's low ranking; I know it's my fault," she said in the softest tone.

"Why didn't I see you until today?" Kalmar said through clenched teeth. He had told himself, if he ever had the chance, he would not yield to the temptation of asking her that question, but he spoke without thinking.

"I knew your sister and Snook would try to keep us apart." She looked down. "What was I to do?" Arasima said barely above a whisper. "Besides," she said with more force as she looked up, "it was best that I stay away . . . you needed to concentrate on the Borrac." She lowered her eyes again and leaned towards him. "To stay away from you was the hardest thing I have ever done."

"It was?" he said. He stopped walking and turned to look at her.

"*Kalmar*, don't talk like that. You know how much you mean to me." She put her hand on his arm. "How do you think I feel knowing it was my fault? I love you so." Her eyes swelled with tears. "It was all I could do to keep from coming to your cabin and begging for your forgiveness."

He looked into her misty eyes and his face lost its hardness. He closed his eyes a moment . . . how stupid of him to have not understood her actions. Now it all made sense; she was the one who had stayed true to their love. He had doubted her promise too quickly. The pain tugging at his heart gave way to elation.

"It wasn't your fault," he said. ". . . I mean . . . well, I am just as much at fault as you are. Really, it is more my fault. I am the one who misjudged my ability to compete without a full night's sleep . . . you were out as late as I was, but you did all right in your first day in the Byrrac."

"Oh, Kalmar." She leaned her head against his chest.

After a moment's reflection, she resisted telling him about the strong herbal tea her Medora had given her the morning after their last sexual encounter. She, too, had been exhausted, but the stimulation of the steaming elixir had postponed the debilitating consequences of their late night activities until after the conclusion of the first day's competition. She, like Kalmar, had recovered with a long night's sleep before the beginning of the second day of the games.

She still had the chance to bring back to her village the winner of the Borrac; that would show them. The memories of her childhood taunters rejuvenated her resolve.

He shrugged his shoulders. "You know, even when I tried to sleep that night . . . after I got back to my cabin, I couldn't. Well, I could, but I was very restless . . . the sleep I did get wasn't . . . real sleep; I kept having this dream. I was as tired when I opened my eyes as I had been when I closed them—"

Arasima tilted her head as she listened intently. For a moment, confusion clouded her face. She started to say something, then changed her mind.

"Well, everything's all right now." She pushed her head harder against his chest, encircled his body with her arms, and squeezed him. Then, all of a sudden, she leaned back. "Everything is . . . all right . . . isn't it?" She studied his face for any signs revealing his thoughts.

He looked down into her hazel eyes as her upturned face rested against his chest. Through her parted lips, he could see enough to make out the gap between her teeth. The gap was the only flaw he could find in this otherwise perfect woman. For some unexplainable reason, he found her imperfection arousing. Her face glowed as it reflected the soft illumination from the two larger moons and profusion of stars. A wisp of hair hanging over her right eye stirred as the breeze from the grassland blew across her face. When Kalmar looked at her, he saw a fragile young woman who was in love with him. Shetow must find him worthy; how else could he be so lucky to have the love of the most beautiful and desirable woman in all of Elom?

"Kalmar, our promise?"

Kalmar reached up and put his finger gently against her lips. "Hush now," he said as he squared his shoulders, which accented the swell in his chest. "A promise is a promise."

"Oh Kalmar, I knew you still loved me. I believed with all my heart that you would not spurn my dedication to our promise. I will make you so happy," she said as she again buried her face in the expanse of his tunic. They stood there for a few minutes. Other couples walking by paid them little attention, as they too were lost in their own amorous thoughts. After a time, Arasima slid her right hand down Kalmar's front. Her hand reached his waist. She leaned back and looked him in the eye as she slid her hand down until it rested on the swelling in his pants. She took the tips of her fingers and softly rubbed them over the tightly stretched fabric covering his bulge. A smile crossed her face. "I see our little friend is also glad to see me," she said.

"Oh . . . if you only knew how glad."

She did not immediately respond to his leading remark, but continued gently stroking the focus of his concentration with the tips of her fingers. She watched as he closed his eyes and slowly tilted his head back. Her feeling of renewed power hardened the lines around her mouth and eyes. "It is difficult to tell how glad our little friend is to see me when you have him covered up."

He grabbed her hand. "We'll just have to do something about that." He quickly led her down the promenade towards the beginning of the Chronicles and the woods beyond.

A s always, a fine mist covered the lake. Kalmar was nearer to the shore and he was turning his head to the left, straining to see if he could ascertain what the movement was to his left. For the first time he could see something; it was the bow of another boat. It appeared similar to the one he was poling across the lake. He squinted to see through the mist. He could make out a shape in the boat—

"*Kalmar, Kalmar wake up!*"

He could feel his body being shaken. His eyes sprang open to see someone leaning over him. It was Snook.

"Kalmar, wake up. You must get ready for the Borrac."

Kalmar's mind cleared; he sat up, and swung his legs over the side of the bed. "Did I oversleep? How much time do I have before the first contest begins?" he said, his eyes glancing towards the door as he made an effort to get up.

"No, you didn't oversleep." Snook grabbed his shoulders and pushed him back down. "You're not late, but you need to hurry if you want to wash up and eat before we leave for the promenade."

"My head." Kalmar closed his eyes as he put a hand to his temple. "I'm so groggy; I feel like I haven't slept at all."

"When did you go to bed?"

"I came back to the cabin a little after midnight and went straight to bed." Kalmar slowly turned his pleading face up to look at Snook. "I don't understand. Even without a full night's sleep, I shouldn't feel this bad . . . the dreams . . . I dreamed all night. The dreams kept me from sleeping soundly. The dreams . . . that's why I feel so bad. That's why I was so tired on the first day of the Borrac. I have had the same dream every night. The last few nights, going to bed early, I was able to get enough sleep to function the next day." He swayed and almost fell. "Ooooh, my head feels like it is inside a Celebration of Life ceremonial drum."

"Do you feel as bad as you did on the first day of the Borrac?"

Kalmar took a deep breath, then let out a sigh. "No, I think I'm better than I was that first day . . . but not a lot better." He sat there a few moments with his face in his hands, and then he stood up. "Guess we had better get moving."

TWENTY-ONE

A chorus of grasshoppers accented the stillness during the lull between the shifting of the breeze as the chill of the twilight-of-night gripped the air. Nutan sat next to Snook. They had not spoken since he found her on the pathway connecting the promenade to the tribe's compound. She had been sitting on a bench under a nutwood tree next to the pathway and barely acknowledged his presence when he walked up and sat down next to her. A knee-high rock fence acted as a barrier between the boodo grass and the manicured lawns of the Gathering's grounds. Nutan had chosen a bench unusually close to the rock fence and the sea of boodo grass beyond. Because of the view, the bench faced the rock fence and boodo grass, not the pathway. After a time, he noticed her shivering and draped his coat over her shoulders.

The dropping temperature signaled a weather change; the breeze now blowing from the grassland was stronger than normal for this early in the evening. The wind whipped across the top of the grass causing a loud swishing sound that could have been mistaken for a herd of prairie buck running through tall grass fleeing a pack of wolves. Dark clouds had moved in from the far side of Alar, bringing with them the smell of rain and ozone. Over his shoulder, in the distance, bolts of blinding energy cut the darkness above the foothills. Storm clouds had gathered above the hills every night since the beginning of the Gathering; this was only the second time the clouds had ventured from their mountainous harbor to block the nighttime skies. The storm was close behind, and soon fine mist joined the bellowing wind; in minutes, chilling rain overpowered the mist and soaked their clothing. Snook and Nutan were oblivious to the rain and to the people scurrying along the pathways trying to get to their cabins. The wind increased in intensity, peppering their backs with watery missiles.

Nutan turned towards Snook. Her hair, now plastered against her skull, hung in wet ringlets around her ears. Small rivers of water trickled down her face. Snook thought it odd that—at a moment like this—he would be noticing how the water dripped from the end of her nose and spattered off the finely curved edge of her top lip. She looked like a half-drowned puppy, yet she was still so beautiful, and surprisingly, so vulnerable.

"Where is Kalmar?" she said.

"Walking . . . he wanted to be by himself."

She nodded, then looked down again. A bolt of lightning lit the sky as it struck close to them; instantly a deafening crack of thunder followed. Snook flinched at the sudden incursion into his reflections. She did not jump at the lightning flash or thunder, but looked up, held out her palm, and caught some of the rain in her hand. "I guess it's time we get out of the storm." They stood as the swirls of gusting wind pelted their bodies with a torrent of raindrops. Nutan indicated for Snook to lean over so she could say something to him. "Let's go to your cabin," she said, just loud enough to be heard over the downpour.

He nodded.

They ran to the cabin, although they could not have gotten any wetter. As they entered the cabin, Snook fumbled around to light a candle. It took a moment for him to get the flame going as the first time he got the wick lit, water dripping from his sleeve put it out. When he turned around, he saw Nutan's wet clothes lying across a wooden chair and her nude body sliding under the covers of his bed. He took off all his clothes but his shorts and spread them across another chair. He looked at Nutan; he could not see her face as she had buried it under the sheets. It was almost summer and until the rain-soaked wind brought cooler weather they had not needed the cabin's fireplace. He lit a few pieces of kindling and covered them with an armload of dried sticks before placing split hardwood logs on the growing flame.

Once the fire was blazing, he was not sure what to do. He was marveling at the grace of her bare shoulders and back when she turned and looked at him.

"Please come and hold me?" she said, as she rose to rest on an elbow and reached out to him with her other arm. As she sat up, the bedcovers fell away, revealing the fullness of her breasts.

He knew she had shed all of her clothing; he could see her wet undergarments drying on the back of the wooden chair. He felt little embarrassment, and she showed no change in her morose expression, as she watched him step out of his shorts. He laid them across a chair to dry, walked over, and took Nutan's outstretched hand. He could feel her warmth as he slid in beside her under the covers. As he lay back, she snuggled against him, placing her silken body between his right arm and chest. Then she laid her head on his shoulder, draping her arm across his torso, while pulling a knee up so that it rested on his hip. Once comfortable, she stopped moving. He positioned his right arm along the length of her smooth back, resting his hand on her bare thigh; then he pulled the covers over their exposed bodies with his free hand.

The cold wet sounds of the rain and blowing wind beating against the roof of the cabin were in sharp contrast to the warm softness of Nutan's body against his. Her bare breast pressed against his ribs. He was keenly aware of every place that their naked bodies touched. He could smell the wetness of her hair and the aroma of her body—a female musk, the fragrance of a woman.

He had often fantasized about sleeping in the arms of a desirable woman. He had even imagined that woman being Nutan; but now, with her soft skin against his, his lust was tempered by the trust and caring she showed him; was this the same woman who almost seduced him the night of the Celebration of Life ceremony? He was sure that he and Nutan had been only moments away from intimacy when Cabyl found them. He desired Nutan, yet the look on Cabyl's face when he had looked up from kissing Nutan had gripped his heart. He jerked when he remembered that look. He felt another wave of self-loathing as he remembered Arasima's look when she smiled at him after seeing the bulge in the front of his pants when they first met. The more he learned about women, the less he understood them, and for that matter, the greater was his confusion about his own sexuality. He had never felt so close to anyone as he now felt to this amazing female clinging to him. He wanted to comfort and protect her—was this love? However, he did understand that what this woman needed from him, at this moment, was not sex; if they were to be lovers, it would be at a different time and under different circumstances. *If holding a woman you cared about but were not going to make love to made you feel this way, how wonderful it must be to hold a woman you loved and were going to make love to*, he thought.

He lay listening to the sounds of the blustery night as thoughts of all that had happened filled his head. The Gathering neared its end and he must soon meet with Berkana and the other Medoras. Berkana had promised to try to find a part for him in the Second Judging, yet unexpectedly, the turbulence in his mind kept sliding into personal matters. He'd never thought being a Seeker would generate more questions than answers. He closed his eyes; sad thoughts of his mother gave way to ones about the confusion he felt over Nutan and Cabyl.

It was not long before Nutan's breathing became shallow and regular. Sleep came slower to Snook.

Kalmar silently entered the cabin and stood, as water dripped from his soaked clothing, staring at his sister and friend asleep in each other's arms. He turned and walked out.

It was the ninth day of the Gathering, the day of the Matage—The Choosing. Those who were to choose sat in one group and those to be chosen sat in another; the females were seated on the right of the dais and the males on the left. All the contestants of the Borrac and Byrrac were seated in the order of their final ranking in the contest. Their ranking was the order in which the females would choose their Pairing Partner. The ranking of the males was a guide by which the females could measure the Concentration of the Traits in the males.

The old woman spoke as those around her listened. "For six Progressions, countless cycles of the seasons, we have gathered for the Matage . . . for the Pairing of our best. Our quest to strengthen the Traits in the People as laid down in Geerna's Covenant with Shetow has been a journey to perfect our species in the Eyes of Shetow the Great Mother. And it is a journey that nears its end," Berkana said from the podium at the front of the dais. Her last words caused whispers to ripple through the seated mass of people. Kalmar turned his head from the second seat in the front row of the males to look at Berkana. She had not said this at the last two Gatherings. Why did she say it now? It was hard for Kalmar to concentrate. He had slept little that night; that, coupled with his exploits the night before, had left his mind a blur. He still could not accept that he had placed second in the rankings.

Why are the people whispering?" Snook asked as he and Nutan sat in a row of seats behind the group of male contestants.

"I think it is because of what Berkana said about the Concentration of the Traits being near its end. Snook, I don't understand what she means." She looked away for a moment, then looked back at him. "What did Kalmar say to you before he left the cabin?" She had not asked about her brother until now. Snook thought she had taken her brother's failure to regain the first place ranking harder than Kalmar.

"He said he thought it was ironic that both he and Arasima were ranked second in the Borrac and the Byrrac."

"He is second place because of *her.*"

"What's done is done," Snook said. He thought about not mentioning what else Kalmar had told him, but after some thought, said it anyway. "He also said that he and Arasima ending up with equal rankings just proves that they must be meant to be together." Nutan looked at Snook with piercing eyes, then slowly shook her head and said something so softly he could not hear it. He started to ask her, but she, realizing what he was about to do, shook her head a second time.

Gwyther sat to his right in the first seat, a man whose higher ranking he could not refute. Kalmar grappled with the conflict between his own shame and his admiration for this humble man who had bested him. He had beaten Gwyther in the two pre-Borracs, and he had often shunned this rival, who seemed to always come up short in the rankings. He had never given Gwyther more than a nod when they happened to meet. Gwyther had always smiled and tried to be friendly, but Kalmar shrugged off his efforts; he had felt Gwyther was jealous of him. The realization that Gwyther had more character than he had was more of a blow to Kalmar's psyche than his placing second in the rankings. The notion of his own arrogance sent spasms of shame through his body. He felt his life had hit bottom; he was not the man he believed he was. It was only the thought of Arasima that made his existence meaningful; her love soothed his wounded pride. She loved him for the man he was; she understood him better than he understood himself. In two days, they would be on their way to her village as Paired Partners, sparing him the humiliation of facing his own village.

Kalmar's mind was overwhelmed with conflicting thoughts. He was a changed man; he would never be overconfident or arrogant again. Yes, he was changed. He was a better man for his humiliation. "Oh, Shetow, forgive my boastful ways," he pleaded silently.

Snook, you know I love my brother," Nutan said.
"I do—"

"As I reflect on how he consorted with that woman, putting him in position to lose the top ranking . . . and what Gwyther did . . . well, I just can't bring myself to feel Gwyther didn't deserve to win the top ranking."

"I know . . . I think Kalmar feels the same way. Until now, I don't think he felt Gwyther was a worthy opponent."

"He was wrong. I overheard Gwyther, when asked why he did it, say that Kalmar had stumbled and he didn't think it right for him to beat someone who was faster than him just because he stumbled."

"Is the race always the last event?"

"Always. Of the four footraces in the Borrac, the Great Race is the longest, being more than three times longer than the next longest race. It tests both the competitor's speed and endurance. Kalmar never lost that race in the pre-Borracs, and would have won yesterday's race if he hadn't been so tired, stumbled, and fell."

"But he *did* fall."

"Yes he did." She pressed her lips together until they turned white. "It took a real man . . . a person of integrity, to stop and help a competitor up and half carry him across the finish line," Nutan said, her jaw set.

"I know. I think it is one of the things upsetting Kalmar. Kalmar knows Gwyther stopped and helped him not knowing the judges would still give Gwyther the win, even though they both, actually, crossed the line together," Snook said.

"I was told you must go back to the Tell of the Fifth Progression to find a Tell of anyone stopping to help another contestant, and then, it didn't have any effect on the top rankings." Nutan's unfocused eyes looked through Snook. "At the time, Gwyther didn't know he wasn't throwing away his top ranking by stopping to help Kalmar."

"He was twenty, maybe thirty strides behind Kalmar when Kalmar fell."

"With Kalmar down, Gwyther had the race and top ranking won, yet he stopped and helped Kalmar up."

Snook nodded. "Kalmar is wondering if he would have done the same for Gwyther."

"What's troubling Kalmar is he knows he wouldn't have."

Snook took a shallow breath. "I cannot say I would have either."

"I hope I never have to make that choice." She tilted her head like a prairie buck listening for a stalker. "Let's listen to Berkana; she might explain what she meant by it being near the end."

When Snook looked back towards Berkana, he saw Cabyl enter the chamber through the corridor door leading to the Medora's Chamber, walk across the dais, and take a seat against the back wall. Cabyl had always looked pale, but now her face appeared almost white. Snook wondered if the strange light originating in the vaulted ceiling of the chamber caused the change in the hue of her skin tone. After he studied the faces of the others on the platform, he realized it didn't; something was troubling her.

"—that Shetow uses to improve the Traits in the people." Cabyl moved to help Berkana to one of the seats lined against the back wall of the dais. Another Medora made her way to the podium.

"The Covenant decrees the females select their Pairing Partners in the order of their ranking in the Byrrac. The first Choosing goes to Dera, of the Long Tusk Tribe."

Dera rose from the first chair in the front row of the female contestants of the Byrrac. She climbed the short set of stairs, stepped on the dais, and walked to the podium. She looked out into the expanse of the Grand Chamber. The view was different than she had thought it would be. She had always believed a person in the audience would be lost and indistinguishable to anyone looking out at them from the dais. To her surprise, she could clearly see the faces of the individuals seated before her. She looked for and, after a moment, found Izzy's face smiling back at her. She smiled at him, hoping he could tell it was meant for him. She closed her eyes. *Verna, thank you for all your love and guidance. I pray I will not disappoint you*, she thought. She opened her eyes. "I, Dera of the Long Tusk Tribe, choose . . . the second-ranked in the Borrac, Kalmar of the Cave Lion Tribe." Whispering erupted in the audience as people turned to talk to those around them.

How wonderful," Nutan said, closing her eyes. "He has been Chosen by the highest-scoring contestant in the history of the Byrrac." She pressed her hand against her chest. "Everything is all right." Her breathing was short and quick. "Shetow is going to get Her Concentration of Traits."

A broad grin spread across Snook's face. "Dera realized Kalmar was the best contestant even though he faltered on the Great Race. Smart girl."

The Medora stepped to the podium and pointed her open hand in Kalmar's direction. "Dera of the Long Tusk Tribe chooses Kalmar of the Cave Lion Tribe as her Pairing Partner."

Still stunned with the turn of events and deep in thought, Kalmar had not heard Dera call his name. It had not occurred to him, with his second-place ranking and his widely known vows to Arasima, that the first-ranked female would choose him. Gwyther slapping his back knocked him out of his stupor.

"What is it? What's wrong?" Kalmar said, blinking his eyes.

"You were chosen by Dera. You are the first chosen."

Confused, Kalmar looked into Gwyther's eyes; they were bright, his smile exuberant. When declared the winner of the Great Race, Gwyther had seemed uncomfortable with the ruling of the judges. It was obvious that Gwyther felt he was not Kalmar's equal. Kalmar knew Gwyther was mistaken.

"Go to the podium, don't keep them waiting," Gwyther said, laughing and pushing Kalmar from his seat.

He glanced at Dera as he walked by her; she had a nondescript look on her face. Her facial birthmark seemed redder than normal, her cheeks flushed. He climbed the steps and walked to the podium. He stood behind the podium in shock—numb. He looked around the chamber until he found Nutan and Snook. Nutan's bright face beamed; Snook's pride for his friend was also unmistakable. He moved his sight to the second-place seat in the female section to his right. Arasima was looking at him; her eyes were big, her face had lost its color. However, most everyone else in the audience was nodding and smiling.

He realized Dera had restored his honor. She had broken many records in her efforts in the Byrrac. Her total score for the Byrrac was far ahead of the old mark. Her name was on everyone's lips as having the greatest Concentration of Traits since the beginning of the Tell. Dera was the culmination of the Traits Geerna and Shetow had hoped the Covenant would produce. To pair with her would restore his damaged pride; their children would be a testament to the glory of Shetow. Kalmar felt confidence flow back into his body. To be chosen by Dera was the key; if she understood he was the best then everyone else would also know it.

He looked at Arasima. Her heaving breast strained against her chemise as she fought for breath. A hint of fear marred her face while finely shaped features testified to her beauty and femininity. He could see the gap in her teeth through her parted lips. He remembered the softness of her naked body against his; his heart beat faster. He ached for her touch. He blinked to regain control of his failing vision and spinning head just like when he faced the cave lion.

He heard his own voice: "I reject the Pairing with Dera and keep myself in the ranking eligible to be Chosen by another." The Chamber went deadly quiet. He first looked at Arasima, whose face was blank. He then found Nutan and Snook. Kalmar expected the look of horror on her face, but he did not expect to find the same look on Snook's.

The Medora moved to the podium, then looked back to Berkana for guidance. There were one, maybe two rejections at every Gathering, but never a rejection of the choices made by the top-ranked females. Kalmar's rejection of Dera was unimaginable to those in the chamber. Yet, Berkana seemed unmoved by Kalmar's actions and raised her hand as a signal for the other Medora to continue. The Medora turned to Kalmar. "If you reject the first female to choose you, you can only be chosen one more time. If you reject a second Choosing, both you and the female who chooses you will forfeit your opportunity for a Pairing and your names will be removed from the rankings. Do you understand?"

"I understand."

"Do you confirm your rejection of your Choosing by Dera of the Long Tusk?"

"I do confirm my rejection," Kalmar said, as he glimpsed Dera standing behind the frail Medora; she showed no emotion.

"Kalmar of the Cave Lion Tribe, you may return to your seat," the Medora said. "Dera of the Long Tusk, you may now make a second choice."

Kalmar walked down the steps as Dera once again approached the podium. As Kalmar took his seat, Gwyther did not look at him, but turned his back towards him. The warmth Gwyther had shown him had now grown cold.

Dera once again stood at the podium. "As is my right," she said in a clear, calm voice, "having once been rejected, I voluntarily ask that my name be removed from the rankings and that I be excused from the Matage."

There was an audible gasp from the audience before a second ripple of whispering crossed the chamber.

"My child." The Medora leaned closer. "Do not make such a rash judgment. Many who were rejected in the past have gone on to be happy with their second choice of Pairing Partners. If you withdraw from the Matage, you'll never have the opportunity to have children . . . your Concentration of Traits will be lost to Shetow and the People."

Dera nodded to the Medora, turned, and walked back to kneel before Berkana. "Medora Roo, I understand the consequences of my actions. Please allow me to withdraw from the Matage as is my right under the Sequa and the Covenant."

"Are you sure you know what you are doing?" Berkana said.

"Yes, my Medora Roo," Dera said, as she bowed her head before the old woman.

Berkana leaned over and spoke in Dera's ear. "Verna often spoke to the Council about you. She believed you to be one of great courage and rare intellect, possibly the possessor of the greatest Concentration of the Traits ever to compete in the games. One truly Blessed by Shetow. Do you believe Verna would have condoned this decision?"

Dera lifted her head and wiped a tear from her cheek. "My Medora Roo, Verna may have questioned my decision but I believe with all my heart she would have supported it."

Berkana leaned back and studied Dera's tear-stained face. After a long pause, she turned to the audience. "Dera of the Long Tusk Tribe," she said loudly, "is released from the Matage." She looked back down. "Rise my child," she said in a softer tone, "may Shetow's love always be with you."

Dera rose, went down the steps, and with head held high, walked towards the back of the chamber. As she walked past Izzy's row of seats, he stood and followed her out.

Dera's actions astonished Kalmar. He never thought she would be so distraught by his rejection that she would withdraw from the Matage. It was unprecedented; neither the Tell nor the Chronicles mentioned such an event. He sat up and rocked his head in a swagger; the trace of a smile etched his lips. He looked around nonchalantly, only to wince when he saw the scowls on the faces of those jeering at him. He lowered his eyes and slid down in his seat.

"I call for The Choosing by the second-ranked female, Arasima of the Red Fox Tribe," the Medora said.

Arasima climbed the steps in perfect posture and glided to the podium. He marveled at the grace and beauty of this woman. The men seated around him hushed at the sight of her. He had waited for this moment for two cycles of the seasons. All was to be set right; the blend and Concentration of his and Arasima's Traits would please Shetow. It might take a little time, but someday everyone would understand his rejection of Dera. In perfect form, Arasima looked towards him—their eyes did not quite meet.

"I, Arasima of the Red Fox Tribe, choose the first ranked in the Borrac, Gwyther of the Brown Owl Tribe," she said in a strong, firm voice.

As Arasima said the words, Kalmar realized she had been looking at Gwyther and not at him. This realization and her words were like a boulder falling on his chest. He could not breathe. His sight faded. Many of those around him did not know he had rejected Dera so Arasima could choose him, but they now guessed it and were telling those next to them. He heard the snickering as the chamber began to spin. He had to have air; as he stood up and stumbled towards the rear of the chamber, the roaring in his ears blocked out the silence that filled the giant hall. He was almost to the exit when supportive arms caught him as he collapsed.

TWENTY-TWO

Mist, as always, covered the lake. A series of ripples interrupted the stillness of the water as they gently rocked Kalmar's boat. The ripples were a new occurrence in his recurring dream. He turned to his left trying to get a glimpse of the object gaining on him. For the first time, through the mist, he could distinguish the outline of another boat. Mist shrouded the occupant of the mysterious boat, but thinned for a moment, revealing other boats in the distance also heading towards the landing. When he turned back, he was approaching the shore. The thick mist billowed around him as he reached the landing. He stepped from the boat onto a wooden wharf that barely rose above the still darkness of the lapping waters of the lake. The mist rolled off a person walking towards him. Straining to see the face of the stranger, he recognized the person; it was Berkana.

"The People need you," she said as she held out her hand. There was movement behind him; he turned to see Snook stepping out of another boat on the other side of the wharf.

Kalmar sprang to a sitting position as he woke up. Disoriented, he looked around the room and saw Snook sitting up in his own bed looking back at him.

———

Snook and Kalmar walked along the promenade towards the Medora's Chamber. "Why didn't you tell me you were also having the dream?" Kalmar said.

"I couldn't. That would have changed your experience in your dream—"

"But we were having the same dream."

"Kalmar, I realized that . . . but I didn't realize we were both in the *same* dream . . . our consciousnesses overlapping. It was a shock to step out of the boat and see you standing on the dock."

"Waking up and finding you sitting in bed looking at me was so eerie." They walked for some time in silence.

"How do you feel?"

"Like dried bat droppings. If we weren't going to meet with Berkana and see if she can explain our dream, I don't think I could've gotten out of bed."

It had stormed that night; however, they were oblivious to the cracks of thunder and the pounding rain against the roof of their cabin. After awakening at the same moment in the dream, they spent the rest of the night talking. At first, Snook tried to be gentle with his friend, but he felt Kalmar had handled the events of the previous day rather badly. As the night progressed, Snook became less sympathetic to Kalmar's plight.

They reached the entrance to the Medora Chamber and Snook knocked on the massive wooden door with his knuckles. The door slowly swung open to reveal a picturesque Cabyl framed by the doorway. He froze in place as his mouth dropped open. He tried to speak but the words would not come. Snook realized he should not have been surprised that Cabyl would be with Berkana, but his mind had been on other matters. He noticed her eyes open wider when she recognized him. As he stammered, he could feel his face flush; he had forgotten how it felt to be near her.

"May we see Berkana?" Kalmar said from behind him.

Cabyl switched her gaze to Kalmar before looking back at Snook. "Please wait here." She closed the door. Snook had detected a tremor in her voice.

"That is odd," Kalmar said.

"What do you mean?"

"Odd that we weren't asked inside."

The door suddenly opened with Berkana at Cabyl's arm. "You wanted to see me?"

Kalmar and Snook looked at each other. Snook raised an eyebrow. They looked back at Berkana and Kalmar stepped forward. "Medora Roo, we were wondering—"

"Wondering *what?*" The old woman's face gave no clue to her thoughts.

"Well." Kalmar hesitated. They had discussed what they would say to Berkana. Both agreed that if she had also had the dream she would readily admit it. Now, she gave no sign anything was out of the ordinary and, it appeared to them, was more aloof than she had ever been to them in the past.

He sensed Kalmar believed Berkana was upset with him about his actions at the Matage the previous day. "We wanted to talk to you about dreams," Snook blurted.

"Dreams, what type of dreams?" she said, eyeing them closely.

"Kalmar and I are in each other's dreams . . . at the same time, and . . ." Berkana looked at Snook, waiting for him to continue. "You are also in our dreams."

"On a lake surrounded by mist?"

They glanced at each other again. "Yes," they said together.

Berkana turned away from them and started to walk back into the chamber. As Cabyl helped Berkana, she turned and looked at them over her shoulder. "Please come inside."

Kalmar and Snook stared at the old woman as she moved away from them. It took a second for them to respond to Cabyl's request; then, they walked through the doorway. In the brightly lit room, the women of the Medora Council sat around their triangular table. As the two walked into the chamber, they saw three other people seated in a group near the table.

"Would you please join the others?" said one of the Medoras as she pointed towards a cluster of empty seats next to the other three people. As Snook and Kalmar turned, one of the three stood up. It was Nutan. They hurried over to her, and after quick hugs, started to speak. Nutan put a finger to her lips and shook her head. Snook and Kalmar took seats on each side of her.

After the initial shock of finding his sister in the council chamber, Kalmar glanced at the other two sitting a few chairs away. The first thing he recognized was Dera's birthmark. He thought he would never see her again, and here she was looking back at him. He expected to see loathing in her eyes; all he got was a faint non-menacing smile. If she was angry with him, her face did not show it. Dera's indifference took him aback. Sitting next to her was a younger male who looked familiar. The young man's eyes were riveted on Kalmar with an expression showing all the rage missing on Dera's face.

The women sitting around the table were talking among themselves in low hushed voices that made it impossible for Snook to understand what they were saying. There was a knock at the door and Cabyl rose from her seat behind Berkana and walked over to answer it. Snook followed the fluid movements of her body; she seemed to glide across the floor to the door. She was so feminine, yet so different from any woman he had ever met.

Cabyl opened the door and talked a moment to someone. She closed the door and walked back to Berkana. When Cabyl finished whispering in Berkana's ear, Berkana stood up, and with Cabyl's help, went to the door. Cabyl opened the door and Berkana talked to the person hidden from view. After a short time, Berkana stepped back to allow someone to enter. Snook could see the person's long hair as Cabyl pointed in his direction. He saw Kalmar's face turn white as Arasima walk towards them. She took a few steps before she recognized Kalmar. She hesitated and averted her eyes as she moved past him, and Nutan, and then on past Dera and the young man to finally sit down by herself.

Izzy had met Dera outside the chamber door. Dera's confession to Berkana about her dreams surprised him. She had not spoken to him about having a recurring dream, but he had not told her about his dreams either. When they entered the chamber, he noticed an attractive young woman sitting by herself twenty or so feet from the Medoras. He could not understand how his vigilant eyes had not discovered her before this. Obeying the instructions of one of the Medoras, he and Dera took seats near the young woman. He maneuvered himself so he had a clear view of her profile. Every time he started to watch the Medoras' activities, his mind and eyes drifted back to her. She held her head and body erect, resting her hands in her lap; her composure was perfect. Her demeanor reminded him of someone, but he was not sure whom.

Later he watched Kalmar and a man he did not recognize, an albino, enter the chamber. Kalmar had shamed his sister; seeing him rekindled his anger. When Kalmar and the albino walked over to the young woman, he watched their interaction closely. For the first time in his life, he felt the pain of jealousy; he wondered if there was a physical relationship between her and either of the men. When Arasima joined them, Izzy was not surprised by

Kalmar's loss of color, but he was mortified by the intensity of the fury in the young woman's face. He felt tightness in his chest. Was it jealousy, he wondered? He swallowed. When he first met Arasima, he could not imagine any other female being so alluring, yet this young woman, with an air of assurance that matched a seasoned hunter, was Arasima's equal.

Dera's lack of emotion when Kalmar appeared was almost as perplexing as his dreams had been. Pushing both these issues to the back of his mind was his curiosity about the enthralling young woman and her relationship to her male companions.

Berkana rose to speak, interrupting his thoughts. "All of you have questions about your dreams. The answer is the same for all of you."

Nutan looked at Kalmar and Snook. She had not missed the stares of the young man sitting next to Dera. For the first time, she let her eyes meet his. He appeared to be her age. Shyness and humility marked his face in a way that reminded her of Snook.

After an extended wait, during which the eyes of the Medoras stayed fixed on the wooden door, the Medora Roo finally focused on the group of six. With the aid of Cabyl, she moved closer to them. The other members of the Medora Council started arranging their chairs to get a better view of their Medora Roo and the group of young men and women.

"My child, I think I had better sit down; please bring me one of those chairs," Berkana said to Cabyl as she pointed, with her walking cane, towards the empty chairs next to Snook.

Without thinking, and before Cabyl could react to Berkana's request, Snook jumped up, grabbed one of the chairs, and carried it to Cabyl. As she stepped forward to take the chair, her hand brushed against his. When their skin touched, their eyes jumped and made contact; for a brief moment, their eyes locked. Cabyl dropped her gaze first and then took the chair and placed it behind Berkana so she could sit down. The Medora Roo eased herself into the chair and rested a moment as Kalmar fidgeted in his seat.

Once settled, the old woman's attention returned to Kalmar and the others. "The six of you have been having the same or similar dreams, the dreams that brought you here. Many others also had the dream, but only you six were compelled enough to come here today. Your dreams"—Berkana swung her right arm and open hand towards the seated Medoras—"were caused by the combined mental projections of this group. Since the last Gathering, we each have been sending out a mental call hoping to determine those among our young with heightened Traits of mental awareness—a Trait the Sequa says Shetow desires in her people, the Trait the council decided to use as the determining factor as to who would represent us in the Second Judging."

Kalmar glanced at Snook and Nutan; their faces were solemn but intense. He stood up. "But Medora Roo"—he dipped his head—"we don't understand, what Second Judging?"

"All of you have questions; in time I'll answer them, but first, I must tell you a story . . . a true story not known by those outside this chamber. It's a story not found in the Tell or Chants of the Sequa; it's the story of the Shetow-ka, passed down through the line of Medoras from the beginning of the Tell." Berkana looked at their questioning faces. "During the time of Geerna, Shetow judged the human race and found them unworthy of existence. Geerna, in a way we do not understand, convinced Shetow to give mankind a second chance . . . she convinced Shetow to perform a Second Judging. The Medoras have been preparing the People for the Second Judging since the first Gathering . . . since the beginning of the Tell. It's the reason we strive for the Concentration of favorable Traits." The youths' attention was set on Berkana, their faces flushed white.

Again, Kalmar started to speak, but Berkana raised her hand. "A few words more before I answer your questions. First, there is nothing false in the Tell or Chants of the Sequa; rather, what we're sharing with you was omitted from these historical pieces. Second, the decision to keep this information from the People was made by Geerna and the Multiped."

Berkana's shoulders drooped. She looked at them, the lines of her face sagging. "Lastly, all of you have been chosen to represent the People at that Judging; our fate rests with you." As her eyes moved from one face to another, she met blank stares. "Kalmar, your question?"

First Kalmar looked at Snook, then Nutan. "I am confused. . . . How were we chosen? What's the Multiped? And I'm not sure I understand the Second Judging."

"We searched for those with the highest mental awareness . . . abilities to sense the feelings of others, those with an acute sense of empathy."

Nutan raised an eyebrow as she glanced at Arasima. Arasima glared back with unflinching eyes.

"We linked our mental capacities together to send out a message to draw you here. We started when we returned to our villages after the last Gathering. Your Medoras selected your names, along with the names of a number of other possible candidates. The call was weak at first but strengthened as we assembled at this year's Gathering. As our call intensified so did the dreams. For most, the dreams were a nuisance; for a very few"—a sweep of her hand indicated them—"they provoked action. You're the ones who came; you possess the highest level of these Traits among the people."

Kalmar frowned and looked down. His arms were heavy, his breathing shallow.

"The dreams," Berkana said, a little more animated, "were only a method to identify which ones of you possessed the highest

Concentration of these Traits . . . the dreams were just a test. As to the Multiped, the Shetow-ka tells us that it was a creature, neither human nor drak, who served as Shetow's representative in dealing with Geerna. What else the Shetow-ka says to us about the Multiped is not understood. We only know it is much larger than a man." She shifted her position in her chair; lines crossed her brow. "And it was engulfed in a green cloud."

The six sat in complete silence.

Then Arasima jumped up. "What did you mean . . . 'our fate rests with you'?"

"As I said, at the time of Geerna, before the First Progression, the People were judged by Shetow and found to be unworthy. Geerna, with the aid of the Multiped, persuaded Shetow to give them, us, a second chance, a Second Judging. Geerna believed if judged unworthy a second time, we would be destroyed. The Covenant between Geerna, again aided by the Multiped, and Shetow, laid out the framework of a plan to increase the Concentration of the Traits, thus improving the People's worth to Shetow. You are the culmination of that process."

"How do you know the time is now?" Dera said in a subdued tone.

"The drak brought us the word. They did not tell us how they knew."

"Why did Geerna think it was so important that the People not know about the judging?" Izzy said.

Berkana looked down at the floor and then turned to look at the other Medoras before turning back to the small group. "She feared it would cause panic. Geerna and the Multiped believed the knowledge of the Second Judging and its possible consequences would only cause despair, despair that could sap the People's will to continue."

Dera shook her lowered head and whispered, "Verna knew all this."

"Verna predicted you would be one of those to answer our call," Berkana said, looking at Dera. "She believed you were our best chance."

Dera looked away, blinking back tears. Nutan watched Dera. Snook looked at Dera, then at Kalmar. Kalmar appeared dazed. Izzy looked at his sister before his eyes drifted back to Nutan. Arasima looked straight ahead.

Berkana's eyes took the measure of each one in the group. She cleared her throat and waited until she regained everyone's attention. "We must continue. The Shetow-ka is an unwritten account of what took place between Geerna and the Multiped, the things not in the Chants of the Sequa. After the Multiped, at Geerna's urging, persuaded Shetow to hold a Second Judging, Geerna and the Multiped felt there needed to be a mechanism to guide and prepare the People. With Shetow's approval, Geerna formed the Medora Council." Berkana stopped and motioned to Cabyl for a glass of water. Cabyl retreated from the room and quickly returned with a small metallic cylinder in her hand. Once finished with her drink, Berkana continued. "The Shetow-ka was passed down through the Medoras by word of mouth, from before the first Gathering, before the beginning of the Tell, and before the first inscriptions on the face of Mount Alar. You three men are the first males to hear what I'm about to tell you. You three women"—Berkana nodded towards Cabyl, whose face became even whiter than normal with Berkana's unexpected reference to her—"will be the first females to hear this, besides Cabyl, who were not Medoras."

Berkana stopped, took in a deep breath, and then slowly let it out. She had the attention of everyone in the chamber. "The Shetow-ka tells us Geerna and the other humans on Elom at the time of the Covenant weren't born on this world. They were born on a world with only one moon and fewer stars, a world that didn't have the draks. It was a cold place bordered by mountains of ice.

Shetow plucked Geerna and the other humans from our home world and brought them to Elom. It was not until after the Covenant that Shetow brought the mammoth, prairie buck, and other animals from our home world to Elom.

"As part of the judging, Geerna was placed in a dark room where she went into a deep sleep. When she awoke, she possessed great knowledge and was able to communicate with the Multiped. Shetow, through the Multiped, made Geerna Her spokesperson to the other humans. When the People failed the judging, Geerna begged the Multiped to intercede for us with Shetow to give her and the Multiped a chance to help us strengthen the Traits Shetow found inadequate. Shetow agreed. Shetow then entered into the Covenant with Geerna, through the Multiped. The Multiped then agreed to aid Geerna in our preparations for the Second Judging. The Multiped told Geerna it did not know when the Second Judging was going to take place so Geerna spent the rest of her life working with the Multiped preparing the People for that day. Since Geerna's death there has been no communication with the Multiped; the draks have been our only link to Shetow's wishes."

"Medora Roo, does that mean the Matage is just a way to prepare for the Second Judging?" Dera said.

"Everything in our society is a preparation for the Second Judging, my child."

"There is something not right about this," Dera said to no one in particular.

"You are correct," Berkana said, "and Geerna felt the same way."

"How can that be, since Geerna is the one who agreed to the Covenant?"

"Correct again, but that doesn't mean Geerna agreed with everything in the Covenant."

"Medora Roo, I am having trouble following you," Dera shot back.

"The Shetow-ka tells us Geerna realized there was a lot that she did not understand. Her sleep in the dark room had made her smarter . . . actually, the Shetow-ka implies it was not that she felt smarter but that she understood more . . . ideas appeared in her head like recalling lost memories. Anyway, Geerna began to believe the Shetow she was talking to on this new world was not the same Shetow she had worshiped on the world of her birth."

"There are *two* Shetows?" Izzy said.

"We do not know how many Shetows there are; maybe each world has its own Shetow. Geerna believed this new Shetow wanted her to believe They were the same so She could control her and the others easier. At first she thought the new Shetow was evil and had stolen her and the other humans from the real Shetow. However, in time, she came to believe the new Shetow was not trying to harm Her new subjects and really was disappointed the People hadn't been judged worthy . . . otherwise, the new Shetow would not have agreed to a Second Judging. Because Geerna believed the new Shetow was trying to hide Her true identity, Geerna engaged in her own subterfuge by putting in place ways to keep the new Shetow from completely controlling the lives of Geerna's people."

"But Medora Roo, Shetow does control every facet of our lives," Arasima said in her sultry voice.

"That's almost correct, but here we are talking among ourselves about the truth, a truth we've been able to keep alive for six Progressions . . . and there is something else." Berkana turned to Cabyl. "Please bring me a wet cloth." Cabyl left the chamber, quickly returned, and handed Berkana a white hand towel with water dripping from it. Berkana wiped her forehead and face with the cloth. Cabyl reached to retrieve the cloth but Berkana shook her head. "Pull up the sleeve of your left arm and look at the inside of your forearm." Everyone in the group did as the Medora said. "What do you see?"

"The Mark of the Covenant," Izzy said as the others nodded in agreement.

"And what does the Mark mean?"

"A sign of our devotion to Shetow?" Izzy replied.

"Or is it a sign of Shetow's control over us," Berkana said as she looked at their questioning faces. "Cabyl, take this wet cloth and rub Snook's Mark."

Cabyl moved slowly as she took the cloth from Berkana and walked over to Snook. Holding her head down, she raised her eyelids to look up into his chalky face. A slight curve formed on his white lips as he watched her walk towards him. As she neared him, he stood up. *Why is Berkana putting me through this,* she wondered. *Berkana knows of my terror of men; all I have ever known from men is pain and degradation.* As the others watched, she started rubbing Snook's forearm; she looked past him and saw the confusion on Dera and the other's faces. She first tried to rub Snook's arm without holding it, but was not able to apply any pressure. After a few rubs, she stopped and looked back at Berkana. Berkana indicated with a flip of her wrist for her to continue. Avoiding Snook's eyes and with slumped shoulders, Cabyl grabbed Snook's wrist with her left hand, and with the cloth in her right hand, started rubbing again. She could feel Snook staring at the top of her head as she tried to keep her attention focused on his arm. Blood rushed to her face. After rubbing a few moments, she lowered the cloth and stepped back as she saw that Snook's Mark had almost disappeared. She heard a gasp behind her and she turned to see Nutan with her hand covering her mouth; beside Nutan sat Kalmar, shaking his head, with a grin covering his face. She glanced at Snook out of the corner of her eye; he was looking straight at her.

Berkana pointed to Snook. "Since Geerna did not completely trust the new Shetow, she had a third of the people slip away and hide until after the first Koo Toc Biren ceremony was performed; at that ceremony, everyone, adults and children—except for the ones that slipped away—were given the Mark. Snook was not born a member of one of the Twenty-Four Tribes. He is a Mookyn—one of the free people. Snook is a descendant of those Geerna had slip away before the first Koo Toc Biren."

Cabyl still held Snook's arm. Entranced by Berkana's revelation, she forgot he was standing next to her. All of a sudden, she looked down, dropped his arm, and jumped back as she turned to face him. Her face revealed amazement laced with a trace of fear. Snook looked back at Cabyl with the sheepish grin of a little boy caught doing something stupid. He glanced at the others in their group. Dera and Izzy's faces showed their surprise. Arasima seemed to be reevaluating him. Kalmar had the satisfied look of someone given the answer to a riddle that had aggravated him for months. Nutan was shaking her head, her lips pulled tight against her teeth. She had the look of a person who knew she had allowed her personal feelings to cause her to ignore the fact that he was very smart to be so dumb.

"The Medora are the only ones among the People who know about the Mookyn's existence. They usually only travel into the lands of the Twenty-Four Tribes to trade or contact members of the Medora Council, and they do that as sparingly as possible. Snook represents one of those rare occasions when the Elders of the Mookyn sent one of their own, what the Mookyn call a Seeker, among the tribes to gather information. That there would be a Second Judging was also a closely kept secret among the Mookyn, only known by their Elders and their apprentices, the Seekers."

Kalmar was the first to recover from Berkana's revelation; really, he was not shocked at all. He had known from the time he had first met Snook that he was different. "Do you really think that Shetow . . . does not know the Mookyn exist?"

Berkana smiled. "Good question. It does try our belief in a Supreme Being. If Shetow is capable of creating and ruling over the stars, how could She not know the Mookyn exist? The Medoras and the Elders have debated this question since the time of Geerna. The Mookyn, after countless generations of being away from Shetow's control, do not believe in Her deity and believe She is fallible. The Medoras, even with much reason for doubt, believe Shetow, if not a God, is still our benevolent guardian. We still believe Shetow knows all, including the existence of the Mookyn."

"We worship a God who either knows we are trying to fool Her, or She is not a God at all," Dera said in a voice just loud enough to be heard. Nutan's face turned pale as she turned to look at Dera.

"I cannot answer your question with certainty. I can, though, give you a few thoughts that will not make your pondering any easier." Berkana paused before continuing.

"First, it is obvious that Shetow exists—or that something greater and more powerful than we are controls Elom. This entity has virtual control over our lives no matter if She, or It, is or is not omnipotent and omniscient . . . the power Shetow has is far greater than we can understand." Berkana raised her hands chest high. "If She has control over the lives of the Mookyn, She has chosen not to utilize it."

"What do you mean?" Nutan asked.

Berkana raised her arm to reveal her Mark. "The Mark of the Covenant—why do we have it?"

"To show our devotion to Shetow?" Izzy blurted out, glancing at the others in the group and shrugging his shoulders.

"The Elders of the Mookyn, and more than a few of the Medoras, think it is for a different reason. Snook, do you have any siblings?"

"No."

The others stared at him. Snook noticed that although the other Medoras showed no surprise at his answer, the look on Cabyl's face revealed she wasn't privy to that information.

"How old was your mother when you were born?"

His knees became wobbly. The Medora Roo would ask about the one subject that he had never discussed with anyone since his mother's death. The Elders had known of this vulnerability and never broached the subject; it was the one flaw in his psyche. A flaw, he knew, he must conquer before joining the men and women who comprised the Elders.

Snook took a deep breath and then counted in his head. "She was twenty-five cycles of the seasons when I was born."

"And your father, how old was he?"

"He was fifteen cycles of the seasons older than my mother."

"Among the Mookyn, many are childless," Berkana said, "but any female who so wishes can bear children and couples choose each other without a Matage. There's no set order for which cycles of the seasons children will be born or the sex they'll be when they are born. . . . Many of the Mookyn men aren't hunters and only a few of their females are artists." Berkana's eyes moved from one to the next. "The Mookyn Elders and most of the Medoras believe the Mark of the Covenant has something to do with the sex and timing of the birth of our children. As best we can determine, the Mark is something that is implanted under our skin with properties that allow Shetow to regulate certain functions of our bodies."

"If that is true, Shetow is not a God, or at least She is not omnipotent and omniscient," Dera said in a matter-of-fact tone.

"How can *you* be so sure?" Arasima said in a condescending tone. "The Mookyn could be part of Shetow's Divine Plan. We don't have any real evidence that Shetow doesn't know the Mookyn exist." She squared her shoulders and glared at Dera.

"Yes my child, how can you be so sure?" Berkana asked in a soft and caring voice.

Dera was oblivious to Arasima's verbal slap and looked at Berkana. "If Shetow knows or does not know of the existence of the Mookyn is not the question; it is the existence of the Mark . . . or more precisely Shetow's use of the Mark."

"I am not sure I understand what you are saying," Berkana said.

"If Shetow were omnipotent and omniscient, She could control the number and sex of our children without the use of the Mark."

There was a long silence. Then Nutan turned to face Dera. "But I wonder if Shetow is benevolent and is controlling the birth of our children because of our reverence for Her by wearing Her Mark . . . I mean, well, maybe it's not the Mark itself that is doing the controlling . . . maybe Shetow only controls those who honor Her by wearing Her Mark. It is possible Shetow is allowing the Mookyn to choose their mates at random . . . like the animals in the wild." Nutan noticed Snook's squinted eyes and scrunched brow but continued talking. "Shetow could know of the Mookyn's existence, choosing not to control their births, and looks with favor only on those who follow the terms of the Covenant." Nutan stopped, thought, and then added, "You know, Shetow could be punishing the Mookyn for their dishonor of Her by not having the Mark."

"Punishing us . . . *how?*" Snook stammered as he switched his attention to Nutan.

"By not concentrating your Traits," Arasima injected. "Without the Matage . . . without a plan . . . a system to have males and females with superior Traits mate, the Mookyn—it seems to me— have a very chaotic method of improving the species."

"If not punishment," Izzy added, "it could be indifference. Shetow might not care about the Mookyn at all and is ignoring them." Izzy beamed as Nutan's eyes met his and she nodded her agreement.

"We do not pair to improve the species," Snook said, gritting his teeth. "We pair out of love for one another."

Dera's heart raced at Snook's words. Then she turned towards Nutan. "Your premise is flawed."

"Flawed? How?"

"You must not forget," Dera said with no malice in her voice, "that Snook was brought here by the same dream as the rest of us. A dream projected to a select few at the Gathering by the combined efforts of all the Medoras as a test to find those among us who have the strongest Concentration of the Traits most desired by Shetow. Snook was the only Mookyn attending the Gathering and he felt the Medora's call. Of all those from the Twenty-Four Tribes, only we five answered their call."

"Are you suggesting," Nutan said, "the Mookyn have a higher Concentration of the Traits than the Twenty-Four Tribes?"

"No, but it does appear that some of the Mookyn," Dera nodded towards Snook, "have some of the Traits that Shetow finds desirable."

Nutan scrunched her face, thought a moment, and then reluctantly nodded.

Dera's eyes moved to Snook. "If Shetow does not know of you now, She will learn soon enough."

"At the Judging," Izzy said.

A weak smile crossed Dera's face.

Berkana raised her hand to stop the whispering. "We must not forget why you are here. God or not, Shetow was powerful enough to transport our ancestors to this planet and no doubt powerful enough to destroy us if She so desires." She raised both arms.

"Whatever the case, the Medora Council has chosen the seven of you to represent us at the Second Judging."

Those in the group looked at each other. "There're only six of us," Kalmar said.

"No, there are seven. Cabyl will also be one of your group," Berkana said. She glanced back at Cabyl, who was standing behind her. Cabyl's face lost what little color it had as she dropped her eyes. After a moment, she raised her eyes; all but two of her new companions greeted her with friendly smiles. Arasima frowned and Snook displayed a toothy grin.

A loud knock at the chamber door grabbed their attention. Berkana's expression revealed trepidation as she indicated that Cabyl should go see who was knocking. Cabyl walked to the door and opened it just enough to look out. She stuck her head out, then quickly stepped back as the door swung open.

TWENTY-THREE

Two draks entered the chamber, looked around, saw Berkana, and scurried over to her. The reptiles' quickness and agility always amazed her; the counterbalance of their long tails allowed body movements unimaginable for humans. She eyed the two intruders. Although it was difficult for humans to differentiate one drak from another, these two appeared to be the same ones who had brought them the news of the pending Second Judging a year earlier and performed the Koo Toc Biren ceremony on the second day of the Gathering.

The larger of the two draks held back a few paces as the smaller one walked up to her. "Medora Roo, these must be the ones the Medoras have chosen to represent your species at the Judging."

The drak's jumbled words were not in perfect synchronization with the movement of the creature's large mouth. Draks spoke in tones impossible to mistake for human speech. The vocal sounds of the reptiles were quite disconcerting for Snook; unlike the rest of the group, he had not spent his whole life around the drak traders—he found their speech unnatural and spooky. He stepped back as the reptiles moved closer to Berkana.

"They are," Berkana said in a commanding voice as she made

a slight bow. "How did you know we had chosen the ones to be judged?"

"We have monitored the situation closely since we spoke with you last year. Your judging is of great interest to us. We . . . the draks think you have chosen well."

"When will you start the Judging?" she said, trusting she showed none of the strain she was feeling. She glanced at the young people, upon whose abilities rested the fate of their race. Their faces appeared anxious as they looked at the drak, waiting for its answer.

"As we told you at our last meeting, we are only the messengers; draks aren't the ones who will judge your people."

Berkana cocked her head. "Then who will?"

A few seconds passed before the drak answered. "We are not sure who will be your final judges nor do we know on what basis the Judging will be scored. As we told you earlier . . ." the drak had no facial expressions humans could read, but it did seem to Berkana that the drak's eyes softened ". . . as we told you last year, we believe there are powerful forces that want you to fail."

The drak's words of warning generated whispers. The information was not new to the Medora Council, but the drak's revelation caught those in the group completely by surprise.

The smaller drak's eyelids flicked over its disproportionately large catlike eyes as its head bobbed in unsettling jerks. "We will collect them at dawn two days from now." Their reptilian visitor stood perfectly still as it eyed the group. Snook stared back at the fearsome lizard and for a moment he felt like a field mouse hypnotized by a grass snake's gaze. "They are to bring only one small bag," the drak finally said, as it turned back towards Berkana, "to carry personal items; they will be supplied with all their other needs." The two draks, with birdlike quickness, turned, their long tails whipping behind them, and hurried out of the chamber before the humans could ask another question.

For a long time no one spoke. The only sound Snook could hear was the shallow breathing of those around him. He turned and found Nutan staring at him, her face painted in confusion.

"What did the drak mean by powerful forces wanting us to fail?" Dera asked.

"We do not know," Berkana said. "I can only tell you it is the same thing they told us at the last Gathering, when they first told us the Second Judging was coming." Cabyl rushed to aid Berkana as she started to rise from her seat. Berkana looked at the group. "Now go and put your affairs in order. Do not talk to anyone outside this room about what you are about to do . . . tell your tribe members we've asked you to stay behind after the Gathering to do some repair work on the Medoras' compound. We will meet with you at dusk on the night before you leave." She looked at them. "Do not worry. We are sure we have chosen the very best to represent us. It is important that you do not let yourselves be overwhelmed by the task before you. Now go," she said wistfully. All of the group but Cabyl stood and made their way towards the outside entrance to the chamber. Cabyl was still at Berkana's side, holding on to her right arm. Berkana patted Cabyl's hand. "Cabyl, my child, you have a new job to perform, now go with the others, I will be all right."

"May I stay with you until it is time for us to leave?"

"Cabyl, you need—"

"Berkana, since . . . since the death of my mother . . . there is no one I need to tell anything to . . . you are the only person I am close to . . . you are the only person who will miss me."

Berkana studied her young novice; a sad, almost pleading look filled Cabyl's eyes. Berkana knew more about Cabyl than Cabyl realized. "Cabyl, you have not asked how you came to be one of those chosen to represent us at the judging."

Cabyl lowered her gaze. "I did not have the dream." She raised her gaze to look at the old woman. "I only have nightmares."

"You did not have the dreams because we did not send you a mental message."

Cabyl started to speak.

"The Medoras chose you at the last Gathering to be one of those who would represent us."

"I—I—" Cabyl sputtered.

"Out of the seven of you who are going, you were the only one we knew, for sure, before today. Cabyl, the members of the Medora Council know and love you; we are all going to miss you . . . every day you are gone. No matter what happens"— Berkana reached up and brushed back a few stray strands of hair hanging across Cabyl's face—"you must never forget how very special you are to us." Berkana watched a smile slowly creep across Cabyl's delicate features. "Cabyl, I would be most honored to have your company until you and the others leave; it will give us time to review what we have been discussing for the last five days."

As Cabyl walked away with her eyes lowered, the red-haired Reva walked up to Berkana. "Why are you allowing the Mookyn to go as one of our representatives?"

Berkana thought of her promise to Snook and turned to face the younger Medora. "The Mookyn's fate is also at stake; they deserve to have a representative and, without Snook, the Equilibrium of the group is even more out of balance."

Kalmar, Snook, and Nutan left the chamber a few steps ahead of Dera, Izzy, and Arasima. They watched Dera and Izzy walk off in deep discussion. Arasima walked by herself down a pathway towards her tribe's compound. Izzy smiled at Nutan as he and Dera walked by her, but Nutan focused on Dera, who nodded and returned Nutan's smile. "I think I am going to like that woman," Nutan said after Dera and Izzy walked passed them.

Snook had made note of the fact that Izzy had been watching

Nutan all that morning. He had also noticed that Nutan had missed much of Izzy's obvious gawking. "I think there is some positive feeling about you, too," Snook said, then chuckled to himself when Nutan completely missed the point of his teasing remark. He shook his head. How was it that some women seemed oblivious to their effect on men while others—he glanced at the accented swish of Arasima's hips as she walked away—were so perfectly attuned?

"Can we talk? I missed the meaning of some of what Berkana said," Kalmar said.

"Good idea," Snook replied.

"I agree. I have some questions too . . . and a few of them are for you, Snook," Nutan added.

"Okay, but can we eat first?" Snook said. The other two nodded in agreement and they started walking back to their compound.

What will Gwyther think about Arasima going off like this right after their Pairing, Kalmar wondered. Fate has also dealt Gwyther a painful blow: Arasima chose him as her Pairing Partner and, before they could return to her village, she is ushered away from him for some unknown time. A spiteful sense of revenge clouded his thoughts. This will cause Arasima problems. Then his thoughts turned to Gwyther. Guilt wrestled with his rage toward Arasima; how could he wish anguish on a man who had only shown him kindness and support. He felt sympathy for Gwyther, who would not be satisfied with the explanation that the Medoras have asked Arasima, his new Pairing Partner, to remain at the Gathering compound to do some repair work. He nodded to himself; of all the members of their group, Arasima would find the next two days to be the hardest.

Izzy and Dera talked long into the night. "I don't understand how you can be so calm around Kalmar . . . now we have to go . . . who knows where . . . with him, to face . . . who knows what, to be judged by some unknown . . . whatever. I just don't understand."

"Izzy, I don't have any hard feelings towards Kalmar."

"I can see that, but why not? I mean . . . you were the highest ranked—"

She held up her hand to stop his ranting. Izzy had always been there for her; why was it so hard for her to be truthful with him now? "If you think so little of him, you should be happy that I didn't end up Paired to him." She raised an eyebrow. "You wouldn't want me tied to someone that unspeakable, would you?" She could tell Izzy knew she was playing with him, but the look on his face showed both his bewilderment about her attitude towards Kalmar and his continuing strong feelings about the subject. She played one last angle to defuse Izzy's anger. "Besides, you had better learn to control your feelings if you hope to have any luck with that cute sister of his."

"Sister . . . she's his sister?" Izzy exclaimed, as Dera grinned and nodded. Izzy rolled his eyes as he exhaled a heavy sigh.

The next day and a half went by fast. Part of the time, Kalmar walked along the rock face of Alar studying the evolution of his civilization; he inspected the handprints, drawings, and ideograms that covered the vast majority of the Chronicles before reading passages of the text, which started near the end of the Fifth Progression, only a few hundred cycles of the seasons earlier. Nutan took Snook to the Koo Toc—the ceremony held the day after the Matage where the choosing females and the chosen males were officially Paired. Kalmar noticed that neither Nutan nor Snook spoke to him about the ceremony when they rejoined him later that day. It was obvious they thought he might be upset if they talked about it. He did not think to tell them he just needed to be by himself.

The three walked together to the Medora Chamber. The hills on each side of Mount Alar were gradually blocking the last rays of the setting Salune. The evening breeze was beginning to flow down the face of Alar, rustling the leaves of the nutwood trees spaced along the pathways that led to the promenade bordering the front of the great mountain. The cool air felt refreshing on Kalmar's face as he and his two companions reached the part of the promenade in front of the Great Chamber. When they stepped off the dirt pathway and onto the promenade, they took a half turn and angled left as they walked across the promenade's close-cut grass surface. The three continued walking while the breeze increased and the last of the day's light ended. A man walked towards them lighting a row of torches along the centerline of the promenade; the flickering flames formed a line of shimmering globes of illumination that stretched behind the man like a trail of giant fireflies. Kalmar, Snook, and Nutan passed the three main entrances of the Great Chamber that interrupted the smooth perfection of the sheer vertical rock face of the mountain before they approached the smaller, solitary doorway to the Medora Chamber.

When they drew near the entrance, Kalmar saw Dera and the young man with whom she had left their last meeting walking towards them. Because of the angle of their approach, Kalmar had not noticed them until they walked through the line of torches. As Dera walked in front of one of the torches, its light shone through the flimsy material of her clothing. He could see the well-defined outline of her body; an unexpected sensation flooded his body. When you could not see her blemish, she's quite lovely, he thought to himself. A flurry of thoughts flooded his mind; with sunken eyes and turned down lips he struggled against his melancholy disposition.

The two groups reached the Medora Chamber doorway at the same time. Dera stopped beside the young man; he gave them a slight bow and indicated with a sweeping motion of his left arm for the three of them to enter the chamber first. Nutan and Snook joined him in returning the bow. Snook opened the door so they could enter. He noticed the beginning of a smile on Dera's face as she first looked at the young man and then at Nutan. The young man also smiled but kept his eyes fixed on Nutan. Kalmar could see Nutan was also smiling; however, Nutan seemed not to notice the young man's look, focusing her attention instead on Dera. It was now clear to Kalmar, by the young man's gawking at Nutan and the amusement it gave Dera, that Dera and the young man were not romantically involved. For the first time in three days, he felt a smile form on his lips; Nutan had an admirer and she appeared unaware of the intensity of the infatuation. A picture of a nude Nutan sleeping in Snook's arms, a scene he had seen three days earlier, flashed in his mind. He looked at Snook and found an unreadable expression covering his friend's face, one more of amusement than of jealousy. He had not broached what he had seen to either Nutan or Snook. If his sister was going to have a relationship with a man before her Pairing, Snook was as good as she could find. There would not be a problem tossing both men into such a small group as long as Nutan did not begin making eyes back at the young man.

All five entered the chamber together. Arasima was already there, as were Berkana and the other members of the Medora Council. Berkana indicated that they should sit in two rows of chairs that had been arranged next to the Medora table—four chairs on the back row and three on the front row. Arasima was already sitting in the first row in the far right chair. The young man and Dera took seats behind Arasima with Dera sitting in the right-inside chair and the young man taking the end chair. Nutan quickly took the chair next to Dera. Dera smiled at Nutan as Nutan laid her hand on Dera's arm. Dera reached over and squeezed Nutan's hand. Kalmar knew Dera and his sister did not know each other, yet, they seemed so . . . so friendly. He wondered if Dera realized that Nutan was his sister. Dera must know there was some type of relationship between him and Nutan, but Dera appeared to hold no animosity towards Nutan. Actually, the only person who seemed to care about his rejection of Dera was the young man who was always with her.

Kalmar studied the remaining seating options, decided not to sit on the row with Arasima, and sat on the back row next to Nutan in the far left seat. He noticed Snook's hesitation before sitting in the far left seat on the front row. Now the only seat not filled was the middle seat on the front row between Snook and Arasima. The doorway leading to the Grand Chamber abruptly opened and Cabyl entered the room; her movements were hurried but deliberate, those of someone who knew she was late.

Hurriedly, Cabyl walked over to her normal place; a chair positioned behind Berkana. As Cabyl took her seat, Berkana leaned over to her. "My child, you must go sit with the others. Your duty to me is now complete. Your duty to the People has now begun."

Kalmar heard Berkana's words and saw what little color Cabyl had leave her face as she rose to walk over to join them. With her gaze at her feet, she took a step before realizing the only unoccupied chair was next to Snook. She averted her eyes from him, walked over, and sat down. Snook sat up as Cabyl took her seat; Arasima only glanced at her.

Berkana cleared her throat as she stood to speak. "Tomorrow morning you will leave with the draks to be judged. We cannot tell you where they will take you or how you will be judged. We do not know how long the Judging will take, when . . . or if you will ever return to us."

Berkana's words struck Kalmar with a force he had not anticipated. His eyes opened wider; up until that moment, he had been wallowing in his own feelings of shame and rejection. He sat a little straighter and squared his shoulders. She was not telling them any-thing she had not already told them. What was different?

". . . as we've told you, we do have the information Geerna passed down to us through the Shetow-ka; Geerna formed the Medora Council and had each member memorize its message. The Medoras have passed that message from the way she first told it to the original Medoras to how we now recite it, unchanged, six Pro-gressions later. Geerna knew the more we understood and the more we prepared, the more we increased the People's chances at the time of the Second Judging."

"Does the Shetow-ka explain what we must do to . . . to pass the Judging?" Snook asked.

"No, the Shetow-ka was not meant to instruct us on how to . . . to pass, as you put it, but was more of a guide to the Medoras on how to prepare for it." Berkana studied the faces of the young people seated before her. "Geerna also thought it important for you to understand that you were to be judged not only for the fate of the People, but also for the fate of the human race that still lives on our home world." She hesitated as the expressions on their faces showed even greater confusion. From what Berkana had told them, Kalmar realized there must still be another world populated by dif-ferent tribes, but still of the People. However, it had not occurred to him that there was still a connection between the peoples of the two worlds.

"Geerna was correct," Berkana started again, "in thinking the Judging could take place far enough in the future that the People would have forgotten or quit believing in the stories of our origin—"

"I do not understand, Berkana," Dera said. "The story of Geerna does not make sense." Kalmar had been thinking the same thing and he noticed Snook and Arasima both nodding their heads in agreement.

"What do you mean, my child?" Berkana asked softly.

"The Tell, and later the text of the Chronicles, say at the time of the first Gathering, the People could not read or write. How could such a primitive society produce someone of Geerna's intellect?"

Berkana nodded as if she had expected such a question. "The Shetow-ka informs us that Geerna was only a young girl when she and the others were transported to Elom. Geerna was in her village on our home world when Shetow lifted her, in a bright light, into some type of transport. Once inside the transport, Geerna found herself in a large room with the floor, walls, and ceiling made of metal. The light in the room alternated between dim and bright for periods that seemed to correspond to day and night. The people were petrified, and at first, were too frightened to sleep. After a few cycles of the lights changing intensities, Geerna and the others collapsed into an exhausted slumber. When she awoke, she was alone and strapped down on a padded table. . . ." Kalmar glanced at the other members of the group. Berkana had their complete attention. "The table was in a small, dimly lit room with walls that were covered with multicolored blinking lights. She was conscious for only a few moments before there was movement at the end of the table behind where her head lay. Seized with fear, she closed her eyes right before she felt something being placed against her temples. She kept her eyes tightly shut and did not see anything that followed. She remembered an odor similar to burning grass that started faint and pungent before slowly becoming sharp and caustic like the stench of mammoth urine. The last thing she remembered before losing consciousness was the suffocating smell and a high-pitched sound like the screech of an eagle. When she awoke, she was again in the large room with the other humans but her head was full of memories of things she had never experienced. Not only was she more intelligent but she was also wiser. She woke up full of questions and the intellect to try to answer them."

"Did Geerna know why Shetow chose her to receive these memories . . . this mental gift?" Snook asked.

"Geerna believed her age was the reason Shetow chose her to communicate with Her intermediary, the Multiped; she believed Shetow chose the youngest adult."

"Why didn't Shetow increase the intelligence of all the humans?" Dera asked.

"The Shetow-ka is silent about this great mystery."

"If Shetow had increased the intelligence of all the humans," Arasima spoke up, a smirk on her face, "there would have been no one for Her to torment." Everyone in the room turned to look at Arasima, but no one responded to her remark. She met the astonishment in their eyes with calculated coolness.

"Berkana," the young man seated next to Dera finally said, "would not it be wise for one of you . . . one of the Medoras . . . to come with us?"

Kalmar sat up. *That's a good idea.* Why had he not thought of it?

"I realize," the young man continued, "it might be hard for you, but maybe another—"

"Some of my Sisters are young enough to take the rigors of the trip, but you seven are the ones who we have chosen to go. The job of the Medoras was to prepare you, not accompany you."

"But Berkana, we go without a full understanding of the Shetow-ka. Surely one of the group should have a grasp of it," Dera added.

"We also believe someone in the group should have this knowledge." Berkana slowly made her way over to stand in front of them. "At the end of the last Gathering, the Council chose the first of your group and started teaching her the Shetow-ka. Until two days ago, Cabyl was my novice. She thought her purpose in life was to serve me and, maybe, someday become a Medora." Kalmar saw Cabyl look down as the attention of the group turned to her.

"It is only now that she understands why she was taught the Shetow-ka." Berkana tottered over, using her cane, and placed her right hand on the back of Cabyl's bowed head.

Sitting behind them, Kalmar had a clear view of both Cabyl and Snook. Kalmar could see the left side of Snook's face as he turned his head to look at Cabyl sitting in the seat to his left. Snook was infatuated with Cabyl the first time the two had met, but the look Kalmar now saw on Snook's face was one of admiration.

"Cabyl will carry the words of Geerna in her head; you will have everything the Medora Council could possibly tell you with you when you leave tomorrow."

Cabyl kept her head bowed. Kalmar remembered what Snook had said after he'd first met Cabyl. "There was something mysterious about this delicate young woman." He could tell by the way Snook looked at her, the same remembrance also filled his mind.

"There is something else the Medoras would like you to carry with you to the Judging." Berkana turned and motioned for a small leather bundle lying on the triangular table to be brought to her. Once in Berkana's hands, she cuddled the bundle like a newborn but held it so it was visible to everyone in the group. "This belonged to Geerna." She loosened the rawhide bindings before carefully unwrapping the leather covering. The last folds of the soft hide unfurled, revealing a thumb-sized object. Berkana held it up for them to see. "This figurine represented Shetow, the Bringer of Life, the Great Earth Mother, to the members of Geerna's tribe. Geerna had it with her when she was taken from her village."

Kalmar and the others strained to get a good look at the carving.

"The carving is crude; the Shetow-ka says the Medora of Geerna's tribe used flint chips to carve it out of a piece of mammoth ivory." Berkana held the figurine a little higher. "It is because of this carving that we hold the long tusks in such reverence. This carved piece of mammoth tusk is the only fragment of our true home that we possess. Geerna tells us that many of the animals on Elom were on Earth, but some of them she did not recognize. Only animals she recognized were used in the naming of our tribes." Berkana handed the carving to Snook; Kalmar noticed how Snook cradled the ivory carving with both hands to be sure not to drop it. "Here . . . you can feel the power that radiates from it. Draw strength from it. This carving represents our home world; it represents who we are." Berkana then looked directly at Snook. "Pass it around . . . feel its power."

Kalmar watched as the carving made its way down the front row to Arasima, who, after looking at it, turned and carefully handed it behind her to the young man next to Dera. The carving then passed to Dera, who later handed it to Nutan, who finally handed it to him. Once in his hands, he turned the carving over. He studied its artisanship; he could make out the feminine form of the figurine. It was hard for him to imagine a female creating the object; he was used to females producing art of an infinitely superior quality. The carving's protrusions accentuated the reproductive areas of the female, while the rest of the anatomy was barely distinguishable or nonexistent. At first, he thought it was a sexual object; the carving's exaggerated breast and the slit of the vulva were clearly visible while the head was disproportionately small and the hands and feet were missing completely. After close study, he surmised the carving's bulges were not meant to excite the sexual nature of a male, but to accent the reproductive attributes of the female body. He tried to comprehend the mind of someone who would see this carving of a pregnant woman as an agent of life. He nodded his head as a look of comprehension settled on his face. The carving represented a goddess of childbearing, a fertile mother to give birth to the people of the world. He felt the ridges covering the small head, depicting braided hair, and brushed the tips of his fingers over the swell of the carving's smooth stomach. He raised an eyebrow as a strange sensation ran through his body.

Berkana stood in silence as the carving moved from one person to the next, but resumed talking after she had given Kalmar, the last in line, a few moments to study it. "Geerna's people worshiped this and other carvings as if they were Shetow Herself. Geerna, after her enlightenment, however, realized the figurine was only a carving. Today we hold the carving in great reverence because it was Geerna's and because it's a piece of our home world." Berkana walked over to Kalmar and held out her hand. He carefully placed the carving in her open palm. She held the carving up. "We do not know if Shetow is the One who brought us to this world . . . we only know that someone . . . or something greater than we are brought us here and that something wanted the people to think It was Shetow. If It wasn't Shetow, why would this Power . . . this God-like entity, want Geerna and the other humans to believe It was Shetow?" Berkana hesitated, then shrugged her shoulders and lowered her hand. "At first, Geerna believed Shetow was behind her abduction, but after her enlightenment, she began to have her doubts." Berkana gazed down at the carving. "Geerna did believe Shetow protected her after she was abducted. She believed Shetow allowed her and the other humans to be brought to Elom. Geerna believed Shetow would protect Her People from this . . . this abductor. She also believed Shetow would protect the ones who were to be a part of the Second Judging."

"Do you think Geerna was right?" Arasima asked as she shifted in her chair.

"Right?"

"Is Shetow going to protect us?" Arasima's voice was thick, revealing suppressed emotion.

Kalmar wondered the same thing. As everyone looked at Berkana, he glanced down the line of faces. Dera's face was solemn, the young man to her right showed no emotion, and his sister's eyes were locked on the Medora Roo. On the front row, the ends of Arasima's lips began to curl up; Cabyl was deep in thought; and as Snook sat in the chair in front of him, his face was blocked from Kalmar's view.

"Geerna believed Shetow caused this Power to choose her when It was abducting humans from our home world. She believed she was the real Shetow's surrogate, selected to comfort and guide those taken. Geerna believed the Second Judging was not only a judging of mankind but also of the supremacy of the real Shetow Herself. Geerna never told the Multiped of her doubts of Shetow's identity, choosing to go along with the ruse. The Shetow-ka instructs us to do the same. We never refer to our benevolent benefactor by any other name than Shetow. We think it prudent that you do the same."

TWENTY-FOUR

The crisp morning breeze felt good against Kalmar's face. For the last four hours they had been climbing a hill southeast of the grounds of the Gathering. The sloped and rocky terrain was rather barren, the sandy soil barely able to support the sparse thickets of scrub brush and scattered clumps of grass that dotted the hillside. Peppered across the dreary landscape were oases of dazzling multi-colored flowers. Weathered ruts left by the large wheels of the drak traders' wheelons marked their path. A short distance from the crest of the hill, Kalmar stopped to get his breath as he turned to look back across the valley. The complete Gathering Compound and the restless expanse of boodo grass lay before him. Kalmar found the delicate changes in color patterns as the wind blew across the grass, the arteries of connecting pathways, and the uni-formity of the trees lining the Promenade fascinating. The rings of perfectly placed cabins around the hub of the central dining halls looked like ripples caused by stones tossed into a still pond—twenty-four sets of expanding waves, one for each tribe. The eight pathways radiating from the dining halls gave an illusion of spokes in a wheel. The emerald grasslands lay before Mount Alar like a vast ocean lapping at the edge of a sheer, rocky shoreline.

"Doesn't look man-made, does it?" Kalmar turned to find Snook standing beside him also looking back towards the point where they had started at daybreak that morning.

"The pathways look like where insects have eaten their way across a green leaf," Kalmar answered.

"I know. It's hard to decide if it's beautiful or grotesque. I have always believed man should blend with nature, not scar it."

"Snook, I believe it is—"

"The layout of the Gathering grounds was determined by Geerna." Both men turned to find Dera sharing their view. "The Sequa states that Geerna did it after consultation with Shetow, which we now know must have been through the Multiped. Since Shetow controls nature, She guided Geerna's hand in the layout; the patterns of the grounds are a reflection of nature."

The two men stared at Dera as she took in the panorama before them. Kalmar could see her eyes move as she studied every feature of the breathtaking expanse. She kept looking for a few seconds, nodded, and without any further comment, turned and continued walking up the path towards the crest of the hill. As she walked away, he noticed how the fabric of her pants pulled tight against her muscular thighs when her legs flexed. He and Snook swapped glances. Kalmar answered Snook's mischievous grin with a shrug and a shake of his head.

The two draks had met them at the Medora Chamber at first light. There had been little ceremony before the group began their journey to fulfill Geerna's agreement with Shetow. The draks separated, positioning themselves so one was at each end of the chaotic band—the smaller leading and the larger bringing up the rear. They followed a drak trader trail. After leaving the Gathering Compound, it meandered towards the hills that lay to the south of Mount Alar—a region which the Tell said Shetow had reserved for the draks.

Kalmar's insides felt as hollow as an empty barrel as they started out; then he saw the anxious look on his younger sister's face. Her pale complexion and hollow eyes prompted him to put his arm around her trembling shoulders. He smiled and winked at her as he pulled her towards him. "Sister, it's comforting to me to have you here."

Nutan lifted her eyes, looked at her older brother, and gave him a weak smile in return; her eyes expressed appreciation for his encouragement. With his jaw set, Kalmar whispered through clenched teeth an oath that no matter what happened, he would not show her any fear or doubt during this precarious undertaking. He must be strong; no matter how ominous the events of their journey became, surely it could not be as frightening as facing a charging cave lion or as painful as Arasima's betrayal. The cave lion left angry scars across his face, an area that still throbbed whenever he exerted himself. The scars Arasima left him were much more painful even though they were undetectable to anyone else. Whatever the Judging entailed, he believed it would not compare to the anguish he felt every time he saw the woman who'd betrayed him. He wondered if this trial of his will was some part of the Judging; it was only the belief that his response to this dilemma could possibly influence the outcome of the Second Judging that permitted him the determination to force one foot after the other.

The seven humans and two draks were spread out as they neared the crest. The smaller drak was in the lead, closely followed by Arasima. Dera and the young man were next with Kalmar, Nutan, and Snook after them. Cabyl brought up the rear only a few steps ahead of the larger drak. There had been little talking among the group as they trudged up the incline. Kalmar could not see the brown line that would indicate the trail on the taller hills beyond the approaching summit; the trail must change directions on the far side of the hill. He reasoned that once they started down the other side of the hill, they would lose sight of the grasslands and be cut off from the world they knew.

Right before they reached the hilltop, Snook broke from the group, walked off the path twenty or so steps, and kneeled down for a few moments. When he stood up and started back towards the trail, he was carrying a handful of purple and yellow flowers. As Snook was walking back, he raised the flowers to his nose.

"How beautiful," Nutan exclaimed as Snook stepped back on the trail.

Snook smiled. "But not as beautiful as you." He handed several of the flowers to Nutan, who took them and quickly inspected their delicate blossoms before smelling them.

"The smell, so sweet and fresh; isn't it strange to find something so beautiful in such a stark place?"

Snook and Kalmar had stopped walking and were looking at Nutan. Cabyl and the larger drak stopped behind them. Kalmar saw Snook glance at Cabyl, hesitate, then, on impulse, walk over to her and hold out the balance of the flowers. "Nor are they as beautiful as you."

Snook caught Cabyl completely by surprise. For a moment, Kalmar was not sure how Cabyl was going to take Snook's gesture.

Cabyl first looked at the flowers then slowly lifted her eyes to Snook's face, which was painted with humility and sincerity. Berkana had told her she should not judge all men by the actions of her father and Pairing Partner. Fate, the old woman said, would not always decide against her. She weighed Snook's action for several seconds before a shy grin shaped her lips. She reached out and took the flowers. For a brief moment, their hands touched. As she sniffed the flowers, Snook's face glowed from the release of so much pent-up emotion.

Kalmar could tell Cabyl's reaction fueled Snook's confidence. "Would you mind if I walked with you?" Snook asked in the softest tones that Kalmar had ever heard Snook utter. Cabyl studied Snook a few more moments; the doubt in her dark and hollow eyes made Kalmar think she would decline Snook's request, but surprisingly she consented with a slight nod.

Nutan had also been a witness to Snook's overture to Cabyl. His sister's reaction perplexed Kalmar. He had assumed, after finding them asleep in each other's arms, that she and Snook were lovers. If Snook's actions upset Nutan, you could not tell it by the way she was smiling at the couple.

Kalmar turned to his sister. "I thought you two were . . . well, together."

Nutan gave him a questioning look. "Whatever gave you *that* idea?" she said, then turned and resumed walking. His jaw dropped as he watched his sister walk away. Kalmar decided he would leave the subject alone as he was now utterly confused; he discarded the idea of confronting her with the knowledge that he had seen her in Snook's bed three nights earlier.

As he topped the hill, he glanced over his shoulder at the vista. Lapping at the shores of the Gathering Grounds lay the inland sea of boodo grass. There was a visible difference between the living and agitated vortex of grass and the motionless Gathering Grounds below him. In the distances, mountains jutted from the flat plain. The mountains looked like the fat fingers of a cupped hand rising from its green palm. As he started his descent down the other side, the world he had always known receded from his view.

It was late afternoon when the apprehensive humans, herded by the two draks, reached a flat area where four tents circled a campfire. For the first time since they had started that morning, Kalmar saw flowing water. On the high side of the campsite was a small spring at the base of an outcropping that jutted from the steep hillside. The water gurgling from the spring fathered a small brook. The lush foliage bordering the ribbon of trickling water stood in contrast to the sparse vegetation strewn across the rest of the hillside. The brook and its encroaching flora looked like a giant dark green serpent slinking down the hill.

Kalmar observed several smaller draks scurrying around as they approached the campsite. He had never seen more than two or three of the imposing lizards at any one time and never ones of this lesser size. The campsite draks appeared to stand no more than half the height of the smaller of their two escorts, and other than a slight difference in plumage coloration, seemed identical to the larger reptiles. After further scrutiny, the smaller draks' movements seemed more erratic and faster than the movements of their larger brethren; the miniature reptiles appeared to flitter about like birds building nests. The sight was a little unnerving to Kalmar. If any of the others in his group had the same uneasy reaction he could not detect it.

The last rays of the setting Salune disappeared as the larger of the binary suns dropped behind the crest of a neighboring mountain. One of the smaller draks motioned with its three-fingered claw for them to place their packs in the tents. The three men were directed to a large tent, and the four females were ushered to an even larger tent, directly across the campfire from the males. The tents were positioned around a crackling campfire that both warmed and lit the surrounding area. After depositing their packs, they all came out to huddle around the fire. The temperature had plunged after Elom's two suns abandoned the cloudless sky, and the human's thin, sweat-stained clothing proved inadequate for the mountainous environment. Moisture clouds formed with their every breath as they rubbed their shivering arms. Kalmar noticed that Snook and Cabyl again ended up beside each other as everyone stood in front of the roaring flames. Three of the campsite draks, carrying heavy hooded coats and matching pants, came scurrying from a tent set apart from the other tents. The humans quickly selected their sizes and pulled the warmer garments over their regular clothing.

After he quit shivering, Kalmar sat down on one of several small boulders ringing the campfire; one by one, the others followed his lead. Three drak cooks who had been working around a wooden table next to a separate, smaller fire brought two plates of food to each of the humans. For everyone but Snook the meal was the same: green and red kappa leaves topped with raw joujou nuts filled one plate; the other plate steamed with cooked vegetables and prairie-buck roast. Snook was given the same vegetables but with baked fish. The draks' knowledge of Snook's eating habits astonished him, and he raised his eyebrows.

"That," Dera said, "answers the question about Shetow knowing of the Mookyn's existence."

A few feet away sat their drak companions with their own plates. The reptiles did not really sit; they leaned against their boulders with their massive tails resting across the top of the stone surface, extending straight out from the back side of the rock without drooping. Kalmar craned his neck but he could not see what the reptiles were eating.

"Do you have a name, or something you would like us to call you by?" Dera asked.

The smaller drak glanced towards the larger one, who swallowed what was in its mouth before answering. "My name is Gogtee; my mate, here," it made a gesture towards the larger drak, "is Dryka." Gogtee's voice was strangely high-pitched but easily understood.

"You *are* female," Dera said. The two draks looked at each other as they both made a wet wheezing sound. After a few moments, Gogtee stopped making the distracting noise and looked at Dera.

"Please excuse us. We find your question amusing. We also have difficulty distinguishing your sex without the aid of a reader." Gogtee handed her plate to Dryka and then stood up. "Yes, I am female. How could you tell?" The resonance of the female drak's voice was definitely not human and Kalmar could not detect any inflections in her voice that sounded in any way feminine. "Is it because I am smaller?"

"No, well . . . you are the one in charge." Dera's remark brought another chorus of wheezing from the two draks.

"I am not, as you say, in charge. My race has to have a voice module implanted in our throats to be able to speak . . . to form sounds humans can understand; even then, it is difficult for us. I have mastered the skill better than most. That is why I was selected to escort you. Dryka is not as comfortable as I am in speaking to you; he defers to me whenever possible." It was the longest speech Kalmar had ever heard from a drak; usually, only the females spoke to the sparsely feathered creatures. Gogtee's speech was raspy but her words distinct.

"Will you answer another question?" Kalmar asked.

The two draks looked at each other once again. He was not sure how, but he sensed there was some kind of nonverbal communication between the two—a look or facial change undiscernable to humans. The draks refocused their attention on the group. Gogtee spoke as her mate looked on. "It is time for some of your questions to be answered, but it's still too soon to try to answer them all."

"Too soon, why?" Arasima blurted out, her face revealing a hardness Kalmar had never seen in all the time he had spent with her. "We are away from all the others of our kind. All of us here"—she moved her arms to indicate the other six members of the group—"are going to the Judging."

"There are questions you will ask that I cannot answer in a way you would understand, things for which there are no words in your vocabulary. You will just have to wait and see for yourselves. Besides, there are many things we do not fully understand ourselves."

A hush filled the chilly night air. Kalmar looked at Snook and then to the others, whose faces were as blank as he realized his own must appear to them.

"What is your role in the Judging?" Cabyl asked in a clear, firm voice. This side of her personality he had never seen. He noticed a smile creep across Snook's face.

"As we have told the Medoras, we are only your guides; we have no part in your Judging"

"Does the outcome of the Judging matter to you . . . to the draks?" Cabyl said tactfully.

Gogtee did not answer for a few seconds. She stood perfectly still. It was as if she had not heard the question. Finally she spoke. "It does matter to us."

"Why?"

Gogtee turned her head to look Cabyl in the eye. "There are many among us who think we are being judged with you."

"How?" asked Snook, sitting up straight.

"That is one of the things that will be easier for you to understand in a few days."

"What—" started Arasima.

"We, the draks, are your . . . servants . . . your friends. I assure you, we will help you, tell you what we can to aid you in the Judging, but you must have confidence in our judgment to inform you in a manner that best helps you understand what we are telling you. A little patience will serve you well . . . in a few days, information will come at you faster than you can assimilate it."

Kalmar recognized that questioning Gogtee further about

what she felt she could tell them was futile. They needed to be asking questions and seeing which ones the reptile would answer. He
decided to begin with a simple inquiry and go from there. "When
will the Judging begin?"

"We are not exactly sure, but it will take a few days to reach
where the Judging will take place."

"Do you think we will be given time to rest from such a long
journey? That many days of walking over mountainous terrain will
leave us exhausted," Arasima said, cutting her eyes from one of
their guides to the other.

"Tomorrow will be the last day we walk." Gogtee's words were
like a frigid wind blowing through the group. For a second, Kalmar
rolled Gogtee's statement over in his mind. Did this mean they
were going to ride in wheelons or travel by boat?

"How far will we be traveling?" Kalmar asked.

Gogtee looked at Dryka before she looked back at Kalmar.
"You cannot comprehend the answer to that question."

Kalmar's face turned white. Her cutting remark stung. Was he
not smart enough to understand?

"What do you mean?" Dera asked, in a soft diplomatic tone.
Her mild manner showed Kalmar that she did not think Gogtee's
answer was meant to be insulting, or, if she did, she was smart
enough not to show it. Dera was smart, but he already knew that.

"To understand something, you must compare it to something
you already know . . . something you understand—you need a reference. The distance we are going to travel . . . you have no point
of existing knowledge, no reference to compare it with."

It did not have to be very far to be beyond his personal experience. Where he sat was the farthest he had ever been from his village.
He tried again. "Gogtee, we can only travel so far in a week. I . . .
we, it is true, have never traveled very far from our own villages, but
we can comprehend the distance to any place we could travel in

seven or eight days . . . any place we could go on Elom." Kalmar felt he had made a reasonable defense against Gogtee's remark and hoped she would now tell them how far they would be traveling. He smiled to himself; it was invigorating to challenge their reptilian host.

Gogtee just stared at him. Kalmar could not read the expression on Gogtee's face; actually, he could not tell if there *was* an expression on her gray scaly face. She blinked and said, "Can you comprehend the distance to Eeo?"

Kalmar did not understand the question. Why would Gogtee use the brown sun, Salune's smaller twin, as a reference? It must be a test. Kalmar tried to be as calm and as self-assured as possible. "Now, Gogtee, I must admit that is a long way, but I don't think it is a distance beyond our mental capacity to comprehend. Surely we are not going to be judged on a sun." Kalmar felt he had stood up for all of them. He filled his lungs and sat a little taller.

Gogtee gave him the same look as before. "No, you are right, Eeo is not our final destination, but if you can comprehend the distance to Eeo, multiply that by a hundred million."

Kalmar reeled from the impact of Gogtee's answer. For a moment, he thought she was joking, but the way Gogtee kept looking at him told him she was not. Except for the crackle of the fire and the movement of the other draks scurrying around the campsite, there was complete silence.

Dera was the first to recover. "You are correct: it is impossible for us to imagine traveling so far."

"Do not feel bad, we cannot comprehend it either." Gogtee hesitated. "Actually, most of the travel time will be used to reach the location where we will start the part of the trip that will cover the greatest distance . . . and that will be covered in, what will seem to you, a few seconds."

Again, Dera was the first to absorb Gogtee's words. "You are serious; we are going to leave Elom?"

Gogtee closed her eyes and nodded. "We thought you realized that."

Dera was the only one of the group who was not too stunned to speak. "No . . . it never occurred to me that we would be leaving Elom." No one else made a sound. "What can you tell us about the place we are going?"

"And how in the world," Izzy piped in, "are we going to get there?"

"As to where you are going, I can tell you nothing."

"You cannot or you do not think we can comprehend it?"

"You cannot comprehend it, I would think . . . but I have never been there, so I cannot tell you about it." Dryka leaned over and put a clawed hand on Gogtee's arm. She looked at her mate; there seemed to be that same inaudible communication between them Kalmar had noticed earlier. Then she returned her attention to the humans. "I think it best that we all get some sleep. Tomorrow will be a day of discovery. By the time we reach where you will be judged, most of your present questions will have been answered and will have been supplanted by new ones." With that said, Gogtee and Dryka stood up and headed towards one of the tents erected away from the two larger tents assigned to the humans.

After a few minutes, the women headed to the brook to wash their faces and prepare themselves for bed; the three men stayed at the campfire. Snook stood up, walked over, and offered his hand to the young man who had stayed near Dera. "I am Snook." Snook waved his hand toward Kalmar. "And this is my friend Kalmar. I guess we had better get to know one another, as it looks like we are going to be thrown together for some time."

The young man nodded and looked at him through cautious eyes. "I know who you are. Remember, Berkana told us all about you." He took Snook's outstretched hand. "My name is Izzy." Izzy shifted his eyes toward Kalmar. "I guess we had better get along if we are going to have any chance in the Judging."

"That's right, and why wouldn't we get along?" Snook said grinning.

"Dera is my sister. Her pain is my pain. What he did"—Izzy nodded towards Kalmar—"was the most painful thing I have ever endured. Your friend is a egotistical fool. It will be hard for me to work past that . . . but I will try." Kalmar could see Snook was caught off guard by Izzy's retort, but Snook's surprise at Izzy's revelation of his relationship to Dera didn't compare to his own utter shock. How could he have been so stupid? Izzy and Dera had been together every time he had seen Dera since the Matage. He had noticed how Nutan and Izzy had exchanged glances. How could he have missed it? Izzy was not Dera's lover; he was her younger brother—the Second Childs.

"I am truly sorry for any pain I caused Dera . . . or you," Kalmar sputtered.

Izzy looked down into the flames for a moment before lifting his eyes to look at Kalmar. "I must be honest with you. I never saw a tear in Dera's eyes after your rejection of her choosing you. I don't pretend to understand it; all I can figure is that she realized that by you rejecting her you proved you weren't worthy of her." He shook his head. "You didn't understand how very special she truly is." Izzy paused to assemble his thoughts. "The sad part is that everybody knew you were the best contestant in the Borrac. You are, supposedly, the cresting of the Traits in the males of our species, yet you reject not only the winner of the Byrrac, but a female at the undisputed pinnacle of feminine artistic ability and intelligence."

Kalmar sensed the young man was becoming emotional.

"For that," Izzy said, raising the level of his voice.

He looked in the direction of Izzy's nod. A little distance from them, he saw Arasima stooped over next to the brook, scooping water up with her hands to splash her face. Her womanly shape was still distinguishable in the weak light cast by the campfire and the twilight-of-night. Once again, he felt a hollow feeling in the pit of his stomach; her sexual allure still grabbed his male weakness. The memory of her touch sent shudders through his body; lust sped the beating of his heart. His cheeks reddened, the scars on his face burned. As he looked at Arasima, he noticed Dera stand up a few steps downstream. A moment before shifting his gaze back to Arasima, Kalmar noted that Dera's curves were every bit as enticing as Arasima's.

Kalmar's mind raced as his eyes moved back to Izzy. Thoughts of Nutan flashed in his head; he had learned a lot about himself. In addition to Dera and Izzy, his actions had also pained one who loved him. He closed his eyes and held them tightly shut. When he yielded to Arasima's seduction, he had only thought of himself. Carnal desire skewed his judgment. He opened his eyes. "Izzy, I was a fool. I ask for you and your sister's forgiveness. I *assure* you, if I had the choice to make over again, I wouldn't make the same mistake."

At first, Izzy showed no reaction to Kalmar's assertion; he only looked at Kalmar, weighing him. Under Izzy's scrutiny, he felt the world around him become strangely distant. Time slowed; jumbled thoughts flooded his mind. He became aware of his own breathing. Things he would normally not notice now demanded his attention. The moths flying around the fire entranced him; they would flitter around the edges of the flames then all of a sudden dive at the lapping tentacles of yellow, red, and gold. The current of hot air flowing up from the flames would push most of the moths back; but, every now and then, he heard the pop of one of the winged insects as the searing heat consumed it.

Reality returned a few moments later when Izzy finally spoke.

"She got to you, didn't she? It seems to me, you were more devastated by Arasima not choosing you than Dera was by you rejecting her."

Kalmar slowly lowered his eyes. He, Snook, and Izzy sat looking at the dancing, iridescent flames—each lost in his own thoughts.

"Arasima," Izzy said, "is one of the most beautiful . . . the most desirable women I have ever seen." He picked up a stick and pushed back an ember, which had rolled out of the fire. "I don't know how I would react if I thought I could have her body next to mine every night for the next twenty cycles of the seasons." Izzy raised his squinting eyes, confronting Kalmar. "But I do know my sister is many times the woman that Arasima is. Dera is a truly wonderful person, something you can't tell by just looking at her or studying her Byrrac scores. There is more to my sister than anybody realizes, a depth we can't fathom."

He listened to the young man's passion. In so many ways, Izzy reminded him of Snook. They both exuded an air of naïveté peppered with indignant righteousness. "I believe what you say," Kalmar said. "Your sincerity speaks for itself. I may have been a fool in my dealing with your sister, but I swear on the Mark of the Covenant, I won't make a similar mistake in *our* relationship." He stood up and offered his arm to Izzy for a clasp of friendship. "That is, if you will allow it."

The young man seemed to run things around in his head a moment, then he stood and grasped Kalmar's arm. "Kalmar of the Cave Lion Tribe, if my sister showed one bit of anger towards you I would be at your throat, but, strangely"—he shook his head—"she seems to have no antagonism towards you whatsoever. I take your arm only because of her total dismissal of you spurning her and the necessity of our present circumstances."

Kalmar arched an eyebrow; he wondered if Izzy's actions had more to do with Izzy's interest in Nutan than it did in forgiveness.

The men's serenity was broken when the four females returned from the brook. Kalmar noticed Nutan kept her distance from Arasima. He had learned a lesson from Izzy; he needed to speak to his little sister as soon as he had a chance. When Nutan reached their tent, she turned and waved at the males. Kalmar noticed Izzy joined him and Snook when they waved back. Dera and Cabyl, after seeing Nutan's wave, also waved at them. He was sure Dera's wave was for Izzy and Cabyl's was for Snook, but all three males answered each woman in kind. Only Arasima failed to look in their direction before she entered the female's tent.

Nutan noticed the men were watching them as she and the other females returned from the brook. She had avoided Arasima, not knowing what she would do if the once-flirtatious woman made a rude remark about her brother. Nutan's lips puckered. In spite of Arasima's aloofness, Arasima still carried herself as if she were in control of everything. Deep lines crossed Nutan's face, followed by a slight crack that forced her lips into a guarded smile. Under the circumstances, it was better that Arasima had rejected Kalmar; it would have been sickening to watch her lead Kalmar around by the end of his manhood. Nutan laughed to herself. She should forget about Arasima; the vain woman had shown the true nature of her inner-spirit. Surely, her actions would now make the males spurn any of her future advances.

Dera, the one who should have been the most devastated by the events of the Matage, seemed unaffected, almost cheerful. The winner of the Byrrac must have the highest Concentration of the Traits, just as everyone had whispered. This was a woman to admire; Nutan could not wait to know Dera better. It would have been nice if Kalmar had accepted her Choosing, but with the way things turned out, it may have been better that they were unpaired.

Cabyl, the strange young woman who had been the Medora Roo's novice, seemed to have lost some of her shyness after

Snook's gift of wildflowers. Nutan thought she would have been jealous of Snook's interest in this pale creature. She pressed her lips together, and then waved at the men standing on the other side of the campfire. All the males waved back. She forced back a grin; she knew it was the eager antics of the youngest male keeping her jealousy against Cabyl in check.

The journey resumed at dawn. A frosty breeze numbed their faces as they continued their ascent. Smoky wisps of condensation formed each time their breath mingled with the chilly morning air; the gusty wind blew the white puffs of moisture into their faces before dissipating. A faint, woody scent from the squatty karpa bushes, which dotted the rocky hillsides, spiced the air. A distant billowing of white clouds to the north—the direction from which they had traveled—was the only imperfection in an otherwise pristine sunlit sky. Kalmar considered the cloud formations and speculated that they hung over the edge of the grasslands on the far side of Mount Alar.

The order of their march had changed from the previous day. The two draks, once again, took stations at each end of column. Dera, followed closely by Izzy, joined Gogtee at the point position. Then came Kalmar and Nutan, trailed by Snook and Cabyl. Arasima walked by herself just ahead of Dryka. Kalmar and Nutan maintained a jumbled conversation; Nutan lost her train of thought and stumbled over her words every time Izzy looked back over his shoulder to smile at her. Kalmar thought it ironic that they had only started the second day of their journey and already Snook and Cabyl had chosen to walk together. Moreover, with the way Nutan and Izzy were eyeing each other, they—unless he was badly mistaken—would be walking together before dark. Was it fate or Shetow's revenge? Dera, Arasima, and he were going to be the odd ones out, and even then Dera seemed completely satisfied to have

Gogtee as a stand-in for a human companion. He vowed to himself that he would walk in silence before he would walk beside Arasima; although, it did not appear that was going to be a problem, as she showed no interest in talking to him either.

Kalmar watched Dera as she walked ahead of him. Before starting that morning, the campsite draks gathered the heavier clothing they had distributed to the humans the night before and exchange them for lighter hiking attire consisting of woolen sweaters and buckskin pants. Kalmar had never seen a woman in leather pants—the clothing of male hunters. A few days earlier, the members of the group would not only have found a female wearing such a garment strange, but a breach of their mores. The pants were loose enough for free movement, yet tight enough to accentuate the shape of Dera's round bottom and long muscular legs as she took full strides only a few paces in front of him. His face flushed; the unexpected exhilaration inflamed by the taut leather across her backside was not only embarrassing, it was also hard for him to fathom. He was accustomed to the raging emotions the curves of a woman's body invoked in him, but, somehow, this was different. He fixed on the outline of her rear and thighs, accented by the stretched leather each time she took a step; then, every few steps, she would turn her body, as she spoke to either Gogtee or Izzy, revealing a silhouette of her torso as her breast strained against the fabric of her sweater. Women were impossible to understand; Arasima was keenly aware of her feminine effect on men, yet Dera seemed oblivious to hers. Only when she turned her head so he could see her blemished face, was Kalmar reminded of Dera's unsightly imperfection. As they walked, he unconsciously took the fingertips of his left hand and traced the outline of the healed but still sensitive wounds left by the cave lion's claws—his, so-called, "Scars of Courage." In the last few days, he had become painfully aware of his other imperfections; Dera had lived her entire life with hers. She seemed to accept her abnormality and did not let it rule her; if only he had such control over his frailties. In a way, Kalmar thought, Dera's blemish was more of a sign of his imperfection than it was of hers. He let Arasima control him; his pitiful naïveté had been no match for her blemishless face and seductive smile. His carnal weakness had betrayed him. A shiver of regret ran through his body.

Dera showed no signs that she was bothered by his presence; actually, she did not act as though she was aware that he was there at all. She seemed completely engrossed in her conversation with Gogtee and showed no interest in what any of the rest of them were doing. He wondered what she and the female reptile were discussing. It appeared as if Gogtee was doing most of the talking while Dera listened intently, nodding her head every few minutes. The female lizard's dialogue was accented by her strangely humanlike and exaggerated arm movements and distortions of her scaly face, visible to Kalmar every time the reptile turned her elongated head towards Dera before she spoke. It was impossible for him to make any sense of Gogtee's gestures when he could not hear what she was saying. Dera walked so close to Gogtee that the two would occasionally bump together if a wheelon rut or uneven place in the path interrupted the smooth flow of their strides. Kalmar studied Dera as she kept her attention on her gray-scaled and green-feathered tutor. He could see Dera's new companion fascinated her; she appeared riveted by the reptile's fractured words and guise of mystery.

TWENTY-FIVE

In the late morning, the hills, played out as an imposing range of snow-capped mountains, confronted the group. The pathway turned and ran parallel with the ridge of the mountains. So far, the incline of the winding pathway had not been so steep that a bovor pulling a wheelon could not manage it. Now, the grade of the pathway running along the base of the mountains was gentler and the course straighter.

In the early afternoon, they overtook a slower group of six drak traders walking beside three bovors, each pulling a loaded wheelon. They had been gaining on the plodding group ever since they first spotted them several hours earlier. When they finally caught up with the small caravan, Kalmar could see, as he had expected, that each wheelon was full of artwork—the pride of the female half of the Equilibrium. Gogtee, Dryka, and the traders huddled while the three bovors and the seven humans took a break from the rigors of their climb. Dera, Nutan, and Izzy went over and surveyed the traders' cargo.

"I think some of these pieces are from my village," Nutan said as she pulled back some of the straw packing. "I recognize the style of one of our best artists. The draks really know how to pick the best pieces. Wonder what they will do with them?"

"I have no idea what they do with it, but I am not so sure how good they are at knowing the aesthetic value of the works they trade for," Izzy replied.

"What do you mean?" Snook said as he, Kalmar, and Cabyl joined them.

"Well—"

Before Izzy could explain himself, the draks broke from their conference. Soon the band of seven humans and their drak guides left the three wheelons, pulled by the steady but slow-moving bovors, and their attendants far behind them.

"Surely the draks don't expect us to climb over this mountain," Kalmar said.

"Maybe there is a gap," said Nutan, who was walking with her brother.

"If there is a breach in the mountains, I can't see it," Snook said.

"Maybe we can't see it from this angle," Nutan answered.

"If there isn't a gap, we will be walking in these mountains for days," Kalmar replied as he surveyed the wall of towering rock that stretched to the horizon in front of them.

"That's not right; remember, Gogtee said we wouldn't be walking after today," Nutan said.

They had walked most of the day when the path leveled out, and then took a downward tilt along a rock cliff. Kalmar's scrutiny of Gogtee and Dera's discussion kept him distracted, causing him to be surprised when they stopped walking. The party had been walking in the shadow of the mountain when the path took a sharp turn and abruptly ended at the rock face. The pathway literally disappeared into the mountain. Kalmar and the rest of the group rambled on until they were all standing next to Gogtee and Dera.

A sense of caution gripped him. Tension knotted his shoulder muscles as he instinctively squared his body in a defensive posture. Animal bellowing and the sounds of commotion came from behind them; he jerked his body around to face the challenge. Just below the path, down the mountain, lay a large boulder not a hundred paces from where they stood. Beyond the boulder was a large wooden fence encircling a plain unpainted barn and small corral. The boulder had blocked their view of the small austere building and enclosure as they approached. Inside the fence were four snorting bovor eating from a long trough. Two draks stood outside the fence pouring grain over the wooden rails, feeding the docile beasts. Kalmar bowed his back, working the kinks out of his muscles as he relaxed his vigil.

"What do you think they're for?" Nutan asked.

"Must be fresh replacements for the bovor used in pulling the drak traders' wheelons," Kalmar answered as he pointed his chin towards the animals in the corral. "The three bovors we passed earlier will probably be exchanged for three of these rested ones." There was movement behind him so he turned back to face the mountain.

The rock surface was smooth and flawless, almost polished, like the walls and ceiling of the Gathering Chamber; too perfect, he realized, to be natural. Gogtee raised her left arm, displaying a bright metal bracelet, which she then covered with the palm of her right clawlike hand. Kalmar was not sure what occurred next, it happened so fast. First, a section of the rock surface as large as one of the entrances to the Gathering Chamber developed a dull, gelatinlike sheen. Then a slight ripple moved across its surface as the rock transformed into a shimmering liquid right before dissolving. It did not roll back or fall down; it disappeared. One moment it was there, the next it was not.

The disappearance of the rock surface revealed a tunnel more than large enough for a wheelon to enter. Gogtee faced the startled humans. "You're about to leave the world you've always known and enter a world you've never imagined." She turned and entered the tunnel without waiting to see the reaction of the humans or if they followed her. Without hesitating, Dera trotted after their quick-moving reptilian guide. Kalmar and the others looked from one to the other. Izzy cut his eyes towards the rest of them and then stepped forward to follow his sister; undaunted, the other five quickly joined him. Dryka lumbered after them.

The muffled sound of their steps against the rock surface caused a muted echo in the confines of the brightly lit passageway. The top and sides of the arched structure glowed with a green-tinted illumination. The diffuse light made it difficult for Kalmar to distinguish shadows. As they entered the strange opening in the mountainside, his emotions matched the pounding of his racing heart; then, the unexpected brightness of their underground walkway lifted his spirits. After walking a few hundred paces into the interior of the mountain, Kalmar stopped to let Snook and Cabyl catch up with him.

"The tunnel doesn't run straight. It seems to slope downwards and gently curve to the right." Kalmar made an arching motion with the back of his right hand and extended arm.

"Yes. And there's no air draft . . . which means the opening at the far end is closed," Snook said.

"Or," Cabyl glanced behind them before looking forward again, "both ends are now closed."

Kalmar looked back, but the evenness of the tunnel lighting made it impossible for him to distinguish the entrance. "If the tunnel was open on both ends at the same time there would be a strong air current," he said nodding. They walked briskly but cautiously through the emerald glow.

"Gogtee seems," said Nutan, after she paused a moment to let Kalmar, Snook, and Cabyl overtake her, "to have picked up her pace."

Arasima followed the others. She had been wondering if being selected to be a part of the Second Judging would equal or surpass bringing the winner of the Borrac back to her Village. On second thought, she did not care if she ever returned to her village; there were no circumstances that would make her want to face her childhood taunters. Her transformation into a beautiful woman had not distracted her female contemporaries; it had only forced them to use other means to humiliate her. In a moment of realization, she understood that it did not matter who she picked as a Pairing Partner or what great deed she did. The females of her village in her age group would never stop their words and acts of persecution. She glanced around her; surely, there must be a way to stop the shunning of the others in this group. The males she understood; they should offer little resistance if she worked at it. However, it was going to be hard to approach the women; the venom she felt for other females was going to be hard to disguise or, for that matter, control.

After they had walked for what seemed an inordinately long time, Kalmar said, "We've gone far in excess of what I'd think necessary to travel through the mountain."

"Kalmar," Snook said, "I think . . . I can see the end of the tunnel. Look"—he pointed—"can't you see the bluish dot ahead?"

"I . . . do. I think you're right."

The events of the last few days had changed Cabyl's life. For the first time since her father started sneaking into her room after her mother went to sleep, she enjoyed the company of males. She wondered if Snook's apparent purity, his whiteness, had allowed her to lower her guard the first time she met him. For all those cycles of the seasons, males had terrified her, but meeting Snook had raised her hopes. Hopes that had been dashed when she came upon him kissing Nutan. Now, Nutan's obvious interest in Izzy and Snook's supportive reaction to their shy glances brought a sense of disbelief. She had only known oppression and uncontrolled jealousy by the other two males in her life. Once freed from her father, she had chosen a Pairing Partner every bit as abusive. Fearing her father and then her new Pairing Partner, she suffered in stifling silence. The memories of the two men, and what they had done to her, often caused her to shiver uncontrollably. It was only when Snook had offered her the handful of flowers proclaiming her beauty, and gave her his bashful smile, that her fear of the Mookyn waned.

Izzy thought he would never meet a female that could match Dera; his feeling for his amazing sister were those of an admiring younger brother. Nutan, though, astounded him. He realized there was something about the young female that reminded him of someone. It had only taken a short time for him to recognize that the things which made Dera special, Nutan also possessed. He glanced at her and her brother as they neared the mouth of the tunnel. He knew this woman was all that he could ever wish for in a Pairing Partner. His heart raced and he thought *if only she can ever feel the same about me.*

The group walked the rest of the way in silence, each person lost in their own trepidations, their nimble minds straining to understand what was happening to them. Nutan hesitated as they neared the mouth of the tunnel. Kalmar walked up to her, put his left arm around her shoulders. "Now is not the time to falter. I'm sure much greater challenges face us than walking out of a hole in the ground." Nutan looked up and gave him a weak smile; then they both walked out of the tunnel.

Her brother had always been the male figure in her life. Then, when Kalmar brought Snook to the village, she was excited but also confused. She had expected it would be two more cycles of the seasons before she would face the realities of the relationship between the sexes. First Snook, then Izzy, brought the deep emotions of a woman out in her. The stirring in her heart she felt toward Izzy seemed to be in conflict with the relationship that had developed with Snook. She was glad that Snook seemed to have chosen Cabyl. She looked out of the tunnel as she and Kalmar stepped through the opening in the mountain. Her feelings toward Izzy caused her to smile as the full force of the sunlight hit her face.

Salune sat high above the horizon, washing out all but the faint ghost of a crescent Boboi. The breeze was gusty, but warmer than it had been at the tunnel's entrance.

After stepping into the daylight, Kalmar had to squint a few moments to allow his eyes to adjust to the bright sunlight. The tunnel had deposited them on the down side of a mountain much closer to its bottom than its crest. At first, the surroundings appeared to be much like what they had seen on the lower levels of the hillsides below the tunnel entrance on the far side of the mountain. It was only when he looked to the horizon that he saw the oddly formed, rust-colored structures.

"Look at that," Izzy exclaimed as he pointed at the unusual objects. "What do you think they are?"

Dera spoke to Gogtee before looking back and addressing the others. "It's where the draks live."

The odd structures covered the side and crest of the next hill like a patch of gigantic mushrooms that sprang up where the wind had strewn the spores of a broken spore case. Their lofty position on the mountainside gave Kalmar a clear view of the pathway, which led down the mountain before winding its way toward the fungi-shaped edifices.

"They're beautiful . . . so . . . so symmetrical," Nutan said, her face radiant.

"You have a skewed sense of beauty," Arasima said, but no one reacted to her snide comment.

"I would sure like to know how they built them," Izzy said.

"It looks like they were grown," Snook responded.

"They look like big piles of mammoth dung to me," Arasima said, without cracking a smile. The others all turned and looked at her. She kept her eyes fixed on the structures, ignoring their stares.

Snook leaned over to Kalmar and whispered, "I hate to admit it, but she's right. They do look like piles of mammoth shit."

"Yes, she's right, but I'd have never seen the similarities without her pointing them out."

"That is because you and I have never paid much attention to what comes out of a mammoth's butt," Snook said, fighting back a snicker. They looked at each other, laughed, and then turned to ogle the stunning female. After a moment, Kalmar's face lost its smirk. "Maybe, it's because we look for what's not there, while Arasima sees things the way they actually are."

"You may be right." Snook's smirk also evaporated as he nodded in agreement.

Arasima smiled to herself as she noticed Kalmar and Snook's expressive glances. At first, her eyebrows rose, and then she forced her eyelids partially shut before turning and smiling at the two males. Then she gave a slight shrug of her shoulders. She could tell by the reaction on Kalmar and Snook's faces that she had softened some of their animosities.

Kalmar knew without asking that their journey would take them to the imposing sight on the far hillside. There was but one pathway leading from the tunnel entrance and it snaked in that direction. Gogtee gave them only a few minutes to scrutinize their new surroundings before she started walking towards the drak dwellings. The humans lined up and followed her.

What kind of birds are those?" asked Nutan, as she nodded towards three large specks soaring in the mountain's updraft hundreds of feet above them. Kalmar had noticed them as he came out of the tunnel, but paid them little attention as he scanned the valley.

"I am not sure," he said after studying them a moment. "With that kind of wing span, they must be some type of vulture—"

"They don't look like any vulture I've ever seen," Izzy blurted. Kalmar nodded. "Nor I. They really look . . . different."

"It's the length of their bodies," Izzy said as his eyes followed the airborne creatures. "Well . . . I mean the length of the body compared to their wings . . . the ratio. That has to be the widest wingspan I have ever seen, but just look at the length of their bodies." They all stared at the birds for a few moments before resuming their descent down the mountain.

During most of their journey, the group had stayed close together; now they spread out along the trail, as one, then another would stop to survey their new surroundings. The lead element of their scattered group reached the foot of the mountain when Kalmar saw Dera, who was walking next to Gogtee, stop a few hundred paces ahead of him. She froze in midstep, staring at something to her left.

"What is it?" Snook asked from behind him.

"I don't know. I can't see what she's looking at." Whatever

commanded her attention was hidden from Kalmar's view by an embankment on the left side of the pathway. Dera's mouth hung open as her eyes stayed fixed on the invisible point of her interest. He had never seen her with such a perplexed expression. Nutan, closely followed by Izzy, darted forward to join her. Gogtee stepped back, allowing the two humans to cluster around Dera. Nutan and Izzy's faces revealed their own bewilderment. Kalmar rushed forward, past the edge of the embankment blocking his view, and in a few seconds reached his sister, Izzy, and Dera.

Dera's head spun; she felt her body slide to the ground. She had been determined not to be shocked by anything they encountered. She had questioned Gogtee in an effort to glean any information that could be useful in their preparation for the Second Judging. The giant lizard had not given her any warning about what lay before her.

Nutan, what is it? What do you see?" Kalmar looked towards the horizon. "All I see is more hills."

"Look down." Then she pointed to a ravine below them that curved away from the pathway along the edge of the mountain. "Art, it is full of artwork."

Kalmar lowered his gaze. Lying below them was a large chasm full of hundreds of house-sized mounds of pottery, sculptures, statues, and other pieces of art.

It took only a few seconds for him to appreciate the gravity of what lay before him. *"This is not possible."* His head began to spin as his legs became wobbly, and then his knees buckled. He cushioned his collapse with his right hand as he dropped to a seated position in the dusty pathway. After a few seconds he jerked his head around to see what the others were doing. They stood around him, staring into the ravine, all, that is, but one. Dera sat, cross-legged, a few paces from him; apparently, her legs had also buckled. Gogtee had been right; they had entered a world he had never imagined. If the piles were composed of human artwork—and it appeared they were—what was it doing here? Something was wrong—terribly wrong.

It was not the first time in the last few days that his world had been turned upside down. It was the first time, however, that he faced something he really had no idea how to start to comprehend. He could think of no reason why the drak would dump the artwork into the ravine. The women's artistic genius was one of the major cornerstones of the People's culture, yet, it appeared, the draks considered the human females' art rubbish.

Kalmar inhaled a slow, deep breath and then stood up. He walked over and looked down at Dera. He was not sure why he did it; really, he did it without thinking. Before this moment, he had never seen confusion on her face; although never cocky, she had always been in control of her feelings. Over the last two days, it had become evident to him that Dera was the brightest person he had ever met. As he looked at her, an unexpected tingle spread through his body. For some unknown reason Dera's confusion gave him a sense of assurance, an intimacy with this enigmatic female. Until that moment, she had just been a member of the other sex; he had never felt any empathy for any female other than his mother and sisters. After a few moments, he leaned over and offered her his hand. She looked up at him but did not make a move to accept his help. Her thick auburn hair hung down her back, tied behind her head with a leather lace; a steady breeze caused the loose strands to flutter around her face. Except for her birthmark, her unreadable face was as pale as Cabyl's. He had never noticed the delicate, yet determined lines of her face. After a moment, she batted her eyelids, regained control of herself, and finally observed his outstretched hand. Her gaze moved from his hand to his face. He felt the full force of her intensity spring at him from the depths of her dark green eyes. He almost faltered under her gaze, but kept his hand out. She hesitated, then reached up and took his hand. Her grip was strong but her skin was smooth, almost soft. He steadied her as she drew her legs under her body and stood up. Once on her feet, she nodded and gave him a slight smile before turning to address Gogtee. He glimpsed Arasima's stern face as she watched them out of the corner of her eye.

Is it all right if I take a few moments to look at that?" Dera indicated the ravine with a tilt of her head.

Gogtee nodded and blinked her large eyes. "Dryka and I will wait here." Dryka had positioned himself next to his mate after he and Arasima caught up with the rest of the group. Dera watched the reptiles as they retreated to the shade of the embankment where they rocked back on their stout legs, balancing themselves with their long, thick tails.

Dera had not asked for consent for all of them to go down into the ravine, but the reptile and her mate's actions implied they expected all of the humans would wish to inspect their find. Gogtee and Dryka were correct; the remaining six humans quickly made their way to the edge of the ravine. Dera noticed wheelon tracks leading from the pathway, which ran parallel to the ravine until they dropped out of sight over a small raise.

Snook also noticed the wheel ruts. He grabbed Cabyl's hand and sprinted off the pathway as the brim of his straw hat flopped around his ears. "Over here. There's a draw that leads down to the ravine bed." The other five ran over to join Snook and Cabyl as they walked down the incline into the ravine. The piles of artwork were even more numerous and massive than they first appeared from the pathway. The humans stayed bunched up as they walked among the discarded heaps of broken pieces of artistic obsession. Snook noticed that Arasima grabbed Kalmar's arm and clung to him. Kalmar looked down at the beautiful woman in amazement before returning his attention to the mystery surrounding them. The seven were hesitant and hushed as if they were walking through a graveyard. Dera walked over and picked up a broken figurine of a male child. She turned the finely formed sculpture over in her hands, studying its artistic lines. Once Dera broke the eerie spell, the others began to gather pieces to make their own inspections. After careful study, Dera returned the figurine reverently to the pile where she had found it. It was obvious those who had abandoned the figurine had done so without any thought of its uniqueness.

There must be hundreds of thousands of pieces here, almost all of them damaged," Dera said.

"Do you think it was discarded because it was damaged?" Nutan said.

"I think not; most of it appears to have been broken when it was dumped here, besides there are a few pieces that are undamaged."

"It would taken a long time to produce this much art," said Izzy. He walked up to stand between his sister and Nutan.

"Six Progressions," Cabyl said in a clear, firm voice. Snook and the other five turned to look at Cabyl. It was one of the few times she had spoken to the group as a whole since they began their journey.

"What do you mean?" Arasima responded in a challenging tone. She also, for the most part, had remained silent. Cabyl shifted her dark eyes towards Arasima but did not respond.

Dera pulled at her chin with her left hand. "What Cabyl means is, this ravine has been used as a dump for our women's artwork ever since the time of Geerna, since the beginning of the Tell."

"From the beginning?" Snook pulled his head back. Both Dera and Cabyl nodded.

"What a waste—it is a travesty," Nutan said, slowly shaking her head.

"It doesn't make any sense. Why would the draks discard our females' artwork?" Kalmar added.

"More importantly, why would they trade with us for things they apparently consider worthless," Dera whispered under her breath. Kalmar's lower jaw dropped as he and the others turned to stare at her, even though she had made the comment more to herself than to the rest of them. "There're no answers to be found here, just questions," she said firmly as she kicked a pebble. She started back towards the pathway.

One person after another turned and followed Dera until only Arasima remained. A single tear rolled down the cheek of the solitary figure. She slowly opened her clenched fingers, allowing a sculpture of a small deer to slide down her pants leg, landing in the sandy soil of the ravine. She stared down at the ceramic product of one of her kindred's skill and patience. Ever since it became evident that her scrawny body would fill out, transforming her to the most beautiful female in the village, she had worked to find a way to silence her taunters. To be the one chosen by Shetow seemed to be the answer. As she looked around her, she knew that everything she had believed was false. After a moment's reflection, she lifted her foot and crushed the fragile figurine under her heel. It crunched like a thin sheet of ice on a fall morning puddle. Her greenish gray eyes slowly scanned the towering mounds of broken porcelain. She jerked her head around, her flowing hair moving in unison, to face the direction of retreat, and followed the others.

As they walked out of the ravine, Kalmar glanced at Snook. His friend arched his eyebrows as he returned the look. Without trying, Dera had become the ad hoc leader of their fledgling group.

"Dera's an enigma; there's more to that woman than I first thought," Snook said as he and Kalmar escorted Cabyl up the incline and out of the ravine.

Kalmar's eyes cut to Snook before turning to watch Dera as she walked in front of him in long even strides. He cocked his head; he had been thinking the same thing.

As the three of them trudged back up the hill towards the pathway, Kalmar noticed a soft smile lingering on Cabyl's lips. His face contorted into a wide grin. *She must think us stupid*, he thought. They had discussed Dera as if Cabyl was not even there.

"Gogtee, would you please explain what this means?" Dera asked as she and the others approached the two draks.

"You must wait until tomorrow for your answer."

"Tomorrow! Why must we wait until then?" Arasima demanded. The other six were taken aback by Arasima's sudden hostility, but looked at the drak for an answer, nodding their approval of her question.

"It will be the time of your first learning," Gogtee said, and with a flip of her long tail turned and started walking with a faster gait than at any other time during their journey. The humans were not expecting Gogtee's reaction to Arasima's question and had to sprint to keep up with the giant lizard. As the group rushed down the pathway, Dryka assumed his place at the rear.

After several minutes of breakneck speed, Gogtee looked back and slowed her pace, realizing the humans could not keep up. "I don't think I could've gone another hundred paces at that rate," Snook exclaimed, clutching his side.

"The Gray Beards claim the draks can outrun a prairie buck,"

Kalmar said, "but I didn't believe it until I saw how effortlessly Gogtee moved when she wanted to."

"You know, if you look at their bodies, you can see their legs are made for running."

"Well, Gogtee never got to a run. I don't think she even hit a trot. She just walked . . . fast, and even with us running as hard as we could, we still couldn't keep up."

Dera overheard Kalmar and Snook's conversation. "Did Shetow give the draks those strong legs so they could escape danger, or do their legs make the draks the danger?" she added.

Kalmar laughed. "The size of their teeth and not the size of their legs may be a better indicator as to the answer to that question."

Dera raised an eyebrow. "I think that's a valid observation." She chuckled and a smile brightened her face, only the second one Kalmar had ever seen from her.

"Look!" Snook said, pointing towards the drak city. "Traders!" They all followed his gaze and saw two wheelons and four draks coming towards them from the city. "What's that in front of the wheelons? Where're the bovors?" All seven humans stared at the approaching column. Stationed in front of each wheelon was a strange mechanical creature—what appeared to be two-wheeled machines instead of bovors were pulling the wheelons. The angle of approach of the baffling mechanisms made it difficult for the humans to get a good look at the bizarre contraptions.

When the strange caravan drew near, the humans followed Gogtee's lead and shuffled off the pathway to let it pass. The strange egg-shaped machines were about a third the size of the wheelons they were pulling and covered with seamless metallic-gray skins. If the wheels had been absent, one would have thought a gigantic metal bird had laid them. The humans had never seen a self-powered machine and, if they had not already been familiar with the wheelon, they would not have known if the unnerving mechanism was doing the pulling or being pushed by the wheelon behind it. The wheels of the metallic eggs were about half the diameter of those of the wheelons—a little over waist high. The wheelons, like all such wagons, had rectangular bodies formed from nutwood planks reinforced with metal rims, angle iron, hinges, nuts and bolts, and other bindings fashioned by the hands of human blacksmiths. In stark contrast, the pulling machines were rounded, constructed from a smooth, unknown material, and fashioned by a craft not possessed by any blacksmith any of the humans had ever met. An axle pierced the underside of the elongated sphere, connecting the wheels of the machines. The smaller, more tapered ends of the egg-shaped objects pointed in the direction they were traveling; on the more rounded and larger ends were hitches for attaching the tongues of the wheelons.

As the pulling machines rambled past the humans—freight in tow—Kalmar could see the drak trading goods stacked high above the wheelons' wooden sides. The four accompanying draks were all adorned with identical leather belts and straps, and their upper limbs sported the same array of metal bracelets as Gogtee and Dryka. All four traders exchanged raspy spurts of unintelligible clamor with the two draks accompanying the humans. The passing draks also acknowledged Kalmar and the others by the lifting of their slender arms and bobbing their feathered heads towards the seven human travelers. As the second wheelon passed, Kalmar spotted a third pulling machine right behind it; the machines were somewhat smaller than the wheelons, so the lone machine had been hidden from his view by the second wheelon. This last pulling machine was not pulling a wheelon, but was moving ahead as if it were. Other than not having a wheelon attached, the third, an unattended machine, was identical to the first two. All seven humans stood in silence as they watched the traders and the loaded wheelons slowly make their way up the mountainside towards the entrance to the tunnel. The third pulling machine trailed like a duckling waddling behind its mother.

"These machines must be used to pull the wheelons through the tunnel where the traders exchange them for the bovors we saw corralled at the other end of the tunnel," Kalmar said.

"These must be scheduled to meet with the wheelon caravan we passed before we reached the tunnel," Snook said.

"How did they work out the timing of when they were to meet? If I am not mistaken, both groups should reach the corral where the bovor are at about the same time," Kalmar said.

"That is why there are three," Cabyl said.

"What . . . three?" Snook asked, smiling at her.

"The third pulling machine . . . the one that's not pulling a wheelon; the draks know they are going to meet a caravan with three wheelons . . . so they took an extra pulling machine with them to pull back the third wheelon when it's relieved of its bovor," she answered. The two men nodded in agreement.

"There must be a constant flow of traders in and out of this valley," Dera said.

"To service all Twenty-Four Tribes, you would think there would be more than this one route," Nutan said.

"I hadn't thought of that. You must be right. There must be other drak villages like this one," Kalmar replied.

"I guess we'll find out soon enough," Cabyl added.

Kalmar continued to watch the monster eggs roll up the hill. He wondered what magic commanded their movement; he also marveled at the oblong-bodied, two-wheeled machines' balance. How do their bodies stay parallel with the ground? Why did one end not tilt down?

"I wonder what powers them?" Izzy asked. "How do they operate?"

"If the draks and our judges fly between the stars"—Snook

made a sweep with his hand—"I'm sure the egg-shaped machines are a small marvel compared to what we are going to see."

Nutan brushed a maverick lock of hair back from her face. "Gogtee said our questions would be answered tomorrow." She glanced up the mountain path towards the ravine. "Besides the questions I have about our journey and the pending judging, the one that is still driving me crazy is why they discard our art after they trade for it. I have been trying to figure out a scenario that would explain it, but the more I think about it, the less logical it seems to be." She compressed her lips until they turned white. "I can't think of any reason that comes close to making sense."

Snook studied her a moment. "There is a second part to your question that's as much a riddle as the first part."

Her eyes drifted towards him, her brow wrinkled. "What is that?"

Snook met Nutan's stare. "Where do they obtain the goods they trade us?"

It was nearing dusk as the group approached the drak village. On the village's outskirts loomed large fields covered by short fan-shaped ferns and bushy knee-high shrubs encircled by thick shoulder-high stone fences. Grazing in the fields were vast herds of large reptilian herbivores whose thick bodies resembled the mammalian bovors used to pull the wheelons. Their tree-trunk-sized legs, however, were closer to those of a mammoth than a hoofed bovor. Their front legs were shorter than their hind legs, causing the creatures to look hunched over. Other than mammoths, the creatures were the largest animals anyone in the group had ever seen. These herbivores—like bovors—walked on all four legs and had horns protruding from either side of their heads, but in the reptiles' case, the horns were not only on each side of their massive skulls—a third, shorter one jutted from the center of their snouts.

Unlike the draks' extended tails, used as a counterbalance, these barrel-shaped reptiles' arm-sized tails hung down almost touching the ground. Fanning out from the back of their heads were tall bony plates, giving the illusion that the creatures' heads were double the size they actually were. The plate started below the ear on one side of their domed craniums, arched over the back of the animals' skulls, and ended below the ear on the other side of their imposing heads. At the end of their snouts, the hard upper lip turned down like a hawk's beak. Kalmar wondered why they had beaks until he saw one of the creatures hook it under the bottom of a bushy shrub, yank it and its roots out of the ground, and start chewing on it. Penetrating soot-black eyes, small in proportion to their large heads, followed the humans as they ambled by. Dozens of identical fields, teeming with hundreds of the fearsome reptiles, dotted the countryside. The creatures roamed the fields freely, but Kalmar spotted a number of draks tending the herds.

There were about thirty of the creatures grazing near the edge of one of the fields bordering the pathway; the enormous animals watched intently as the band of two draks and seven humans walked towards them. As the group approached the creatures, Kalmar took the opportunity to study them closer. The creatures kept chewing their feast of ferns and shrubs but stopped pulling them out of the ground. Their small black eyes fixed on the humans as they drew nearer. When the band was about to pass right in front of them, one of the larger animals stopped chewing and bellowed a long deep challenge. Kalmar noticed he was not the only one of the group who jumped at the loud resonating sound.

"Well, we know which one is the bull of the herd," Kalmar said, laughing.

Dera cupped her right hand against the side of her mouth so that Gogtee and Dryka could not hear her as she whispered back to Kalmar, Snook, and Cabyl. "Well, reptiles don't produce milk so I think it's safe to assume these creatures serve as one of the draks' meat sources. It answers any question we had about the draks' teeth and what they do with them."

As Dera turned away from them, Snook lifted an eyebrow. "She sure doesn't hold a grudge long. If I didn't know better, I would swear this isn't the girl whose choosing you rejected."

Kalmar nodded, shrugging his shoulders. "In a way, it makes it even harder for me to come to grips with the fluctuation in my emotions about all that has happened . . . I mean, you know, about what happened before we knew about this journey."

Snook avoided Kalmar's eyes. "Have you noticed anything odd about the plant life since we came out of the tunnel?"

Kalmar looked around, shaking his head.

"Do you see anything missing?"

Kalmar looked harder at the foliage. "Well, I don't recognize any of the trees, but other than that, I don't notice anything different."

"You're correct, the trees are of a kind that I've never seen, but that isn't what I was taking about. Have you not noticed? There's no grass."

Kalmar stopped walking and took a closer look at his sur-roundings. There was an abundance of vegetation, but the closer he looked at it, the less familiar it looked. There were no nutwood trees and, what was now even more obvious, there was indeed no grass. When Kalmar, Snook, and Cabyl stopped walking, the others paused to see what the three were doing. Kalmar told them of Snook's observations concerning the plant life.

"Snook, I've also been studying the fields and the hillsides," Dera said. "Everything looks . . . normal until you look closer." She bent over and picked up a leaf that had been blowing across the path and gave it a quick glance. "Under closer scrutiny it's easy to tell we're in a land where the plants and trees are different from the ones we've known all of our lives." She glanced down at the leaf one more time, then let it flutter out of her hand on a gust of wind. "The land of the draks isn't like the one we know and understand."

"How can plant life be different on each side of the mountains?" Izzy asked.

Dera looked towards the mountain peak. "The mountains must act as a barrier between our two worlds."

"Any physical obstacle will act as a barrier for both plant and animal life," Arasima said sarcastically.

"It seems impractical that a mountain range could stop all the flying animals, along with the plant seeds spread by the wind," Snook said, "but, other than the draks, I've never seen any of the animals or plants on this side of the mountain before today."

Gogtee made a clicking sound and an arm motion indicating they should continue. The group did start, but for the first time since they left the Gathering Compound, they walked in a tightly packed cluster as they resumed their conversation. Without anyone suggesting it, they spoke in hushed tones so the two draks could not hear what they were saying. Arasima stayed close to Kalmar, bumping into him several times.

"Izzy, what did you mean this morning?" Nutan asked.

"About what?"

"As we left the drak caravan, you said you weren't so sure how good the draks were at knowing the aesthetic value of the works they traded for."

"Well—" Izzy didn't seem to know what to say. "I have heard the draks sometimes give excessive trading value to art that's . . . well, not that good."

"What do you know about the value of art?" Arasima said, her voice as sharp as the tip of an eagle's talon.

Izzy lowered his eyes. "I know—"

"Izzy knows," Dera interrupted. "I had an inferior piece of

sculpture with me the last time I traded with the drak traders because it was a piece I meant to destroy. By mistake, a drak trader saw it in my bag and offered me an exorbitant exchange value for it."

"That proves nothing," Arasima said in a condescending tone as she walked over and joined the others. "Everyone knows you excel at *everything.*" She crossed her arms and squinted her eyes. "Even your worst art is better than many other artists' best." Kalmar bristled at the venom in Arasima's little bites of sarcasm.

"No, the drak trader was valuing the art higher than he should have," Dera replied calmly, not rising to Arasima's attack.

Arasima knew it would be a mistake to attack Dera, but her insecurity prevailed. Her eyes opened wider and the ends of her lips turned up. "Dera, surely you are not criticizing your own artwork?" Her words dripped with false sincerity.

"No . . . it wasn't my best work . . . believe me, it wasn't worth what the drak wanted to value it." Dera looked and sounded a little flustered. Her agitation surprised everyone.

Snook turned and whispered to Kalmar. "What's going on?" "I don't know."

"Dera's holding something back," Cabyl whispered to Snook, but loud enough for Kalmar to hear. Cabyl did not say much, but when she did, both Snook and Kalmar listened. "Dera knows something she's not telling us."

"How does perfection not find everything else flawed?" Arasima pushed her point. Dera had stopped talking, thus allowing Arasima free rein to keep on making her little stinging remarks.

Kalmar did not understand. Why did Dera not defend herself? Arasima's remarks should have been easy for someone as smart as Dera to parry.

He had heard all he wanted to from Arasima. "I think you've said enough, Arasima." Arasima's eyes cut to him, and Kalmar braced himself for her next hail of cynicism, but to his surprise, she lowered her large eyes and took a step backwards.

Arasima panicked. She had let her dislike of other females rule her words. She should be less confrontational, she thought. She was not used to having to deal with both males and females in the same group.

Not seeing Arasima's reaction to Kalmar's outburst, Izzy stepped in the middle of the melee before Arasima could respond. "The reason the art piece wasn't up to her standards was . . ." Dera gave her brother a stern look ". . . was because the art . . . wasn't hers."

Everyone looked at Izzy; confusion cloaked their faces. Then Kalmar smiled; they had been arguing over nothing.

"Why didn't you tell us that, Dera?" said Nutan, in her most consoling voice. Nutan had taken a real liking to Dera and Kalmar could tell his little sister was ready to defend Dera if Arasima resumed her assault.

Izzy took in a deep breath and released a little of it. "She didn't tell you because I was the one who molded the piece."

TWENTY-SIX

Stunned by what Izzy had told them, Nutan was having a hard time sorting it out in her mind. "Kalmar, I'm not sure if I am more shocked that Izzy would try to create art or that the draks couldn't tell the difference in what Izzy made compared to Dera."

"You like Izzy, don't you?"

"Sort of." Her face revealed lines of concern. "But I don't know what to make of him—his flagrant disrespect of Shetow's commands . . . his doing something Shetow has allocated exclusively for females."

"Do you think it makes him less a man?"

Her head tilted forward, muffling her response. "I don't know what to think."

"Do you remember when you were ten or so and I caught you trying to shoot my bow behind our cottage?"

Nutan lifted her head, covered her open mouth with her hand, and yelped. "Oh, I had forgotten about that."

"An act that's as barred to females as being an artist is to a male."

"I didn't want to be a hunter; I just wanted to see what it was about."

"If Shetow is all knowing, she hasn't forgotten it. The Medora Council believes Shetow guided their hand in selecting us to represent the People at the Judging." Nutan flashed her eyes up at her brother as he kept talking. "The draks knew Snook didn't eat red meat when we were so sure they didn't even know Snook and the Mookyn existed. If the draks knew that, they are not concerned about Izzy and Dera's transgressions . . . or yours. Shetow, or whatever higher power the draks answer to, didn't instruct them to reject any of us."

"But when I played with your bow I was a small child; Izzy is a man. A man who was trying to be an artist." There was a tremor in her voice. "I feel like he assaulted me . . . my personal privacy . . . of what it is to be female. The wrongness of his act is so embedded in my mind"—she tapped her temple with a finger—"I—"

Kalmar shook his head. "Sister, Izzy's actions were of no consequence." He made a casual flip of his hand. "Of more importance is this: how does it make you feel to learn that, for the last six Progressions, the draks have been dumping that *exquisite* art—what you feel is the soul of our females—into a trash heap on the backside of that mountain?" Kalmar pointed over his shoulder.

She walked with her head lowered, "I'm still in shock, I—"

"It can only mean but one thing."

"What's that?" Her eyes darted towards him.

"The worth of art is only, as you say"—he mimicked her tapping of her temple—"up here." They walked a few more steps. "It's only valuable to us. To appreciate human art, apparently, you have to be human."

Her face drew into a scowl and she blurted, "Then why would they want us to think they believed the art had value to them?"

The other humans turned towards the sudden outburst. "Because they had to have something to trade for," Dera said, with no inflection. "There can be no other rational explanation."

"Huh?"

"All those things we don't make for ourselves: metals, medicines, glass bottles, and hundreds of other things. They needed a way to supply them to us. The drak traders were always there when we needed something we couldn't manufacture for ourselves."

"But why art? The way they treated it"—Nutan reached down and picked up a fist-sized stone from the side of the path—"it would have been smarter to have us gather rocks so they could use them when they needed to build one of their rock fences."

"I'm not sure," Dera said, "but there has to be a reason they settled on our females' art as the trading item."

"There also has to be significance to the fact that they traded with us in the first place," Kalmar said.

"How do you mean?"

"While it is of importance that the draks trade for our females' art, it's just as important that they trade with us at all."

Dera's cheeks hollowed as her eyes stayed fixed on him.

"They're trading us things of value for things they don't value," Kalmar said, with a little animation.

"And?"

"It would have been much easier for them to just give us the goods." Kalmar rubbed his forehead. "They spent as much time transporting and disposing of the art as they did in bringing us the trade goods; without the ruse, they could have delivered twice the goods for the same effort."

"Or the same amount with half the effort," Snook added.

Kalmar nodded. "We have two mysteries." He held up a finger. "Why did they choose art as the thing they traded for, and"—up went a second finger—"why do they trade with us at all?"

"They trade with us," Cabyl said, "because Shetow designed the system to make us feel productive, to give us a sense of worth, while in reality, we have been tended like chickens in a pen."

There was a long silence.

"We're forgetting Snook's earlier point," Dera said.

"What's that?"

"Where do they obtain the goods they trade us?"

The group voiced many questions but produced no answers. After the initial flurry of speculations, the group slowly spread out into smaller bunches trailing behind Gogtee as she led them towards the drak village. Kalmar and Nutan walked together, a little ways away from the others.

Kalmar noticed Nutan's troubled expression. "Still thinking about Izzy?"

Nutan looked down as they walked, a slight toss of her head her only response to Kalmar's inquiry.

"Sister, I cannot tell you what kind of *man* he is, but I can tell you he is a person of integrity."

"Why do you say that?" She glanced at him with large, quizzical eyes.

"He didn't have to say anything when Arasima was grilling Dera about the reason Dera knew the artwork was inferior. Dera wasn't going to reveal what he, or they, had done, but he still stepped forward to protect his sister from Arasima's taunts."

"He did, didn't he?" A guarded smile crept across her face.

"That's the action of a courageous person, one who cared more for his sister's honor than he fretted about the fear of being ostracized by the rest of us. We all could learn from this young man."

Nutan's face burst into an expansive smile. "Thank you, brother," she blurted. She flung her arms around his neck.

For the first time since before the Matage, Kalmar felt his outlook lift. As Nutan slowly relaxed her hug, he said, "We must not doubt the others. The slightest doubt about one another is the surest way to guarantee our failing the Judging." He forced a grin. "You must help me pull the group together. We must be an example to the others. We must act in a way that would make our parents and grandparents proud, not only for ourselves but also for every person in the Twenty-Four Tribes." Nutan looked at him questioningly. He grinned again. "Yes, also for Snook and the other Mookyn, plus our distant relatives on our mother world."

Nutan smiled and nodded.

As the humans and their two drak guides drew close to the strange structures, they began to meet other draks on the pathways, which now branched in every direction connecting the mushroom-shaped buildings. The converging draks would squawk at Gogtee and Dryka as their little group walked past. The two draks answered their kindred with equally unintelligible guttural sounds. The onlookers began to follow the group in ever-larger numbers as they neared the settlement. Many of the draks were small, not over knee-high; the smaller versions of Gogtee and Dryka would dart from one spot to another in greenish gray blurs; when the small lizards were not running, they walked and moved in fast, jerky birdlike motions.

"Do you think the smaller ones are another species, or just their young?" Kalmar asked.

"I would guess they are the young, but I can't see any signs of age other than size; the small ones appear to be lean replicas of the larger ones," Snook responded.

"*Signs of age.* How about the ways the little ones are always moving?" Nutan interjected as she pointed to a pair darting in and out of view. "That's either youthful tension or they're playing."

Kalmar and Snook watched the pair of miniature draks scurry

around the knurly trunk of an immense tree. One was chasing the other. The first one stopped and its pursuer froze in midstep and stood perfectly still. The one doing the chasing then craned its head to one side and watched, through unblinking eyes, the one it was trying to catch. In a few seconds, before resuming their game of chase, they bobbed their heads in jerky motions and hissed at each other. After witnessing the antics of the two undersized draks, Snook reevaluated his comments and then both he and Kalmar nodded their agreement with Nutan's conclusion.

"They are playing all right," Kalmar said. "However, their game is one based on learning how to hunt, not just on youthful playfulness. I think if we look hard enough, we could pick out their equivalent of our Gray Beards among the onlookers."

"The young play hunting games, have razor sharp teeth, and the adults can run down a prairie buck," Dera said. She, along with Izzy, had overheard Kalmar, Snook, and Nutan's conversation. "It becomes even clearer that our friendly draks are much better suited to be predators than they are traders."

"Just like humans, born to hunt," Izzy added.

"Maybe so, little brother." She raised her eyebrows, wrinkling her forehead. "But I judge their physique far superior to ours in environments where survival depends on being able to track down a meal."

"Hunting is a masculine art; it's as much up here"—Kalmar tapped his temple—"as it is in an animal's physical prowess."

"No offense meant to your masculine self-esteem," Dera said, "but if I were a prairie buck, I think I would stand a much better chance with you after me than one of them." She tilted her head towards the mob of draks following them.

Kalmar responded with a weak grin and a shrug.

"That brings up another question," Snook said.

"What do you mean?" Kalmar's eyes jumped to Snook.

"Why are there drak traders in the first place?" They all looked at Snook; no one ventured a guess.

The pathways narrowed as they wove their way among the imposing buildings. Kalmar caught glimpses of draks peeping out of the windows that ringed the round towering structures. The head of a large drak protruded from one of the annular openings; the lizard turned and looked back into the interior of the structure as if distracted by something behind it. The drak made a raspy squawk, pulled back, and was quickly replaced by the chirping heads of four smaller draks who assailed the humans below with their warbling.

"What is that?" Izzy shouted, pointing to something off to their right.

Kalmar stopped and saw something bulky move out of the shadow of one of the mushroom-shaped buildings. It turned and scooted along a pathway that intersected with the one they were traveling. All the humans gawked at the curious craft as it glided along about as fast as a young man could run. The only noise generated by the strange contraption came from the commotion and squeals of the draks forced off the pathway by the passage of the unimaginable vehicle. It looked like an enchanted boat, swept along by a swift current, sailing down an invisible river. The land-boat floated knee high above the ground and was as wide as a wheelon and about as long as two wheelons placed end-to-end; the top of its sides were about chest high and its contents were uncovered. Standing on a platform that jutted out of the rear was a drak clinging to two metal poles that stuck up from the end of the vehicle. The drak's tail stuck out behind it like a rudder and Kalmar would have found the spectacle humorous if he had not been so astonished. As the land-boat neared them, they scurried off the pathway. When it whisked by, Kalmar glimpsed various objects that appeared to be trading goods.

"It doesn't have any . . . I don't see any wheels," Dera said.

"That's because it doesn't have wheels," Gogtee responded.

"How can that be?" Kalmar grimaced. Gogtee did not stop to answer but continued at her grueling pace. The apparent proximity of their destination seemed to have lengthened her strides. He was now walking as fast as he could; it was all he could do to keep from jogging and he became disoriented as they zigzagged through the forest of domed buildings and the squawking assemblage of reptilian onlookers.

Gogtee finally halted in front of one of the larger structures and waited for the others to catch up. Arasima and Dryka were the last to arrive. Even though he was only panting, Kalmar gave mental thanks for the physical conditioning he had undertaken in preparation for the games. Snook and Cabyl were not as fortunate—they were both bent over gasping for breath. It was evident by the strained look on Snook's face and the way he was holding his side that he was in the worse condition of the two. Nutan, Izzy, and Arasima were also breathing hard but otherwise seemed all right. Dera stood a few steps away, studying their surroundings in her uniquely inquisitive way and appearing unfazed by their ordeal.

After a quick survey of her flock, Gogtee pushed on a large oval door. It split down the middle, with one half swinging to the right and the other to the left. The doorway was wide enough for a wheelon to roll through and stood twice as tall as it was wide. Without hesitating, Gogtee led them down a dimly lit hall into a large, vaulted room.

"Please wait here," Gogtee said. She and Dryka walked out, leaving the humans alone for the first time since they'd left the Gathering Compound two days earlier. Everyone but Snook and Dera sat down on one of two wooden benches lined end-to-end against the left side of the room.

Still panting, Snook walked around, carefully inspecting every object in the room. He brushed his hand down the surface of one of the walls. "It's stone."

"What's stone?" answered Kalmar, who had been watching Arasima out of the corner of his eye while trying to hide it from the others, especially her.

"The walls, the floors, the whole structure . . . everything is made of seamless stone."

Kalmar and Izzy jumped up and rushed over to where Snook was inspecting the wall. Both ran their hands over the grainy surface before stepping back.

"It's rock all right," Izzy said. Snook nodded.

"Guess if they can hollow out Mount Alar, they should be able to build these buildings out of rock," said Kalmar.

"Maybe," Dera said, "but it's one thing to form a hole by digging clay out of the ground and another thing entirely to take that clay, mold it, and fire it to produce pottery." At the sound of her voice, the three men turned to face Dera. She walked towards them, after she carefully set down a metallic device she had discovered lying on one of the tables lined against the other side of the room. "Our Gathering Chamber is essentially a hole in the ground; this building's more like molded pottery."

"I don't know much about making pottery, but I do know hollowing out Mount Alar or fabricating these buildings is beyond our capabilities," Kalmar said.

"I'm not sure you're right," said Dera, in a firm yet easy voice.

"How . . . what makes you think that we could—" started Kalmar.

"Gogtee told me she was one of the very few of her race selected to deal with humans. It seems being a trader, or to take part in our Koo Toc Biren ceremony, is a great honor to the draks. She also said she was chosen for this assignment because of her high intelligence and intellect." Everyone else stopped talking to listen to what Dera was saying. "I have spent the better part of the last two days conferring . . . no, more like chatting with Gogtee. I like her. She has a wit that is sometimes hard to follow, but basically, we could be friends. As a mental superior, though, she falls short."

"Dera, we all fall short of you," Nutan said, without a hint of sarcasm in her voice.

Arasima rolled her eyes.

Dera smiled at Nutan. "Thank you, I have been blessed with many talents, but I understand the talents we're judged by during the Byrrac and the Borrac aren't the talents that make us"—she lifted her hands and arms to indicate them all—"into who and what we are as a species. You may not recognize them, but I see talents in each of you that are far superior to those same talents in me. All of you employ your talents in your everyday lives far better than I do." Her gaze met their questioning eyes. "But the point I was trying to make about Gogtee wasn't because I had judged her against me, or for that matter, against any of you. What I'm trying to say is that the draks, if Gogtee's a fair example, aren't our mental superiors."

"How do you mean?" Snook said.

"Well, during our conversations, either she was playing me for a fool—and I'm *very* sure that was not the case—or she couldn't grasp many of my questions. There were a number of questions she did understand, but was not able to answer. There were times when I asked her questions, after I had already determined the answers, only to find *she* did not know the answers. A few times, after I suggested an answer, she seemed surprised and said she would never have thought of it, and that it was obvious to her after I pointed it out. Often she seemed unable to fathom complex concepts; other times, even obvious conclusions escaped her. When we talked about anything beyond rudimentary subjects, she was lost.

After we entered the tunnel, I asked her what made the rock wall disappear. She said, by waving her bracelet in front it. I laughed and said, 'No, what made it disappear? How does it work?'" Dera looked away. "She couldn't begin to explain it to me."

"Maybe she was evading the question," Cabyl offered.

"I don't think so, she was . . ." Dera paused and seemed to be searching her mind for the right word ". . . embarrassed that she couldn't explain it to me. I also felt she was embarrassed that she hadn't wondered how it worked before I asked her."

"It's possible," Snook offered, "she was embarrassed for you and not for herself, not wanting to humiliate you by talking about things you wouldn't understand."

"I realize that is possible, but I don't think so. I don't think Gogtee had any idea how the rock wall disappeared, she—" Dera was quiet for a long time. She sat staring at the wall as if she were seeing a vision invisible to the rest of them. The others did not speak as they exchanged glances.

Kalmar knew Dera would return her attention to them once she had worked it out in her own mind. He noticed Arasima watching him as he waited on Dera's next observation.

Dera stood up. "I believe that the draks think in very simple patterns, really. There's something . . . an intuitiveness missing from their thought process." Her eyes traced the outline of the room; then she made a sweeping motion with her hand. "If the draks can fabricate these buildings, we can too. It's not beyond our capabilities."

"Dera, how could we build these structures . . . what about the floating wheelon we saw as we entered the city?" pressed Nutan.

"I think we could build the structures if we had the tools. And I know any one of us could operate the floating wheelon after we had a chance to study it."

"But Dera, every craftsman knows the tools are what's important," Snook said, throwing his hands up, "and we haven't a clue how to make such tools."

"That's my point; I don't think the draks made them either."

"By the Mark of the Covenant, you don't think the draks were the ones that Shetow used to bring Geerna and our other ancestors to Elom," Kalmar said, his eyes searching for a reaction.

"Of course they didn't." She scrunched her face. "Gogtee said the draks weren't the ones who were going to judge us. The ones Shetow is going to use to judge or help Her judge us are the ones who did bring us to Elom. I think Shetow uses surrogates like the Multiped to do Her bidding. Those surrogates are the ones who brought Geerna to Elom. The draks are just our caretakers; the surrogates may have even brought the draks to Elom just for that purpose."

"And you're right . . . or mostly right," bellowed a raspy, barely intelligible voice from behind them. They turned to confront the largest drak any one of them had ever seen, at least a third larger than Gogtee, who stood behind and a little to the left of the imposing stranger. A feathery purple crest topped the creature's head and a smaller remnant ran down the back of its neck. The customary leather belts and metal bracelets draped its body. Kalmar wondered how the three-toed giant had been able to enter the room without them hearing it; he also wondered how long the creature had been listening to their conversation before it spoke. He drew his head back as he stared at the creature's finger-long teeth. Something to his right distracted him; he cut his eyes in that direction and saw Dera.

Her darting eyes found his. "Pre-da-tor," she mouthed. Dark lines etched her pallid brow.

Ten or more smaller draks had also entered the room. The gaggle of attendants carried an array of bundles, bags, and instruments. Without a visual or audible sign, one of the minions jumped and then scurried over to the giant, reached into a leather bag, and pulled out a mud-colored, fist-sized object, and handed it to the giant lizard, who promptly popped it into its mouth. Kalmar stood transfixed as the creature lifted its massive head and swallowed the morsel whole. The towering creature seemed surreal, out of place even in the land of the draks. The color of drak plumage, or at least every drak he had ever met was, for the most part, a rich moss green with parts of their heads, claws, and feet a dark gray. The adults' heads—or what the humans thought were adults, the larger draks—were topped with multicolored crests, and stripes fanning out across their backs in varying hues of black, red, brown, and yellow. The feathers of the giant drak, however, were muted, washed out, many shades lighter than the other draks; they also lacked the sheen of Gogtee, Dryka, or the draks they had passed as they entered the city. Kalmar assumed the creature's torpid coloration indicated a sign of advanced age.

A twitch of the reptile's massive mandible signaled the creature was about to speak; Kalmar leaned forward as he strained to understand the next words.

"I'm Adurrell, the Bora, or male leader, of the draks. Zalibar, the Davar, our female leader, will join us shortly."

Out of the corner of his eye, Kalmar saw Dera take a small step forward. Since she had been the one Adurrell had spoken to first, Kalmar figured Dera felt she must respond.

"My name is—"

"Dera," said Adurrell, in a harsh, croaky voice harder to understand than Gogtee's softer speech. He had made a slight bow to Dera as he addressed her, and then he addressed each one of them in turn, identifying them all perfectly. After finishing, he returned his attention to Dera. "Gogtee tells me you are the only one she has had a chance to evaluate. She thinks you are smart; you have given her hope for a favorable outcome in your pending Judging."

"Gogtee is kind; you can be sure that I and my friends will do our best to represent our race at the Judging."

"We hope that is the case; more than your race's fate is to be decided by the Judging."

"I . . . we"—Dera looked around at the others—"we don't understand what you mean."

"Much I need to tell you, but first sit down. I will have food brought."

"We're ready to listen *now!*" Arasima exclaimed. She moved forward a step.

"Eat first, talk soon. We wait for the Davar, Zalibar," said the drak, in his jumbled syntax, as he turned his broad back to Arasima with a flip of his blue-tipped tail. Kalmar chuckled at Arasima's rebuff. Here was a male not swayed by her seductive charms. She turned and gave him a scolding stare. Adurrell motioned to Gogtee. Gogtee gave a slight dip of her head, turned, and quickly scurried out of the room. Adurrell made a shallow bow to the small group of humans and followed Gogtee. Each one of the smaller attending draks bobbed, then followed Adurrell. In a few moments, Gogtee returned, leading a host of even smaller draks carrying platters of fruits, raw and cooked vegetables, and roasted meats. Scaled down from the size of Adurrell's attendants, the servers were smaller copies of Gogtee, except leaner and only about half her height—barely a third the size of Adurrell.

Kalmar leaned towards Snook. "I still can't tell if they're all the same species and the discrepancies in their sizes are a matter of age, or if each different size represents a different species."

Snook frowned thoughtfully. "The draks' size and color variations could be the result of more complicated variables than age. They could be like ants, and divided into different types where workers, nurses, soldiers, males, and queens all vary in size according to their function." Snook stopped talking as their reptilian servers placed the platters on the large wooden tables and stepped back to stand in silence along the walls.

Gogtee shepherded the humans to the tables and indicated they should start eating. Nutan eyed the banquet of unknown fruits, vegetables, tubers, fish, and meat before giving Kalmar a questioning look. Eager to disguise his own anxiety, Kalmar nodded with as reassuring a smile as he could muster. After scrutinizing his choices, he reached for a brownish gold, slightly pear-shaped piece of fruit, hesitated momentarily, then took a bite. The draks had known Snook did not eat red meat; surely, they knew if this food was palatable to humans. The group had not eaten since early that morning, but the pandemonium of the day's events had camouflaged Kalmar's hunger until the taste of the sweet, juicy pulp of the exotic food exploded in his mouth. It was completely different from anything he had ever tasted. He promptly filled his plate. The others followed his lead.

The food was fresh and filling, but puzzling to the humans; some of it had a strangely familiar flavor, other morsels had exotic delicate tastes that they tried to savor. At first, they talked sparingly as everyone took their fill.

"I don't recognize any of the fruits or vegetables," Snook finally said.

"Neither do I, and the meat isn't prairie buck," Kalmar answered.

"But it is good . . . it has a . . . different texture and lighter color," Nutan said.

"I bet it's from a relative of one of those horned brutes we saw in the fields outside the village," Izzy said.

Nutan scrunched her face in a shudder.

"I do not recognize the fish either," Snook said, as he picked up a thin-skinned reddish fruit. He held the fist-sized sphere up as he turned it over in his hand. "It doesn't look like any fruit that I have ever seen."

"The food must have been grown on this side of the barrier," Dera said.

"Dera," Snook asked, "do you really think the mountains impose such a barrier that all animal and plant life are barred from traveling from one side to the other?"

"You mentioned that point earlier today and I have been thinking about it. You are correct; the mountains aren't tall enough to stop every bird or windblown seed." Snook smiled at Dera's verdict, but she had not finished. "The answer has to be that the mountains are not the only thing stopping them. The draks or their masters must have created a barrier which extends beyond the crest of the mountain peaks."

"Correct again."

Kalmar and the others turned to find that Adurrell had reentered the room.

"How does something so big move so quietly?" Kalmar whispered, shaking his head. Snook and Nutan shrugged.

"Predator . . . the deftness of a predator," Dera replied, even softer.

At the muted sound of her voice, the oversized saurian jerked his head to the right in what Kalmar surmised was an effort to orient the left side of his head towards them. *Another attribute of a predator is acute hearing*, Kalmar thought to himself. He glanced at Dera and their eyes met; the intensity of her gaze revealed the same thought had just crossed her mind. Kalmar wondered if the drak's hearing was so keen that Adurrell was oblivious to the fact that the humans had tried to conceal their comments from him. He was convinced, however, that Adurrell had heard and understood their mutterings; whatever the case, the reptile chose not to offer a retort and, after a moment, turned his head to once again face them.

"There's a nuz-energy generator that produces an ionic partition that reaches to the upper strata of the planet's atmosphere, making it impossible for any life-form to move between the land of the draks and that of humans."

"We do not understand what you are telling us," said Dera, after she gave a questioning glance to the others.

The massive creature shifted its weight from one foot to the other. "It is an invisible barrier where the wind, dust, and clouds are not hampered, but any life-form, down to the very smallest, is kept from passing between the two sectors. There are four tunnels— including the one you used today—that serve as portals between the two sectors."

Nutan looked at Izzy, who raised an eyebrow.

The reptile took no notice of the reaction of his soft-skinned audience. "These tunnels are the only way for us to have access to your sector of Elom, and for that matter, the only access humans have to ours. The tunnels also act as a cleansing chamber for those who walk through them; any seeds that cling to your clothing, any rodent, or insect that might have hidden in a wheelon . . . any life that is present is selectively sterilized in the tunnel by a force you do not, as yet, comprehend."

"So living things . . ." Nutan said slowly ". . . can pass through the tunnel, but they . . . can't—"

"That's right," another raspy voice intruded. Kalmar twisted his body to confront a second enormous drak who was just entering the room. "A foreign life-form cannot reproduce if it is an animal, or germinate if it is a seed, once exposed to the cleansing force in the tunnels . . . it can't change the balance of life between the two sectors by multiplying in its new environment." The latest reptile loomed over the humans as it stopped next to their table. The drak was adorned with their customary leather belts and straps along with bright metal bracelets encircling its spindly arms and was accompanied by its own cadre of attendants. Kalmar realized who the newest contributor had to be.

"This is Zalibar, the Davar, the female leader of the draks," Adurrell announced. The Davar was not as massive as Adurrell but she was somewhat larger than Gogtee. She also lacked Adurrell's purple coloring in her less pronounced crest. Dingy gray feathers, like Adurrell's, covered her body, but they were not as dull as her male counterpart's. Faded black stripes ran along her back and joined at her posterior to form a solid line on the top of her tail. Kalmar glanced to his right and saw Dera's jaw drop open as she studied their newest visitor through squinted eyes.

Nutan slowly lifted a hand. "That means . . . we're now sterile?"

Zalibar, Adurrell, and Gogtee exchanged quick glances as they made the wheezing sound of drak laughter.

"No, you're not sterile. The cleansing force is calibrated to prevent harm to either humans or draks," Zalibar finally said, in a voice with the clearest diction of any drak Kalmar had heard speak. He noticed his sister lowered her head as she let out a sigh; he could also see relief on the faces of the others. He took a deep breath before letting out his own moan as he wondered if it really mattered if they were sterile or not. What fate awaited humanity if they failed?

"Why's it so important that the two sectors not exchange any life-forms?" Snook asked.

"Each sector has its own distinct system of plants and animals. The introduction of a foreign life-form could have a destabilizing effect on the unique life that already exists in each sector," Adurrell said.

"I can see how a plant or animal that was more adept," Dera said, "might overpower and weed out a weaker competitor for the same resources, but why would that matter?" She moved her hand in an arc to indicate the food on the table. "This food is obviously grown in this sector. The plants and animals you used to produce this meal would serve us just as well as the ones found in our own sector."

"True, but what if the plant that overwhelmed an edible plant was a weed . . . a plant with no nutritional value," bellowed the male leader.

"I guess"—Dera frowned—"that could endanger the food supply of the affected sector." She thought for a moment. "But it would seem procedures could be implemented to control any harmful contamination from taking place . . . it still seems exceptionally zealous measures are being used to keep the sectors separated."

Izzy nodded. "My friends back in our village would love this food. Couldn't you just be selective with what was introduced from one sector to the other . . . allow only some of these choice fruits and vegetables to be introduced into our sector?"

Zalibar took a moment before she answered. "That's not possible."

Izzy shrugged his shoulders. "But why? What harm could it possibly cause?"

"The answer is beyond our ability to explain."

"You're not making sense. It can't be that complicated."

"It is when we do not know the answer to your question," Adurrell said.

"You don't know why you can't introduce fruit and vegetables from one sector to the other?" Snook asked.

"We . . . that is not quite right," Zalibar said. "We do not know why we are not allowed to introduce our plants and animals into your sector. As to our sector, the decision was made by us; we chose to keep the plants and animals from your sector out of ours."

"Please explain to us what you do know," Dera said in a slow, calm voice.

"Our continuing instructions, initially given to the first Bora and Davar when humans were brought to Elom, were to keep your sector free from any contamination from any life-forms from our sector. There were no such instructions to keep us from bringing plants and animals from the human sector to ours. As I said, that decision was ours and was made by the first Bora and Davar during the time of Geerna."

"Why did the Bora and Davar make that decision?" pressed Dera.

"They reasoned, if it was important to keep the human sector free of outside life, then it might be prudent to do the same for our own sector."

"Then, if you're to keep the plants and animals from your sector out of the human sector," Kalmar said, "isn't it strange that humans and draks relish the same food?"

"Draks are more carnivorous than humans."

Kalmar, Snook, and Dera's eyes locked. Dera raised an eyebrow.

"We can easily survive on a diet of nothing but meat, but you are correct, both races could live off the same food supply." The Bora did not seem to notice their reaction to what he was saying. "However, it would be virtually impossible for us to subsist only on fruits, vegetables, and fish like he does." The Bora pointed at Snook with the middle claw of his three-digit left hand.

"Then there must be a simple, rational reason why our sector is isolated," Dera said.

"Maybe Geerna's abductors are worried about their planet being contaminated by life-forms from our sector," Kalmar said. He turned to face their drak host. "The draks aren't the ones who brought Geerna and the other humans to Elom, are they?"

The two enigmatic reptiles looked at each other before Zalibar spoke. "No, it was not the draks. It was the peeri. But they're not concerned about being contaminated by any life-forms from your sector, and besides, I told you we are to keep your sector from being contaminated, not to keep your sector from doing the contamination."

"Then if the peeri are not concerned about being contaminated, why aren't they our caretakers instead of the draks?"

"Without the aid of special equipment, the peeri would quickly die if they were to come to Elom, and, for that matter, humans and draks would die if we tried to live in an environment suitable for the peeri."

"We and the peeri can't eat the same food?" Izzy asked.

"You cannot eat the same food, but that is not the only reason they cannot live on the same world as you . . . this may be more complicated than you imagine," Zalibar said. "Humans and draks can eat the same food, breathe the same air, live under the same sun. These facts do not seem extraordinary to you; we draks have always been part of your culture. In the wider scope of the universe, however, different species are unable to utilize many of the same resources without modification."

Kalmar first looked at Snook, then Dera, and finally at the others in their group. All their faces were as pale as Elom's moons on a foggy night. He squared his shoulders and again examined the two saurians. "We are struggling, trying to understand what you are saying."

The female drak leader made a muted trumpeting sound as she exhaled. "Life has spread to an unimaginable number of planets across the expanse of the universe; the smallest components that comprise the majority of that life are similar."

As Kalmar listened to the giant reptile, he realized the Davar's intellect vastly exceeded what Dera was able to glean from Gogtee.

"Even though similar, this multiplicity of life developed along many variations. Every planet developed its own unique creatures. For the most part, these creatures, unaided, can't readily survive on a world different than that of their origin."

"Temperatures aren't suitable?" Snook offered.

"Differences in home planet temperatures are the least of the incompatibilities." Zalibar swished her tail. "Although not confined to it, the vast majority of life flourishes between the temperature of freezing water and the kindling point of wood." The massive lizard had a sudden twitch that sent ripples along her left side from her shoulder to halfway down her thick tail. With what seemed like a reflex to Kalmar, she scratched the annoyance with the middle claw of her left hand, but the distraction did not deflect Zalibar from her lecture. The giant female lizard again shifted her immense weight from one tree-trunk-sized leg to the other.

"Food—other life—must have developed along the same life path as the creature that eats it; which means the chances of life-forms that originated on a different planet being able to digest the same food is mathematically remote. Animal life on most planets is like the animal life on Elom; we cannot take our sustenance directly from the minerals in the air and soil, as plants are able to do. We must eat the plants that can process the minerals, or eat animal life lower on the food chain, which obtained the minerals and essential substances from eating plants. With the thousands upon thousands of possible combinations of these minerals and essential substances, life is always different on every planet."

Dera was sitting on the opposite side of the table from Kalmar. He could see how absorbed she was as they listened to what the Davar was saying.

"This is hard for us to grasp so quickly," Dera said as she sat up. She looked around at the other humans; Nutan was nodding her head in agreement. This show of support caused a visible change in Dera; she straightened her shoulders and took in a shallow breath. "My brain tells me what you're saying makes sense, but it's still hard to comprehend."

The Davar fixed her eyes on Dera. "Have you ever cut down a tree and dragged its branches home to eat?"

"Of course not, we can't . . . animals can't eat wood. We can't digest it." Kalmar could see by the way Dera winced that she knew she had spoken before thinking.

"Termites do it, as do a number of rodents; even your long tusked mammoths thrive on leaves in addition to grass—another thing you humans cannot digest."

As the reptile spoke, Dera grimaced. It was obvious she felt she had made a stupid mistake. Zalibar seemed indifferent to Dera's humiliation. Kalmar looked from one human to the other; none paid any attention to Dera's blunder. Zalibar held their complete attention.

"If you ate sawdust, it would only pass through your bodies with little change and with no nutritional value to you. Humans cannot digest wood or grass, the two things that comprise the vast majority of the bulk of the plant life on Elom. You must eat the things that can be digested, like the prairie buck and the other creatures of the grasslands. Life that originated on another world would be even more incompatible to you than wood or grass. You could eat a wheelon full of animal and plant life from another planet and you wouldn't receive the essential substances needed to operate the functions of your body. Anything that you ate that didn't poison you outright would enter and pass through your digestive track just like wood or grass. Your stomachs would be full, yet you would not receive any nourishment . . . you would starve to death."

"What you say makes complete and rational sense except for one point," Snook said.

It was impossible for Kalmar to read the facial expressions of the reptiles, but by the way she hesitated before she spoke, he sensed Zalibar was weighing what she was going to say next.

"How are humans and draks able to eat the same food?" Izzy asked.

"I've already given you the answer to your question."

"You're still not making any sense," Izzy protested.

Dera sat up and let out a gasp. "We're both from the same planet. That's what you've been trying to tell us, isn't it?"

"That's correct. We both come from the same planet."

"Wait a moment," Izzy protested. "Both the Tell and the Chants of the Sequa say Geerna indicated there were no draks on our home world, that . . . that the draks were here on Elom when she and the other humans arrived."

"That is also correct."

"How is this possible?" Snook asked.

"We were already here when the peeri first brought humans to Elom. Our ancestors have been on Elom since long before the time of Geerna," Zalibar said.

"That—that's—" Izzy stuttered.

"But," Snook interrupted, "why didn't Geerna know about the draks on our home world?"

"Because there were no draks on Geerna's home world."

"But you just said—" Izzy said.

"The peeri allowed a devastation to occur on our home world that killed all of the ancestors of our species long before the time of humans." Sadness permeated the massive creature's voice.

Up until this last sentence, it had been impossible for Kalmar to sense any feelings in the drak's speech. For a brief moment, Kalmar wondered if his failure to pick up on the draks' emotions had been by their design.

"The peeri murdered your ancestors?" asked an unnerved Nutan.

"Why?" added an equally shaken Izzy.

In the same somber tones, Zalibar said, "We failed our Judging."

"But to kill an entire species—for what possible purpose?" Dera exclaimed.

In an eerie monotone bellow, Adurrell replied, "To make way for your species. If our ancestors had passed their Judging your species would never have had the opportunity to evolve."

"What does evolve mean?" Izzy asked, his eyebrows drawn closer together. The others in the group pulled on the reins of their galloping thoughts and waited for the drak's response.

The giant reptile swung its massive body around so one of its oversized eyes could focus on Izzy. After a moment's scrutiny, the drak blinked and cocked its head towards its questioner. "Your race strives to Concentrate the Traits by bearing children that are pleasing to Shetow. Your society has a system that all but forces two people who appear, to you, to possess qualities that strengthen the race to mate, a system that denies children to one out of ten Pairings because their children would dilute the concentration of those favorable Traits. Your system is an example of controlled evolution: you follow a predetermined plan. In nature, however, species adapt to their changing environment by concentrating their favorable traits, both physical and mental, that make them better able to survive those changes. Over millions of cycles of the seasons, animal and plant life can change dramatically, so much that it would be hard to recognize the species they once were." Zalibar shifted her head and body to face them all and said in a lower tone, "Now this knowledge is beyond your ability to grasp." Zalibar seemed to lose some of her rigidity. "In a few days, though, you will understand it better than I do."

The members of the group exchanged glances and were quiet for several minutes.

"The peeri destroyed all life on the planet?" Dera asked, her voice cracking.

"No, not all life, but the planet-wide devastation extinguished most of the planet's species . . . including all of our kind."

There was a moment of silence. The humans looked at one another, and then, in a polite yet guarded manner, Izzy asked, "Then . . . how did our species evolve?"

Zalibar did not answer at first; she stood perfectly still, looking away from the humans. Kalmar wondered if she had heard Izzy's question, but was glad that he did not repeat it. Without any visible cue, Zalibar broke from her trance and shifted her colossal form to face the humans sitting at the table. "As I said, some species were spared: a minute portion of the sea creatures, a few birds, a small number of cold-blooded reptiles, and small fur-covered warm-blooded scavengers." Zalibar stopped talking. Kalmar wondered if she was going back into her trance when she started again. "Those fur-covered animals, who lived in shallow burrows in the ground . . ." The great lizard paused, let out a low, bellowing sound that seemed to emanate from deep in the reptile's chest. "Those scurrying little nocturnal vermin who feasted on the carcasses of our ancestors during the time of the Great Death . . . from those insignificant animals . . . humans evolved."

Silence crept across the room like a dark shadow. Zalibar's revelation dazed Kalmar. For a moment he was flushed with fear of the surrounding drak; he could feel hate in Zalibar's voice. He took a quick inventory of the other six humans seated around the table. By the looks on their faces, it was hard for him to tell if they were stunned or just deep in thought. Cabyl was clutching Snook's arm and had leaned her head against the left side of his shoulder. He had not seen the two touch before this moment. If the circumstances had been different, the tenderness of the sight would have warranted a smile on Kalmar's somber face. Izzy and Nutan appeared sedated as they looked down at the table, their eyes focused on some unseen thought.

As Kalmar moved his attention from his sister, his gaze collided with two unblinking greenish gray eyes staring back. His view of the others in the room blurred as he winced from the power of Arasima's cold and calculating countenance; instantly he felt small and insignificant. No emotion, no shame or message could he decipher in the furrows on her brow or in her piercing yet haunting eyes. It was as if she were trying to make a decision and he was the last piece of evidence she needed to analyze before reaching a verdict. The wily look on her face gave him the feeling her thoughts had skewed from what the Davar had just said. His body tensed, apprehension flooded his mind; he felt the awakening of lust, something he thought had been permanently squelched. She looked capable of chewing him up and spitting him out. Why did that look excite him? Why would he have such thoughts now? The pure sexuality of this woman astounded him. The fact he had caught her looking at him did not seem to affect her; whatever her decision was to be, she would make it without any consultation with him. Her eyes were slightly squinted, her face unflinching; she did not avert her gaze. The only reaction she exhibited was the raising of her left eyebrow. His eyes stayed locked on hers until his nerve broke and he turned away. He cursed himself for his cowardice; his face flushed. He had faced the fury of a charging cave lion and had not flinched, yet he could not stare down a young woman's scrutiny. It took him a few moments to regain his composure. As he looked up, even though he tried not to, he glanced at Arasima for a split second before his frantic, darting eyes found the safety of Dera.

The difference between the two women could not have been greater: Arasima's look was calculating, Dera's pensive. Arasima seemed self-absorbed; Dera looked as if the weight of the future of her species rested on her shoulders.

Kalmar shuddered as a strange chill flowed through his body; he had an epiphany, a mental flash of why the Medoras had chosen these two contrasting women to represent humanity at the Judging.

Between the two rested the culmination of six Progressions of concentrating the strengths of the female Traits. In that instant, as he looked at the two women, it became clear to him that it was impossible for all the Traits to reach their fullest potential in any one person, or, for that matter, in either of the sexes. Some Traits were diametrically opposed to other Traits. You could not be the most compassionate, like Dera, and at the same time, be the most conniving, like Arasima. The Medoras must have believed that for this small band to be successful during the Judging they would need the mental and physical strengths and dexterity of Dera's Traits, but also the crafty, intuitive strengths Arasima's cunning exemplified. The clarity of Kalmar's thoughts filled him with a strange blending of conflicting sensations, energizing him, but at the same time, he felt the serenity of understanding.

"We will stop talking now; it is time for you to rest," Zalibar said, giving no other reason for ending the session. She stood perfectly still, her head cocked to the right like a bird watching a bug. As she stared at them, her long massive tail stopped its normal side-to-side swaying motion. Her relentless gaze bore in on them for a few uncomfortable moments. Kalmar felt a bead of sweat run down the side of his face; he fought back the fear that she was going to charge them. He noticed her eyes blink; she then began moving her head back and forth in a rocking motion as she shifted her gaze to the blank wall on the opposite side of the room. The saurian looked at the wall a moment, and then she turned and walked out of the room. Adurrell started to follow her, but stopped, looked back at the confused humans, and gave them a slight bow before leaving the room.

If the humans had not been so solemn after Zalibar's revelation, what happened next would have seemed comical. The draks in Adurrell and Zalibar's entourages scurried around frantically, as if each one were determined not to be the last one out of the room. In the mad confusion, the last two scampering reptiles ran headlong into each other, producing a loud crack when their heads collided. The collision knocked both of them to the ground amid tumbling legs and whipping tails. One of them recovered quickly, jumped up, and was out the door in seconds. The other seemed dazed and when it tried to stand up, lost its balance and flopped back on the floor like a fish out of water. More successful on its second try, the teetering creature finally staggered from the room on wobbly legs.

The humans were left in the room with the small reptilian food servers, who lined up against the near wall as Gogtee and Dryka stood motionless in the same spots they had occupied since before the exodus of the scurrying entourage. The sudden departure of their leaders seemed to surprise their drak companions as much as it did the seven humans.

The distraction caused by the comical withdrawal of the attending draks interrupted Kalmar's train of thought; with the break in his concentration, his fleeting, pristine moment of complete comprehension began to wane. His ability to grasp the complexities of his revelation concerning Arasima's and Dera's Traits began to elude him; it became impossible for him to corral all the various concepts together in his mind. He did however, fight to retain a glimmer of the essence of his mental discovery; he kept a firm grip on the realization that both Dera's and Arasima's Traits were essential to their success at the Judging. He stopped trying to remember all of the reasoning that led him to his conclusions and closed his eyes as he burned its significance into his mind.

Kalmar's eyes popped open at the sound of Gogtee's voice. "Your accommodations are ready." She motioned towards the door on the other side of the room from where they had entered. "If you will come this way. . . ." The seven humans got up from the table and followed their hosts.

"Gogtee, Zalibar doesn't like us, does she?" Dera asked as she rushed ahead to catch up to their guide.

Gogtee did not answer at once, but instead looked at her mate. There seemed to be that silent communication the two draks had exhibited ever since the beginning of their journey. After a few moments, Gogtee refocused on her human questioner. "It is not you, it is what you represent."

"But," Snook said as he caught up with Dera and Gogtee, "we didn't have anything to do with the failure of the draks at your Judging. Even Zalibar said the draks' Judging happened long before our species evolved. How can she hold the death of your ancestors against us?"

"She does not hold the death of our ancestors against you," Dryka said. "She holds our knowledge of the Great Death against you." The humans all turned towards their male guide. What he said was even more shocking because he was the one who had said it. Gogtee had told them Dryka did not speak because he felt inadequate with his command of the human's language. From the clarity of his words, there had to be a different reason for his having been mute. Kalmar knew the other humans had to be thinking the same thing. He wondered if they also realized it was the least important bit of information just revealed to them.

"She holds the knowledge of the Great Death against us," Nutan sputtered. "We didn't know of the Great Death until she told us about it . . . we didn't tell the draks. How can she hold it against us?"

The two draks exchanged another subtle glance before Gogtee said, "You must rest now; your question will be answered tomorrow."

"But—" Izzy started.

"*Tomorrow,*" Gogtee said.

Izzy first looked at his sister, who gave him a reassuring nod, and then at Nutan's stately smile. Kalmar noticed his sister's acquiescing to the situation seemed to bolster Izzy as much as Dera's nod. With Izzy's acceptance of Gogtee's command the others, who all seemed to understand they would have to wait for an answer, trudged out of the room.

TWENTY-SEVEN

Gogtee and Dryka led them up a stairway sized for the largest draks and then guided the humans along a cavernous hallway before stopping at a series of doorways. Once again, the draks separated the men and women. The draks opened two of the doors, leaving a third doorway between the two unopened. Kalmar entered the room assigned to the males and looked around to find it furnished with unassuming beds, tables, and chairs.

After the draks left them, Kalmar spotted a door on the wall towards the females' room. The door also had Snook's attention. He immediately walked over and placed his ear against it.

Snook could not detect a sound as he pressed his ear against the thick wooden door. He was not sure what he expected to hear. The Elders had told him he must be ready to face a far different world than he was accustomed to once he entered the lands of the Twenty-Four Tribes. His journey had now led him to a world inconceivable even to the venerable leaders of the Mookyn. The Elders had not conceived of the possibility that he would be one of those the Medora would pick for the Second Judging. Seekers searched for the truth about Shetow. Snook knew he took his duties seriously, but unlike most of his kind, he had chosen to do his quest as an aloof spectator. He shook his head; apparently fate held another role for him in this bewildering saga. Circumstances demanded that he become more involved. Would he be the Seeker who first solved the great mystery?

Kalmar was not sure what Snook heard but Snook shook his head before stepping back and grabbing the door handle.

"Do you think that's wise?" Kalmar asked.

With his white-knuckled hand gripping the door handle, Snook furrowed his brow. "I'm a Seeker . . . it's what I do." He yanked and the door swung open. Kalmar hesitated a second, then joined Izzy as they cautiously followed Snook into an even larger room. After all their concern, their entry into the room proved anticlimactic. It was an expanded version of their bedroom minus the beds. Tables and chairs lined the walls; a counter mirroring the curve of the outside wall of the building stood in front of an oval window filled with straw-yellow tinted glass. Two baskets woven from thin wood strips sat on the countertop filled with a kaleidoscope of unrecognizable fruits. A squat, sturdy wooden table dominated the center of the room, encircled by four mud-brown sofas smothered with billowing teal pillows. Opposite the door they entered through lurked another door. The three males stood their ground as the door creaked opened. Nutan peeked in as the other three females peered over her shoulder.

Izzy made a deep bow and motioned for them to enter. "We would be most honored if you ladies would join us in our own miniature Oonoc Lodge . . . our Oonoc Room." Although he had spoken to all the females, his gaze lingered on Nutan. Kalmar observed his sister returning Izzy's notice along with a shy smile; a second later, she pried her attention away from her admirer to study their discovery.

The females entered the room bunched together and moving

sideways like a sand crab on the beach. Once inside the room, Arasima broke from the others and after a quick evaluation said, "This place could use some color; it's about as drab as a gray fox's winter coat." After a second look, Kalmar had to admit the walls and furniture were dowdy, mostly browns and melancholy tones of charcoal speckled with the gray found in campfire ashes. Only the vivid hues of the fruit in the baskets fought the monotony of the dingy room. Arasima's first appraisal seemed to satisfy her curiosity and she walked over and plopped down on one of the cushiony sofas.

Snook headed for the fruit, and he picked up several imperfect purple spheres. He turned towards Cabyl. "Here, try this. I ate one downstairs and they're wonderful." He tossed her one of the lilac orbs. Cabyl caught Snook's offering, raised it to her undersized mouth, and took an oversized bite. Her ambitious efforts filled her mouth with the meat of the unknown fruit. Her eyes grew large as she shed the placid expression that usually shrouded her face. Tiny bits of ripe pulp and juice trickled down the sides of her cheeks as she chewed and swallowed the mysterious fruit. For his efforts, Cabyl rewarded Snook with a pixie grin. The effect on Snook was immediate; his pale cheeks reddened. For the first time, the white of his albino face yielded to color.

Kalmar noticed Dera responded with her own broad smile to the interaction between Snook and Cabyl. Dera seldom smiled. Her smile flattered her; it revealed a side she kept hidden, a tender and human side. Dera exuded the manner of someone who tried to control her outward emotions; he wondered: if she knew how powerful her smile was, would she keep it to herself so much? Her teeth were the whitest he had ever seen; was it an illusion produced by their contrast to the scarlet mark on her cheek? Dera smiled after seeing the sparkle in Cabyl and Snook's eyes. She had lowered her guard revealing a frailty or just maybe . . . a strength; was she a romantic at heart? The question provoked the ends of his own lips to curl up as he chuckled, and then he turned to see what the others were doing.

Of the four sofas, Izzy and Nutan had sat down on the one with its back toward him. Surprisingly, the two youngest members of their group were not pressed against each other but barely touching, both their backs straight as nutwood saplings. The tension from their mutual attraction provoked a swelling in his chest. As he looked at the two, he realized Arasima was sitting on the sofa across from them—the sofa facing him. She was also smiling, but it was a much different smile than Dera's. Focusing on Arasima, he realized it was more of a smirk than a smile. She had watched his reaction to Snook and Cabyl; she would have also seen his reaction to Dera's smile. Arasima raised her eyebrows, not averting her eyes once hers met his. A hot flush spread through his body; his fingers tangled. Why did she still make him so uncomfortable? For a second time that day, he was the one who broke eye contact, something he had vowed to himself he would never do if ever put in that situation again. As he looked away he made a mental shake of his head and thought, *You nutless pile of bovor dung . . . this woman has taken your balls again.* With desperate eyes, he looked around to see if anyone else had witnessed his humiliation. To his relief, the remaining five seemed oblivious to his degradation.

The two sets of couples were absorbed in their own thoughts while Dera slowly walked around inspecting the room. She finally walked over and opened the third door. It was obvious the door opened into the hallway, but Dera opened it anyway. Kalmar had thought about doing it, but had failed to do so. Standing in the hallway were four human-sized draks. The startled reptiles stepped back at the unexpected intrusion, but Dera nonchalantly closed the door before they could react further. Dera showed no reaction to the guards standing outside their doors; she acted as if she had just closed the door to her own home after opening it to look out and check to see if it were raining.

After confirming what was beyond the door, Dera turned and addressed the group. "So, what do you think?" She waited a second, then walked over and collapsed on the sofa next to Arasima. As she flopped down, her long hair bounced and an auburn lock fell across her marred face. She reached up and casually brushed the unruly strands back behind her right ear.

Verna had spoken to Dera of her dreams and the fact that she believed there were changes coming to the Twenty-Four Tribes. Dera's mind filled with a flurry of convoluted ideas about the possible changes dreamed by her old mentor. Dera rolled a lock of her hair around a finger. Could Verna have envisioned the marvels Dera's group had discovered? What role had Verna foreseen for her in the coming events? Whatever that role was, Verna would expect her to stay focused and be resourceful until it became clear to her what actions she needed to take. She closed her eyes and could see the loving face of her beloved Medora.

Arasima glanced at Dera out of the corner of her eyes for a moment, then crossed her arms and slumped down in the cushions. After burrowing into the softness of the sofa, Arasima lowered her head, resting her chin on her chest, and seemed to slide into deep thought.

"Well, to me, there seem to be some holes in what Zalibar and Adurrell said," offered Izzy.

"How so?" Snook asked, quickly adding, "Not that I disagree with you." Then he and Cabyl, after an exchange of unconscious looks, walked over and sat down on one of the two remaining unoccupied sofas. They followed Nutan and Izzy's lead, keeping a hand's width of space separating them.

"Well, for one thing, what about the idea the draks have lived on Elom ever since they failed their Judging? I thought the fate of the People was in our hands . . . I mean, we were led to believe that if we failed, the humans on Elom were to be exterminated, along with our kindred on our home world." Izzy looked at Kalmar, then at Snook and Cabyl, and finally at Dera, seeking concurrence. Finally, they nodded in agreement. Izzy squared his shoulders. "These peeri, or whoever they are, didn't destroy the draks on Elom after they failed their Judging. If we fail, maybe we'll be spared too."

"I agree with you," Snook said. "It's odd the draks on Elom were spared, but for some reason, I don't think we should put too much faith in being spared if we fail. The way Zalibar feels about us, she would do away with us herself if she had her wish."

"Yeah," Nutan said, "that's only because she believes the draks on the home world were destroyed because of us."

"And if we fail," said Cabyl, who seemed to glow from Snook's attention, ". . . and if she truly does believe her kind was exterminated so we could evolve . . . well, she will feel her ancestors died for nothing." The change in Cabyl's demeanor since the start of their journey was remarkable, thought Kalmar.

"I don't think she will change her feelings about us even if we do pass the Judging," Izzy said.

"Perhaps that's true," Dera said, "but we mustn't forget what Gogtee said about Zalibar."

"And that was?" Arasima asked, lifting her head as she emerged from her mulling.

Dera glanced at Arasima, but Kalmar could not detect any animosity in her demeanor towards the irksome young woman. "Gogtee said Zalibar holds the knowledge of the Great Death against us, and that can only mean one thing."

Arasima raised a condescending eyebrow and studied Dera for

a moment. Then her face softened. "The draks didn't learn of the destruction of their kind on the home world until the time of Geerna . . . long after it had happened." For a fleeting moment, Kalmar detected a tinge of admiration for Dera in Arasima's voice.

Dera nodded. "Which means their myths of the home world would have been diluted to the point where they wouldn't have been believed by the draks, or even more likely, they would have been totally forgotten ages ago."

Cabyl spoke up. "That's so sad. The draks lived millions of cycles of the seasons in ignorant bliss, only to learn of the annihilation of their species on the home world when the peeri began preparing Elom for the arrival of Geerna and the other humans."

"It's also sad that their lives revolve around humans," Snook interjected.

"And that is why Zalibar hates us," Dera said, nodding. "The coming of humans ended that bliss, and in exchange they received the pain of the knowledge of the annihilation of their species. . . ." She paused and bit her bottom lip. "Zalibar blames us, as Gogtee said, not for 'the Great Death' but for their knowledge of it." She paused again. "There is something else—when we were all around the campfire two nights ago, Gogtee said the fate of the draks also rested with our Judging."

"Hmmm," Snook said. "I do remember. You would think Zalibar would be friendlier."

"Especially since the fate of their race rest with us," Izzy added, with a little bafflement detectable in his voice.

"They are supportive," Dera responded, giving her brother a stern look.

"But Zalibar—"

"Zalibar's the only drak that has shown us any hostility."

"I'm not so sure," Kalmar said. "What about Dryka? When he

spoke, I picked up something . . . something that wasn't so friendly." Everyone looked at him, most with expressions of agreement.

Dera's expression hardened. "I don't think Gogtee, or Dryka for that matter, wish us anything but success. What we're reading as disdain may be only the outward signs of the pain they carry." Her eyes dropped for a moment. As she raised them again she added, "Zalibar said the Great Death took place so we could evolve, but she also admitted that if their ancestors had passed their Judging, the destruction of their kindred on the home world would have been prevented and humans would never have had the chance to evolve."

Nutan shrugged. "They're transferring the blame for their failed Judging from themselves—or their ancestors—to us."

"Possibly," Dera answered, her face rigid. "But what Dryka said may be the extent of it. It was learning of the Great Death that causes them pain, and they, rightly or wrongly, blame us for that."

Something had been eating at Kalmar ever since their meeting with Zalibar and Adurrell. "Dera, you said Gogtee, who claims to have been chosen to work with us because of her intelligence, isn't any smarter than we are." He grimaced. "I hate to admit it, but Gogtee isn't anywhere near as intelligent as Zalibar and Adurrell. Do you think there is a correlation between size and intelligence?"

"Well," Cabyl responded, lines of deep thought crossing her brow, "there's no such correlation among humans, so I don't see why there would be one in the draks. After puberty we don't get smarter just because some of us grow larger than others; I don't see why they would." As Cabyl finished talking, she noticed the others in the room were staring at her. "What . . . what is it?" Lines cut across her brow as she looked from one grinning face to another. Then, as if on cue, the other six burst out laughing. She jumped up, red-faced. "What did I say that's so funny!" It was hard for Kalmar to tell if they had made her mad or just hurt her feelings.

For a few moments, Cabyl recoiled from their laughter, misinterpreting it as a cruel jab. The verbal and physical abuse she had endured, first from her father and then from her Pairing Partner, raced through her mind. She felt trapped, held down by a fear as paralyzing as the calloused, groping hands of her father. She had misread these people. Then, Snook stood up, towering over her as did everyone else in the group, and put his arm around her shoulders. "Don't be mad. We just thought it was humorous that you, the smallest among us, are the one who pointed out that size and intelligence aren't related."

Cabyl looked up into his face and recognized his compassion. She looked around the room and was greeted by smiles and understanding eyes. A sparkling tear trickled down her cheek; she lowered her head and sat back down. The laughter seemed to lift everyone's spirits; it was several minutes before the chuckling subsided.

I want to go back to the difference in intelligence among the draks," Dera began. "Really, up until we met Zalibar and Adurrell I was sure the draks weren't as intelligent as humans. How is it possible that two of them are so much smarter than all the others?" She glanced at Cabyl. "And I agree with you, it's a reason other than size. Within certain limitations, many reptiles continue to grow throughout their life depending upon food supply, but it doesn't make sense that intelligence would correspondingly increase." The others, including Cabyl, nodded. Dera shrugged. "We're missing something." The skin on her face tightened as she squinted; her voice dropped to a harsh whisper. "If we could just figure it out."

D era's mind raced. *There is a Trait I possess that must be needed . . . perhaps I was chosen as a member of this group because of my ability to see things without letting emotions get in the way.* She lifted her head and observed Kalmar gazing at Arasima's legs. The ends of her mouth drooped as she looked away. *Without letting emotions or lust deflect my . . . our mission. Some of us . . . I must not lose focus on the reason we are here.*

S tillness filled the room as they all thought about what Dera had said. Kalmar walked over and sat on the remaining unoccupied sofa. Now all seven humans sat on one of the four sofas that encircled the wooden knee-high table. They all looked at each other, waiting for someone to speak. Kalmar noticed Nutan and Izzy had moved a little closer and, although no closer, Cabyl had reached over and rested her left hand on Snook's right thigh. Arasima sat with a barely detectable scowl on her face. Dera, her jaw firmly set, leaned over to rest her chin in her palms while propping her elbows on her knees.

"We need more information," Snook said, breaking the silence.

"Just what I was thinking," Kalmar replied.

"We need a scouting party," Dera said as she straightened up.

"A what?" Arasima said tartly.

"We need some of us to go and find out as much as they can about the draks and what's going to happen to us next."

Nutan noticeably stiffened. "But Dera, there are guards standing outside our doors. How can we do that?"

"We'll produce a diversion to distract them so a few of us can sneak out and look around. The guards' mental dexterity, if our hypothesis is true, should be lower on the scale than the draks we've been dealing with."

"Who goes?" Nutan said, still uneasy.

"Three should be enough." Dera's eyes sought out Kalmar. "I would think Kalmar should lead, as he is the most experienced hunter and tracker. His skills in stealthy movement should be invaluable."

Kalmar sat up at the mention of his name, his face reddening. Was Dera mocking him? If she was, she would be moving at a right angle to the way she had been acting towards him since they started their journey.

His fears were put to rest when she said, "I'll go, since I made the suggestion; I wouldn't ask anyone to do something I was afraid to do myself."

Kalmar studied Dera's expressive face a moment before concluding that she made the suggestion because she thought it correct and for no other motive.

"That leaves one more," Izzy said, his excited eyes betraying his own desire to join them. "Dera, who do you think it should be?"

"Any three people in this room are as good as anyone could ever hope to find for this project and we only need one more. Who would like to come?"

Izzy's face became even more animated, but before he could speak, another's voice beat him to the mark.

"I'll go," Arasima said with a tinge of contempt. Her coolness sent a chill through the room.

Kalmar's brow furrowed as the whites of his eyes grew to overshadow his small dark pupils. Both Nutan and Snook gave him reassuring glances.

"That settles that. Now we need to find a way to create a diversion," Dera said, her voice not wavering. If the idea of Arasima joining them bothered her, she showed no signs of it.

Nutan lifted her head. "What kind of diversion?" she asked, showing her first enthusiasm for the project.

"It doesn't matter, just something that'll distract our guards long enough for us to sneak out and creep down the stairs without being noticed. It'll have to cause enough of a commotion to draw the guards into this room while we slip out the door of one of the bedrooms." She scrunched her face. "Izzy, you and Nutan look in the men's bedroom. Snook and Cabyl look in the women's bedroom. We three"—Dera moved her hand, indicating Kalmar, Arasima, and herself—"can look around in this room." Everyone but Kalmar bolted—as if coming out of starting blocks—to his or her allotted task.

Kalmar was still not sure what he was looking for. He hoped he would be better at knowing what to do once they had gotten out of their rooms than he was at figuring out how to get out. As he stood by the sofas trying to decide what to do, Dera was scrounging around in the cabinets under the fruit baskets, and Arasima was turning a padded chair over, studying its construction.

"In here . . . come in here," beckoned an excited voice from the men's bedroom. Kalmar followed the two females into the room only to find it empty. "Over here," called Izzy, although Kalmar still did not see him. The three walked towards the sound of Izzy's voice. They had only taken a few steps when Nutan's head popped out of a hidden alcove.

"In here," she said, then stepped back into the hidden area. When he, Dera, and Arasima followed Nutan into the recessed space, they found Izzy on his hands and knees inspecting what appeared to be a waist-high masonry wall. Looking closer, Kalmar could see the partition formed one side of a steaming water-filled bath. The bath was spacious, more than large enough to hold nine or ten people; however, the bath was not what held Izzy's attention.

The side of the masonry bath was several feet thick, and the object of Izzy's excitement was a small opening near its base.

"I can see a row of small flames used to heat the water," Izzy said as he pointed to the opening. Kalmar dropped to his knees beside Izzy and peered into the gap between the stones.

"Pretty clever," Kalmar said as he stood up. He bent over to stick a finger into the water. "And just the right temperature too."

Dera rubbed the tips of her fingers along the grout between two of the stones. "The mortar's fresh; the bath's new—constructed just for us."

"Doesn't seem like the actions of someone who hates us," Izzy said as he rolled over from his kneeling position, sat on the floor, and leaned back against the side of the bath.

"They don't like us," Nutan said, her voice flush with irony, "but they take good care of us. Why? That's another reason for you to go and have a look around." She sat down on the edge of the bath and crossed her legs, causing the cuff of her tight-fitting pants to brush against Izzy's arm. The muscular calf of her right leg dangled only inches from Izzy's face.

Nutan didn't seem to notice how close her leg was to Izzy, but Kalmar could tell by the whites of Izzy's eyes he was very well aware of the proximity of the feminine leg almost touching his face.

Izzy stared at Nutan's shapely limb a moment before realizing Kalmar was watching him. Izzy quickly redirected his gaze and tried to fake his way through the situation. He licked his lips. "The draks went to a lot of trouble, even though they say we're not going to be here long." Izzy's eyes jumped up to Kalmar for a second; then he seemed to wilt from Kalmar's stern look.

Kalmar kept his intimidating gaze on Izzy for a few moments longer, never showing a crack in his rebuking glare. He chuckled to himself at how well he had played his charade. In reality, he found Izzy's fascination with his sister amusing, not offensive.

"We need something to burn . . . something that will produce lots of smoke," Dera declared.

"How about one of the bath towels?" said Nutan, reaching over and pulling a towel off a shelf that ran along the wall next to the bath.

"No . . . no, I know what we need," Arasima said, her eyes opening wider. She darted around the side of the alcove. Kalmar, Dera, and Nutan stepped out of the alcove just in time to see the back of her body disappear as she darted through the door leading into the middle room. Arasima's excitement was unexpected. Kalmar had noticed a decrease in her aloofness ever since Dera had accepted her as part of the group that was going to sneak out and snoop around the draks' building. Arasima's change in demeanor was unsettling to Kalmar; he had not realized it until that moment, but he felt more comfortable when she was quiet and aloof.

"Where is she going?" Izzy asked, after he had gotten up from the floor and followed them out of the bath area. Nutan looked back at him and shrugged her shoulders. When the four walked into the middle room, they found Arasima bent over pulling at something from the bottom of an overturned sofa. Kalmar found it hard not to stare at the outline of her shapely bottom, revealed by her tightly fitting pants. Nutan's eyes shot him a scolding rebuke.

Arasima stood up holding a handful of what looked like clumps of wadded up golden-brown grass. "We can burn this stuffing; it should make plenty of smoke!"

Dera went to Arasima's side, took a little bit of the material, and studied it. A wide grin spread to the corners of her lips. "Arasima, that's perfect."

"What's perfect?" Snook said as he and Cabyl entered the room from the girls' bedroom.

"We have everything we need to create our diversion," exclaimed an excited Nutan. "We're going to start a fire to produce smoke. If that doesn't distract our guards, nothing will." Snook and Cabyl joined the other five around the four sofas in the center of the room.

Dera flipped over another one of the sofas and motioned to Arasima and Nutan. "Help me pull out more of the stuffing, but take care not to take too much from any one sofa. We want to be able to sit on them later." Then she bent over a second overturned sofa and started pulling at the padding. "What made you think of this?" Dera said. She looked over and smiled at Arasima. "You couldn't have found a better material; this stuff will smoke like dried nutwood leaves." Arasima was, along with Nutan, tugging large handfuls of the stuffing from the other two sofas and tossing them into a growing mound on the center table. Kalmar noticed Dera's question seemed to catch Arasima off guard. She stopped yanking at the stuffing and stared at Dera openmouthed, her face shrouded by astonishment.

Kalmar could not believe it; Arasima was blushing.

"I don't know. I saw the stuffing when I turned the sofas over looking for something to create a diversion." She shrugged, and then added giddily, "I made the connection when you asked about needing something to burn and make smoke."

Kalmar had seen Arasima flushed before, but it had always been in different and more personal circumstances. Did Arasima know how to respond to praise coming from another female? After another moment's reflection, he wondered if another female had ever praised her. Had she only filled her need for approval through the accolades of males? If Dera had set out to pull Arasima into being a working member of the group, she could not have been more successful. As Kalmar watched the interaction between the two females, he wondered if Dera was truly open to Arasima, or just crafty. If there was subterfuge in Dera's actions, he could not detect it. He knew Arasima was smart enough to realize Dera could be using her, but she seemed not to care if Dera had any hidden motive. It appeared Arasima was tired of being shunned. The relief from being ostracized visually improved Arasima's attitude.

Snook leaned over and whispered in Kalmar's ear. "As I have been telling you, there is more to that woman"—he tilted his head towards Dera—"than she wants you to know."

Kalmar peered at Dera, studied her, and then whispered back, "As I said before, I think you're right."

The three females had produced a sizable pile of stuffing. Dera grabbed an armload and headed towards the males' bath area. A string of onlookers followed her. When they reached the bath, Dera started looking around. "We need something fireproof to hold this."

"Here, use this container," Cabyl said, walking over and picking up a knee-high open-topped urn that was sitting next to a sink and placing it in front of Dera. Dera dumped the stuffing into the container. Snook dropped to one knee.

He ran his fingers gently across the container's gray surface. "It appears to be made of the same material as almost everything else around here, some kind of formed stone." He thumped it. "But thin and light."

"Nutan," Dera said, "you and Izzy can stay in here after we light the stuffing and see if the container is combustible. If it is, you can splash water on it from the bath." She used her foot to push the object across the floor and against the side of the bath. "Izzy, see if you can find something flammable to stick through the opening"—she indicated the hole in the side of the bath he had found earlier—"so we can use it to light the stuffing." Izzy nodded, and after looking around, picked out some of the longer fibers in the stuffing and started weaving them into a stiff rope. Dera watched her brother; when it became evident that it would only take him a few minutes to complete his task, she turned to face her two accomplices.

"You two ready?"

"*Ready*," Arasima blurted. She began shifting her weight from one foot to the other—rocking her body to release built-up tension. The woman's enthusiasm for the pending venture seemed reckless to Kalmar. He had doubts about the wisdom of sneaking around the draks' quarters in the middle of the night. Reluctantly he nodded his readiness.

Dera surveyed the room a final time, then turned to rally her troops. "Izzy will start the fire and let the smoke fill the males' bedroom. We three"—she indicated Kalmar, Arasima, and herself— "will go into the females' bedroom, shut the door, and wait there. Once the fire starts producing smoke, Izzy, you'll join Nutan, Snook, and Cabyl in the middle room. When the smoke pours through the bedroom door and starts to fill the middle room, you open that door." She pointed to the door leading into the hallway from the middle room. "Then, and only then, the four of you start yelling and waving your arms and try to draw our four feathered guards in from the hallway. It's doubtful they understand our language, which will only confuse them further."

"But what do we do if they don't come in," Nutan asked, her voice laced with doubt.

"I'd bet my finest piece of artwork they will."

Kalmar glanced at Dera and wondered if she had forgotten what filled the ravine outside the draks' city. Even if it had occurred to Dera after she said it, she did not flinch.

"The guards should stay in the room for a few moments before running for help, but that's enough time if we move fast. To make sure we know when to go, Snook and Cabyl, you must tap on the bedroom door the instant the last of the four guards enters the room from the hallway." She hit the door a few quick licks. "When you give us that signal, we'll sneak out the bedroom door into the hallway and head down the stairs. If the draks don't see us then, I think the smoke will confuse them long enough for us to get away clean. Besides"—she shrugged her shoulders—"if they catch us we will just protest and say the smoke drove us into the hallway."

"Dera, I should go with you," Snook said, his pallid face appearing paler than normal. "I am a Seeker, I have trained all my life to study and understand this world of ours. If I do not go, I will be turning my back on the reason the Elders sent me to the land of the Twenty-Four Tribes." A solemn look masked his face; his eyes widened as he looked down to see Cabyl slipping her tiny hand into his.

Snook's eyes locked with Dera's. The Elders charged him with learning about the pending Judging, and then returning to them with as much information as he could. Since he had not returned, the leaders of his people must think some calamity had befallen him. He looked around at his companions and noted the strength and resolve in Dera's face. He had learned much from the people of the Twenty-Four Tribes, but oddly, the most of what he had learned was about himself.

Dera studied the albino. "Seeker? I'm not sure what that is, but it sounds like you're probably the one person who should go." She glanced at Cabyl. "I guess you will have to bang on the door by yourself."

Cabyl's eyes flashed up at Snook for a moment before shifting them back to Dera and nodding.

Dera gave Cabyl a supportive smile. "All right, let's do it."

Izzy and Nutan went into the men's bedroom. In a few minutes Nutan came rushing back through the bedroom door, her face flushed with excitement. "Izzy has it lit." She glanced at Arasima. "You're right; the stuffing is going to give off plenty of smoke."

Kalmar noticed his sister had addressed Arasima for the first time since the beginning of their journey. He found Nutan's warm remark to Arasima eroded some of his own animosity towards his longhaired nemesis. He smiled to himself; maybe he could tolerate the pending excursion.

The four conspirators went into the females' bedroom, but Dera left the door cracked after instructing Cabyl to signal them when Nutan was about to open the hallway door in an effort to distract the drak guards.

Dera could see smoke rolling through the door of the far bed-room. The pungent smell of the burning padding had a hint of a scent that reminded her of smoldering hardwood. Visions of Verna's burning pyre grabbed her thoughts and deflated her resolve to continue. Her heart pounded at the base of her throat. What folly was she undertaking; was her self-reliance about to lead them into danger? Verna's words crept into her thoughts; she was to play a part in the coming change. Could there be a correlation between the smoke billowing from the male's bedroom and that of Verna's burning pyre? There was a touch of flint in her angular smile.

I'm shutting the door now," Cabyl said. "Izzy just came back and the smoke is pouring into the middle room. Nutan will be going out into the hall any second now." She shut the door.

"Dera, how are we going to create a diversion so we can get back into our rooms?" Snook asked.

"Oh, we won't need one," Dera answered matter-of-factly.

"How do you mean?"

"We don't care if they see us go back into our rooms. I'm sure our guards only have orders to keep us in the rooms." Dera shrugged. "Once we've had our look, we don't care that they know we got out; besides, what are they going to do? Kill us?"

Kalmar saw the look on Snook's face; he wondered if his own face revealed as much anxiety as his friend's. Their eyes locked. "Kill?" Snook mouthed, as Kalmar heard Cabyl's tap on the door. For a split second, their eyes met; then Dera pushed open the bedroom door leading into the hallway. Kalmar followed the other three adventurers as they darted—like wild children at play—out the door and down the hallway towards the stairs.

It had been easy, thought Kalmar, as he and his three companions plastered themselves against a wall in the shadows of a corridor they had found after racing down four flights of stairs. They had not encountered any draks in their frantic dash; it appeared they had gotten away without being seen.

"I think," Snook whispered, "that we're below ground level. We didn't go up but two flights of stairs when we were led to our rooms." Kalmar made an affirmative wave of his left hand.

"Try to make as little noise as possible," Arasima said. "Only one of us should check out the rooms down this corridor while the others stay here." She gave Kalmar a quick glance as Dera nodded her agreement.

"Kalmar," said Dera, "you're the hunter; if any of us can sneak down this corridor without being heard, it would have to be you." They were all speaking in whispers; Kalmar had to strain to catch every word.

Kalmar clenched his lips into a thin line and nodded. He wondered if Arasima had made her suggestion for spite or whether it was just an obvious conclusion on her part. He did have to admit, logically, he was the most qualified of them for the task. However, there was something about Arasima's calculating manner that made him believe there was more to her suggestion than that.

He dropped to the floor, pulled off his prairie-buck skin boots, and handed them to Snook. Snook used his other hand to help Kalmar up. He peered down the long hall and wondered how he had gotten into this predicament. He gave a barely audible sigh; he had been against the idea of this venture from the beginning. As he eased out of the shadows, Dera touched his arm. "If you see something you think we all should see, step to the middle of the corridor and signal us."

Kalmar nodded, then cautiously started down the corridor. His body instinctively coiled into a lower profile, and he walked by putting his weight on his heels, then shifting it to the balls of his feet, as if he were tracking a prairie buck. After several steps, he realized he was not going to step on a twig and give away his location, so he stood more erect as he continued down the hall.

Kalmar's bare feet produced no distinguishable sound as he glided along the cold stone floor. He stopped after thirty or so steps and approached the first door. Illegible script marked the door. Draks could read human text; it never occurred to him the draks might have a written language different than the one used by humans. He glanced back at his compatriots. Dera motioned for him to hurry and open the door. He forced a smile, grabbed the door handle, and yanked. The door was not as heavy as it appeared and swung open easily. What he saw startled him, causing him to step back. It took a second for his eyes to adjust to the shadowy, daunting shapes confronting him. He blinked and took another step backwards before his vision adjusted to the dark recesses beyond the opened door. His heart raced as his vision cleared. He gasped.

"Brooms! By Shetow's Mark!" he hissed under his breath as he faced four large sticks with bundles of straw and bristles bound to their ends. "It's a broom closet." Kalmar could feel the pounding of his excited heart. This was worse than tracking the cave lion; at least with the cave lion he knew what he was facing. He glanced at Dera, Arasima, and Snook and gave them a cocky, tooth-filled grin. "Next time one of you can be the bait," he said under his breath. He hoped they were unable to see his nervousness. His cohorts were all leaning away from the wall with their heads out of the shadows, Snook's bright face shining in the light, the three's attention fixed on his slightest move. Snook and Dera responded with encouraging, if not goofy smiles. Arasima was harder to read; her eyes were round and unblinking. *Show them no fear*, he thought. *I'll not be the butt of anyone's recount of this calamity.* This adventure did not make sense to Kalmar: why were they out tromping about the draks' building in the first place; had not Gogtee encouraged them to be patient, saying their questions would be answered in due time?

Kalmar tried to calm himself; why was he so anxious? He took a deep breath, trying to regain control over his emotions. All that had happened to him in the last few days must be why he was so apprehensive. He shut his eyes for a moment. In a mental flash and for the second time that day, he had an overpowering insight: how he dealt with his circumstances was entirely up to him. Everyone makes mistakes in their life—it's how one handles their mistakes that's the true measure of their character. He opened his eyes and forced his thoughts to refocus. He finally admitted to himself that he had made a mistake in picking Arasima over Dera. Arasima had been a choice of the gonads, not one of the head. She had also not been, for that matter, a choice of the heart, but that had not bothered Kalmar, for the heart played no part in choosing a mate in Shetow's world, at least not before your Pootash. He had made his choice for the wrong reasons and paid a price for his mistake, and to wallow any further in his anguish only compounded his original blunder. Dera showed no outward signs of concern over his rejection of her and he was not responsible for Arasima's situation—she had made her own choices. A feeling of calmness moved through his body like a trickle of warm water running down the middle of his back. He vowed to himself not to forget this epiphany.

He caught a glimpse of Snook waving his arms, trying to get his attention. When Kalmar looked at Snook, Snook made a questioning gesture. He motioned to Snook that he was all right. He looked away from his three companions and concentrated on the task ahead. Kalmar remembered what Dera had said earlier— "besides, what are they going to do? Kill us?" He smiled and whispered to himself, "Dera, I hope you know what you're talking about." He shut the closet door and crept down the corridor towards the next door. Once in front of the door, he kneeled down so his head was lower than the door handle; he thought this crouched position would make him harder to spot by anybody or anything that might be inside. Kalmar pressed his face against the doorframe and slowly opened the door just enough for him to peek through the crack.

The room glowed with a pulsating green light that blurred the lines of the space; at first, he could not distinguish any firm shapes. The emerald illumination gave Kalmar an uneasy feeling; the eerie hue was unlike anything he had ever seen in nature. No leaf or blade of grass had such an incandescent appearance. The unnatural radiation also made it difficult for him to detect movement in the room. He swallowed and opened the door just enough for him to crawl into the room on his hands and knees. He flinched as the door clicked closed behind him. He should have been more careful and eased it shut. For a split second he closed his eyes and shook his head at his careless blunder. Quickly his eyes popped open and he surveyed his surroundings. The Grace of Shetow was with him for the room was empty.

He was in a small enclosure where the far wall was about

twenty feet from him, but it curved and attached at each end to the flat wall behind him. The arched surface was solid to about waist high, and then a seamless, curved-glass plate extended to the ceiling. In the center of the curved wall was another door—the only blemish on the otherwise flawless surface—also constructed of glass. He marveled at the transparent wall; he had never seen so much glass, at least not in such a large sheet. There was no furniture or other articles in the room. Kalmar wondered if this was just an anteroom leading into what was beyond the glass door. Even though the wall was mostly glass, he still could not see what was on the other side; he was still squatting and the level of his head was below the beginning of the glass portion of the wall. He crept over and slowly stretched his neck so he could peep over the lower, solid section of the wall. He had to stick his head up more than he wanted to get a clear view of the next room. The floor level of the adjoining room was fifteen or so feet lower than the anteroom. He could see steps leading down from the glass doorway. The room was expansive, somewhat larger than his tribe's Oonoc Lodge. Long polished metal machines, with rows of blinking multicolored squares on panels along their sides, lined the room.

As Kalmar contemplated the function of the machines, he caught movement out of the corner of his left eye and jerked his head down. After waiting a few minutes, he lifted his head and peered over the lower wall again. Less than fifty feet from him, he saw a group of male and female draks—whose sex was now recognizable to him because of the coloring of their plumage—helping a larger drak climb onto the flat top of one of the machines. His eyes narrowed; it appeared to be Gogtee.

Once settled, she lay on her side on the smooth bed of the metal apparatus. In a few seconds, what appeared to Kalmar to be an elongated glass bubble lowered to cover her body. One of the attending female draks pushed a few buttons on the side of the machine as Gogtee lay perfectly still under her transparent enclosure. When the female drak pushed an orange button, purple illumination filled the bubble, immersing Gogtee's body in a shimmering violet shroud. As Kalmar strained to see what was happening, a yellow gaseous cloud began to fill the clear container. When the drak finished with the controls, she and all but one of the male draks turned and scampered out of the room. The remaining drak took a station at the end of the machine and appeared to be standing vigil over the confined Gogtee. Gogtee had offered the smaller lizards no resistance when they led her to the machine. Kalmar was puzzled; was Gogtee in danger? What could the strange contraption be other than some form of punishment?

He knew he had to show the others what he had found. He quietly crawled back into the corridor and motioned for them to join him. As they started towards him, he put his index finger to his lips. In response to his signal, they tried to walk on their tiptoes. With their best efforts, they still sounded like a herd of black boar tramping through a thicket. Kalmar grimaced. Smart they were; hunters they were not. Dera and Arasima were females. Females were not taught the skill of silence. However, Kalmar knew Snook, even though he was not a hunter, could move stealthily; he had been undetected by the cave lion on the day they met. When the three reached Kalmar, he gave Snook a questioning frown. Snook just looked back and angled his eye towards the two women before shrugging his shoulders and shaking his head.

"What is it? What did you find?" Dera whispered. Arasima and Snook leaned closer to hear his answer.

"I don't know . . . and I'm not sure I want to know."

"What's that supposed to mean?" cracked Arasima.

"You're about to find out," Kalmar answered. He kneeled down in front of the door to the green room. Snook and Dera dropped to their knees beside him. The three of them looked up at

Arasima, who hesitated, giving them a half-hearted smile, before following their lead. Kalmar cracked the door and, after confirming the room was still empty, opened it enough for them to enter. The three crawled in behind Kalmar and followed him as he crawled over to the curved wall. When he reached it, he turned around and leaned against the wall. Dera had been close behind him and crawled up just as his back touched the cool smooth surface. Arasima came next. She kept craning her neck to look up at the glass section of the wall. Snook, like a doting mother, brought up the rear. A little over halfway across the room, Snook stopped crawling. Mesmerized by what he saw, his jaw dropped. His eyes rolled as he gazed at the glass-walled room.

"Snook, come on," Kalmar whispered softly. Snook did not respond. He tried a second time but to no avail. Transfixed, Kalmar stared at his friend, not knowing what to do next. There was movement to his left; Arasima, whose own emotions were now well in control, quickly crawled to the middle of the room, grabbed Snook's shoulder, and shook him. Arasima's unexpected jolt caused Snook to jerk as he snapped out of his trance. Snook glanced at Arasima for an instant with a puzzled expression, then he closed his eyes and shook his head. With an apologetic grin, Snook nodded to Arasima, and they both crawled towards Kalmar and Dera. Dera glanced at him with a raised, questioning eyebrow. Kalmar noticed Arasima sported a sly smirk when all four of them were finally leaning against the wall. Kalmar could not decide if it was because Arasima thought what had happened to Snook was funny, or had just revealed a side of herself she had kept hidden.

"I'm a Seeker, but I've never seen anything like this room before. All this glass," Snook said, moving his hand in a circular motion. "As a Seeker, it's my duty to study things I've never seen . . . and try to understand them."

"But you stopped short of seeing the thing that will make your

Seeker curiosity go crazy," Kalmar said. "The mystery of the glass is minuscule; what's on the other side of the glass is the reason I brought you in the room."

"What do you mean?" Dera asked, glancing at Snook before her gaze settled on Kalmar.

He looked up and tilted his head toward the wall behind them. "Peek over the solid portion of the wall and look through the glass and tell me what you see." The three looked at Kalmar with different expressions: Arasima's face was impossible to read, but seemed to have lost some of its color; Snook's face bubbled with curiosity; Dera's face held an aura of apprehension. In a few seconds, their attention shifted from him to what he had said. As if on cue, they all slowly raised their heads enough to see over the lower section of the wall and look into the room beyond the glass.

For a time no one spoke. Then Snook broke the silence. "I don't understand what it is." The only color in the room, besides the haunting green glow and purple spotlight, were the multicolored blinking buttons on the side panel and the swirling yellow gas that filled the glass dome of the strange machine next to the lone drak attendant. "Is that a drak in the glass enclosure?"

"Yes . . . I think it's Gogtee," Kalmar said cautiously.

"What makes you think that?" challenged Arasima, wrinkling her nose. "You can't see enough from here to tell that it's Gogtee."

"I saw her when they led her into the room and watched as she climbed onto the machine."

"Hmmm." Dera narrowed her brow. "Then she's only been under the dome for a few minutes."

Kalmar nodded. "And she didn't appear to offer any resistance when they led her in."

"What can they be doing to her?" Snook craned his neck to get a better look.

Since the drak attendant was below them and, for the most part, kept his attention on Gogtee and the machine, it was easy for the humans to conceal themselves. As they watched, the yellow gas clouding the dome began to dissipate. After several minutes, only a wisp of the strange vapors remained, allowing a clearer examination of the drak lying inside. Even with their unobstructed view of the encapsulated saurian, it was still impossible for the others to confirm Kalmar's belief that the prone subject under the dome was indeed Gogtee. Kalmar strained to see every detail of the sedated reptile. Then he saw Gogtee's legs twitching.

"She's having convulsions," Dera said, a little louder than Kalmar would have liked.

"What should we do?" Snook chanced another look.

"I vote we do nothing," Arasima said in a matter-of-fact manner.

Kalmar opened his mouth to speak. "I—"

"Arasima's right. We should do nothing," Dera said, scrunching her face.

Kalmar forgot what he was about to say and could only wonder, "why?"

"We've far too little data to come to any conclusions about what's happening to Gogtee. For all we know this is how draks take a bath."

"*Bath,*" Snook protested. "That yellow cloud was gas. It looked like the deadly sulfur jets that spew from the vents around the Aja hot pools. That foul stuff can drop a mammoth."

"Or it might be a way of killing mites under their plumage." Kalmar had volunteered the first thought that popped into his mind. His words surprised him even more that those around him. Snook, Dera, and Arasima stopped bickering and looked at him.

"Now, *that's* a possibility that hadn't crossed my mind," Dera said with a chuckle, "but it's as good as any that I can think of. We just don't know what they're doing to Gogtee. Prudence demands caution; as Arasima said, it's best we don't interfere."

Arasima's pouted lips curved into a devilish smile.

"I believe you are right," Snook said. He lowered his voice. "As it seems we don't understand what our little foray has discovered, it might be wise for us to return to our rooms." The others nodded. They crept out of the room and raced up the stairs to find the hallway outside their rooms empty. They opened the middle door and found Izzy, Nutan, and Cabyl sitting around the central table talking. The three jumped up and rushed to meet the returning adventurers.

"What did you find?" Izzy blurted.

"Nothing." Kalmar grimaced. "Well . . . nothing we could understand. What happened after we left?" He caught a whiff of a pungent, acetic odor; burnt grass scent permeated the room.

"The draks rushed in just as you had predicted." Nutan nodded towards Dera. "After a moment of confusion one of them bolted out the door, apparently to get help. In a couple of minutes the room was full of chirping draks who finally put out the fire and opened the windows to let the smoke escape."

"What did they say to you?" pressed Kalmar.

Nutan and Izzy shrugged their shoulders. Cabyl answered, "They didn't say anything."

"*Nothing?*"

"Nothing."

"By Shetow's Mark . . . you'd think they would have said something," said Kalmar as he plopped down on one of the sofas.

"Maybe the draks were so mad they wouldn't talk to you," Arasima said. "If it had been me, I know I would have been angry."

"That's the strange thing; after the first frantic minutes, the draks seemed to take the fire and smoke in stride. They acted as if we weren't there." Cabyl giggled.

"That's strange all right," Snook said, tilting his head. "Did they realize we were missing?"

"If they did, I couldn't detect it," Izzy replied.

"I couldn't either," Nutan added. "It was like we were invisible."

"Do you think they were snubbing you?" Kalmar questioned, his eyes searching for the faintest response.

"No. They—they—" Izzy sputtered.

"They acted," Nutan interrupted, "as if we were unrelated to the smoke and fire."

There was an uneasy silence. "You haven't told us about what you found." Izzy's eyes scanned the four adventurers, looking for clues. "What did you learn?"

"We . . ." Dera's face hardened; deep creases dented her forehead. "We concluded the draks are right, we're not ready to try to understand all the information they have to give us."

Kalmar straightened his back. "We must pool our efforts to understand what we see and hear." His tone stayed level. "We must become one mind." He interlaced his fingers. "The only way for us to succeed is to do it together . . . for we will surely fail if we don't work together." His eyes wandered from one to the other before settling on Dera. "I concur with Dera; we are as smart as the draks . . . probably smarter. The gap is in our knowledge. A gap we must close."

Dera stared back as she studied him. With steady eyes, and her expression unreadable, color drained from her solemn face; her facial blemish, more apparent than ever, contrasted against her unusually pale complexion. "Yes, we must focus our efforts, combine our skills," she said. The deep lines in her face evaporated; the ends of her lips showed the slightest arc of a smile.

It was the first time Dera had ever taken him seriously. She had requested that he go with her to gather information, but he had not sensed that she valued his opinion. Her unexpected grin gave him an unfamiliar sensation—strangely pleasant. He felt his cheeks flush and looked away.

He winced when his drifting gaze collided with Arasima's torrid glare. Her eyes squinted, her pouted lips jutted from the taut skin of her rigid face. She made an unconscious nod.

TWENTY-EIGHT

The smaller, hyperactive draks quickly cleared the breakfast plates from the table. The humans had been awakened at sunrise after having talked late into the night. Kalmar was surprised at how well he had slept, but came to the breakfast table full of apprehension. The humans were whispering among themselves when a drak strolled into the room arrayed in the same color and plumage patterns as Zalibar, but its feathers were sleeker. The smaller size and rich luster of the reptile's guise indicated this drak was younger than the female Davar. Their guest moved toward the table in the fluid and flowing gait of the larger drak, not the jerky, sudden movements of the adolescents of her race. The seven humans stopped talking and stared at the stranger. The stately lizard, with clear and bright eyes, looked back at them.

"You don't recognize your guide Gogtee?" the drak said, a familiar resonance in her voice. Kalmar's eyes sought Dera; for an instant their eyes locked. A feeling of astonishment passed between them.

"I trust you slept well and are rested," Gogtee said. "Today we begin your enlightenment."

Kalmar sensed more of a change with the saurian than her

plumage color. Obviously, the previous night's ordeal was not to kill Gogtee's feather mites, as he had suggested. It was a few moments before anyone responded to Gogtee's statement. The other humans were as stunned by the female lizard's physical appearance and demeanor as he was.

"Gogtee," Dera asked, after she shook off her astonishment, "by enlightenment do you mean you are going to be answering our questions?"

"Your enlightenment will answer many of your questions, but the answering of your questions is not what I mean by enlightenment." Gogtee turned and started walking towards the door; after a few steps she stopped and glanced over her shoulder at them. "If you would please follow me." The seven humans quickly pushed back their chairs from the table and, like baby chicks, dropped in behind the regal reptile.

"This," Kalmar whispered, "isn't what I expected to happen this morning."

"You didn't expect a smarter Gogtee," replied Dera in a hushed tone, "and you expected some mention of our late night escapade."

"Well . . . yes." Kalmar shrugged. "Precisely."

Dera dropped back to walk next to him. "It's obvious whatever happened to Gogtee last night changed more than her appearance; as for our little scouting party, she could mention it later."

"It's hard to believe she wouldn't say *something* about it," Kalmar persisted. As they moved closer to whisper, the backs of their hands brushed. It was the first time Kalmar had ever touched Dera other than the time he had helped her stand up at the ravine full of artwork. She did not seem to notice the innocent graze; however, for a split second, all of Kalmar's senses focused on the remembrance of the unintended contact.

———

Kalmar's touch surprised her; surely, it was not intentional on his part, Dera thought. He appeared as cold as ever, but she could still feel the warm caress of his touch.

Kalmar regained his train of thought. "It might have something to do with where Gogtee is leading us."

Dera's luminous eyes flashed as she looked up at him. "Maybe this *enlightenment* Gogtee speaks of will make all of our questions seem trivial."

Kalmar nodded. He realized he had never had a real conversation with Dera. Once again, he had the same tingle as when she had smiled at him the night before. Was it sexual? He had made love to Arasima, slept with her warm naked body pressed against his, and never experienced this sensation.

Dera had not really thought much about Kalmar since his rejection of her Choosing, which she had expected. She now wondered if she had underestimated this complex man. She again thought about the momentary touch of their hands. How could something so insignificant have caused such a strong emotional reaction?

Kalmar contemplated his confusion as Gogtee led them down several flights of stairs to the hallway of their previous night's exploits. Snook glanced back at Kalmar but did not utter a word. Kalmar studied Dera; she was biting her lower lip. Why was it only now that he found her appealing? Gogtee did not slow down but pivoted around on the landing and started down the next flight of stairs. At the bottom of these stairs, Gogtee walked down a hallway that ran under the hallway the four humans had explored only hours earlier. After walking about three-fourths of the way down the hallway, Gogtee stopped and opened a door. Kalmar, Snook,

Arasima, and Dera traded looks. They knew what lay beyond the doorway.

With some trepidation, the seven humans followed Gogtee into the hygienic room of gleaming glass-domed machines. She quickly led them to the area where she had undergone her procedure the night before and turned to face them. Kalmar shifted his eyes up and saw the glass door to the observation room from where he and the others had witnessed Gogtee's ordeal. As he lowered his gaze, he noticed a dome darkened by swirls of brownish-yellow gas. He worked his way behind the others to get a better look. It was Dryka.

"These machines will begin the first stage of your enlightenment. There is no reason to fear them." The giant lizard hesitated. "Four of you have seen them in operation and know they are harmless."

Kalmar's eyes darted to Dera's face to catch her reaction to Gogtee's revelation. She blinked once, though her stone features did not betray the volcano of emotions he knew were erupting beneath her placid exterior.

"What did the machine do to you?" Arasima said. "And can you be sure they are safe for us?"

"These are learning machines, but they are capable of much more. The process I went through was different than the one you will undertake."

"Yeah—" started Snook, but Gogtee interrupted.

"The machines can teach, heal, and modify our bodies," Gogtee said. She used her clawed hand to indicate both she and the humans. "Besides the obvious changes, the process I underwent modified my brain, along with filling my memory with information. My deductive reasoning was increased by a factor of ten and the knowledge to use my enhanced mental power was also increased many times."

"How," questioned Dera, "will our procedure be different from yours?"

"The machine modified my brain to a degree only a select few of my race has undergone."

"Zalibar and Adurrell," Dera said.

"Yes, they are the only other living draks who've been through as much modification as I now have. My mate," she pointed to the machine holding Dryka, "will finish his transformation to the fifth level in a few hours. All of my race are modified at least once, some more than once. Our modifications are so we can perform specific duties, the traders being a prime example. The Learning Machines, through cellular sculpturing, modified my trachea so I can produce sounds you can understand . . . so I can talk. Trachea modification is limited to those of us who have direct interaction with humans."

Cabyl's almond eyes were wider than normal. "You've been modified many times before this?"

"Yes. Actually, four times; the first when I was quite young. Our society revolves around a successive series of modifications. If we perform well at one level, there is the possibility of modification to a higher level of intelligence and responsibility. It takes five modifications to produce our Bora and Davar."

"Then, with these last modifications," Nutan said softly, "you and Dryka are set to take Zalibar's and Adurrell's places?"

"No. Our fifth modifications were to prepare us to accompany you to Pandeelee. Our future after that"—the reptile's plumage fluffed—"is unclear."

"Pandeelee?" Izzy said. The skin of his face tightened as he moved closer to Nutan.

"Pandeelee is the end of your journey, the place where you will meet the peeri."

———

Arasima felt uncomfortable with the idea of the procedure. She tried to block the memory of the prankish giggles of her childhood enemies; she did not trust other humans and the feathery draks even less.

"Must we go through this?" Arasima asked, a quaver in her voice, as she motioned towards the mysterious machines.

"Your brains and bodies won't be modified; only draks are modified in that way. Your procedure will only enhance your knowledge."

"*Why not* modify us?" Snook exclaimed. "It would make us smarter. It would give us a better chance to pass our Judging."

"You do not understand. The only reason we were modified is so the peeri can use us to interact with you. The peeri are interested in how you will evolve as a race. To modify you would adulterate the purpose for you being on Elom."

"Gogtee," pressed Dera, "with your newfound intelligence, tell us what purpose the peeri have for us." The other humans' eyes shifted to the feather-covered saurian as they awaited her answer.

"The machine did not give me the answer to that question, but it did give me some insight concerning the matter. The fact the peeri wanted you unmodified may be a larger piece of the puzzle than I first thought." There was dead silence for a few seconds.

"I don't understand how the machines are going to increase our knowledge without modifying us," Arasima said. A few of the others nodded.

"The Learning Machine used cellular sculpturing to increase my intelligence by changing the capacity of my brain and how it functions. I now understand things I could never have understood no matter how long or hard I studied. On your part, the machines will only increase your knowledge by placing information in your minds; it will plant knowledge into your memory that you could have learned by reading and studying. It would have taken many cycles of the seasons but you could have done it. My capacity to learn and understand has been enhanced; your capacity to learn will be the same. It is your reservoir of knowledge that will expand."

"How can a machine do this?" Nutan asked, a challenge in her voice.

"I don't have a firm grasp on how it's done, but I can feel the difference."

"How can we, all of a sudden, deal with new information in our brains?" Kalmar asked.

"Most of the new information will be stored in your memory. The information will not overpower you, but will be there—in your head—when you need it. You will think about something and"—she flicked her wrist—"you will remember the new information."

"What if we don't want to go through the procedure?" Arasima said, almost frantic. Kalmar was not surprised by Arasima's question. It was obvious from her demeanor that she had serious fears about the Learning Machines.

"If you choose not to go through the process, your decision will be honored."

"Good. I choose not to," she said. The hard lines of her face softened.

"Very well," Gogtee said pleasantly. "Is there anyone else who chooses to not go through the knowledge enhancement process?" To Kalmar's surprise, the reptile brushed by Arasima's choice.

"What effect," Dera asked, her face set and her voice slow and deliberate, "will Arasima's not going through the enhancement process have on our chances of passing the Judging?"

"Again, I don't know, but I would think she would become a nonfactor."

"What do you *mean?*" Arasima asked, with added firmness in her voice.

Kalmar had not distinguished any inflectional changes in Gogtee's voice until the lizard turned to face Arasima. "They," Gogtee said in an unsympathetic voice as she indicated the other six humans, "will become the most intelligent humans to ever live. You . . . you will not grasp many of the things you will see and hear in the next few days. With their enhanced knowledge they will quickly assimilate to the world you are about to enter. Their intellect will soar; yours will falter. You will become even more isolated from them than you already are." Gogtee's words fell hard on Kalmar; he knew they must have been devastating to Arasima. He had wondered if the draks were aware of Arasima's strained relationship with the other humans. The draks seemed to understand humans better than he had thought.

"But you said our intelligence wouldn't change, just our knowledge. Our memory of facts would be what was increased," Arasima sputtered.

"I said your reasoning ability; the mental functioning of your brains would not change. Your companions' intelligence will increase because intellect is brain capacity nourished with knowledge. Your brain capacity will be equal to theirs, but your knowledge will be infinitesimal when compared to theirs. You will become as a child surrounded by adults." Gogtee paused. "And as time passes, the gap will only grow larger."

"The procedures change your plumage color?" Snook interjected, after several minutes of seeming distracted. "The draks, you're all the same species, aren't you?"

Kalmar was thankful Snook changed the direction and intensity of the conversation and wondered if that was Snook's aim. Kalmar was, nevertheless, very interested in Gogtee's answer. He noticed Arasima shrink to the back of the group, where she slumped against one of the metallic machines.

"Yes, of course. Did you think differently?"

"We weren't sure, with so many different color patterns in your plumage. We wondered if duties were assigned to a variety of differently related species."

"In a way that is correct. The differences in plumage are modifications made by the Learning Machines to differentiate among us what brain and body modification any one individual has had. Draks are a conglomerate of different varieties, not the result of natural evolution. We are a product of the Learning Machines, creations of the peeri. As hatchlings, we peck through our egg shells emerging almost identical; cycles of the seasons later we return to dust as a hundred different breeds." If Kalmar had ever picked up a hint of sadness in Gogtee's voice, it was now.

There was a long silence.

"Gogtee," Dera said, "before we face the machine, would you answer a question?"

"The machines will—"

"Please, Gogtee; it's a simple question."

The saurian hesitated. "What's your question?"

"Our guards didn't realize some of us left our rooms last night, yet you knew we had seen you under the glass dome. How?"

"The domes aren't glass, and those who were outside your rooms were not guards, only attendants. They were there to help you if you needed anything. They're modified to react to situations, not analyze why they happen. When you started the fire, they knew to put it out. It never occurred to them to wonder how the fires started."

Kalmar wrinkled his brow. "You said the attendants were there to help us. Would they have stopped us if we had just walked out of our rooms and gone exploring?"

"No, but they would've followed you to make sure you didn't put yourselves in danger."

"*Danger,* how could we have been in danger?"

"They would have made sure you didn't grab an energy wire or step in front of a fast-moving transport machine."

"Then how did you know we had seen you under the dome?" Snook asked.

"You were tracked by the hall and room viewing devices." Gogtee pointed to a small black spot on the ceiling above the doorway into the room. "After your enhancements, you'll understand how they work, but with the viewing devices we can observe what happens in this building."

Kalmar had no idea how the mechanism could possibly work, but he did understand its implications. "Then we were watched when we stared the fires?"

"No. If we had, we would have come to you and requested that you not put yourselves in danger. Your rooms are unmonitored; we respect the human need for privacy."

Kalmar noticed Dera, Nutan, and Cabyl nod their heads. The thought of being watched in his room bothered him, but he knew that females were more self-conscious than males. Arasima was not listening to the conversation and appeared lost in thought.

"Are you ready to begin the enhancement procedure?"

The six humans looked from one to the other before nodding. Gogtee tapped a silver button on her leather body strap. In seconds the room was full of draks with the same plumage as the ones he had seen aiding Gogtee the night before. The draks separated like drops of shimmering mercury into small groups, and then converged on the seven humans. Gogtee made a soft unhuman squeal towards the draks who had gathered around Arasima. The draks looked at Gogtee, and she made a slight motion with her right claw while making a few more unintelligible sounds.

"That's all right," Arasima snapped at Gogtee indignantly. "I've changed my mind; I'll undergo the enhancement process."

Gogtee did not respond to Arasima's decision other than to

make a few more chirps to the draks surrounding Arasima. Then each human was led to a machine and helped onto its metal bed. The ominous apparatuses had more than enough surface area for a human; they were big enough for the largest drak, thought Kalmar.

From the moment Kalmar first lay down on the cool flat metal surface, he was uncomfortable. He remembered Gogtee had lain on her side and wondered if it mattered that he was on his back. There were four draks stationed around his platform, one on each side and one at each end. None made an effort to get him to change his position on the table, so he decided to stay the way he was. In a few minutes he heard Gogtee's muffled bark. He turned his head and saw the drak on his right moving its clawlike finger over a portion of the machine just below his line of sight. His attention shifted to the clear elongated dome above him as it started to lower. He felt a jolt of panic; a sense of being encased in a tomb rolled over him. When the edges of the transparent dome touched the metal of the machine's flat bed, purple illumination flooded the enclosure. He was thinking how soothing the unusual glow was when a hissing sound preceded the hazy yellow gas that he knew would start billowing into his confines. He got a whiff of a musky fragrance that reminded him of the flower of the penree bush. He smiled; the yellow gas was not the nauseous sulfur fumes Snook had feared. As his sight blurred, the increasing weight of his eyelids forced them shut.

TWENTY-NINE

His right arm twitched. He pried his eyes open, fighting back tears, as he dragged his left arm over his face to block the piercing light that burned into his skull like smoldering coals pressing against his pupils. He heard a distant moan, then realized that he had uttered the eerie sound. Booming pain gripped his head; it felt like someone was blowing hot air into his ears in an effort to expand his skull. Memories of regaining consciousness after his traumatic encounter with the cave lion flashed through his mind. Unseen hands grabbed his arms and legs and pulled him to a seated position. Unable to force his eyes to anything more than a squint, he detected a faint phosphorescent tint to the things around him. Then, remembering where he was, he understood why the room was bathed in the fluffy green light; anything brighter would have blinded those who awoke from the Learning Machines. He knew where he was and why he was there; however, the relentless pounding in his head deflected any efforts for further thought.

Several hours later, the drak attendants escorted the humans back to their rooms and put them to bed. Kalmar slept soundly and awoke famished. He walked into the middle room wearing only his shorts. He found Dera, Nutan, and Izzy reclining on the sofas and eating exotic fruit from bowls that ringed the edge of the round table in the middle of the room. Izzy was also in his shorts; the two young females wore sleeping skirts and their chemises. Dera's chemise clung to the front of her torso; the gauzy fabric strained to conceal the dark area around her nipples. She seemed unaware of her provocative pose; she had never been the recipient of a man's lusting glances. The sight of her sent a shudder through his body. Whatever the Leaning Machine did to him, it did not change his hunger for the touch of a female.

"How do you feel?" Nutan asked, giving her brother a comforting smile.

"Better than I did when I first woke up, and I hope we never have to go through that again."

"And to think, Gogtee has gone through it five times," Nutan responded.

"Surely," Dera's eyes darted up to met hers, "Gogtee's procedure was worse than ours, more traumatic with both her body and brain going through the modification process."

"Oooh, I'd forgotten about that," Nutan responded.

"Well, does anyone feel smarter?" Kalmar broke eye contact with Dera.

"I do *remember*," Dera answered. "It will take a few days before our brains and bodies recover enough from the ordeal to put our enhancements to the test."

"You know," Kalmar said, the skin around his mouth wrinkling, "I remember that too. By the Mark of Shetow, the procedure worked."

"Why are you so loud?" Snook asked as he walked in from the males' bedroom. He looked at the four of them. "Where's Cabyl?"

"She and Arasima are still asleep," Nutan answered.

"Not anymore," said Cabyl as she opened the door to the

females' bedroom. She was also dressed in her sleeping skirt and chemise. Snook's mouth dropped when he saw Cabyl's body only partly covered by the flimsy material of her undergarment. Kalmar spotted Arasima walking behind Cabyl. The sight of Arasima's perfect body pressing against the confines of her chemise had its normal effect on him. Kalmar had a funny thought; he had seen this woman nude—in a strange way, this was even sexier. The two females walked over and joined the others. What a sight, Kalmar thought to himself, a feast of delicious fruit in the company of the most beautiful under-clothed women he could imagine.

In a few minutes, they were all laughing and Kalmar could feel the mood of the group soar. Snook was sitting next to Cabyl. He bit into a grapelike fruit and the pulp flew out from the skin and hit her on the cheek. Everyone saw what had happened and the surprise of the event quieted the room. Nutan covered her mouth to keep from laughing as the slimy substance slowly slid down Cabyl's startled face. Cabyl regained her composure and saw Snook's lips curved into a silly smile. She laughed as she grabbed a handful of grapes and threw them at Snook. Snook ducked, allowing the ripe fruit to splatter Nutan, who took the full force of Cabyl's volley up and down her breasts and arms. Cabyl covered her mouth in shock over her mistake. Cabyl pulled back as Nutan reached for the grapes, but instead of throwing them at Cabyl, Nutan pelted Izzy, who was holding his sides as he rolled around on the next sofa laughing. In seconds, smashed fruit covered everyone and the room was in shambles. They all laughed until they were too tired to laugh anymore.

"I'm going to take a bath in the large tub," Izzy said as he jumped up and headed for the male's bedroom.

"Now that's not a bad idea." Snook jumped up and followed Izzy.

"They're not going to leave me out," Kalmar said to the girls as he stood up and followed his two roommates.

The four females exchanged glances. After a few moments, Nutan jumped up. "Anyone coming with me?" she exclaimed as she headed for the males' bedroom.

When Kalmar got to the bath, Izzy and Snook were splashing each other. He slipped out of his shorts, dropped them next to Izzy and Snook's, and climbed into the tub. Izzy and Snook ganged up on the straggler, splashing him as hard as they could. The tub was large; each one took a side, and they were able to extend their legs and feet toward the middle and barely touch each other's toes.

"Make room," Nutan said, grabbing the male's attention as she walked from behind the alcove. The three men exchange cautious smirks.

"Come on in. The water is warm and there is room for all of us," Izzy said, the pitch of his voice higher than normal. He motioned an encouragement. The three other females appeared behind Nutan a moment later.

"I'll bet you could find room for us even if it were smaller," Nutan said with a sultry pout that melted to a shy grin. Kalmar had seen his disrobed sister asleep in Snook's arms, but he had never witnessed the raw sexuality she was now displaying. She walked over, sat down on the edge of the bath, swung her legs over the side, and stepped into the bath. As a big brother, he wondered if he should be alarmed. After a few seconds of considering their circumstances, he decided that he was proud of her grace and composure. As Nutan kneeled into the water, the thin fabric of her chemise became invisible. She rose out of the water eight or nine inches so she could pull her legs up under her. The water-soaked material clung to her body like another layer of skin. The outlines of her erect nipples were almost as visible as if she had been nude. The dark rings around her nipples looked like large brown eyes.

Cabyl entered the water next. Her chemise also seemed to disappear as it soaked up water. Her actions were causing her a great deal of embarrassment; her flushed face was radiant. She moved quickly to sit next to Snook. One there, she lay her head against his chest.

Arasima looked down and saw the pile of men's shorts. She stepped to the edge of the bath, peeled off her chemise, and then slowly shimmied out of her sleeping skirt. Kalmar had been wrong; she looked better without her clothes. He re-ran the scene of the chemise dropping from her shoulders and catching on the feminine swell around her hips before dropping to the floor. No, it was the moment of her disrobing that seemed to excite him the most. Arasima gave him an inviting but defiant look before moving her gaze and staring down the other two males. Kalmar stared transfixed as she skipped the routine of sitting on the edge of the bath and swinging her legs over the side by simply stepping over it as the males had done when they had entered the bath. When her foot touched the water, her lips parted in reaction to the soothing feel of the warm liquid. The small gap between her front teeth— her only imperfection—stirred his baser emotions even more. Kalmar marveled at the perfection of her body. The swell of her breasts and the lines of her legs and bottom would rival the greatest creation of the finest sculptor. The dark mat of her pubic hair looked perfectly symmetrical, as if it had been trimmed and combed. Arasima slipped gracefully into the water and retreated to the one unoccupied side of the bath.

Dera, standing alone, looked at her six compatriots. Kalmar had never seen her ever do anything provocative, but there was no way for her to not be looked at sexually if she entered the water. He knew her pride would not allow her to turn and walk away. He could not imagine Dera backing down, but he did not think she would do what she did. She looked at the piles of the men's shorts and Arasima's chemise. She then looked at Nutan and Cabyl's water-soaked, almost invisible chemises. After a moment's hesitation and in contrast to Arasima's sensual stripping, Dera nonchalantly untied the string to her sleeping skirt and let it fall, pulled her chemise over her head and dropped it on the floor, and then stepped over the side of the bath. If Arasima's body had set him on fire, Dera's naked body did nothing to douse the flames. If anything, she stoked the blaze. It had never occurred to him that if a female had a head full of red hair, her pubic hair would match. The auburn ringlets stood in sharp contrast to her pale skin. The sight of this unexpected treasure left him breathless. He did feel rather foolish at his naïveté as his enhanced understanding of genetics flowed into his brain. He smiled to himself; you would think the Gray Beards would have mentioned the possibility of such a wonderful discovery.

After Dera entered the bath nude, Nutan stood up, pulled her skirt and chemise off, and threw them over the side of the bath, where they hit the floor with the loud splat only a wad of wet cloth can make. After a few seconds of silence, Cabyl stood up and followed Nutan's lead. They were all in the bath nude. Kalmar sensed the lowering of one of the last barriers between them. It never left his mind that the female members of their group were sitting in the bath in the nude; however, he did gain a respect for the females and their show of independence. He *remembered* the importance of that understanding when dealing with the other sex. For the next few hours, the group laughed, retold the story of Snook squirting Cabyl with the grape pulp, and splashed each other until the floor next to the bath was drenched in water. For a time it was the happiest night Kalmar could remember.

As the night grew long, their gaiety settled into a more somber mood. Kalmar found he had to fight to keep a smile on his face. As his eyes moved from one of his companions to the next, it was obvious to him that the seriousness of their situation was beginning to smother their levity as their thoughts moved to the rapidly approaching dawn and the next stage of their journey. Arasima, the first of the females to shed her clothes, he noticed, was the also the first to succumb to her thoughts and sit with her back against the side of the bath, her eyes fixed on a distant thought. He fought a moment of desire for the devious young woman. It was the first time he had ever seen her truly frail. He quickly shifted his gaze to his sister, then to Dera, who seemed the most focused of the group. Her obvious strength grabbed at his heart. Females who needed his strength had always surrounded him; stunned by Dera's poise, Kalmar felt an unexpected sense of sadness. Dera brought out a feeling in him he had never felt, one he could not explain. On second thought, he wondered if the dawn might bring some clarity to his clouded mind.

THIRTY

A flawless golden sphere, as reflective as a polished mirror, sped towards the heavens, rising like a bubble racing to the surface of a mighty ocean. The only sound was the whoosh of air rushing out of its way, but even that was inaudible to its passengers. It was a strange, unnerving sensation; really, it was the lack of sensation that made the event seem unreal. Kalmar, the six other humans, and the two draks looked at the view of the planet falling below them as the craft ascended from the surface of Elom. They could see they were accelerating, although no other sensation betrayed their movement.

When they were first led to the craft, it was floating several feet off the ground. From the outside, the sphere had looked solid and impenetrable, a brilliant shiny golden ball casting back all light that fell upon it. As they approached, a ripple rolled across the perfection of its outer membrane and a round orifice appeared in the craft's side. The six attendants who had escorted them to the craft lifted a long boarding plank, stuck one end through the opening, resting it on an unseen prop. The other end they set on the ground. Kalmar chuckled; the most basic technology was going to be their bridge to the most advanced technology on the planet. Two of the attending draks carried a small metallic cylinder up the walkway and set it on the landing of the craft. The bottom edge of the opening hovered several feet above Kalmar's eye level, partially obstructing his view of the cylinder. After the two smaller draks started back down the plank, the silver cylinder slowly sank into the landing floor. When the attendants reached the bottom of the plank and hopped off, the two larger saurians did not hesitate and walked up the plank into the craft. The seven humans followed them.

Kalmar resisted the impulse to reach out and touch the side of the sphere; it did not matter, the edges of the opening were beyond his reach. When Kalmar stepped on the landing, he looked down at the place where the two draks had placed the cylinder; there was only a smooth surface. The inside of the sphere was sparse; nothing but an unblemished floor and a circular railing. The area where they were to stand was marked by the curved railing situated approximately ten feet from the edge of the circular floor. It was obvious that the rail formed a barrier to keep the craft's passengers from getting close to the sides of the craft. The floor was a gray translucent plane and separated the bottom third of the sphere from the vaulted dome of the craft above them. The golden walls disappeared once they were inside the craft; the curved sides of the bubble were transparent from the inside, making them invisible to the travelers. They appeared to be standing on a gray circular disk. Only the translucent floor gave the passengers a sense of firm support, something Kalmar began to believe was for their benefit once the craft started its ascent. He closed his eyes to fight back vertigo and only opened them when he felt a firm feminine hand grab his shoulder. He looked up and kept his attention focused on what was in the direction they were traveling; he soon discovered it was the only way he could control his feeling of falling without closing his eyes. He felt clammy, and sweat rolled down his face. Beads of liquid trickled down to his scars and then followed the ruts in his skin like rainwater guided by furrows in a field. He had not sweated this much when he faced the cave lion. The spinning of his head was an unexpected sickening feeling—one he fought to control. His enhancement had not prepared him for this. He could tell by the way that Snook and Cabyl were talking to each other that they did not share in his dilemma. Was he the only one stricken with this infirmity?

"Artificial gravity," Snook said to no one in particular. Several of the others nodded. The new memories of the intricate mathematics needed to comprehend the complexities of the event came easily. Things unfathomable only a day earlier were now quite understandable. Moments after the vessel left the planet's surface they neared the upper atmosphere and the heavens began to lose its bluish tint. A few seconds later, the last remnants of Elom's sky dissolved, leaving a picture of the night sky, a black sea strewn with the distant embers of a hundred thousand suns. The spectacle engulfed them, and the multitude of stars near the galaxy's core was undistorted. The craft's transparent sides allowed them to have unobstructed views in every direction, except for the small area blocked by the gray disk they were standing on.

"It's more beautiful than any Jara Oow," Cabyl said. The others did not respond. Silenced by the visual majesty, each person was lost in their own thoughts.

Their destination soon became obvious; centered above them was a point of light that grew brighter as the others stayed the same. "It's Mystery; we are going to Mystery," Izzy said as he pointed to the expanding light.

"Yes, once there we'll change to another vehicle," Gogtee said.

"Mystery's artificial, isn't it?" Dera asked.

"Yes, the peeri placed it in orbit during the time of Geerna."

"Gogtee, what's it like?" Izzy asked.

"We don't know. We are like you; this is our first time to leave the planet's surface. From this point in the journey"—Gogtee looked at her mate—"we all meet the unknown together."

"Then why are you going if you don't know how to lead us to the peeri?" Kalmar asked.

"For two reasons," Gogtee's mate answered. Because of his latest modification, Dryka's diction had become much easier for the humans to understand. Energized by his new verbal dexterity, Dryka had made up for his earlier silence. "First, although we've never been to Pandeelee, instructions on how to lead you there were imprinted in our minds. Second, because of the importance of your Judging on the fate of our species, the peeri granted permission for two draks to accompany you for the rest of the journey."

"As I told you on the first night of our journey, we wish only to help you," Gogtee added.

Their ship was rapidly closing on the moon. The size of Mystery doubled every few seconds until it filled their forward view. "We're going to collide," Nutan whispered. She pressed her body against Izzy and closed her eyes, but there was no impact. Their craft did not decelerate; one moment its velocity was thousands of miles an hour, the next it was approaching Mystery at only a few feet a second. The craft, a thousand feet from Mystery, moved closer.

"Our bodies—" Snook said in a state of awe. "There's no inertia; we should've smashed into the side of the bubble when it stopped moving so fast."

"Snook, it's that artificial gravity you mentioned earlier," Dera said. "Inside our little sphere we have our own gravity field independent of any forces beyond this enclosure. Up, down, and—" Dera reached over and pushed Kalmar so hard he had to struggle to keep from falling.

"What is that for?" Kalmar exclaimed.

Dera ignored Kalmar's protest as she observed his efforts to remain standing before finishing her thought. "The rules of inertia only apply inside this gravity shell." Kalmar grabbed Snook's outstretched hand and steadied himself.

Nutan giggled at the confused scowl on her brother's face. Dera once again seemed oblivious to Kalmar as a person. She had used him as an object to prove a theory. He was confused because he thought his and Dera's relationship had improved. Did she use him in her experiment because he was the one easiest to push, or was it just an opportunity to make him look foolish?

Behind him, Arasima raised an eyebrow as she watched Kalmar's reaction to Dera's treatment.

"I think it even affects the light in the sphere," Dera said after she had thought a moment.

"What do you mean?" Nutan said.

Gogtee and Dryka listened closely to their conversation.

Dera's eyes darted as she looked around the inside of their enclosure. "The outside skin of our craft, did you notice how it seemed to almost glow? How polished the sphere was?" Dera waited until Nutan nodded. "Don't you see? The gravity field even controls the light in and around the craft. I don't think the craft even has sides, at least not physical sides; the envelope is the edge of a gravity field. Look into your memories: there is only one possible explanation. There's some kind of artificial gravity generator"— Dera pointed to the floor below them—"And it's probably there, in the only part of the craft we can't see through. The gravity generator produces the bubble of gravity waves that holds in the air and moves the bubble, and it bends light, causing its outside appearance."

Everyone just looked at Dera. Gogtee swished her tail. "I think she is right. At least the information imprinted in my brain, as far as it goes, agrees with her."

Snook turned to Kalmar. "She must have been enhanced more than the rest of us."

"No." Kalmar cut his eyes towards Dera, who had dropped to a knee and was inspecting the craft's floor. "There was just more to her to begin with." *The more I learn about Dera*, he thought, *the less I know about her.* His eyes moved to the radiant Arasima, who just pursed her lips. Kalmar thought it was so much simpler when a female's beauty and sexuality were the only things he considered.

Snook looked at Kalmar. He could tell from the tone of his friend's words that Kalmar's respect for Dera had grown. Snook wondered if Kalmar was thinking about the Choosing, and how things might have been different if he had chosen Dera. Some things might be different, but Kalmar and Dera would still be here; the Medora would still have selected these two no matter if they had been Paired. Snook gave his head a slight shake and switched his attention to the display playing out above him.

It was impossible for the passengers to continue their discussions as their attention was drawn to the foreboding Mystery, which filled their view. The name of the fourth moon was appropriate; even this close, it was still a conundrum. Mystery, like their craft, was a sphere, but it lacked the polished exterior. The dull gray skin was dotted with rows of lights that appeared to circle the small moon. To see it up close did not answer any of the questions running through Kalmar's mind—it added more.

"They are windows," Nutan said.

"What?" Izzy asked, as Nutan's statement drew him out of his trance.

"The lights, they are windows."

"You're right, unbelievably large windows. Each one appears

to be larger than our craft," Cabyl said. She looked up at Snook as she clutched his arm.

"If the lights are windows, then Mystery is hollow," Snook said. He knew as soon as he said it that it was an obvious conclusion and his statement was trivial. He was relieved when no one commented; the others must have taken his remark as nervous chatter. *Really*, he thought, *that is what it was—nervous chatter.*

Other than the rows and rows of lights, there were no distinguishable features.

It's small." Cabyl shook her head. "No, I mean it's big, but it's not nearly as large as I thought."

"Its reflective quality and low orbit make Mystery appear larger, from Elom, than it is," Dera said.

As their craft moved closer, Kalmar spied a large round opening between two of the windows on a row near the top fourth of the gray moon.

"It's so unbelievable. Why would the peeri have put it here?" Nutan said.

"To watch us, I'll bet," Izzy answered.

"I'm sure you're right, but there must be more to it than that," Kalmar responded.

"I'm curious to know how they watch us," added Dera.

In a few moments, they entered the opening in the side of Mystery.

Even Gogtee and Dryka seemed unprepared for what they found inside Mystery. Kalmar assumed, although he was not told, that they would finally meet the peeri, Geerna's abductors. But it soon became clear that this was not the case.

———

The craft passed through the orifice of the artificial moon and entered a large chamber. The entryway closed behind them. The sphere stopped and floated in the center of the massive chamber, which also appeared to be spherical. The chamber's stark white walls presented a ghostly appearance, and there were no markings or other features marring its smooth surface. An entrance appeared, breaking the plainness of the wall; first, a small hole opened in the surface of the interior wall at the same level as the floor of their craft. In seconds, the hole expanded to half the size of their craft. They moved closer to the side of the chamber as a walkway quickly extended from the opening until the end of it reached and then rested on the floor of their craft.

Kalmar turned to Snook. "Could you tell when the gravity field of our craft opened so the walkway could reach us?"

"No, but I haven't seen the walls of our enclosure since we entered the craft. It's as if they're not there. It must have been when the railing folded out of the way."

Gogtee and Dryka were the first to step on the walkway. The two saurians quickly crossed the bridge that led into the interior of Mystery. Kalmar moved to be the next one to cross. The walkway was about two feet wide, and it looked to Kalmar that the span between their craft and the doorway was a good fifty feet. He stepped on the walkway and walked about five feet past the edge of the circular floor of the craft before he stopped and looked back. Dera was right behind him. The golden shell of their craft was visible. He looked back through the opening in the side of their craft and out the other side. As he already knew, he could see the craft's shell from the outside but not from the inside. If the shell of the craft was not a controlled gravity field, it did have to be something that manipulated light. Dera's theory was probably right. For a split second, he admired the long fine auburn hair that flowed down the back of Dera's head as she also turned to study their craft. The sheer feminine image she made gave him an unexpected tight feeling in his chest. As the Gray Beards said, women were such a wonderful, bewildering gift from Shetow. Kalmar smiled to himself as he turned back to finish his march across the span, then his eyes glanced off the edge of the narrow walkway. Again, an overwhelming fear of falling hit him; his head spun and he began to stagger. Kalmar was about to drop to his knees to keep from falling off the walkway when he felt two arms encircle his waist.

"Close your eyes," Dera said, as the side of her face pressed against his back and her hands locked against his stomach.

Kalmar did as she commanded while she steadied him with her body. Even with his eyes closed, his head kept spinning; Kalmar felt Dera pull his body hard against hers. She felt as immovable as the trunk of a nutwood tree; she became his stability. His head was still spinning but Dera's body against his kept him from falling off the narrow walkway.

"Now squint and look straight ahead at Gogtee and Dryka."

He did as commanded and slowly opened his eyes enough to make out the outlines of Gogtee and Dryka standing at the far end of the walkway. The two saurians were motionless, their attention focused on him. He fought back an impulse to glance down.

"Turn your body a little to the left." Dera wrestled with his body as she squared him with the walkway. "Kalmar, you must do what I say. I know you're brave, you faced a charging cave lion; you can do this."

He felt her warm body and the swell of her breasts against him; her closeness gave him a strange feeling of confidence. "Now walk very slowly. Barely pick your feet up. Slide them. I'll tell you if you are going wrong." Kalmar knew he had to move and even though he had never known such fear, he slid his right foot forward. On reflex, he started to look down.

"Don't look down, look at Gogtee."

Kalmar knew the memory of Dera guiding him across the walkway would be etched in his mind forever. When they reached Gogtee and Dryka, Kalmar spun around to face Dera. "You saved my life. You risked your life for mine."

Dera looked at him for a moment before she reached up and brushed a drop of sweat off his forehead. "No, I really didn't. There's no doubt our hosts, with their technology, have an energy field around the walkway, which would have kept you . . . kept us from falling."

Kalmar looked at Dera. He could see compassion in her eyes.

"That makes sense," he said almost inaudibly. A strange feeling invaded his awareness. "Then why didn't you tell me this out there on the walkway?"

"Because you wouldn't have believed me."

Kalmar thought a moment. "No, I guess I wouldn't. I was paralyzed with fear." Dera looked deep into his eyes in a way he could not read.

"We all have our fears; it's being able to control them that show our true strength. Most people would have panicked in that situation, but you didn't. You pulled yourself together and made it across the walkway."

"But I wouldn't have without your help."

"Again you're wrong. Either a person has the internal strength or they don't. If they don't have that strength, no one can help them. You have it; all I did was make it easier for you. I helped you focus your thoughts, just as you did when you faced that charging cave lion." Dera reached and lightly touched the scars on his face. "You learned to control your fear of the cave lion because you understood your fear and you had time to learn how to control that fear. You, and we as a race, haven't had the opportunity or the reason to learn to deal with a fear of heights. I'm sure it affects every human, but to different degrees. I felt a little queasy in my stomach when the craft left the surface of Elom, but I was able to control it. If, on the other hand, the walls of the craft hadn't been transparent and I had felt enclosed, I would have been the one who would have needed help. As you have a fear of heights, I have a fear of being in enclosed places." She reached out with her left hand and grasped his right arm above the elbow. "You would eventually have overpowered your fear; I just sped it up and made it less painful."

Kalmar was not sure he understood her answer, as his mind was still fuzzy, but he had developed a great respect for her mental prowess; he would yield to her rationale. "One last thing: if you believed I was in no danger, why didn't you just let me fall?"

"The fall wouldn't have hurt you physically, but it would have hurt your pride more than your pride could be damaged by me helping you across the walkway . . . and it was time for me to help you. I owed you that much."

"I don't understand. How could you possibly owe me anything?" After he had said it, he wished he had not. Dera had every reason to owe him something—her contempt. Contempt she had never allowed herself to show him. In her own way, she was a greater mystery than this artificial moon.

She gave him a soft smile. "We'll talk about it later."

Kalmar nodded. Dera was right; this was not the time to talk about such things. He returned her smile, gave her a final nod of thanks, turned, and walked towards their two reptilian companions.

Izzy and Nutan had finished their crossing of the walkway and heard the end of Dera and Kalmar's conversation. Izzy put his hand on Dera's shoulder. "Do you really believe there's an energy field to protect you from falling?"

"No, there's no energy field. The system was built for a race that has no fear of heights."

"How do you know that?" Nutan asked.

"A race with any traces of that phobia in their psyche wouldn't have built a craft or walkway that could bring such terror to its members. Not the peeri, or whoever build this." Dera moved a hand in a circular motion. "They didn't build an energy field around the walkway for the simple reason that they wouldn't need it."

"Then why didn't you tell him the truth?" pressed Izzy.

"It didn't matter if the danger was real or not; the fear was real. I didn't tell him the truth because I didn't want a barrier to form between us. A barrier could cause problems that we don't need going into our Judging." Snook and Cabyl crossed the walkway in time to hear what Dera said to Izzy.

Although Snook did not hear everything, he heard enough to understand the implications of what Dera had said to Izzy concerning how she had handled Kalmar's predicament on the walkway. He could not detect any malice towards Kalmar in her words, but there was also something not quite right; her actions and emotions were still guarded.

The humans and their two reptilian companions stood in the landing entrance. No one, or thing, was there to welcome them. Like the chamber where their craft docked, the small room was featureless. The opening from the chamber to the room closed like a healing wound once all the passengers entered the room; the edges of the opening seemed to melt and flow back together, leaving no trace of where the breach had been. A few days earlier, the event would have shocked them; now it did not even bring a comment.

"There are no shadows," Izzy said.

"What do you mean?" Nutan asked.

"I mean there are no shadows."

Nutan looked around. "How can there be any shadows? The light's not bright enough to cast any."

Izzy and Nutan's conversation prompted the other members of the group to start studying their surroundings. The floor was flat, but the curved walls and ceiling flowed together without demarcation. Cabyl walked over and ran her fingertips over the surface of one of the walls. "The surface texture is much smoother than the rock facing of the Grand Oonoc Chamber." She looked up; her eyes followed the arched lines of the ceiling and walls. "It does have the feeling of the Grand Oonoc Chamber though. . . . I mean on a much smaller scale."

"That's because of the curve of the walls and ceiling," Snook said.

"It looks like an egg," Arasima added.

"An egg?" Nutan questioned.

"The curved ceiling and walls, their texture and color . . . it is as if we are inside an egg." Kalmar had to admit to himself that he could not argue with Arasima's observation.

Izzy, lost in his own thoughts, had not paid any attention to what the others were saying. "Nutan, you are right. There isn't any bright light, but can you tell me where the light we do have comes from?"

Nutan jerked her head around looking for a light source. Izzy dropped to his knees, cupped his hands together, and placed them on the floor, leaving a small opening between his right thumb and the index finger of his left hand. He leaned over and put his right eye to the opening. "By Shetow's Mark, that's why there are no shadows."

"What is it; what have you found?" Nutan asked.

"Light radiates from, well, everywhere," he said as he looked up at Nutan. After a moment, Izzy moved his eyes to his sister. As he stood up, the surface of one of the walls started to melt.

Standing on the other side of the opening doorway were three ghostly figures. The waist-high creatures had scarlet oversized eyes and stood on their two hind legs; their skin was colorless, almost lucent, like the petals of a juka flower. After a moment's scrutiny, Kalmar could tell the irises of their eyes were pink and the pupils were blood red.

"They are albinos," Snook whispered.

When the doorway finished forming, their three hosts walked through the rounded opening. They appeared reptilian, but they were different from any saurians Kalmar had ever seen. Their scant plumage consisted of white fluffy down feathers. Their three-fingered claws appeared delicate and much more suited to working with intricate objects than the larger claws of the draks. It took Kalmar a moment to recognize another difference between these reptiles and the draks. The draks walked with their upper body leaning forward, counterbalanced by the weight of their sizable tails; these reptiles walked as erect as a human and had stubby tails only a few inches in length. A sweet, almost antiseptic, odor accompanied the three-albino reception committee. The middle reptile walked up to the group while the two flanking it stayed back.

"Welcome to Bar' rah. We will make every effort to ensure your short stay with us is as pleasant as possible." The creature's voice was not human, but was clear and quite understandable.

The humans looked from one to the other. Finally, Dera stepped forward. "May we ask how long we'll be here?"

The docile creature studied Dera. It blinked its enormous red eyes, which was more noticeable than a human or drak blinking their eyes. The contrast between the red in the creature's eyes and the stark whiteness of its skin and sparse feathers made that instant when the creature's eyelids were shut stand out.

"You could leave now, but all of your party has not arrived." The humans looked at each other and then at Gogtee and Dryka. It was obvious that their two drak companions were as shocked by this revelation as their human charges.

"Who else is going with us?" Dera asked, a guarded inflection in her voice.

"Why, the rest of the human contingent. We are to send all of you at the same time."

Dryka moved up beside Dera. The white saurian looked up at the towering drak before taking a step backwards. Kalmar had the distinct impression the small reptile was more anxious with the closeness of its fellow reptile than it was with the humans. If Dryka noticed the smaller reptile's reaction to him, he did not acknowledge it. "We and the humans believed this group was the only one going to Pandeelee."

"You are but one of three groups that will represent mankind on Pandeelee. Since you were unaware of the existence of other human colonies on Elom, you had no reason to think that others of your kind would accompany you on your journey." The saurian made a motion with its head to its companions; upon which, they stepped to the sides of the entranceway. "Follow us to your quarters. After you've had time to freshen up, we'll take you on a tour and also try to answer your questions."

THIRTY-ONE

The humans and draks were told they were being led to an observation deck. The humans wore shorts and sleeveless pullover tops made from a soft thin material. Except for the fabric's coloring, the outfits were the same for both sexes: the males' were a forest green and the females' a rich purple. They all wore the same brown slippers. The humans bunched together, walking behind the two draks, who followed the three albino saurians.

"Even if I could get accustomed to these monotonous walls, I don't think I could ever become accustomed to the eerie way the doors—or whatever they are—open and close," Nutan said.

"I think the clothing is going to be harder for me to adjust to," replied Arasima, as she picked at her blouse.

"I think I understand the clothing a lot better than I do the doors," Snook said. "They gave us these flimsy coverings because of human modesty. With the temperature being perfect, we don't need them for anything else."

"Well, that shows they don't know everything," Snook said. "If they knew about our little party in the hot bath, they would know we don't have any modesty left."

"Speak for yourself," responded Cabyl as she punched his arm.

"Even though I pushed aside my inhibitions last night, it makes me blush to think about it now."

All the rooms and hallways were the same bone white. The irregular dimensions compounded the perplexing qualities of their austere surroundings; all rooms had more than four walls, and none were the same size; hallways would narrow at one point then balloon out a few feet later. There was no pattern to these variations; it was as if they were trapped in a piece of fruit, walking through tunneling bored by a hungry worm that showed no reasoning behind the direction of its eating.

Without warning, they walked into an expansive room. Their walkway transformed into a catwalk that bisected the room above its floor at the height of a man. The room, as voluminous as a meeting hall in an Oonoc Lodge, was the largest they had seen and followed the same baffling architecture as everything else. The room vibrated with the bobbing heads of hundreds of white reptiles milling around below them. Many of the reptiles stood in front of panels checkered with multicolored lights. The blinking panels bulged along the sides of numerous stunted walls molded from the same material as the room's floor and other walls. The contorted walls rose from the floor and ran the length of the room. They were extrusions, varied in both height and width—large wrinkles in the very fabric of Mystery itself—and looked like mud forced up between the toes of some unseen giant and left to dry. There was no symmetry; most sections of the walls were thinner than a man's chest and few reached the height of the pasty reptiles watching the panels.

"Looks like organized chaos," Izzy said.

"What's that on their heads?" Nutan asked.

After his sister's comment, Kalmar looked closer and saw the reptiles standing before the blinking panels wore small skullcaps, the same dreary grayish color as everything else on Mystery.

"Only the ones watching the lighted panels," Snook said, "are wearing them."

They walked through several smaller rooms before they reached the observation deck where a panorama of the planet lay below them. The front half of the wall on their right was also transparent. Kalmar could not tell if the front wall was glass or an energy field, but he could see light refracted by the clear sidewall, giving him reason to believe it was glass. Since the floor of their craft on their ascent stayed between them and the planet, they now had their first unobstructed view of Elom. The three albino reptiles walked to the front of the room and turned to face the group of humans and draks. The sight of their three hosts set against a backdrop of Elom turning behind them looked unreal to Kalmar.

"You have many questions," the middle reptile said. "I will try to answer them as best I can."

"Are you draks?" Gogtee asked, before any of the humans could speak. The smaller reptile appeared startled by the question.

"We both spring from the same ancestors. We share a genetic history until the time when the peeri placed humans on Elom; at that time our gene pools were separated."

"Separated? How?" pressed a visibly unnerved Gogtee as she shifted from one foot to the other.

"The peeri genetically modified the draks that were left on Elom and our ancestors who were brought to operate this moon." The reptile looked at Gogtee and Dryka before its eyes moved to the humans. "Many of the draks on Elom are enhanced an additional three or more times during their lives. Our modifications, however, are passed from one generation to the next." The reptile waved its upper limbs to indicate the two draks and then to indicate itself and its two companions. "As you can see, now we're not the same race. We could not mate and produce offspring."

"Why were your modifications permanent and not the draks'?" Dera asked.

"The draks have many duties on Elom, requiring many different levels of skill. The peeri needed not only traders to barter with the humans but also workers to manufacture their trading goods. Draks are evaluated as to their suitability to perform the needed task and then they are modified to reach their greatest potential." Gogtee and Dryka had put their heads together and were conversing in a flurry of whistles, clicks, and grunts. The small, pale reptile waited a moment before continuing. "We, on the other hand, have a much narrower responsibility."

"Responsibility?" Kalmar asked.

"Why, we control the experiment."

"*Experiment?*" Dera questioned.

"Please excuse my bad choice of words. I'm the first of my race to ever speak your language. We monitor what happens on Elom and report it to the peeri. We control the environment on Elom, the weather and the barriers between the lands of the draks and humans. We evaluate the draks for modification. We also activate the hormonal sequencing in you humans."

Kalmar could feel the tension build in him, and he sensed it in the others. Dera's eyes shifted to meet his. Except for the blemish on her cheek being redder than normal, her face masked her feelings.

"Hormonal sequencing?" she asked.

"Hormonal sequencing controls the checks and balances that keep mankind on the path to reach its potential."

"All right, but what is it?" Kalmar said.

"We, at the proper time, activate the hormones in your bodies which allow you to accomplish certain things."

"*What things?*" Snook said, clenching his fist in a rare display of emotion.

"The most important are who can have children, when they can have them, and what sex those children will be." The reptile's answer stunned them. No one spoke; each dealt with the revelation in their own minds.

Finally, after gathering her thoughts, Nutan asked, "How can you control our hormones from up here?"

The reptile looked at her. "Through your implants."

"What implants?" Izzy said.

"It's the spot, the Mark of the Covenant," Dera replied, as she lifted her arm and looked at the small mark on the inside of her left forearm. After a slight pause, five of the humans turned their arms over to look at their own marks. Only Snook did not move.

"I have no mark. How do you and the draks know so much about me?"

"From Bar' rah, we can see everything that happens on the planet's surface. We have known about the Mookyn from the time that Geerna first snuck them away from the rest of the humans in her group. After we evaluated the variables, we allowed the Mookyn to exist outside our direct control. We thought they could serve as a control group, a way for us to know how humans would develop outside a system structured to Concentrate your Traits."

"We're a control group?" Snook said.

"It didn't turn out that way. The Mookyn did pair and mate outside any structured plan, but they were aware of the story of Geerna and became mindful of their special place on Elom. We believe that awareness caused them to Concentrate their own Traits in a completely unplanned fashion. Even though your"—the reptile indicated Snook—"raw mental powers are not equal to Dera and some of the others in the group, you and the other Mookyn have developed certain Traits that are much stronger than the other humans."

"Stronger Traits?" Snook said.

Kalmar could see the reptile's last statement deflected his friend's line of thought.

"They are Traits that will become obvious during your journey." Snook furrowed his brow; there was a moment of uneasiness.

"Uh, what should we call you?" asked Nutan, breaking the silence. "What is your name?"

"As a race we call ourselves the quel; as an individual, please call me Arno."

"Arno, you told us about the two other groups of humans," Kalmar said. Arno had information and there were things he wanted to know; he planned to have as many questions answered as possible.

"Geerna and her group of humans were taken from our home world over eighteen thousand cycles of the seasons ago. Another group was gathered from a different section of the planet about two thousand cycles of the seasons later, and a third about five hundred cycles of the seasons after that."

"But why three groups, and why weren't we put together?" Arasima asked.

"That was by the direction of the peeri. We assumed the peeri didn't want to disrupt the Trait Concentrations that had already taken place within your group of humans for over two thousand cycles of the seasons." Kalmar listened to the reptile's explanation, thinking there was something not right with its answer.

"What are the peeri like?" Izzy asked.

"We do not know; we have never seen the peeri."

"But you said you were directed by the peeri," Cabyl protested. Kalmar noticed Snook look at the woman standing beside him; his eyes softened as he studied her face.

"The peeri communicate with Bar' rah; Bar' rah communicates with us."

"How can you talk to the moon?" Izzy asked. Kalmar saw Nutan brush up against Dera's brother.

"Bar' rah is alive—"

"*Alive,*" the group exclaimed in unison.

The reptile placed its right claw on a section of the floor that jutted up into a cup-shaped chair. "The floor," the reptile moved its claw and pointed its middle finger, "ceiling, and walls is the flesh of a conscious, responsive, and feeling being. In fact, all material in Bar' rah, besides the energy and gravity generators, constitutes a living organism. Bar' rah has lived in its orbit around Elom since humans were first deposited on the planet."

"That seems impossible . . . living?" Nutan said.

"It's hard for you to understand when you have only known carbon-based life on Elom. Bar' rah is a life-form different from any you have ever seen—"

"But, how can it . . . Bar' rah . . . live in space . . . the vacuum, the extreme variations in temperature?" Snook asked.

"Bar' rah is silicon-based. The compounds of silicon are not as versatile as the compounds of carbon, but many are impervious to the extremes found in space. Unlike carbon-based life, Bar' rah is able to adapt to those extremes. Bar' rah is aware of its own existence, it thinks, it stores the data we gather about you, and when it needs to, it can reconfigure its own structure. But more importantly, Bar' rah communicates with the peeri."

"But how does . . . Bar' rah eat?" Izzy asked, shaking his head.

The white reptile shivered. It emitted a wheezing sound the humans had heard so many times from the draks. "Bar' rah doesn't eat; an energy generator embedded near its center, and passing space dust, supply all the nourishment it needs."

"How can an energy generator supply it with nourishment?" Izzy's eyes begged the other humans for support.

"Humans, draks"—Arno looked at Izzy, then at the two draks—"and all animal life on Elom eat carbon-based foods and breathe oxygen-rich air so their bodies can produce chemical reactions that give off energy. Billions of cycles of the seasons ago, in its evolutionary past, Bar' rah's species, whose energy needs are electrical, developed a more efficient manner to get that energy; their energy generators produce all their electrical requirements for hundreds of thousands of cycles of the seasons before needing to be refueled."

"If Bar' rah's alive . . . a member of a species . . . how did it get here and where are others of its kind?" Kalmar said.

"Bar' rah traveled here the same way you are going to travel to Pandeelee, and as to its kind, there are billions scattered throughout the galaxy."

They peppered Arno with questions until the reptile became visibly exhausted. As if by some unspoken signal, the humans fell silent and stopped their badgering. For a long time they sat in the observation deck's chairs, which were extensions of the floor, gazing at Elom turning below them.

Nutan stood and rubbed her backside. "I hope Bar' rah doesn't find my fat bottom as uncomfortable as I find its living chair." Her unexpected comment unleashed a cascade of laughter, a much-needed release of pent up apprehension. Their circumstances magnified the humor of Nutan's offhand remark.

"My dear little sister," said a smiling Kalmar, winking at her, "of the many things you have, a fat bottom is not one of them."

"*That's right,*" Izzy said, nodding his head. Those in the room stopped laughing and looked at Izzy. Surprised by their grins, he added, "Well, she *doesn't,*" which only reignited the chorus of booming laughter. A shadow of growing anger crept across Izzy's face. Finally, he noticed Nutan; her effervescent smile and radiant eyes, glistening with tears of delight, softened him. Izzy's hard expression melted into momentary confusion.

"Izzy, you say the sweetest things to me." She leaned over and

lightly kissed him on the cheek. Izzy blushed, realizing why everyone was smiling at him. His reddening face launched an even
louder round of laughter.

A flicker of movement caught Kalmar's attention; he turned and
looked through the glass sidewall. He gasped; a group of five
humans and two quel entered the adjoining room. The humans
surged forward, seeking a better view of the wonder before them.
His gasp caused Snook and the others to look at him; after a split
second, they looked to see what had drained the color from his
face. The new group of humans was unaware of Kalmar and those
in his group staring at them; Elom, in all her majesty held the new
group transfixed. The astonished looks on their faces showed this
was their first view from the observation deck.

The jolt of seeing a second group of humans was unexpected.
Kalmar knew another group of humans had already reached Mystery, but it never occurred to him they could be so different from
his group. A sobering thought raced through his mind; he should
have been more curious when first informed of the existence of
two other groups of humans. He assumed all humans were pretty
much the same. He was wrong.

B ewildered, he could not move his eyes off them. They were
dressed in the same flimsy clothing as he was. Their tall, lean
bodies moved with a surprising grace, but something else traumatized him; their skin was black as soot. Salune often tanned the
skins of Gray Beards to the color of leather, but the skins of these
humans were rich, almost-shiny ebony. The closest male turned his
head as he spoke to the female on his left, and he spotted the spectators. He flinched as his mouth squeezed out a muted sound. The
other four responded to the inaudible alarm by whirling around to
face Kalmar and his companions. The two groups, separated by the

glass barrier, stood less than twenty steps apart. Stunned, they stared at each other.

"How magnificent," Dera whispered.

Kalmar studied the dark-skinned humans. Two were females and the other three, males. They had traded their animated expressions for somber ones. The men were lean, almost majestic, and taller than any persons he had ever seen. They towered over their quel attendants. The females stood a head shorter, but he guessed they topped his own height by several inches. Their hair was also black; short on the males and tied back on the females. He and these strange people evolved on the same planet, yet they looked so different. Would he find they had more in common than was first apparent?

On impulse, he walked to the glass. After a moment's hesitation, the male who first spotted him responded by also walking to the glass and facing him. Only an arm's length separated them as Kalmar looked up at his counterpart; the man's steady, dark eyes returned Kalmar's probing gaze. Strong features added to the man's mystique: His broad nose and thick lips first drew Kalmar's attention. His hairline produced a precise line of demarcation between his skin and his short frizzy black hair. His small ears lay close to his head. Broad shoulders squared his body and anchored long, muscular arms. His tall stature sported no excess weight; his skin was taunt, his body lanky.

The man also took Kalmar's measure, but Kalmar detected no reaction in the stoic dark face. The pupils of his charcoal eyes focused on Kalmar's facial scars—his still-healing gift from the cave lion. The man lifted his right hand and gently brushed his fingertips across his cheek in recognition of Kalmar's disfigurement. Then he reached down and lifted the edge of his pullover shirt to reveal a muscular, flat, ebony stomach. The man turned his body to the left so Kalmar could see four healed claw marks that started high on the man's rib cage and ran to his thighbone; this man had also faced death.

Kalmar sensed the strength in this man. Calmness spread through Kalmar's body; he realized the fate of humanity also rested on these strong, dark shoulders. He did not know this man, yet he did. Kalmar had been wrong; he and this man were not different at all. Kalmar raised his left hand and placed his palm, fingers spread, against the glass. The man looked at Kalmar's hand, then raised his own left hand and brought it towards the glass. On the inside of the man's arm, a few inches above his wrist, Kalmar saw a disk-shaped discoloration; even against his dark black skin, the Mark of the Covenant was clearly visible. Right before the man placed his left hand opposite Kalmar's, Kalmar saw the man's dark eyes dart between the two hands. After a moment of reflection, he dropped his left hand, replaced it with his right, and pressed it against the glass. Right hand on left, the fingers matched. Kalmar could see the man's larger hand and longer fingers extend beyond his own. He looked up into the stranger's face; their eyes traded a silent message. Kalmar dipped his head in a slight nod; his counterpart did the same, acknowledging their unspoken understanding.

Whatever they were to face, one could count on the other.

THIRTY-TWO

Their craft resembled the golden ball that brought them to Mystery; however, this one was much larger. From the inside, the invisible walls, like those on the first craft, allowed an unobstructed, panoramic view of everything around or above them. The only direction hidden from their sight was the area below them—the direction blocked by the ship's floor, or "deck," as Gogtee called it. The deck on this craft, like the deck on the first craft, looked like a large round tabletop bordered by a short railing. There the similarities stopped. Inside the smaller craft, the deck had been bare except for the railing. A labyrinth of chest-high partitions covered the three-hundred-foot-diameter deck of the larger craft; the pattern of the stubby partitions also divided the floor area into three sections—one section for each group of humans. There were no private quarters; Kalmar could look across the top of the maze, see every passenger on the interstellar vehicle, and then look up and witness the glory of two hundred thousand stars.

Kalmar, Snook, and the other humans in their group lounged on a grouping of benches and chairs in a spacious cul-de-sac near the curved edge of the deck. Snook stood, looked up at the endless night, and gazed over the edge of the deck less than thirty feet away.

"It's like standing on the summit of the tallest mountain," he said. Kalmar looked at his friend. Snook cocked his head; his eyes glazed as he focused on some vision extracted from his memory. "When looking from a mountaintop, just like here, the skyline is lower than you are." Snook looked toward the edge of the deck. "Close to the edge, we see stars above and below us." He continued looking off the edge of their craft and drifted again into deep thought.

Kalmar knew it was a time to listen and resisted the urge to respond to his friend's philosophical ramblings.

"And now, we are higher than any person from our world has been since the time of Geerna." As Snook looked at Kalmar, his expression softened. "I know there is no up or down between worlds"—he lifted his hand to indicate their surrounding—"here thousands, maybe hundreds of thousands of miles from the nearest planet's surface."

"Millions," Dera said. Kalmar and Snook turned to find her listening to their conversation.

"What?" Kalmar said.

"Gogtee says her implanted memory tells her we're millions of miles from the nearest planet and moving farther away."

"Did she say where we're going next?" Kalmar asked.

"Eeo."

"Eeo?"

"If you'll remember, Gogtee told you Eeo wasn't our final destination."

"I remember; it was the first night of our journey. It was when she was answering my question about distance. I thought she was using Eeo as a reference point."

"Well, it seems Eeo's gravity field is what supplies the energy to bend space-time and send us to Pandeelee."

Kalmar looked at Snook, then at Dera. "This implanted memory is downright spooky. I actually understand what you are talking about."

Dera pressed her lips into a sheepish smile and nodded. "Yes, every second I'm fearful of what I'll remember . . . what I'll know the next minute."

Kalmar looked into her pale face. He moved towards her. In the next moment, they wrapped themselves in each other's arms. There was no passion in the action, just a reassurance of their humanity, a release of tension, the ebb of an emotional tide. It would probably have happened between any member of their group if the circumstances had been different. Others in their group saw what happened and understood its insignificance.

All that is, but one. Arasima sat across from them, watching with a smoldering anger.

Why are we kept apart?" Nutan asked, as she leaned back on one of the benches. Izzy sat next to her. He lightly brushed her skin with his fingertips as he traced an outline on her bare shoulder.

"Surely, we aren't meant to compete with the other two groups," Cabyl said.

"I hope not," Snook replied, as he turned to face her.

"Did you see their eyes? They're just slits," said Arasima, who sat in a chair, as did Kalmar and Dera.

"First dark-skinned and now yellow-skinned people. I'm glad there are only three groups; if there were more, they would surely be red and green," Nutan said in a humorous tone that implied no animosity.

"They have the most beautiful hair," Izzy responded with obvious admiration. "So fine." The three males of the last group had shoulder-length hair while the three females' hair reached past their waist.

Kalmar agreed with Izzy: the females' hair was beautiful, so straight and smooth. Their hair had a clean, healthy sheen. Their yellow skin had not been as much of a shock as the black skin of the first group, but their eyes were so squinted, Kalmar wondered how they could see out of them.

Nutan sat up and looked at Izzy. She did not try to hide her displeasure at his interest in the yellow females' hair. Izzy had not specified the females with his remark. The males' hair appeared to be just as straight and fine, but the females' long hair was what was so striking and obviously the subject of his admiration. "It's nice if you want every female to look alike. You can't tell them apart." Nutan's verbal slap at Izzy went over his head.

"Well, at least they aren't taller than we are," Snook said. Cabyl gave him a weak smile. Cabyl was shorter than anyone else in the three groups of humans. She was self-conscious of her small stature; however, Snook found her petiteness appealing.

Izzy stood and made a quick visual sweep of the deck. He stretched his arms, acting as if that was the reason he stood up. Kalmar knew the ruse was not for their group but was Izzy's way of looking at the other two groups of humans without openly showing them his curiosity. "Oh no, they are looking over here," Izzy said.

"Which ones?" Dera asked.

"Both. Now one of the yellow people is waving at me."

"One of the females no doubt," Nutan said.

"No, one of the males," answered Snook, ignoring Nutan's sarcasm.

"What are they doing now?" Arasima asked.

"Most of them are standing and talking among themselves. One of the black men is pointing towards me and talking to one of the black females. She is nodding and laughing . . . man what a smile."

"Would you sit down and quit making a fool of yourself," Nutan said as she grabbed Izzy by the arm and pulled him back down to the bench.

"What did I do?"

"The reason," Nutan sputtered, "they are keeping the three groups separated is because if we were all put together, you, Snook, and Kalmar would be preoccupied with either the yellow females' hair or the dark-skinned females' smiles and bodies."

"I think you're right," Dera said. Kalmar had noticed that their brightest member had been unusually quiet.

"I am?"

"I think we are being kept separated to keep us focused on the Judging ahead of us. If they put us together, we would disintegrate into rabble; all we would do is talk about our differences or stand around gawking at each other."

"I'm sure that's some of it, but there must be more to it than that," Cabyl said. "If they didn't want us to gawk, as you say, they wouldn't have let the different groups see each other." Dera reflected on what Cabyl said for a moment, and then nodded her head in agreement.

"It's by plan," Kalmar said.

"Plan?" Snook replied.

"Dera's right; if we were thrown together, there would have been chaos; but Cabyl is also right. They could have avoided any difficulties by just not letting us see each other—"

"So you are saying they are both right. Hard to be wrong if you agree with everything others say," Arasima said, with a trace of taunting, the gap in her teeth plainly visible between the lips of her challenging yet sultry smirk.

"What kind of plan?" Snook said, ignoring Arasima.

Dera's eyes opened wide and the lines of her face became animated. She held her hand up, indicating she was about to join the discussion. She glanced at Arasima, then looked at Snook. "What Kalmar means is we're being prepared before we're put together."

"Prepared," said Arasima, with open skepticism.

"Prepared one step at time," Kalmar said, standing up for himself. "They knew it would be a shock for us to find there are other humans on Elom, so they have slowly been preparing us for when we are put together."

"First, Arno lets it slip there were two other human groups going to Pandeelee," Snook said, his face showing he was following Kalmar's reasoning.

"Next," Kalmar said, "the black group walks into the adjoining room on the observation deck and then we see the yellow people as we board this craft. Each of these events was spaced to give us time to adjust a little before they hit us with the next one. When they feel we're ready, they'll put us together."

"By ready, you mean all three groups being ready," Nutan said.

"Exactly."

"Understanding what they're doing tells us two things," Dera said, looking at Kalmar.

"First, the three groups," Kalmar said, "aren't going to compete against each other when we reach Pandeelee." He winked at Dera in recognition of their identical conclusions before looking at the rest of them.

"How can you be sure of that?" Izzy asked.

"Because they wouldn't care how we get along with each other if we were to compete. We wouldn't have seen them before the Judging."

As Kalmar spoke, Dera nodded her head. It was an odd sensation for her; her thoughts had never been in accord with anyone other than Izzy, but this had a different feel. She looked at her brother; she could tell by the expression on his face he was still trying to grasp what was so plainly obvious to Kalmar and herself. No one had ever understood her reasoning better than Izzy. A shiver ran through her body. Dera was not sure she liked this feeling.

All right, I'll accept that," Snook said. "What's the second thing it tells you?"

Dera looked at him, her lips pulled tight. "There's a higher intelligence on this craft instructing the quel in this process."

Kalmar had not been forced to face his vertigo again as this time they entered their craft by a tunnel, which turned out to be a large tube that extended through an opening in the craft's side and was withdrawn once they were all aboard. Once again, the craft's gravity field robbed its passengers of all sensations of movement; only the rapidly expanding face of Eeo testified to their great speed—the vast distance to the background of stars made them appear motionless.

Two hours into the flight, Gogtee and Dryka ushered them towards the center of the deck. They could see the other two groups of humans also moving towards the same area. Two quels were leading the dark-skinned group and one quel led the yellow-skinned group.

"Wonder why we have draks and they have quels?" Snook said as they walked down a run of the maze.

"Gogtee said the peeri allowed them to come with us," Dera said, "because the draks' fate is tied to ours. Maybe the peeri allowed the draks only two representatives."

As they moved towards the center of the deck, it became obvious the design of the network of waist-high partitions was not to confine them but more to differentiate each group's area.

Kalmar's group trailed behind the two draks, who were

somewhat larger than they were; whereas, the other two groups of humans followed their child-sized quel guides, whose heads barely topped the short partitions of the maze. Around the center of the deck, the partitions formed three large circles some twenty-five feet apart. The humans in each group eyed those in the other groups as they moved to their designated circle. An arrangement of strange elongated pods filled the center of each circle. The symmetrical cluster of ten pods looked like a flower, each pod being petal-shaped and radiating from a cylinder-shaped pistil. The pods reminded Kalmar of caskets, but the pods' lids were clear. Gogtee motioned for each one of them to stand next to one of the pods. The end of the lids next to the pistil popped open and rose with the hinge of the lids away from the center of the cluster. The two reptiles climbed into their pods and lay down with their heads pointing away from the center of the cluster.

"You don't have to be enhanced to know what we are expected to do," Izzy said as he reached across his pod, took Nutan's hand, squeezed it, and then climbed into his pod. The others cautiously did the same.

Kalmar lay on the inclined interior surface of the pod with his head several feet higher than his feet. The pods' positioning, with their heads on the outer edge of the cluster, insured their visibility to the occupants of seven of the other pods. Two pods were blocked from view by the metal cylinder in the middle of the flower-petal grouping, and Kalmar had to rise on his elbows and turn his head to the right or left to see the pods on either side of him.

Gogtee lay in the pod to his left, and then Dryka, followed by the unused pod, and then Arasima, Nutan, Izzy, Dera, and Cabyl, with the circle of pods ending with Snook to his right. Snook, the last to climb into his pod, lay back as the clear lids of all the pods closed with the slightest of sounds.

Kalmar closed his eyes to compose himself. Lying perfectly still, he forced his body to relax. A soothing sensation flowed over him; he felt like he was floating in a warm bath, the water gently lapping along his body. After a moment, the pleasant feeling turned to tingling, which eased into numbness. His eyes popped open when he realized he could not move his head. He strained to move his hand; it also refused to budge. He could not move any part of his body other than his eyes. His eyes darted to Dera's pod, which he could see without moving his head; her eyes, nose, and mouth protruded from a flesh-colored oval surrounded by the black bottom of her pod's interior, her blemish reddened by anxiety. She appeared to be floating in a pool of darkish-colored oil with her body just beneath the surface, the blackness almost reaching the corners of her eyes and lips, hiding all but the front of her face. The flooring material inside the pod had liquefied, allowing her body to sink into its darkness. He snapped his eyes shut with the realization he had suffered the same fate. He opened them again and peered through the pod's clear covering; his eyes danced from one pod to the next, seeing his companions' faces hanging, like masks on black walls. He struggled to breathe as anxiety engulfed him. His heart pounded; the roar of the blood surging through his ears invaded the solitude of his alien womb, a sound he last heard waiting for the assault of the cave lion. The stab of terror at the cave lion's charge flashed in his mind. Bridling his fear had been easier when his fate lay in his own hands; being held motionless by an omnipotent force petrified him.

Now, as he neared the judgment of all humanity, he felt frail and impotent; his stomach churned, and the sour taste of bile filled his mouth. Frantic, his eyes again sought Dera's face; her wide eyes met his. He was such a fool; he would beg her forgiveness if they lived through this ordeal.

———

Dera fought back claustrophobic panic. The substance binding her muted the feeling from her body's extremities, but she knew it covered her feet, body, and arms. The gentle roar in her ears confirmed that the substance also covered them. The metallic cylinder at the center of the cluster of pods, and the vise holding her, limited her view to six pods: the empty pod, Arasima, and Nutan to her right and Kalmar and Gogtee to her left. Through a clear lid, Dera saw Gogtee's eyes and snout; the reptile's body lay hidden by a black shroud. Dera shifted her gaze to the next pod only to find Kalmar gazing back at her. She looked into his pleading eyes; she sensed his pain and anguish. Remorse flooded her thoughts. Tears trickled down her cheeks; some left glistening trails over her scarlet blemish before they reached the dark substance holding her in its relentless grasp. She knew what she must do; only the truth would free him.

Arasima observed the glances between Kalmar and Dera. Her breath quickened, but she gave little thought to the substance binding her to the bottom of the pod. She had underestimated the blemished Dera. Or, was it that Kalmar believed her spurning him at the Choosing meant she had no interest in him? She gritted her teeth. Izzy and Snook had their minds set on Nutan and Cabyl; there was only one available male left in their group. She forced her eyelids shut; the gnawing laughter of young girls filled her solitude; the thought of being scorned again produced an invisible shudder. She would not lose him to the most hideous female born to the People of the Twenty-Four Tribes in a thousand cycles of the seasons. She set her jaw as she opened her eyes to gaze at Kalmar. The Second Judging might make it a meaningless effort, but as long as she had breath in her lungs, she would not stop until she regained Kalmar's affection.

————

The accelerating craft fell towards Eeo. At twenty-eight thousand miles a second and one hundred fifty thousand miles above the smoldering brown sun, the craft changed its vector. The dark sun loomed over the confined travelers, its immense gravity radiation bombarding the tiny craft's gravity field. The vortex created by the clashing gravity waves corrupted the uniformity of space. The turbulent struggle surged as the minuscule craft approached the dark star. Five thousand miles above Eeo and milliseconds before their collision, the craft emitted a gravity radiation pulse twenty million times stronger than the brown sun's gravity battering the craft. The craft's gravity pulse disrupted the fabric of the universe ahead of it—the craft slipped between the folds of a space-time rift. A nanosecond later and one hundred thousand miles above a red dwarf in another binary star system, the craft reappeared on the far side of the galaxy's core.

THIRTY-THREE

The pod lids sprang open as the craft slowed its descent upon entering the planet's atmosphere. Kalmar felt his restraints melt away; he could move his head and arms. There was movement in the other pods; they all survived the trip.

"Now, that wasn't very pleasant. I hope we don't have to do that again," Nutan commented as she climbed out of her pod.

"Pleasant or not," Izzy said, as he helped Nutan stand up, "if we ever return to Elom we will travel the same way."

"I didn't think of that."

"That must be Pandeelee," Snook said as he looked up. A yellow-hued globe with wisps of green, red, and blue filled most of their view. In relation to the planet's surface, they were upside down; the craft moved with its dome pointed in the direction it was traveling. Kalmar instantly closed his eyes and leaned against his pod, struggling with his vertigo. The craft plunged through the atmosphere, its gravity field shielding its occupants from the planet's pull and the craft's own inertia. In less than a minute, the craft hovered near the planet's surface; when the craft was a few feet above its docking area, it rotated to align the deck with the planet's surface.

Kalmar peered through squinted eyes and saw that they had landed. He wrenched open his eyes to find Nutan, Izzy, Gogtee, and Dryka cowering besides their pods, their eyes clamped shut. Arasima and Snook were slouched next to their pods, their arms covering their faces. Dera and Cabyl stood, braced against their pods, eyes lowered, and staring at the deck. Evidently, the visual trauma triggered by the craft's rapid, inverted descent took its toll on his companions. Kalmar smiled, remembering the terror of vertigo; he wondered which one of his companions hid their eyes last. "We've landed; it's safe to look around," he said, aware of the irony of being the first to recover from the craft's dive to the planet.

"You don't do that every day," Snook said, as he pulled his feet under him.

They looked at the world beyond the transparent shell of their craft. "It looks like Elom, the trees and all," Nutan said.

"What happened to the yellow world we saw before we landed?" Izzy asked.

"We're in the Elom enclave," Dryka answered.

"An area on Pandeelee altered for human and drak life," Gogtee added.

The craft had reached the enclave before the middle of the day. The members of each group had watched the members of the other two groups as they disembarked from the craft. Three walkway tubes rose from the landing platform, one for each group. Kalmar stopped right before entering the walkway and looked towards the two other groups of humans. The dark man he had first seen on Mystery stood looking back at him next to one of the other walkways. Motionless, the statuesque pose of the stately man exuded unfaltering confidence. Kalmar had the same sensation of trust of this man that he had had when they placed their palms against the glass of the observation deck on Mystery. For a second time, they exchanged nods. Then each group's drak or quel guides, following mental maps, led the three separate parties through a forest of trees indigenous to Elom before reaching three multistoried buildings.

Once settled, the draks told Kalmar's group the peeri would summon them in a few days and that they should use the interlude to recuperate from their trip. Much too excited to remain in their assigned rooms, the seven explored the area surrounding their quarters.

The transformation in Arasima's demeanor surprised Kalmar. The same overt sexual overtures that had enthralled him at the last two Gatherings now made him uneasy. The flawless example of feminine beauty turned the full force of her charm on her male companions but, obvious to all, the point of her interest lay with Kalmar.

Six members of the group sat around a circular stone platform with a diameter close to that of a wheelon wheel. A small Life Fire sat in the center of the knee-high structure while a funnel-shaped hood collected the smoke from the crackling blaze. A pair of couples sat across the fire from each other, with Kalmar between them on one side and Dera between them on the other side. The reaching flames pulled back after consuming most of the wood. A glimpse of Dera's somber face between the wiggling fingers of the blaze interrupted Kalmar's confused thoughts. At that moment, Arasima strolled into the room with a broad smile adorning her face. She eyed the sitting positions of the others and headed for a chair next to Kalmar. Izzy and Snook stopped talking to the females beside them and watched the fluid movement of her slender but curvy body. Both Nutan and Cabyl noted the way their potential lovers' attentions wandered as Arasima approached. Nutan pinched Izzy's arm. When the oblivious male turned to voice his objection, Nutan's raised eyebrow and undaunted scowl wilted his protest.

Snook witnessed Izzy's debacle, thought of Cabyl, and turned to find the fragile female with her head bowed. He put his arm around her trembling shoulders and whispered that he loved her.

Love her." What did men know of love? Cabyl kept her head bowed. The men of her past only demanded one thing from her; they had only caused her pain. She had been a plaything, used and hurt at their pleasure. Her few moments of reprieve came when her mother was near, and then later, after her Matage, when the relentless desires of her Pairing Partner were met. She had thought Snook might be different; that illusion evaporated when she witnessed the effect the mere presence of Arasima had on him. His unflinching stare prompted memories of him kissing Nutan to overwhelm her thoughts. Before tears could fill her eyes, she pushed Snook's arm aside, jumped up, and ran from the room.

Nutan heard the footsteps of Cabyl's rapid retreat. She glanced at Snook as he watched Cabyl disappear down a hallway. After a few moments, he turned towards her. His mouth hung open, his red eyes now large circles. Confusion blanked his face. He slowly shook his head and gave her a slight shrug of his shoulders. The skin of her forehead gathered; then she jumped up and raced after Cabyl.

Arasima plopped down in a chair an arm's length from Kalmar in an effort to regain the attention lost to Cabyl's sudden departure. When Kalmar did not react to the exaggerated sound of her taking her seat, she reached over and gently touched his hand. He jerked his hand back from the unknown sensation and turned to see Arasima's bewitching face. The lines of surprise radiating from around his eyes melted.

A rasima smiled. "Is there something wrong with Cabyl?"
"I don't know," he answered, shrugging his shoulders.
"Kalmar, I think we need to talk."
He squinted. "What about?"
"There are things that I need to tell you. Things I must get off my heart before we face the uncertainty of the Second Judging." She parted her lips just enough for him to see her one, tantalizing, imperfection. He could see the tip of her tongue touching the gap in her teeth.
"What . . . what do you need to tell me?"
She quailed. "I don't think I can talk with the others"—she tilted her head towards Dera and spoke a little above a whisper—"being able to overhear our conversation." She motioned towards the terrace with her eyes.
There is no reason for me to talk to this woman, he thought. Then he remembered how he preached to Nutan that they all had to work together if they were to have a chance with the Second Judging. It would be easier if the tension between them could be softened. He nodded and stood. Arasima smiled and reached out her hand so he could help her up. He hesitated and then took her hand. Out of the corner of his eye, he glimpsed the stark expression on Dera's face harden as she looked away. For an instant, his gaze crossed Izzy's chiseled features. Was his conversation with Arasima only going to fragment their small band further, he wondered? His eyes moved back to Arasima; his concerns evaporated in the warmth of her radiance.

N utan found Cabyl lying on her bed with her face buried in her pillow. She rushed to cradle the distraught woman in her arms.

"What's wrong?" Nutan asked. Cabyl refused to pull her face from the pillow. "Surely it cannot be that bad."

Cabyl raised her head and looked at Nutan. "I have no desire to live."

Nutan recoiled from Cabyl's unexpected words. "What do you mean?"

Streaks of moisture covered her ashen cheeks. "I allowed myself to hope," she said in complete despair.

Nutan shook her head, her mouth open. "What's happened?"

"Snook just wants to use me. I didn't think so at first. I should have realized it when I saw him kissing you, but I knew for sure when I saw how he looked at Arasima."

"Kissing me?" Then she remembered the night Cabyl found her in Snook's arms. She puckered her lips as the skin of her face drew taut; she felt the force of her own mischievousness. She grabbed Cabyl by the shoulders and made the tearful woman look at her. "Cabyl, I cannot imagine the trauma you have suffered; seeing your father kill your mother would cause any woman to be fearful of men. Trust me; Snook is not like your father, or for that matter, any male I have ever met. Snook would never hurt you. I believe he loves you."

Cabyl used the back of her hand to wipe her face. "Do you know why my father killed my mother?"

Nutan slowly shook her head.

"Late one night, she caught him holding me down as he forced himself on me. She screamed and he jumped up and slammed her against the wall, breaking her neck." Cabyl looked down. "I never told my mother what my father was doing because I was petrified of him." She shivered as she took a shallow breath. "If I had only told her when he was not around, she might be alive today."

Nutan hugged Cabyl and cried with her.

Izzy stood up, walked over, and took a seat next to Snook. Snook stared at the fire, seemingly hypnotized by the dancing flames. Not knowing what to do, he put his hand on Snook's shoulder. "I'm here if you want to talk."

Stunned by Cabyl's unexpected actions, Snook's mind reeled. The haunting anguish on her pallid face slammed images of his dispirited mother against his thoughts. Why had the Elders chosen him to come to the Twenty-Four Tribes? They said they needed to understand if the Second Judging was truly about to take place. The Elders preached that Shetow did not know about the Mookyn; therefore, She could not be a god. He shook his head. *The Elders . . . we thought we knew so much more than the members of the Twenty-Four Tribes. We thought them so foolish. However, neither the Elders nor the Medoras know of the two other groups of humans. How many other mysteries still lay uncovered?* In the last few days, he had discovered that the beliefs the Elders had always trusted as truth were no more correct than those of the Medoras'.

He gasped as if he were drowning. *The Elders thought the Medoras would mishandle the task of facing the Second Judging. So they sent me, their "most gifted" student, to insure the Medoras did not let their misguided belief in the deity of Shetow interfere with rational judgments.* He closed his eyes and bowed his head. *Me, who cannot understand the feelings of an irreproachable young woman. How can I represent my race when I cannot understand my own feelings nor judge the feelings of others?* He pressed his eyelids shut as tight as he could. A swirl of haunting images of his mother and Cabyl flashed before his closed eyes. *I have cared about two females in my life and have seen the same pain in both their eyes. Pain that I have no ability to understand. What use can I be at the moment of Judging?*

He raised his head to find Izzy hovering over him. He nodded

a thank you and then stood up and dragged his barely responsive
body toward the stairs.

A cool breeze welcomed Kalmar and Arasima as they strolled
through double doors and out on the terrace. Unlike the seamless shaped stone of the Gathering Hall and the structures of the
drak, this building's construction rivaled the artistic work of the ma-
sons and carpenters of the Twenty-Four Tribes. Irregular-shaped
hard stones covered the surface of the terrace. Kalmar could see the
grout between each flagstone but was unable to feel a break in the
smoothness as he purposely dragged his foot across the tile. A chest-
high rail skirted the edge of the terrace. Arasima took his hand and
led him to the railing; he could see that both the railing and its supporting spindles were wood. The rail was nutwood and the spindles
had the reddish hue of roder saplings.

Kalmar's face did not hide the bewilderment he felt. Arasima
pulled his hand under her arm as she leaned against the rail and
peered into the starlit night. He could feel the softness of her breast
as she kept his hand between the railing and her warm body. He
wanted, with all the will he possessed, to pull his hand away from
her grasp, but didn't.

He glanced down at the silhouette of her face. "What did you
want to tell me?"

She turned her head slightly and cut her gaze up at him.
"Kalmar, there is something I want you to believe before we face
the Second Judging."

He wet his lips and nodded.

She squeezed his hand. "I don't know why I didn't choose
you. My heart screamed for me to call your name but my anger
would not let me."

"Anger?"

"This is hard for me to talk about." She glanced down before looking up; a tear trickled down her cheek. "I was a scrawny child. The gap in my teeth seemed larger when I was young." She lowered her head again. He could see her gasping in short shallow breaths; her body trembled.

Instinctively, he put his other arm around her and pulled her closer. As he did, she turned so the length of her body pressed against him.

"The other girls of the village teased and taunted me, called me ugly, called me rabbit-toothed, called me bird legs." She buried her face in his tunic. In a few moments, she lifted her stained face to look into his eyes. "All those cycles of the seasons ago, I swore to them I would Pair with the winner of the Borrac. They all laughed, and called me more names and shunned me even more. As I grew older and it became apparent that I would become as you see me now, their taunting words changed to sneers and remarks behind my back." Her eyes grew larger as the tone of her voice became frantic. "Don't you see? I had to choose the winner of the Borrac to show them . . . to show them all that I didn't need them . . . that I didn't care what they thought of me." Her shoulders dropped as her body lost some of its rigidity. "Then you lost." She raised her fist and pounded his chest.

He was speechless; had he misjudged her again?

She ceased striking his chest and collapsed against him sobbing. "I love you so. I'm so sorry that my anger at you for losing the Borrac made me do such a horrible thing. If I had only followed my heart instead of my prideful anger, I would now be Paired to the man I love."

He squeezed her tighter; it was hard for him to breathe. For a split second, a wave of vertigo almost made him fall.

———

Arasima could feel his heart beating faster. With the side of her head against his chest and her face hidden from his view, her trembling lips stilled and slowly formed an impish smirk.

"We are moving at an incredible speed," Nutan said, staring through the glass-covered rear of their cylindrical apparatus as light from their subterranean transporter flickered against the receding walls of the rock-faced tunnel. The metal cylinder, which measured less than fifty feet end-to-end and had a diameter close to twelve feet, offered an unobstructed view out each end through glass panels. The flat plane of the floor broke the symmetrical lines of the smooth curved sides of the cylinder. The walls, ceiling, and floor offered no place to sit or handholds to grab. Light flickered against the tunnel in front of them; however, the illumination shining in the direction of their travel only reached out a few feet and failed to convey the same sense of speed as when looking through the rear port. The seven humans and their drak companions stood in the transport staring out the front end of their shuttle. Snook and Cabyl stood on opposite sides of the transport, Izzy and Nutan leaned against each other, and Kalmar and Dryka stood towards the rear of the cylinder, while Arasima, Dera, and Gogtee stood at the front end.

"Unlike the golden spheres," Nutan said, "the walls aren't an energy field; they're made of metal."

"But," Izzy said, "inside the cylinder, like the golden spheres, there's no sense of motion. One moment we are still, the next we're hurtling through this tunnel. When we started, the inertia should've splattered us against the rear glass."

"The cylinder's metal," Dera said. She looked to the rear of the cylinder. "Obviously, however, the propulsion system, like the golden spheres, is based around the manipulation of an artificially generated gravity field. The gravity fields around the golden spheres were constant; I think the cylinder's gravity field activated when the door shut. Like the spheres, when we're inside the gravity field, we're impervious to any movement outside the field."

"The cylinder was built with no specific race in mind. Only size controls who or what can ride in it," Snook said, after he pulled his gaze off Cabyl long enough to study the interior of their transport. Without warning, the amount of light shining through each end of the cylinder increased dramatically; they had stopped moving and rested next to an exit platform. After a side door opened, Gogtee stepped out of the cylinder and hesitated as she studied the three hallways leading from the platform. Although smaller, the surface of the hallways resembled the smooth rock face of the tunnel. Kalmar walked over and rubbed his fingers on the gray finish. Gogtee's eyelids flickered as her implanted memory prompted her and she led them down the middle corridor.

Nutan leaned over and whispered to Izzy as she squeezed his arm. "I think we're nearing the end of our journey." Izzy nodded. The group did not walk a hundred feet before coming to a doorway. Kalmar stayed at the back of the group, but kept his eyes on Dera, who avoided looking at him, a behavior unlike her usual indifferent manner. Arasima walked by and brushed her arm against his.

The door slid open without a sound, revealing a darkened room. "You're to enter without us," Gogtee said. "Inside you'll find some half-circle devices which you are to put over your heads with the ends covering your temples." She turned and walked back through the members of the group to stand next to Dryka. For a moment, no one moved. Then Kalmar said, "We did not travel halfway across the galaxy to falter at the last few feet." He stepped to the front of the group and entered the room. He could hear the others shuffling in behind him.

Once inside, the door closed behind them and now looked just like the other three walls—smooth gray stone. It slowly got brighter, revealing a square room with sides about half the length of their cylinder transporter.

Nutan scrunched against Izzy. "I don't like this." Izzy put his arm around her waist; the muscles in his jaw tightened.

Kalmar had the strangest sensation. The fate of humanity hung in jeopardy, yet his attention focused on Dera. The way her eyes avoided him made him think he also filled some of her thoughts. He had to do something. He walked over and stood behind her. Out of the corner of his eyes he could see that Arasima had turned towards him, but Dera did not know he was there until he grabbed her shoulder and spun her around to face him. He took her hand and pulled her a few feet away from the others. Everyone's attention shifted to them, and even though their mood was somber, all but Arasima grinned. Dera looked back at him, the whites of her eyes more noticeable than normal. "We have only a few seconds to talk, but I think it's important we get something straight right now. I do not know what's about to happen to us, but I want to face our Judgment with a clear head and one thing understood." He held her shoulders. "Right here, right now, we must forgive each other for all that has happened between us." Kalmar looked deep into Dera's eyes and squeezed her shoulders. "Agreed?"

For a second Dera did not answer—Kalmar's forcefulness had taken her completely by surprise. She considered the strong lines of his face. The pale scars on his cheek contrasted against his skin's pink blush. She looked away and glimpsed Arasima's pinched face. She knew Arasima was trying to work her way back into Kalmar's heart. Then she pulled her eyes back to Kalmar. There just might be more to this man than she had expected. "Agreed," she said. Then the light in the room softened and took on a yellow tint.

———————

Kalmar and Dera turned to see the gray rock surface on the front wall sliding away to reveal a glass barrier and a room on the other side filled with an illuminated greenish cloud. A moment later, a large creature appeared through the haze. Numerous appendages jutted from its hard elongated body. Its exoskeleton had the look of dull metal. As it neared the glass barrier, it rose up with the first third of its body standing erect, facing them like a snake ready to strike. In addition to a pair of antennae, eight black-stalked eyes covered its fearsome head. Under a flat plate covering the crown of its head hung a pair of bristly mandibles moving in collaboration with a pair of smaller under-jaws. Attached to each body segment after its head was a pair of multijointed legs.

"It's a giant centipede," Snook said.

"It does look like an arthropod," Dera agreed.

"It's the Multiped," Cabyl said as she stepped forward. "The Shetow-ka has been misinterpreted. Multiped isn't a name, it's a description." Izzy, Dera, and Nutan nodded; the other four just stared.

After regaining his nerve, Kalmar walked over and picked up a curved object hanging with other identical objects from a rock peg on a sidewall. The semi-circular object was as thick as his little finger and bulged on each end to three times that size. "This must be what Gogtee told us to put on our heads." He handed each member of the group a headset before he pried the ends of his apart and pulled it over his head, resting the bulges against his temples.

"Kurrrish," popped into Kalmar's head. He turned to see the others also looking around. "It is I, Kurrrish, Third Sub-link of the Scarlet Order, mate to Pathpuu, and Overseer of Elom, Earth, and a host of other worlds." Kalmar did not hear the words; they just popped into his head like air bubbles bursting as they reached the surface of a pond.

They all turned to face the large arthropod. "Are you of the peeri?" Dera asked, as she stepped closer to the glass to look closer at the strange creature.

"Yes, I'm of the race the draks calls the peeri."

"Are you Geerna's Multiped?" asked Cabyl.

"Yes. One of my ancestors is the one who guided your first Medora."

Kalmar stepped beside Dera. "Are you here to judge us?"

"No, Kurrrish is not your judge. The peeri do not judge other species."

"Then why have the draks brought us to you?"

"I'm to help you to the next level."

"How will you do that?" Izzy said.

"By answering your questions so you're mentally ready to grasp what you're going to discover on Pandeelee."

"When are we to be judged?" Nutan asked.

"That will be clear to you soon enough."

"Another race will judge us?" pressed Snook.

"That will be clear to you soon enough."

"I thought you were here to answer our questions," Arasima blurted. "You're not answering our questions at all; you're just telling us everything 'will be clear to you soon enough.'"

"You're not asking the right questions," the peeri answered, as its antennae moved like two stalks of boodo grass in the breeze at the foot of Mount Alar.

Kalmar pushed his fingers through his long hair. "Did the peeri bring Geerna and the other humans to Elom?"

"We did."

"Why did you do that?" Kalmar continued as the others listened.

"We did as we were instructed."

"Who instructed you?"

"That which we serve."

"And you serve?"

"That will be clear to you soon enough."

Kalmar shook his head, not knowing how to proceed. Dera leaned over and whispered in his ear. When she finished, Kalmar asked, "Can you give us the answers to what questions would best help us?"

The creature swayed side-to-side on the other side of the glass before responding. "The peeri are not an intellectual race. We are a race used by a greater intellect to do Its will."

"Does this greater race have any relationship to Shetow?" Dera asked.

"Shetow is one of the many names used by your race for a power greater than yourselves."

"Is Shetow real, does She exist?" blurted Snook.

"In the sense that there is an entity greater than humans and the peeri which has an interest in what happens to them, yes." The peeri's answer stopped the questions for a moment as the humans gathered their thoughts.

"Why were our ancestors taken to Elom; why does this 'greater intellect' desire to judge our race?" Snook asked.

"A billion cycles of the seasons after the birth of the universe the First Race put all of Its intelligence and energies into spreading life across the cosmos. During the next five billion cycles of the seasons, the First Race nurtured the peeri and a number of other races. We and these other races now serve the First Race in their quest to spread intelligent life across the entire universe."

"Why did the First Race wish to spread intelligent life across the universe?" Snook asked.

"We do not know; we never asked."

"You never asked? Why not?" Nutan said.

"The First Race is not like the other races. We do not have a dialog with them; we receive mental instructions on what to do and never try to ask questions."

"How were you and the other races nurtured?"

"We don't know; we only know that races, such as yours, are the end results of the First Race's efforts." The peeri's statement stunned them.

"Is that why we were brought here, for the First Race to judge its efforts in spreading intelligent life across the universe?" Dera asked.

"You are on Pandeelee to meet the First Race."

Kalmar's head reeled; his mind could not process his thoughts. He stared at the giant creature. "When will this take place?"

"I cannot answer; it has been over two billion of your cycles of the seasons since a peeri has had direct communication with the First Race." The creature swayed as if keeping time to some unheard music. "But, it will be clear to you soon enough."

They were all dazed as the transporter silently whooshed them toward their quarters. Arasima moved closer to Kalmar but did not touch him. Dera noticed Kalmar, who was lost in his own thoughts, made no response to Arasima's subtle overture. Snook glanced at Cabyl, who kept her eyes lowered. Nutan leaned against Izzy, encircled by his arms.

"If the peeri could not tell us when we will meet the First Race, it's for sure the draks will not know," Snook finally said.

"Don't you find it strange that the races—the drak, quel, and peeri—who have controlled our lives since the time of Geerna, do not know why they are doing it?" Dera said.

"It's a large puzzle with one major piece missing," Izzy commented.

"The most important piece," Nutan responded.

"The drak and the quel control our lives and the peeri control theirs and a Being that has not had a conversation with the peeri in billions of cycles of the seasons controls them all," said Dera.

"Which means we are the least important beings in the First Race's minds," Arasima said in a flat tone, her face unreadable.

"Or," Kalmar said, "it could mean we are very important to the First Race." Dera and Snook looked at him and both nodded after a moment's reflection.

"We are important to the First Race?" questioned Nutan.

Izzy's eyes grew larger and he looked down into Nutan's upturned face. "If we aren't important to the First Race, why would there be so much effort to take care of us?"

"Instructing the peeri," Dera said, "to guide us through six Progressions while allowing the Mookyn to think they were hidden from view."

Arasima pursed her lips. "And we must not forget our dark and yellow companions."

Dera stood looking out the front of their transporter, lost in her own thoughts. Her face regained some of its color and she turned to the others. "We are not here to be Judged."

Arasima raised an eyebrow and said in a cutting tone, "Then why are we here?"

"All I mean is that I don't think we are being Judged so much as being evaluated."

"Evaluated?" asked Nutan, wrinkling her brow.

"I think the First Race has some purpose for us and we are here to see if we are ready for whatever that purpose is." Dera bit her lower lip as she scrunched her face and again looked out the front of their transporter. She added, "I cannot think of another explanation considering all the facts."

No one else spoke as their transporter stopped at their quarters.

———

Kalmar sat in a thatched chair on the terrace mulling over the morning's events. He wondered if Dera was right. Did Shetow . . . the First Race . . . have something planned for them of greater importance than the Second Judging? Was the Judging more to "evaluate" their level of development than to see if humanity should continue to exist? He followed her logic, but his ingrained preconceptions bothered him. Since the morning when Berkana spoke to them of their mission, he had tried to prepare himself mentally for the rigors of the anticipated Judging. Now the tension was even greater; what *did* they face?

He heard footsteps and turned to see Arasima standing by the terrace doorway. The pale skin of her solemn face and slender arms seemed to shimmer in the late afternoon light. As he gazed at her, the morning's tribulations faded from his thoughts. He did not know how to respond to this baffling woman whose actions waxed and waned like the phases of Elom's three larger moons. His own actions were just as confusing; since the Gathering, he discerned that he was more of a spectator to his romantic and sexual follies than a participant.

After her hesitation, she slowly walked over and gently placed a hand on his shoulder. "Please reopen your heart to me. Surely I deserve a second chance."

He looked up at her and forced a smile. "Arasima, you must give me time. It is hard for me to focus. The peeri, the First Race . . . my head doesn't seem big enough to hold it all." He covered her hand with his. "Just give me time."

She dropped to a knee, laid her head and one hand on his leg, and gently stroked the inside of his thigh with her other hand. After several minutes, he placed one of his hands on the top of her head and let the ends of his fingers intermingle with the fine strands of her soft light-brown hair. She turned her head, propping her chin on the top of his leg, and continued gently stroking the inside of his thigh. As he looked down at her delicate features, the gentle strokes of her fingertips quickened his breathing. The smile on her face as she spied the growing bulge in his pants did not escape his notice.

Nutan and Cabyl lay across Cabyl's bed. "It wasn't Snook who pursued me," Nutan said. "I was the seducer. Your anger should be directed at me, not him. If I had not met Izzy, and Snook had not met you, I would have pursued Snook until he succumbed." She shrugged her shoulders. "I guess I wanted to see if I could do it. Sure, I liked him. He is *truly* a special person." She looked down. "I was just a young girl who had not gotten used to the attention of men. The effect I had on Snook invigorated me." An anxious smile parted her lips. "But I knew when I saw how he looked at you, you were the one who held his heart. And, as for Arasima, it's like my mother says, men are always going to look. Only judge them by their actions, for if you begrudge them for their stares, your heart will always remain broken."

Nutan sat up on the bed, grabbed Cabyl's trembling hands, and held them tight against her breast. "Cabyl, Snook loves you. He has not one idea of why you fled yesterday. We are about to undergo the Second Judging and if Dera's correct, experience the greatest occurrence in the history of our species." She pulled Cabyl's hands away from her body and squeezed them as tight as she could. "My mother also told me only a few of us are ever blessed with something greater than passion. Let this man love you. Open up to him and tell him all those dark secrets you keep buried inside you. Don't face what is before us alone." She pressed her lips together until they turned white. She nodded, then began to speak again. "And don't let an innocent man be guilty of your pain; face it knowing that it is not him that you ran from."

Cabyl lifted her contorted and tearstained face, peered into Nutan's forceful eyes, and nodded.

Snook almost walked onto the terrace but stopped when he saw Arasima kneeling at Kalmar's side. He turned to walk to the pedestaled fireplace when he heard the soft steps of someone coming down the stairs. Even with his untrained ear, he knew only a female could make such light steps. His heart seemed to move to his throat as he waited to see which one of the females would appear. To his joy, Cabyl stepped from behind the stairwell wall. She took a step back and dropped her eyes when she spotted him. She stood fixed in place like a statue on display. He could see her struggle to slow her breathing. She elevated her proud face to look him in the eye and started walking towards him. She stopped at arm's length. He felt short of breath; his white face flushed. She closed the distance between them and gently placed her head against his chest. He wrapped his arms around her petite body.

He felt as if he were suffocating. "Can we go outside to get some air?" he said.

She pulled back without looking him in the face, put her tiny hand in his much larger one, and turned towards the door.

Izzy walked down the hallway looking for Nutan. He found her still sitting on Cabyl's bed, the lines of her face mirroring her deep deliberation. He watched her a moment without her knowledge. He had thought he could never find a female he could admire as much as he did his sister until he met Nutan. She had Dera's quick mind and kind heart. Even though Nutan reminded him of Dera, she stirred a much different feeling in him.

"Well, if it isn't the prettiest female I know." His words pulled her from her thoughts and she jumped up, ran to him, threw her arms around his neck, and kissed him. After a minute, they stopped kissing and looked into each other's eyes. "If I had known how you would respond to my flattery, I would have started doing it sooner."

She giggled and kissed him again. When she pulled back, her lips lost some of their smile. "Promise me that whatever happens, you will never leave my side."

His eyes closed slightly as lines crossed his brow. "That is a promise I will gladly make." He pulled her against him.

As the side of her face rested against his chest, the lines around her eyes and mouth deepened. "I persuaded Cabyl to go to Snook and explain to him why she ran from him."

"That is good . . . isn't it?"

She pursed her lips and whispered, "I hope so."

Izzy left Nutan to find Dera and tell her of his feelings for Kalmar's sister. He found Dera as she was leaving the building. "Hello sister," he said with his old joviality.

She studied him a moment. "Okay, tell me why the sudden exuberance."

"I love Nutan."

She grinned. "That has been quite evident for some time."

"No, it is more than that." His smile faded. "Nutan and I have decided that we will never go through the Choosing even if we do return to Elom. We have all changed too much. Distance is not the only way to measure our journey; it is also the revelations we have experienced that will guide our future. Nutan and I will Pair out of love and not because of a timeless custom. If we return to Elom, we must take with us the truth we have discovered and liberate the People from Geerna's Covenant with Shetow." He had a thoughtful look. "That may be one of the reasons we were brought to Pandeelee; this might be the next Progression."

Dera looked at him a long time before nodding.

Nutan found Kalmar on the terrace with Arasima. She watched through the glass panes in the terrace door as Arasima rubbed the inside of his pants leg, slowly moving her hand toward his genitals. His head teetered as if it were an eagle's egg balanced on its end.

"Brother," she said. She burst through the door as if she had just found him. She strolled towards the two as Arasima stood up.

Arasima forced a smile and she started towards the door. "There is something I need to do." She looked back over her shoulder. "Will I see you later?" she asked, prompting his reassuring smile.

Nutan thought of scolding him but remembered her words to Cabyl. After a moment's reflection, she took a different tack.

"Looks like you will get Arasima after all."

He shrugged. "She seems to always know how to play me. Every time I think I have her figured out, I learn that I have misjudged her." He shrugged again. "She knows how to excite the male in me."

"Are men always controlled by their drive for sex?"

"It *does* play its part."

"We are about to face the fate of our kind. If sex is the thing that is foremost in your mind, we should hope that Dera is correct and that this is not a Judging but more of an evaluation. Minds that can control the destinies of millions of species, I'm afraid, are not going to be overwhelmed by creatures whose only thoughts are of carnal desires."

"I am so confused. At the time when I should be most focused, I can barely think. Every time Arasima comes close to me, I remember Gwyther, her Pairing Partner, and how wrong my desires are. Then she touches me and I can think of nothing else but her." He lowered his head and sighed.

Nutan cocked her head and bit her lower lip. "Then your

problems are inconsequential," she said in the most pleasant tone she could muster.

"Inconsequential." He raised his head. "I realize things have changed since we left Elom. We have discovered that the Choosing is nothing more than what we do when we breed bovors to improve their strength or milk production. Even understanding this, I cannot force from my mind the idea that my thoughts are wrong. The Choosing may end after our journey, but there were vows made at their Matage, vows that I cannot easily disregard."

"As I said, it's inconsequential. Did she not tell you? There were no vows made between Arasima and Gwyther." He looked at her in disbelief. "Kalmar, Gwyther rejected Arasima's Choosing."

"Gwyther *rejected* her?"

Nutan nodded.

The bitter taste of bile filled his mouth as he dropped to his knees and emptied his stomach. "Gwyther really is the better man," he said in words Nutan strained to hear.

"If you had not rushed from the Gathering Hall after Arasima chose Gwyther, I'm sure you would have been her second choice. You would be Paired to her now."

His mind suddenly cleared. "Maybe some things are not meant to be," he said. Something caught his eye. He turned his head and looked through a window and across the open expanse of the first floor to where Izzy and Dera were talking at the entrance of their building. After they finished, Dera turned, walked out the door, and headed towards the forest.

THIRTY-FOUR

Dera gazed into a clear pool created by a row of small stones damming the brook. Perched on a rock outcropping jutting from the bank, she sat with her legs pulled to her, her arms wrapped around her shins, and her chin resting on her knees. The jagged shadows of the towering nutwood trees lengthened as the alien sun neared the horizon. Below her, a trout leisurely swished its tail to hold its position against the docile current. Behind her, water trickled over the stone dam, a sound that sparked memories of her hideaway in the nutwood grove on Elom. She heard movement and lifted her head to find Kalmar watching her.

I didn't see you. I was taking a stroll. I hope I didn't startle you," he said.

"No, it's all right," she answered, lowering her eyes back to the brook below.

"It looks so much like Elom," he said as he awkwardly scanned their surroundings.

"Yes." She raised her chin off her knees. "I wonder how long the enclave has been on Pandeelee?"

"Some of the nutwood trees appear hundreds of cycles of the

seasons old," Kalmar said as he brushed his hand across the knurly bark of the closest tree.

"Why would the peeri have built the enclave so long ago if we're the first humans from Elom to visit Pandeelee?"

"And why build it so large?" Kalmar stepped closer to Dera. Her blemish seemed redder than normal. "May I sit down?"

She hesitated. "Of course."

Kalmar climbed onto the rock outcropping and knelt in front of her. She seemed uneasy with his nearness. Did she sense his discomfort or did his mere presence agitate her? She had reasons to shun him, yet, she had only showed restraint in his presence. Since the beginning of their journey, she had refrained from confronting him. He would have to make the first move.

"I've not been truthful."

"What do you mean?"

"I didn't stumble upon you. I wasn't taking a stroll."

Dera looked at him. She shook her head to show she did not understand what he was saying.

Kalmar breathed deeply. "I followed you. I need to talk to you. I need to apologize."

She cocked her head as if she were straining to hear a faraway sound. "We agreed to forgive each other on the transporter as it carried us to meet the peeri."

"I know, but I think I owe you more than that. You deserve an apology made without the stress we were under."

She pursed her lips. "I didn't think the strain had slackened."

He shrugged. "It hasn't, but I feel the need to reiterate my apology at a time that is not so hectic."

"Why?" The force of Dera's answer surprised him. After a few seconds, her face changed from a look of surprise to one of understanding. "Oh, about your rejection."

"Dera, you are truly an extraordinary woman, the Traits are

strong in you. And you are so beautiful"—as the word slipped from his lips, Kalmar realized he *did* find her beautiful—"any man would be fortunate to have you as a mate." He looked past her, avoiding eye contact. "I see that now. When you chose me at the Choosing, I was a fool to reject you." He shifted his eyes and gazed at her. "I am sorry that I was so stupid." He lifted his hands and shrugged his shoulders. "I am truly sorry I hurt you."

Dera measured him in silence. He could tell she was evaluating what he had said. After a few moments, he dropped his eyes. He could not tell if she was angry with him or just lost in thought. A chorus of insects—who began their serenade as the last feeble rays of the setting sun faded—was the only sound competing with the melody of the gurgling brook.

"There is something I must tell you," she whispered.

He knew what she was going to tell him; he deserved her impending tirade. He lifted his head and tried not to wince as their eyes met, but the fury he was expecting never came. What he saw in her face was not loathing but compassion. In spite of her obvious strengths, he detected vulnerability. He studied her. To him, the majesty of her auburn hair and green eyes overpowered any distraction caused by her scarlet blemish. As he peered into her eyes, it struck him; to really see her, he had to look past her blemish—and past her beauty. Elegance lay not only in her emerald eyes, but also in the sparkle of compassion behind them; not only in her lips, but also in the wisdom that came from them; and not only in her auburn hair, but also in the intellect it surrounded. A strange feeling of remorse gripped him. He hoped she would forgive him.

"When I chose you," Dera said in a measured tone, "I expected you to reject me."

"You expected me to reject you? I don't understand."

"This didn't turn out exactly as I planned it."

"Planned what?"

"I planned on you rejecting me."

"You chose me but you didn't want me as a Pairing Partner?"

"It had nothing to do with you as a person . . . as a male. I chose you because you were the most likely male to reject me." Kalmar listened to Dera in disbelief. "Everyone knew of your relationship with Arasima; you both made it very clear you planned to Pair." Dera tilted her head and made a gesture with her right hand. "You started telling the other males in your group, over a year ago, at our second Gathering, that you and Arasima had pledged to Pair at the time of our age-group's Pairing. You told them you would reject any female who tried to choose you before Arasima had her chance at the Choosing. I counted on your pledge, and your desire for Arasima, to ensure you would reject me if I chose you."

"And I did as you expected. I rejected you," he said with no emotion in his voice.

"Arasima's very beautiful; any man would have succumbed to her charms."

"Gwyther didn't," Kalmar said, and then looked away.

"You're right, he didn't," she answered softly. "He should be commended for his high principles, but remember, you are the one the Medoras chose for this journey, one of those they believed would represent humanity's best."

"They also chose Arasima." Kalmar's eyes darted to Dera.

"It is obvious she has her strengths."

"I think," Kalmar nodded, "I have figured out why both of you are here. The combination of your Traits is—" He hesitated. "The Medoras didn't select us to be the ones to be Judged. It was the dreams. Those who reacted to the Medora's mental call, the ones led to the Medoras' Chamber, were the ones chosen for the Judging." He smiled. "I was chosen by the Medoras' dream to be one of those Judged and chosen by you to be the one stupid enough to reject you."

"My plan went astray," she said again, lowering her eyes.

"Astray? But I rejected you, just as you planned."

"Yes." Her eyes moistened. "But I also planned on Arasima choosing you after you rejected me. I was to be free of the Pairing and you and Arasima would have each other. No one was to get hurt; we would all have what we wanted." She glanced down at their faint reflections in the pool and then back up at him. "So you see; it is I who must apologize to you. You're innocent. I pulled you into my web of deceit without your consent; you're the one who suffered."

Still dazed by her confession, Kalmar said, "Arasima also suffered."

Dera stiffened. "That is regrettable, but Arasima took a gamble and came up short. You kept your pledge; you rejected my choosing so she could choose you. You followed your heart, you loved her; you did what you told everyone you were going to do. Your actions were pure; you have no blame." Dera tilted her head. "Arasima had the chance to do something denied to most of us. She had the chance at the Choosing to choose a man who loved her and she threw it away."

Minutes later, they sat looking at the shimmering shadows dancing on the surface of the water each time a ripple disturbed the tranquility of the pool. After the sunset, the reflected light from two large moons illuminated the night. The croaking frogs around the water's edge competed with the sound of the flowing water.

"I don't think it was love," Kalmar finally said. "I thought it was love, now I'm sure it was only lust."

"Is there a difference?"

"I didn't think so, but now I believe there is." He leaned back, resting on his elbows. "I learned one thing from my fiasco with Arasima. Love, if it exists, is what remains after the passion is spent;

it's that incredible feeling you have when you've exhausted your physical desires, are drenched in sweat, and still reach out to touch the one lying beside you."

Dera's gaze moved to him. "You've had that feeling?"

"No." He took a short breath. "But I know I'm capable of such a feeling."

"Is that what you think love is like?"

"I believe love's possible between a man and a woman, love that'll last past the passion. If there are no feelings after the passion then . . . then the feeling was only lust." Kalmar picked up a stick and tossed it into the water. "It's time for you to tell me the reason you wanted to be rejected. Why did you want to avoid the Pairing and throw away any chance of having children?"

Dera pulled her knees closer to her chest. "It was my way of rebelling against Shetow, a way to take control of my life."

"By not taking part in the Pairing?"

"How we dealt with each other, how we chose mates, was all wrong. In my heart, I knew it was not right to force a person to pair with a partner they did not know, one they may despise a day later. We have done this for eons all in the name of Shetow. We are devastated if our frantic efforts to chose, or be chosen, by the highest-ranked potential partner fails. In Shetow's world, we lived only to Concentrate our Traits. We lived in a world where we knew the sex and birthdays of our great-great-grandchildren. Humans are the only animals on Elom whose lives aren't their own. Wolves mate for life and have pups every spring. Because of this mark"—she lifted her left arm to show Shetow's Mark—"the number and sex of our children are set." She dropped her arm. "The procedure to determine our Pairing Partners was set thousands of cycles of the seasons ago."

"But we only learned a few days ago how the Mark of the Covenant is used to control us."

Dera raised her eyebrows as she let out a shallow breath. "No, I knew the purpose of the Mark long before the start of our journey."

"But how is that possible; did you meet a Mookyn?"

"No, I was told by my closest friend." The thoughts of Verna made her eyes fill with tears.

"A Medora?"

"Yes. She thought it would make my life easier." Dera touched her blemish. "Verna told me there was a reason for everything— even for my blemish. She said my blemish was Shetow's way of indicating to everyone that I was special. Verna believed deeply in Shetow's Will and the importance of us honoring Her." Dera slowly shook her head. "The other children did treat me 'special': When I was small, they taunted me; when I was older, they shunned me; and now people avert their eyes away from me. I never believed my blemish was anything other than a curse, a blight on my face that's built a barrier between me and every other human besides Verna, Izzy, and my mother." She averted her eyes from Kalmar. "Even my own father spurned me—" Dera's voice cracked and she cleared her throat. "Would any God who loved us scar us"—she placed her right palm over her heart—"to the point where even one of our own parents is repelled by our looks? Shetow, or whatever is Judging us, doesn't love us. It has a different motive. Our judge is less than a God."

Kalmar did not know what to say. The words of this young woman moved him, the shame of his rejecting her deepened. "Y-You may be right," he stuttered.

She turned and stared at him with unblinking eyes. "I know I'm right. If Shetow was all powerful, She wouldn't need Her Mark on our arms to control our births; She wouldn't need a living moon manned by little white lizards watching everything we do." She ran the fingers of her left hand through her hair. "I'm no fool. I understand that whatever commands the draks and quels has mental powers far beyond ours." Dera bit her lower lip. "Even so, I refuse to worship a Being who doesn't care about us as individuals. People say I have the greatest Concentration of Traits, a mental prowess unmatched by any other human, yet if my intellect tells me anything, it tells me something is horribly wrong with the way we're propagating the species."

"Dera, I understand most of what you say, but the Choosing pairs those males and females with the strongest Concentration of Traits. Those Pairings ensure our species will grow stronger. How can that be wrong?"

"Our system of ranking males and females by their performance in the Borrac and Byrrac ensures the Choosing of mates is based on mental and physical Traits. I believe that there are important Traits not evaluated in the Borrac and Byrrac, and therefore not considered in the Choosing. We choose mates based on the performances of their minds and bodies, and we neglect their Traits of compassion, gentleness, and inner strength." She put her hand on his knee. "The Borrac gives points for how straight a man shoots an arrow but not how straight is his character."

Kalmar nodded. "That would explain why so many Pairings dissolve after the Second Childs reaches maturity."

"The Pairings are based on Shetow's—or whatever controls our lives—wishes for the Concentrations of those Traits It considers important."

"Isn't the Concentration of Traits necessary for our Judging? Wasn't that why Geerna started the Choosing in the first place—to develop those Traits?"

"That's what we're told, but what God would base Its Judging on human strength and mental dexterity over love and compassion? I decided not to worship an entity that judged us on our performance in the games—Traits I found to be of little importance when compared with those Traits found in the noblest humans."

"Then why did you strive to excel in the Byrrac if you find the Traits it highlights to be of little importance?"

"I had to be sure I was right. If I ranked low in the Byrrac, I couldn't be sure my feelings weren't based on envy and resentment. When I won the Byrrac, and I still felt the same way, then I knew I must be right. The Choosing and the Pairing aren't for our benefit; they don't increase our humanity; they just make us stronger and smarter. There's more to us . . . to humanity . . . than what the countless cycles of the seasons of selective breeding have produced."

"There may be a flaw in your thinking."

"What do you mean?" she asked, her eyes narrowing.

"You have, as you pointed out, the greatest Concentration of the Traits as ranked by the Byrrac. I think you also have the greatest Concentration of the Traits not ranked by the Byrrac: those you think are important. You're the most compassionate person I've ever met. You speak of being shunned, yet your actions towards others show no signs of animosity. The mere fact you find these unheralded Traits so important confirms that they are strong in you. As for concentrating both types of Traits, the process may work better than you think."

Dera seemed taken aback by Kalmar's assessment of her. "If what you say is true of me, the Concentration of the other Traits must be purely by chance."

"Don't misunderstand me; I'm not defending the process. I understand why you wanted to be rejected."

"There's one more reason." The lines of her face tightened.

"What's that?"

"I didn't want to be a victim of the process; I didn't want to share a bed with a man I didn't love, to bear his children, and later have him leave me after twenty cycles of the seasons when our children were grown." Dera reached out and gently touched the scars on his face. "We both have blemishes on our faces. Yours is a testimony to your manhood, a sign you're all our race has strived for these last six Progressions, a sign of bravery, skill, and determination. My blemish adds nothing to me but memories of heads turning away when they see my face. Your blemish scarred your face but gave you honor. My blemish covers my face but scars my heart. You ask why I wanted to be rejected." Dera looked into his eyes. "Because I knew I would never be loved by a man in the light of day, and I refused to yield my body to a man who would only desire me in the dark of night, groping me when he didn't have to look at my face." Tears filled her eyes.

"I am not as strong as you," he said, his face strident. "I could never cut myself off from the touch of the other sex."

"You cannot miss what you have never known."

"Women are different than men," he responded, with a tone of authority. "Men think and dream about women all the time. I've dreamed sexual dreams that were so real I'd wake up covered in sweat."

She averted her eyes. "I have had such dreams," she whispered. Her body relaxed as her mind wandered. Their legs touched; Kalmar could feel her trembling. Her blemish and the other features of her face blended into the darkness. He remembered the feeling of her touching his scars. He reached up and gently stroked her blemished cheek. He felt her warm, trembling skin; a tear touched his finger. He squinted as he sought her water-filled eyes, but the darkness masked them. She reached up and laid her hand over his. He shifted his body, keeping his hand in hers. He could now see the moonlight glistening off the tears trickling from her closed eyes; he felt their wetness as they rolled against his hand. He leaned over and gently kissed her wet, blemished cheek. As his lips touched her skin, the tip of his nose brushed against her silky hair. A delicate fruity scent invaded his senses. He remembered the females sometimes used fruit extracts when they made shampoo; he never thought such a smell could be so arousing. He felt weak; his eyelids grew heavy. It took a moment for Dera to realize the unfamiliar feeling on her cheek was Kalmar's lips. She opened her eyes to see Kalmar's half-closed eyes. She turned her head and their lips met.

Their kiss started as tender and gentle, but their pent-up emotions quickly surged forward. The kissing became wet and hard. Kalmar pulled Dera to him and encircled her with his arms. His left hand found the edge of her chemise and went under it to feel the softness of her warm bare skin. His hand roamed over her body until it stopped to cup her right breast. For a moment, he remembered how Arasima's breast felt. Dera's breast felt much the same, yet the emotional charge was so much more intense. Kalmar finally pried his lips from Dera's to catch his breath. In the twilight, he could only see the outline of her face. He gently kissed the tip of her nose, then each of her closed eyelids. He could just make out the movement of her opening eyelids. Her body became rigid and then she pulled back. Her hand reached under her chemise and grabbed his hand and jerked it away from her breast.

"Not in the dark. I won't be groped in the dark by any man." She pushed him away and in a second had rolled off the rock outcropping and vanished in the night.

THIRTY-FIVE

Kalmar could not sleep. His conversation with Dera kept running through his head and he was awake when Snook tiptoed into their bedroom. When he heard Snook's bare feet against the smooth floor, Kalmar rolled over and passed his hand over a small metallic cube sitting on his bedside table. The room instantly filled with a soft glow, which slowly increased in intensity.

"How ingenious," Snook said, standing next to his bed with his shoes in his hands. "The lighting gives your eyes time to adjust before reaching its full brightness." He turned to Kalmar. "Sorry if I woke you."

"No, I couldn't sleep." Kalmar rolled over and sat on the side of his bed.

"Wide awake myself." Snook dropped his shoes on the floor.

"Good, let's go out on the balcony." Kalmar stood up and walked towards a glass wall. Before he reached it, a panel slid out of his way, opening a doorway to a balcony several hundred feet above the ground. Their quarters were in a cylindrical building Kalmar guessed to be twenty stories high. Kalmar and Snook chose to share a room rather than staying in separate rooms. Each of the outside rooms on the top third of the building opened onto a balcony. The two sat down and surveyed the surrounding terrain.

"That's the building where the dark-skinned people are staying," Snook said, pointing to a building several miles to their left, which looked identical to theirs. "And over there is where the yellows are staying." He swung his arm around to point to another matching building in the other direction.

"Just like it was on the craft; each group is assigned to a specific area. When do you think the groups will be mixed together?"

"Soon enough, I'm sure," answered Snook, who seemed distracted. Kalmar decided against questioning his friend about what was troubling him and sat back to collect his own thoughts. A different pattern of stars lit the night, but their number rivaled those seen from Elom. He scanned the darkness-shrouded enclave; the dim lights from the other two building broke the otherwise uniform black landscape.

The chilly night air on the terrace invigorated Kalmar. He glanced at Snook, who sat bent over, elbows propped on his knees, resting his chin in his palms. He could not remember his friend ever being so quiet. A cool breeze rustled the leaves in the forest of nutwood trees surrounding the building. The enclave was a wondrous place. Other than the three buildings, the enclave looked, smelled, and sounded like Elom. He recognized every tree and the call of every bird. The model for the enclave was the human section of Elom, not the draks'. Kalmar wondered if this meant the sections of Elom where the other two groups of humans lived was similar to his section. A distinctive fragrance, the sharp aroma of freshly cut boodo grass, flared his nostrils. The strong plant scent reminded him of the Gathering Campground and the unpleasant memories he now associated with it. He closed his eyes in an effort to push the events of a week ago from his mind. His eyes sprang open. It had only been a week. The pain of Arasima's rejection still gripped his chest. This did not make sense; Arasima was not the woman he had thought she was. How could he pine over a female he was not sure he even liked? Two weeks ago, he could do anything; at that time his bulging ego was deserved. Now, he was confused and anxious with only his growing resolve to lift his spirits. He thought of Dera and smiled; his arms could almost feel the weight of her body against them. How strange, this woman had not wanted him when she chose him, yet tonight her lips were quick and eager. She'd run from him thinking he only kissed her because he could not see her blemish in the dark. He slowly shook his head. There was no doubt; he would have desired her just as much in the light. He should have known she would run; she told him she believed a man would only want her in the dark. He closed his eyes and again shook his head. How foolish could he be? It was a mistake he would not make again—that is if he ever had another chance.

You all right?" He heard Kalmar's easy voice say. Snook turned his head to see his friend speaking to him. "Your face, it's even paler than normal."

"I'm fine. Must be the cool air." Snook shivered as he shrugged his shoulders.

"Did Gogtee say if the Judging would start tomorrow?"

"She said she didn't know when the Judging would begin. And if I'm any judge of drak disposition, I'd say she is apprehensive."

"What do you mean?"

"It's hard to explain, Kalmar . . . I just feel it."

"You're probably just picking up on my anxiety and crediting it to her."

"We're all anxious, but this is different."

"Well, I say we have enough things we only halfway understand to worry about. There is no reason to agonize about something we don't understand at all."

"You're right of course." Snook stood up and walked to the railing of the balcony. Kalmar stood up, walked over, and joined him. From the distance, a wolf's call permeated the cool night air.

"If I hadn't watched our craft enter the atmosphere of this planet, I would argue we're still on Elom," Kalmar said as he gazed into the dark.

"The enclave must be hundreds of cycles of the seasons old; it would take that long for the trees to grow to their full size."

"That's what I told Dera."

"You've been with Dera?"

"Just for a little bit. I took a stroll and came upon her in the forest."

"And?"

"And what? I just stumbled into her. It's not like I was trying to find her."

"Kalmar, I have never said much about it, but you really made a mistake when you didn't accept her Choosing."

Kalmar's face pulled into a grimace. "Dera didn't want to Pair with me; in fact, she wouldn't have chosen me if she thought I was going to accept her Choosing." He braced himself for Snook's peppering questions, but they never came.

Cabyl and I walked," Snook said in a dry hollow tone as he tilted his head in the direction of one of the towers, "towards the yellows' building." He coughed to clear his raspy throat. "We thought we might see some members of their group." Snook avoided Kalmar's eyes. The starlight accented his ashy, gaunt face. "Even though Gogtee told us not to speak with members of the other groups, I didn't think there would be any harm in getting a better look at them." As Kalmar's interest rose, he leaned forward to ask

Snook a question, but before he could speak Snook answered it. "It didn't take long for us to decide the building was farther away than it looked and we sat down near the crest of a small hill overlooking an open meadow."

Kalmar slid back to listen. Snook turned towards him; his colorless complexion and the dark sockets of his albino eyes, which were squinted, startled Kalmar.

"You're the closest friend I have," Snook said, as his stare drifted to the floor, "and the only person in our group I can talk to."

"And you're my closest friend," answered Kalmar, not knowing what else to say. Snook did not acknowledge Kalmar's response; his hollow stare lost none of its intensity.

"I promised Cabyl I wouldn't tell anybody, but I have to talk to someone. If I tell you something"—he looked Kalmar square in the eyes—"you mustn't tell anybody."

"I promise." Kalmar could not imagine anything bad enough to upset his friend to this degree. "What is it?"

Snook took a shallow breath before settling back in his chair. At that moment, a lull in the breeze accompanied by a muting of the night sounds produced an eerie backdrop to his obvious torment. "You know I care for Cabyl. I thought I loved her—" Snook hesitated as he stared into the night.

Kalmar waited a few seconds, then prompted his friend. "You sat on the crest of the hill. What happened then?"

Snook smiled. "We leaned against the trunk of a large moss-covered nutwood tree and started kissing." His white animated face seemed to gain color. "I picked her up—she's so light—and sat her so she straddled my hips with her knees on the ground on each side of me. I pulled her to me and we kissed for a long time. Then she sat back, unbuttoned my shirt, and started kissing my chest." Snook paused a moment and ran his right hand through his snowy white hair. "After a few minutes, she sat up and pulled her chemise over her head. She sat straddling me, naked from the waist up." He raised his hands and held them as if grasping her imaginary thighs. All signs of anguish evaporated from his face.

"Kalmar, she's so beautiful; at first, I just stared at her. She must have mistakenly thought I felt she was being too forward in her actions, because she blushed and then dropped her eyes and crossed her arms, covering her breasts." He paused as the memory flashed in his mind. "I gently pulled her arms down and stroked her breasts as I kissed her nipples." His voice began to falter. "I told her I loved her and wanted her as my partner." He brushed away a tear from his pallid cheek. "She covered her face with her hands and started crying; I could tell her sobs were not ones of joy. I stammered, not knowing what was wrong or what to say. I tried to explain that the Mookyn choose their own mates, but that didn't stop her sobbing."

"Would she not tell you what was wrong?"

"Not at first; she wouldn't even put her hands down. Not knowing what else to do, I pulled her to me and she sobbed with her face against my chest." He pressed his right palm against the middle of his chest, indicating where her face had rested. "I could feel her warm tears run down my body." Snook brushed his fingertips down his ribcage.

"Did—"

Snook raised his left hand, stopping Kalmar's question.

"After a few minutes she stopped crying, but she kept her head against my chest and, a moment later, with her head still pressed against me," he said so softly Kalmar had to strain to hear him, "she whispered that she also loved me."

"But Snook, that's wonderful. I thought something was wrong."

"That's when she told me." Snook's fingertips twitched. "She said it's haunted her since she did it."

"Did what? Snook, what did she do?"

"Cabyl's Pairing Partner left her when she didn't have a child."

"I know; if you'll remember, I'm the one who told you about Cabyl that day I first took you to see Berkana."

Snook sighed and nodded his head. "She made sure she never became pregnant."

"How could she do that?"

"She said her Pairing Partner abused her—"

"Not why. *How?*" Kalmar said.

"Each morning after she and her partner had had sex, she drank a potion brewed from an herbal mixture that prevented pregnancy. She knew her Pairing Partner would leave her if she didn't produce children and when she didn't have the First Childs, he left her." Snook lowered his head. "She said that ever since she prevented her pregnancy, she has been gripped with shame."

"How did she know about the herb?"

"Berkana told her."

"How would Berkana know about an herb that would keep a woman from becoming pregnant? I've never heard of such a thing in the history of the People, and even if Berkana *did* know about the herb, why would she tell Cabyl how to use it and go against the Will of Shetow? The Medoras are the ones Geerna used to perpetuate the system of the Borrac, Byrrac, and Choosing to Concentrate the Traits. For a woman to prevent her pregnancy goes against all of our traditions."

"The Mookyn females have used such a potion for generations. Kalmar, the Mookyn Elders and Medoras have been in league since the time of Geerna. The People weren't told about the Mookyns' and the Medoras' efforts. They believed humanity's survival depended on our keepers—Shetow, the peeri, or whoever—not knowing about our resistance to their control."

"Snook, why are you so upset? If Cabyl had become pregnant and had her First Childs, she would not be with us now."

"There is one other thing. Cabyl was also repeatedly molested by her own father." Snook looked at his feet and shook his head. "I don't know; I realized she had a sexual life before I met her, but I kept it pushed out of my mind."

Kalmar's jaw dropped and he made a slight shake of his head. He turned to face Snook. "You're upset because she had sex before you met her?"

"No, yes; I don't know, I'm so confused." He looked up at Kalmar. "I looked at her and she seemed different."

"Because she had *sex* with her Pairing Partner and was forced to submit to the unforgivable demands of her father?"

Snook drew back. "She plotted to deceive her Pairing Partner, and she broke her vows . . . and the sex thing too."

Kalmar stood up and stared at his anguished friend. "Snook, I believed you to be the most compassionate man I had ever met. I marveled at your wisdom, insight, and courage. Other than my grandfather, you are the person I revered the most. However, the last few minutes have shattered my faith in my own judgment. The person I thought I knew would never have such thoughts. You're the lowest kind of dog to judge Cabyl so harshly for things beyond her control." Snook looked up as Kalmar continued to accost him. "Have you lost all reason? Either your jealousy of another man having sex with her or your corrupted sense of piety about her decision to take the herb has shown a warped scorn that's not only wrong but unjustified."

Snook opened his mouth, but Kalmar hit his shoulder. "If you say one word"—Kalmar drew back his right fist—"I will hit you where you stand."

Snook's eyes widened as he scooted back in his chair.

"Everyone knew that Cabyl's father murdered her mother, yet I never heard a word of gossip about her father molesting her. I also knew Cabyl's Pairing Partner; he lived in our village for almost three cycles of the seasons. After Cabyl won her Byrrac, she made the first Choosing in her age group's Choosing. She picked the winner of the Borrac, the one the system said was the perfect partner for her." Kalmar lowered the tone but not the intensity of his words. "It did not take long for us to realize the man she chose was a ruffian, but we were unaware that she traded one monster for another—a molesting father for an abusive Pairing Partner."

Kalmar sat down and looked over the rail of the balcony. "We were so proud and happy for her. She was the first winner from our tribe of either one of the games in thirteen cycles of the seasons." Kalmar kept looking over the rail, his eyes fixed on the darkness. After a few seconds, he again turned to Snook. "Cabyl's choice, the system's choice, *Shetow's choice*, turned out to be an abomination to everything we thought sacred. The man Cabyl brought home from the Choosing was boorish, arrogant, and condescending. It doesn't surprise me that he also abused her." Snook did not move as Kalmar's eyes bored in on him. "We thought Shetow found Cabyl and her partner unworthy of children. We felt she shamed our tribe when she didn't produce children. I can't imagine the torment he must have put Cabyl through for her to resort to drinking the herbs." Kalmar lowered his voice. "I'm ashamed I judged her." Kalmar shook his head. "With her mother dead and her father taken away by the draks, she brought this perverted man back to the village to deal with without anyone to help her. She must have lived a tortured life."

Snook stared at Kalmar for a long time before speaking. "Why didn't you tell me this before now?"

Kalmar glanced back at Snook. "It was something the members of our tribe didn't talk about." He shrugged his shoulders. "To not talk about it meant we didn't have to deal with it."

"You should've done something about Cabyl's predicament; somebody could have talked to her partner about his behavior."

Kalmar rolled his eyes. "We knew he was bad but we didn't know he was abusing her."

"But when she didn't have her First Childs, didn't that tell you something was wrong?"

"Yes, it told us that Shetow found her and her partner not worthy of having children," Kalmar yelled.

"But your women's pregnancies are controlled through those Shetow's Marks on your arms," Snook yelled back.

"We didn't know that." They glared at each other. Kalmar lowered, then closed his eyes for a second, before he looked back at Snook. "As I think about it now, I realize it was watching the horrors of Cabyl's Pairing that caused me to cling to the idea of Pairing with Arasima. I don't know, maybe it was my way of trying to fix it so I knew my Pairing would be a happy one."

Snook smiled. "And Dera threw a rock into that plan."

"There's a lot I need to tell you, but it can wait until later."

"Kalmar."

"Yes."

"Would you have hit me?"

"With all the force I could muster."

"Good, I deserved no less." Snook reached over and put his hand on Kalmar's knee. "What do I do?"

"How do you feel towards her?"

"I love her." Snook's face tightened as his eyes glistened. "I love her so."

"Then just love her. Love her and she'll know it."

Dera and Cabyl lay across matching twin beds. "And you told Snook all of this?" Dera asked.

Cabyl nodded as she brushed a tear from her cheek. "He told me he loved me; I had to tell him what I'd done. I care for him;

I couldn't keep such secrets from him; but, when I told him, he grew cold and distant."

"The night of confessions," Dera said under her breath. "Mother said, in matters of the heart, the truths about past indiscretions are the sharpest daggers."

"What did you say?"

"Nothing . . . no, that's not right; I need to tell you something." Dera sat up. "I chose Kalmar knowing"—she shook her head—"bad choice of words—not *knowing*—but *counting* on Kalmar rejecting me. It was what I planned. I told him that tonight. You see, it was also my night of confession."

"You *wanted* him to reject you?"

"Cabyl, you and I did the same thing. We both chose not to bear our partner's children. I just did it before the Choosing paired me with a man I knew didn't love me. You paired with a man who only loved himself, a man who forced himself on you." Dera rolled on her side, facing Cabyl. "We both realized Shetow's system for choosing our partners isn't the best method for us as individuals." Dera rolled over and sat on the side of her bed. "You said Berkana gave you the herbs to keep you from becoming pregnant and I now understand how Verna's counseling led me to hatch my scheme to have Kalmar reject my Choosing." Dera jumped up. "Don't you see what that means?" Cabyl looked puzzled and shook her head. "It means the Medoras were behind, or partly behind, our actions." Dera's face flushed. "The Medoras may've doubted Shetow's good intentions for humanity, but they believed with all their inner-spirit that Geerna's plans to prepare us for the Second Judging were in the People's best interest." She looked at Cabyl. "Geerna's plan must have foreseen"—Dera pointed to Cabyl, then herself—"our predicament."

Cabyl nodded. "I think you're right. It gives me hope that things might work out in the Judging. Geerna must've been a very smart woman."

"Until I learned of the Multiped and saw the draks' enhancement machines, I doubted the stories of Geerna's intellect. I didn't see how it was possible for a person from a primitive culture to produce the Sequa. Now I wonder why other humans weren't enhanced like Geerna and the draks. You would think the enhancement machines could have negated the need for our six Progressions."

"Maybe that question will be answered here on Pandeelee. The question I'm wrestling with now is what do I do about Snook? I never thought I would have another chance to love . . . or be loved by someone." Cabyl, her eyes open wide, looked at Dera. "I don't want to live without the feeling"—she pressed a fist against her bosom—"he gives me."

Dera smiled. "I'm sure if we work out the small problem of humanity's survival, we can solve the problem of Snook's hold on your heart. My mother, who was always trying to give me hope"— she unconsciously put the fingertips of her left hand on her blemish—"told me men are simple creatures. If they're worth having, women just need to give them a little time and they'll use their"—Dera slowly cocked her head from side-to-side—"simple minds to ponder their shallow thoughts and somehow come to the correct conclusions. If that doesn't work, she told me to stick my hand down the front of his pants, grab him by his manhood—and then I can get him to do anything I want."

Cabyl covered her reddened face with her hands as she let out a shrill cry. They both sank to the floor laughing. A moment later, Cabyl leaned over and hugged Dera. "Let's always be friends," she said. Tears filled Dera's eyes.

A knock on the door startled them. They separated and Dera jumped up, walked over, and opened the door. Snook stood in the hallway, his face as nondescript as the white fur on a prairie buck's stomach.

"Can I talk to you?" he said, his eyes locked on Cabyl. Cabyl just stared back at him. Dera grabbed his arm and ushered him towards the balcony. When Dera and Snook reached the stunned Cabyl, she grabbed Cabyl's arm, jerked her up, and escorted the two through the glass doorway. Once on the balcony, Dera turned and walked back into the room, leaving the two dazed lovers gazing at each other. As Dera closed the balcony's glass door, Cabyl and Snook embraced in a passionate kiss.

Mother, thought Dera, *you are smarter than I ever gave you credit.* She closed her eyes as she relived her earlier moments with Kalmar. Her hands slid across the front of her chemise; the bulge of her breasts pulled the cloth tight against her skin and her breathing quickened as she remembered the caressing and gentle probing of Kalmar's fingers.

THIRTY-SIX

Kalmar lay in his bed in the dimly lit room, looking at the ceiling. The room's cool temperature did little to stop the beads of perspiration from forming on his face. His brain and body ached from the mental exhaustion of the day's revelations. Snook had left the room earlier; Kalmar guessed he was with Cabyl. He heard the door open but did not look to see who entered. He felt a soft warm hand touch his arm. He turned his head to see Arasima standing next to his bed. As he looked at her, she quickly shed her clothes and stood naked before him.

"I made a mistake," she said. "We now know our lives have been manipulated; it wasn't my fault. The system dictated that I not choose you even though that's what my heart yearned for me to do." She bit her lower lip. "Please believe me."

Kalmar gazed at the perfection of her alluring body, a body that had haunted his dreams so many nights. "I believe," he said, the lines in his face unyielding, "that the system caused you not to choose me." His words brought a smile to her face, but the gap between her teeth did not have the same provocative effect on him it had had in the past. She reached down to pull back his bedcovers but he reached out and grabbed her hand. "We had our opportunity and let it slip away."

She looked at him for a moment with her mouth open, then reached down, picked up her clothes, and hurried out of the room. He turned his back to the door. In a few seconds, the door opened again.

"It's *over*, Arasima," he said, without turning his head.

"That's what I heard you say." Dera's voice came from behind him. Kalmar turned to see her standing just inside the doorway to his room.

"I—"

"I was outside the door. I heard what you said to Arasima." The chiseled lines of her face camouflaged her thoughts. "You said you followed me into the forest so you could apologize for rejecting me."

He propped himself up on an elbow. His weary but alert eyes scanned the pleasing features of her face, seeking a break in the rigid composure masking her temperament. "That was my intent; I know I was wrong declining your Choosing." All of a sudden, he felt a chill and pulled his blanket over his bare shoulder. As he did this, he noticed the first break in her unreadable expression—a slight rise of her eyebrows. "Now I must also apologize for the way I acted in the dark as we sat on that rock."

"I told you that I expected you to reject my Choosing; it is what I planned for you to do."

"Dera, I realize that, but I didn't know it at the time. I rejected you without any thought for your feelings; I only cared about my own."

"I guess that could be said for both our actions."

He nodded. "Then I only need to apologize for my actions this afternoon."

"What actions," she asked, her feelings still a mystery to him.

"What do you feel you need to apologize for?" She stepped to the middle of the room and, without breaking eye contact, calmly brushed his hastily shed clothing off a chair. She sat down a body length from him. Her back stayed straight, not bending with the contour of the chair. Her scrutinizing eyes made him feel exposed, uncovering his every frailty.

This was not the Dera he thought he knew; assured yes, but there was more to her than the trembling woman he had held only hours earlier. "You told me you would not be"—he broke eye contact for a moment—"groped in the dark by any man. I apologize for not being sensitive to your wishes." He felt uncomfortable as she continued to stare at him. He could see her jaw move back and forth; the lines of her face stayed well defined.

"Then why *did* you grope me?"

"It seemed like the thing to do at the time," he answered. "Your nearness sparked a feeling in me; I reacted to it." Her unblinking eyes stayed fixed on him. "When I touched your cheek and felt the softness of your skin, the dampness from tears, I reached for you."

"Why did you wait for the darkness to reach for me?" she whispered.

"I didn't wait for the darkness; that is just when the impulse hit me."

"But why did it only hit you after it became dark?" she said a little more forcefully.

As he looked at her, he could see the moisture in her eyes begin to glisten. "Dera, I have wanted to reach for you many times in the past few days. Today was the only one of those times that it was dark."

She blinked, squeezing out a tear. "I don't know if I should believe you . . . my blemish." She reached up to touch the afflicted side of her face.

He knew what he said next could be the most important words that he would ever utter, but he had no idea of what to say. Then he heard his own voice. He spoke without thinking; he spoke from his heart.

"To know you, to be around you, to see the kindness in your heart . . . when I look at you I don't fixate on your birthmark." He wet his lips. "When I first met your brother he told me there was more to you than anyone realized. Dera, now I look past your birthmark and I see the woman Izzy was talking about. However, I see a feminine side that Izzy would not recognize. To me you are the most desirable woman I have ever met." He was out of breath and his heart was pounding when he stopped talking.

Dera looked at Kalmar and thought about what he had said. She remembered Izzy's unblemished sculpture of her head. That was when she realized Izzy did not see her as a person with a blemish. Now Kalmar was saying he also looked past her birthmark. She stood up and took a step towards him.

"Do you think you could ever love me?" The tone of her voice was tender, yet questioning.

His face softened as the ends of his lips slowly turned up. "I don't think I could ever fall in love with anyone else."

She took another step forward and she stood but inches from his bed. "Before I take my clothes off," she said with the wisp of a smile, "I guess I should ask you first if you're going to run me off as you did Arasima." Kalmar did not answer, but pulled his bedcovers back, exposing his nude body, rolled over, and sat on the side of his bed. He pulled the front of her chemise up and started kissing the soft skin of her flat stomach. She reached down and pulled the chemise up and over her head, and then wiggled until her skirt slid down enough for her to step out of it. Then Kalmar pulled her down to lay beside him.

THIRTY-SEVEN

The end of the round wooden push pole felt smooth, as if polished by many cycles of the seasons of use in a boatman's hands. Kalmar's arms flexed as he pushed against the pole, propelling the boat slowly across the satiny surface of the lake. He immediately recognized the illusory state of his surroundings. He realized, in a different consciousness, Dera's warm naked body lay asleep in his arms. In this consciousness, however, he once again stood in the boat on the lake, having the same recurring dream he had had on Elom. This time, though, his senses betrayed him; they perceived everything as real. The air drawn through his nostrils carried the unmistakable fishy odor of a shoreline; the dark water lapped against the side of the boat from the tepid splash made by the push pole as he pulled it up then lowered it again to reset the submerged end on the lake bottom. He blinked when a fallen strand of hair fluttered against his right eyelash as a soothing breeze skipped across his face. He reached up and brushed the hair back out of his eyes. When he started another thrust, his hands squeezed the pole and he felt the reassuring sensation of his tingling shoulder muscles; he experienced the gratification of physical exertion. Once a source of tension, the dream now brought comfort, ease only felt from a sense of familiarity.

The mist hung just above the lake's surface, parting as the bow of the boat penetrated the vapor barrier. He soon detected the faint silhouette of the island ahead. He never doubted the island would appear, but only when its dark outline became visible did he begin to wonder what awaited him on its shore. He tried to relax his cramping jaw muscles; instinctively, he knew Berkana would not be the one greeting him. The appearance of the island did not dampen his serenity; he felt safe in his dream refuge. Memories of Dera's touch rolled over him, causing him to consider trying to wake up. The thought of Dera also reminded him that he had not been alone on the lake in his earlier dreams and he turned to look behind him. This time he could see no other boats trailing him, but the mist was much thicker than in his earlier dreams and he wondered if the fog hid them.

When the boat reached the island, it bumped against the wooden landing. After stepping on the dock, he attached the boat's moorings. He walked along the dock until he reached the shore, where a stone pathway led away from the water and up the side of a hill. Kalmar looked back at the lake, but the mist already hid his boat and most of the dock. He turned and studied the hillside. The mist dissipated a few feet from the shoreline, allowing him to follow the stone pathway with his eyes. The path weaved up the hill, entered a wooded area, reemerged, and then disappeared over the top. He started walking up the pathway but stopped and looked up when he heard the screech of a split-tail hawk. He spied the majestic bird soaring near the crest of the hill, riding the warm air currents rising off the water.

Seeing the bird brought memories of his childhood: a time when life seemed simple, a time when the warmth of a loving family surrounded him. The death of his grandfather had not diminished the love of his mother, grandmother, and older sister—in many ways it intensified it—but the tragic, unexpected event cast a shadow of sadness that none of them had ever been able to shake. The event also traumatized a younger Nutan even though, as a female, she spent most of her time with their mother and grandmother learning the mysteries of womanhood and had never had the opportunity to know the grand old man as he had.

The hawk hung close to the crest of the hill above the cliff facing the right side of the pathway; he could see individual feathers in its wing tips bend against the air currents. *Were the details of all dreams this complete and he just did not remember them?* he wondered. For the moment, the answer seemed unimportant with the cobbled pathway beckoning. After a ten-minute climb, a drop of perspiration trickled down his forehead, caught the bridge of his nose, and ran to the tip before he wiped it away with the back of his hand. At the crest of the hill, he stopped to study the view of the other side. The pathway disappeared after entering a stand of nutwood trees less than three hundred feet down the hillside.

He lifted his head and, after a pause, sniffed; yes, he smelled the lingering scent of burning wood. A quick scan did not reveal the fire's location, so he resumed following the pathway. Halfway to the stand of nutwood trees he met the aroma of cooking meat, a smell any hunter could distinguish. He thought of his boyhood, half his life, when he, the other boys in his age group, and the Gray Beards had gathered around a campfire with meat from a freshly killed prairie buck cooking over an open flame. Roasting prairie buck on a spit produced an aroma he would recognize every time, an aroma unmatched by the women cooking meat in an urk at the families' Life Fire, an aroma to raise the hunter instinct in a man, an aroma that defined what it meant to be a man. The smell of the cooking meat kindled his hunger and he scanned the hillside trying to find the source of the alluring scent. The fullness of the smell told him the campfire was near. A light breeze brushed the left side of his face; the redolence of the cooking meat now permeated the air.

The smell came from the stand of nutwood trees. Stepping off the path, he walked into the trees, the breeze kissing his face. The thick underbrush tempered the wind and also forced him to follow the remnants of a deer trail until he came to a spot where he could peer over the undergrowth enough to see that a clearing lay ahead. Wisps of gray smoke rose from the middle of the clearing before melting away near the treetops. A different tangle of scents reached him; the smell of joujou wood was also distinguishable, burning with the nutwood: a combination of fruity woods experienced hunters used to bring out the best taste from meats cooked over a campfire. It was evident that the scent of burning wood and the aroma of the cooking meat originated in the clearing. As he walked closer, he could make out the movement of a person, but the leaves of a thick bush obscured most of his view. He reached out and pushed aside the guilty branch; the backlit figure of a squatting man facing away from Kalmar blocked the campfire. The idea that the person could be a woman never entered his mind. This person was a hunter; by the mores of the People, only men were hunters. Kalmar observed a bow and a quiver full of arrows leaning against a tree trunk a few feet away from the hunter. The bow showed the same workmanship instilled into every young male of the People by the Gray Beards. It looked just like the bow he used to bring down the cave lion; Kalmar knew he and this hunter would have much in common. The man put a few small sticks on the fire, then he reached out and appeared to be cutting off a piece of meat from the cooking prairie buck blocked from Kalmar's view. There was something familiar about the man. As Kalmar stepped into the clearing, the man stood up and turned around to meet him.

It was his grandfather Urga. "I cut this for you," his grandfather said, holding out a knife with a piece of skewered meat on the end of its blade. Dazed, Kalmar did not move; he just stared at the man. "Come, eat. Fill your belly; we have much to discuss."

"Is it you?"

His grandfather took a step closer and held out his other hand. "First, come warm yourself by the fire and eat some of the prairie buck I cooked especially for you." Kalmar did not know what to do until he remembered it was all a dream and decided there was no harm in playing his part. He walked towards the campfire, took the knife from Urga, and bit into the meat.

"Now, I've missed that," Kalmar said, as the salty juices filled his mouth and a few drops ran from the corners of his lips. "It tastes fresh-killed."

"I thought you would like it." His grandfather sat down on a large rock and pointed to another rock to his left. "Sit, I'll cut you another piece." Kalmar settled on the rock his grandfather had indicated. The old man pulled out a second knife, leaned over, and started cutting on the meat, which was held over the coals by a forked green tree branch propped up and anchored by two large stones. "Bet you could smell the burning joujou wood I added after the meat was cooking. You always liked it cooked that way." He shook his head. "Joujou wood adds the perfect zing to the meat. Your mother never understood why we liked to eat under the stars; I once told her it was because it was what men do." He dipped his head to add emphasis. "I sometimes wonder if it's because it's the only time we do the cooking and have a chance to taste meat roasted over a fire with joujou wood added to it. She never understood; women never understand the need of men to hunt and cook over an open flame." As Urga spoke, he looked up into the starless sky as if he were talking to the towering trees that surrounded them.

"You're not my grandfather. You look like him, you even sound like him, but the words are wrong."

His grandfather straightened his back and his face sobered. "Does that cause you fear?"

"Fear . . . no. Is there a reason I should be fearful?"

"No, I mean you no harm."

"Then, you aren't my grandfather."

"No, I am not your grandfather, but I thought you would feel more comfortable speaking to me if I looked and acted like him."

" 'More comfortable speaking to me.' I'm dreaming, aren't I?"

"This isn't exactly a dream. Your body is still asleep but your mind is awake."

"Awake? Who are you? What's happening to me?"

"I'm the First Race the peeri told you about." The man smiled, trying to soothe Kalmar's possible anxiety. "Our physiology is different; the best way for us to communicate is through a direct mental link."

Kalmar fought to keep his composure. "The draks told us how different life-forms require different environments to survive; I guess I would die if I were in a room with you."

"No, we can live in the same environment—or rather I can live in your environment—but you can't survive in the wide range of variations I can tolerate. Actually, we've been together many times."

"I don't understand," Kalmar said, studying Urga's face.

His grandfather picked up a long stick and poked the fire. His movements and facial changes were identical to those Kalmar remembered his real grandfather making. Urga noticed his scrutiny. "Would it be better if I weren't in this form?"

Kalmar thought a second. "No, it's all right; but why use human form at all?"

"For us to communicate there must be a common point of reference; otherwise, you wouldn't understand anything I have to tell you. You can't grasp something that you can't imagine; you can't conceive of what you can't conceive."

Kalmar scrunched his face; there was a familiar ring to the old man's words.

Urga leaned over to rest his arms on his legs. "You have a kindred bond with the draks; you comprehend a number of their emotions because you share many of the same perspectives. You can eat the same foods; breathe the same air; you both have two sexes, which can develop a love bond; you both care for and love your offspring; you both have two eyes, arms, and legs; you both need the same environment to live." His eyebrows narrowed. "Yet with all these things in common—and even after their genetic modification—you still have difficulties articulating your perception of an idea to them. Imagine trying to communicate with a species that has four stalked noses, no eyes, looks like a large slug, secretes toxic acid, breathes methane, mates only once in their five-thousand-cycles-of-the-seasons life, and converses with others of its kind by passing different combinations of odorous gas." Urga reached down, picked up a small stone, and started rolling it around in his hand. "Not only would it be difficult for you to convey your thoughts and feelings to such a creature—even though it's your equal in pure intelligence—but what thoughts and feelings you were able to convey, without a common perspective, would be interpreted by them in a way that would be far from your meaning." The old man raised his hands to emphasize his point, just as the real Urga had. "How do you describe the beauty of a flower to a species that sees only by sound echoes? Or speak to them of the love of a child, when their only reaction to one of their adolescent offspring is one of terror, and the need to fight them to the death."

He flipped the stone in his hand over the campfire. "And that pleasant fellow has more in common with your species than most."

Kalmar thought a moment, before asking, "Then what perspective do our two species share? I think I have a harder time understanding your species than I do the creature you just described."

"Actually, we share almost none, but by channeling my thoughts through the perspective of your grandfather, there's a better chance of us understanding one another. This way we not only share a human perspective, but one with a common background."

"I know you aren't my grandfather, yet I find it hard not to think there's a little bit of him in you." Kalmar's brow wrinkled. "I guess that's why it's easy for me to talk to you."

His grandfather lowered his head and nodded. "That's what I hoped."

"How are you able to use my grandfather's image; how can you act just like him?"

The old man's hand moved in an upward arc. "This isn't real; I'm only an image in your mind, an image that isn't an exact re-creation of him. I used your own memories to create this vision. I'm not just like your grandfather; I'm as you remember him. The perspective I have in talking to you is the one that you believe he would have."

Kalmar studied the chiseled face of his companion. "You said we had been together many times."

"On Mystery and in the golden spheres."

"I didn't see you."

"You saw me; you just didn't know what you were looking at," the old man said with a fatherly smile.

Kalmar stared at his grandfather.

"The draks told you Mystery is a living entity and you saw the draks place containers on the two golden spheres; all of those are me."

"Mystery. You're a *moon?"*

"Among other things. You see, I'm spread throughout our galaxy, in many forms and sizes. I'm in every solar system that's spawned even the simplest life."

"There must be billions of you."

"No, I'm just one with parts of me in billions of places." His grandfather let his statement sink in before continuing. "Just as your body is made up of millions of cells, my body is composed of many parts but only one consciousness."

Verna's face lacked the stress lines that Dera remembered commanding her old friend's expression during the last months of her life. It pleased Dera that the bit of memory used to re-create her confidante depicted Verna happy and relaxed. Dera marveled at Verna's image, the way her fine, gray hair fell in little tresses against her neck. Each time Verna turned her head the ringlets bounced just as Dera remembered them doing on the real Verna. If the First Race chose Verna's image to calm her, it worked. They sat in Dera's spot in the nutwood grove, a place Verna never visited during all those cycles of the seasons she counseled Dera. To a troubled child with a marred face, the nutwood grove had offered solitude, a place to hide from the prying eyes of people who did not understand the pain inflicted by their curiosity; even though it was only a dream, sharing the serenity of her hideaway with her old friend now seemed natural. Dera wondered why she had never invited Verna here while she had the chance. She studied the illusion of her mentor's image. The apparition never tried to fool her, admitting during the first few seconds of their meeting that she was only a mental projection into Dera's sleeping brain. She readily accepted Verna's explanation for the need to meet during her sleep, and even though she knew the familiar surroundings were only a figment, their familiarity freed her mind to once again feel the safety of her childhood sanctuary—a contentment she had never felt in any other place. She smiled as she looked away from Verna to listen to the music of the brook's babbling water; Dera recognized every note.

"If I hadn't held you in my arms when you died, and watched the flames consume your body, you could convince me you are Verna."

"As I said, it's not my intent to deceive you, but only put you at ease as we communicate."

"To appear in the image of someone who . . . who's not now living could make someone uneasy. Your efforts could have frightened me."

"I considered that possibility, but isn't it normal for humans to dream about someone who has died?"

"You're right." Dera nodded, grimacing. "I knew I was dreaming—even though everything's so real—and it was easier for me to accept seeing Verna and my mind keeps reacting to you as if you were Verna."

"That's why I came to you in a dream. I could've projected myself into your mind when you were awake—"

"No, you're right; it's easier this way."

"Good, it's best if these first meetings are as undisruptive as possible."

"You speak as if you have a lot of these . . . meetings."

"A few. It's what makes my scattered existence bearable," Verna said as she put her hands on her hips. She straightened her back, making a slight moan. "Joints are sore."

"Do you feel the pain or is that a resonance of Verna's personality I hear?"

"A little of both," the old woman said, as she laughed at Dera's hint of sarcasm. "I can't share your perspective without feeling the aches and pains, as well as the power of the intellect, of the image I borrowed from your memory."

The lines of Dera's face became more angular. "These 'few' you speak of—tens, hundreds?"

"Millions," the old woman said. Dera's facial reaction prompted Verna to continue. "I've communicated with every species in the galaxy that has evolved to a point where they might be of significance."

"We might be significant?"

"Possibly. Ask again in a million cycles of the seasons."

A part of me travels in the golden spheres, transferring gathered information to other parts of me like the nerve impulses in your body. The container placed on the golden sphere by the draks right before you left Elom carried a piece of me small enough to put in your knapsack; encapsulated in that piece was all the information I had gathered since the last transport left Elom. When the sphere came to retrieve you, it brought a part of me that held all of the new information I needed to function on Elom properly."

"Then each piece of you must have its . . . their own con-sciousnesses. . . ." Snook argued with his childhood mentor. The two sat on the tree-covered peak of a ridge overlooking the turquoise waters of Lake Dorad; Ardly's Member, an eighteen-mile-long strait, connected the lake—actually an inland sea—to the Great Ocean. The ridge ran south along the crest of a chain of foothills that shadowed the Tarton Mountains before they both veered to the west, forming an escarpment bordering part of the massive lake. The Mookyn village nestled between the sparkling lake and the eastern base of the hill below the ridge. Snook and his mentor had made the four-hour climb to the ridge top two to three times a week for most of Snook's life; from this pinnacle,

Snook's mentor taught him how to hold himself above the frays of ordinary men and let loose the Seeker that resides repressed in every person. Named Olum by his mother, but dubbed Snook by his mentor, who gave him the nickname early in his training because the antics of the hyperactive youth reminded his tutor of the small darting snooker fish that schooled in the shallows of the lake's shoreline. In time, Snook's mind proved to be nimbler than even his name implied. After his mentor's revelations on the ridge top, Snook cast off his worldly shackles and dedicated his life to finding the truth about Geerna and the myths of her abduction. He had lived his short life for this moment.

"It's a concept you may never fully understand . . ."

It's a concept you may never fully understand," Urga said. "Humans think about one thing at a time. You might think about something as you walk down a trail and have a second thought when you need to step over a fallen tree limb, but for the most part, you think along a single plane. My thoughts occupy millions of planes, evaluating countless situations simultaneously. Just as your brain utilizes millions of specialized cells, acting as receptors for your senses of taste, touch, sight, hearing, and smell, I also utilize parts of me to gather the data I need. Your body transmits information to your brain by nerve impulses in an infinitesimal amount of time. You live a scant hundred cycles of the seasons; during that life you may face dangers, situations where your decisions can mean life or death." Urga pointed to the scars on Kalmar's face. "You must gather and process information fast; you must do this in order to survive." The old man turned his whole body towards Kalmar. "I face no imminent danger; a supernova could destroy part of me, but since I am spread among billions of star systems, I would scarcely know it. I've lived since the dawn of the universe, for billions of cycles of the seasons, and I'll live for many billions of cycles of the seasons in the future. I will be there when the last stars in the universe finally flicker out; only then will I share the fate your race faces every day. To you, the passage of time is a dreaded inevitability; where, to me, the flow of time is my one trusted companion." Urga looked at the cooking prairie buck, then leaned over and turned the nutwood branch so another side of the meat faced the flame. "From the senses in the extremities of your body"—he lifted his hands and wiggled his fingers—"your body gathers information at a fraction of the speed it takes me to receive information from all of my parts. The golden spheres are my nerve's synapses; they fold the fabric of space-time and jump across the vastness of the galaxy carrying information to all the parts of my body, the information I use to make my decisions. It may take several cycles of the seasons for a single bit of information to spread across the galaxy to all my parts, but as I said, I'm not in danger; unlike you, I don't have to make quick decisions." He grinned. "I've been mulling over you humans for several hundred thousand cycles of the seasons. And, considering the scale of time—the length of your life compared to mine—I make my decisions faster than you do."

"Then you're not a god?"

"I suppose it's all in how you define 'god.'"

"You're not the ultimate Being?"

His grandfather seemed to mull over his answer before answering. "I believe there is Something greater than me. Something that has had as much to do with my existence as I've had with yours. Before my life fades from this universe, I hope to have the same kind of discussion with It as you are having with me. All that I am yearns for that event."

But the golden spheres and their gravity generators couldn't have been formed by nature," Dera said.

"No, but you need to understand a few things not revealed to you by the learning machines. In the universe's infancy—with the death of the first fledgling stars and the supernovae of the larger ones—the newly created heavier elements were flung into the expanding void. The ashes of these stars collected around gravity pits and in time formed large, swirling, cosmic clouds. These clouds provided the materials for the next generation of stars, and the first planets. In one of these cosmic cauldrons of hot gases, a concentration of cooling silicon vapor mixed with traces of nitrogen, lithium, cobalt, potassium and a few of the metallic elements . . ." Verna lifted and shaped her hands as if holding a small globe. "While this mountain-sized concentration of gaseous soup cooled, subatomic particles—formed during the first seconds of creation— continually bombarded it. The subatomic particles energized the agglomeration of elements. When the first planets solidified, among the debris left over was me. The chances of my creation, of an elemental mixture having a chemical reaction sparked by subatomic particles, must be a quadrillion to one. I am an aberration; I have discovered no other life like me. If it were there—in this galaxy at least—I would have found it." Verna smiled, and then chuckled. "From Verna's viewpoint, what I just said sounds pretty outlandish." Her expression hardened. "Only a great species can ever learn to see truth from the perspective of another species. That will be your . . . humanity's . . . greatest test."

"At our judging?"

Verna ignored Dera's question.

Sometime during the first billion cycles of the seasons, I became aware of my own existence, but it took another five hundred million cycles of the seasons before I was able to sense my surroundings. During much of this time I floated in interstellar space, drifting between star systems." His grandfather's words mesmerized

Kalmar. Urga used the same inflections in his voice as his name-sake. Kalmar stopped trying to separate them and mentally treated the person sitting in front of him as a reincarnation of the real Urga. Kalmar knew that was not the case; however, it made it easier for him to rationalize everything in his mind.

The campfire crackled as Kalmar stared at the hypnotic dance of the flames. His mind raced. "Then you weren't always spread throughout the galaxy."

"That only happened during my third billion cycles of the seasons of existence. After spending almost all of my second billion cycles of the seasons theorizing on how to travel faster than the speed of light, I discovered how to use gravity generators to fold space-time. I divided into billions of segments and embarked on a quest to find other life."

Cabyl sobbed as she clung to her mother, even though she knew the woman she held was only an illusion. In time, her mother gently pulled herself from Cabyl's grasp and kissed her on the forehead.

"You judge yourself too harshly."

"But if I had just said something, you . . . my mother . . . would still be alive."

"All I know about what happened is what I glean from your memories, even those memories you suppress. I think you know your mother knew something was wrong between you and your father. It was her choice not to confront him with her suspicions." The image of her mother stroked her hair as Cabyl closed her eyes and leaned her head back.

The sound of the waves pounding the beach made Snook realize how much he missed the place of his youth. "I left here seeking truth. The only truth I've really found has been within my heart," Snook said, talking as if the man with him was the one who had guided him through his adolescence.

"How do you mean?"

"Cabyl."

"Cabyl?"

"When I'm near her my heart beats faster, yet my inner-spirit feels at ease."

The face of his old mentor became animated. "Is it love you feel?"

"If it isn't love, I'm not sure my heart could stand it if I ever did find it."

"I don't wish to offend"—the old mentor made a slight bow—"but she's not perfect; she has many imperfections." The tone and inflections in the voice were just as Snook remembered them, yet the logic behind the voice was unfamiliar. He would not have been surprised if his mentor had mentioned Snook's imperfections; however, it was totally out of character for the old sage to speak negatively about someone not there to defend them-selves. For the first time, Snook recognized a different intellect behind the words of his mentor. Snook did not think the words unduly harsh, just directed in a way his mentor would not have gone.

"I'm aware of her imperfections," he said stiffly.

"And yet you continue to love her?"

Snook studied the old man; the visual illusion still revealed no flaws. In a way, he was glad he could distinguish the fact that he was talking to someone other than his lifelong teacher. "I don't love her despite her imperfections; I love her, in part, because of them. If she were perfect, she wouldn't need my love . . . only because of her imperfections is she human . . . perfection doesn't love. Perfec-tion stands on its own." Snook was not sure from where the words came; he said them without thinking, but once he'd said them he recognized it was how he felt.

"You have grown."

"You know such things?"

"Not normally. I can tap your memories, but your emotions are much more difficult." The old man pulled at the end of his beard. "Your feelings are of a species which has grown past the primitive reflexes of survival."

The Gray Beard shrugged his shoulders. "I know little of such things. I do know, however, that Nutan's feelings are as strong for you as yours are for her."

Izzy watched the movements of his companion; he was in every way an exact personification of his old tutor. "Teacher—if it is all right to call you that—" The Gray Beard nodded. "Why didn't you appear to us when we were conscious; perhaps you could have communicated with all seven of us at the same time?"

"I am communicating with all of you at the same time, and as I said earlier, your minds are conscious; it is your bodies that are asleep. Moreover, at some point, I will communicate with your group when everyone is in a fully conscious state, at a time when I can better explain what plans I have for you."

I found a fragile carbon-based life form," Verna said. "I nurtured them until they reached a high level of intelligence, but the species did not endure. My interference and modifications sapped their motivation for life. I took their genetic structure, modified it one last time—to its most basic components—and placed it in the ice heads of countless comets across the galaxy. Over time the comets collided with billions of planets; that genetic seeding produced most of the carbon-based life in the galaxy." The memory enhancements allowed Dera to understand what Verna was saying, but what she was saying did not answer all of Dera's questions.

What about the Judging?" Nutan asked.
"Your Judging is not on Pandeelee. Humanity's judging is on Earth, your home planet."

"Then why did you bring us here if not to judge us?"

"To prepare you for your role in your species' future." Seldan, Nutan's father, lifted an eyebrow. "And I'm not the judge of their fate."

"But you judged the draks and when they failed you destroyed their ancestors."

"The destruction of the draks' ancestors on Earth was caused by an act of nature. I had the peeri prepare Elom for the draks but they never evolved on their own to a point that would allow me to communicate with them. I left Elom as a sanctuary for the draks. When your species evolved to a sapient level, I had the peeri modify a portion of Elom for your ancestors. The peeri also modified the draks to give their lives a purpose besides just existing. I grasp the draks' disillusionment and frustration." The man shifted his jaw to one side as his eyes drifted. Then he turned to Nutan. "Perhaps there is still a place for them in your lives." Seldan pursed his lips as he nodded. "They possess many attributes that might aid you and your group." A broad smile slowly commandeered his face. "And your and Izzy's children."

Nutan blushed, then looked at what she knew was only an image from her memories. "Thank you, father." A tear crept down her cheek. "I miss you."

For the most part, I leave species to develop on their own," Verna said. "From time to time, I do remove a few specimens to communicate with and study as I did with Geerna and your ancestors.

I've sworn to myself not to repeat the mistakes of the past. I only take specimens before the species is fully developed. Only under extreme circumstances do I modify them, and I seldom reintroduce them to the general population of their home planet."

Dera stood up. "Then why have you controlled our lives since the time of Geerna if we're not to be judged?"

"That was Geerna's wish."

"Geerna?"

"She's the first one of your species with whom I communicated. She was convinced I was a god and that I had taken her to be my acolyte. Many races have mistaken me for a god."

"I can understand that." The lines of Dera's face hardened. "You meet the criteria to be Shetow. You live forever, you're spread across the galaxy, and you did play a part in our creation."

"True, but I am not a god in the true sense. I do not know nor can I change the future."

"Your knowledge seems so vast."

"That is only because of fifteen billion cycles of the seasons of reflection and the collective intellect of the millions of species to whom I am mentally linked."

But why did you appear as her?" Arasima sputtered. The lines of her reddened face contorted.

"She was the one who had the paramount presence in your memories," Raya answered.

"But I loathe her." She shook her fist. "She was my major taunter."

"And the primary influence on your character."

Every hair and feature of her childhood nemesis was unchanged, as was the effect she had on her.

"You had no female friends in your village. Your younger brother was ashamed of you until you grew older and, by that time, you had cut him out of your life. The mores of the People kept the males of your own village out of reach; however, from them you learned the effect you had on men. Your parents were preoccupied in their own turbulent relationship. Who else was I to choose but the one you wanted to impress the most?"

"I don't care what you . . . Raya thinks of me."

"You tell yourself that, but your deeper feelings show that is not the case."

Arasima's bottom lip protruded past her upper lip as she gritted her teeth.

Raya smiled. "Arasima, you have much to offer this group. They will meet you halfway if you will give them the chance."

Her puffy eyes considered Raya's likeness. She dropped her head after she convinced herself there was no reason for her to fight the obvious. "The other three females have secured themselves a partner; there are none left for me. I will always be considered a rival."

Raya walked over and put her arm around Arasima's shoulders. "Perhaps your romantic future lies beyond your group of seven."

Arasima turned her head to look into Raya's eyes, only inches away.

"Your group is about to expand. Don't forget the lessons you have learned in the last cycle of the season and you will find a man who will love you with all his heart." Raya cocked her head. "That is, if you will desire him with your heart as well as your body."

"There is someone for me?" Arasima said, as meekly as a child.

"At this moment I'm in the thoughts of one I would think could love you if you can breach the walls he has built around his own heart."

"Do you mean someone from the other two groups?"

Raya stroked Arasima's hair and did not answer.

Y our blemish gives you great pain," Verna said.

"It seems so unfair."

"Is life meant to be fair?"

"You . . . the real Verna always told me I was the culmination of thousands of cycles of the seasons of Concentrating the Traits. If I am so special, why must I also be hideous?"

"I have found there's a purpose behind almost everything," Verna said softly.

"A purpose behind my hideousness? Even a mind that stretches across the galaxy can't conjure up an explanation"—Dera placed her fingertips against her blemish—"for this."

"Do you remember where you're sleeping?"

Dera paused. "Kalmar's bed."

"In Kalmar's bed," said a taunting Verna. "In the arms of the man who would have won the Borrac if not for Arasima's scheming; and why, pray tell, if you are so hideous, did he bed you— pity?"

The bite in Verna's words stunned Dera.

Verna's hard expression softened. "My child," she said in a tone reminiscent of the counselor Dera had loved, "Verna wanted you to believe there was a reason for everything—even for your blemish. I believe she may have been correct. Your blemish is what gave you your humility and molded your character. Without a counterbalance to your overwhelming Concentration of the Traits and a bridle on your beauty, you would have become an arrogant person. A person detested by others and one useless to Geerna's plan."

Verna reached out, grasped Dera's chin in one hand, and turned her face to the side. With the fingertips of her other hand, the old woman gently stroked the scarlet discoloration covering the young woman's cheek. "I can remove your facial blemish if you wish, but you must never forget the person it has allowed you to become." A soft smile formed on Verna's lips. "It's essential that you remember true beauty is invisible to someone who does not take the time to learn to know you. As you have already discovered, those who love you don't do it in spite of your blemish— they no longer see your facial imperfection." Verna released Dera's chin and pushed Dera's auburn hair behind her ear, revealing all of the birthmark. "My child, everyone has blemishes. You are fortunate that the one that gives you the greatest anguish is one that all can see. Those with troubled hearts or conflicted inner-spirits are not as lucky as you; they often don't recognize their blemishes, much less know how to rectify them."

The flames made repeated attempts at leaping beyond the cooking meat, but they always fell short. Kalmar felt the fire's radiation; his freshly healed claw marks were more sensitive to the heat than the rest of his face. He leaned back to distance himself from the source of his discomfort. He never saw the sunset, but it was now dark and the firelight cast giant shadows of his grandfather and him on the stand of tree trunks behind them. Urga studied Kalmar's face. "I perceive that you're not proud of the scars the cave lion gave you."

"People made more of them than they should. They think they're a sign of bravery."

"And you think they're a sign of what?"

"Without Snook there to distract the cave lion, it would have killed me."

"Possibly." The old man nodded. "But the creature died from your arrows. Your bravery's the same."

Kalmar shook his head. "Maybe, but Snook was the brave one. He faced the cave lion without weapons"—he turned his palms up—"with only his bare hands."

"Snook doesn't see it that way. He thinks you are the bravest man he knows."

"He does? But he knows the scars are more of a sign of my stupidity than of courage."

"Snook knows that courage isn't something you can see in a person's face; people make a mistake when they try to read a person's valor by outward appearances. The courage Snook sees in you is invisible to the eye."

Kalmar smiled. "I guess you're right; since the day I met Snook, I've thought him the bravest person I knew and—"

"He shows no outward signs of his courage."

Kalmar looked hard into the eyes of the old man. "You have the wisdom of my grandfather."

"No, I have the wisdom you remember him having. Courage is a concept that has no meaning to me. It doesn't take courage for me to face life when I have no concept of fear. My perception of courage is the one I get from you, Snook, and the rest of your group. Thank you for that insight."

Cabyl's mother pulled the end of her own chemise from where it was tucked in her skirt and used it to wipe Cabyl's face. "I can sense from his own memories that Snook is a considerate and tender man, a man who would never hurt you, a man who loves you deeply." The woman reached over and pushed a wisp of Cabyl's hair away from her eyes. "Your mother would be happy for you."

For the first time, Cabyl smiled.

But you modified Geerna," Snook said, with the ring of challenge in his voice.

"Yes, she pestered me to the point I didn't know what else to do. It was after her genetic modification and knowledge enhancement that she, with the peeri's help, developed the plan the humans on Elom have followed for these many thousands of cycles of the seasons."

D o you know why my grandfather hunted the cave lion?"
The stately old man sat a little straighter. "I don't know for
sure, but I think it was just another sign that I had to act. The soci-
eties Geerna and the peeris created began to deteriorate. Things
that had never happened before began to happen: Cabyl's father
molested her and killed her mother, Snook's mother committed
suicide, and the girls of Arasima's age group teased her to the point
that it warped her personality. Dera's blemish caused her to withdraw into herself, and both the Medoras and Elders began to doubt
their purpose. Your grandfather went on a hunt knowing he would
die, and you, foolishly, did the same. The system would have completely collapsed in another hundred cycles of the seasons. If I was
ever to communicate with your species, I had to do it now."

B ut why? Why would Geerna inflict this controlled life on us?"
exclaimed Dera.

"She felt it was the best way to ensure the survival of the race,"
Verna said.

There was a blank look on Dera's face.

"Geerna was an extraordinary woman, even before her modification. Once exposed to vast knowledge, she came to believe
there would come a time when humanity would falter. She knew
her species to be not only bright, cunning, and resourceful, but also
capable of unspeakable cruelty, and she feared that cruelty could
lead to its own genocide."

Shaken, it was a few moments before Dera could respond.
"But how could directing our lives on Elom save humanity?"

"It was her plan to send the best of you back to Earth if the
time ever came when the future of your species was in doubt. Even
though I told her I would not intervene if the situation ever arose,
I could counsel those who were going to be sent back to Earth.

She knew from my earlier failure that modification of the race would only exacerbate the problem, so she devised a plan to concentrate the finest human traits; she believed that by keeping your numbers small, and by selective mating, the humans on Elom would surpass those on Earth in intellect."

The Judging that Geerna prepared for—" His grandfather reached over and patted Kalmar's knee. "It's one on Earth, and your fellow humans there will dictate their own fate—I'm only a spectator, but I have a plan that should increase your wisdom to match your newly acquired knowledge."

THIRTY-EIGHT

Geerna and the peeri even foresaw the need of bringing members of other human races to Elom," Nutan said.

"I wonder why the races weren't mixed?" Kalmar asked. He looked around the room at his companions. They had all awoken from telling dreams. Each person's story was different, but the knowledge gained was similar.

"Evidently that was also in Geerna's and the peeri's plan. We just hadn't reached that far until today," Cabyl said.

"And that is what's about to happen," Arasima said as she cut her eyes towards the two towers visible out the windows.

Dera sat leaning against Kalmar, lost in her own thoughts. Kalmar put his arm around her waist and she turned her head and smiled at him. Kalmar's actions brought her back into the group's conversation. "It lives vicariously through us," she said.

"What?" Kalmar exclaimed.

"It has no emotions of its own. The reason it links with our minds is to experience our feelings."

"Well," said Nutan, "this group should have filled its needs for many cycles of the seasons." They all laughed.

———

Were you told how many planets we would visit before we go to Earth?" Izzy asked.

"I would think," Nutan said, "we will go to as many as it takes for the First Race to feel we have broadened our ability to empathize with other species."

"The First Race thinks we will be of greater use to our kindred if we have an appreciation of different viewpoints," Kalmar added.

Dera looked around the room, her eyes meeting theirs, each one in turn. "The image of Verna told me 'only a great species can ever learn to see truth from the perspective of another species.'"

"And that," added Snook, "'will be humanity's greatest test.'"

Silence covered the room like a morning fog.

"Do you think we will ever return to Elom?" Izzy asked.

"I don't care if we ever go back. There is nothing for me there," Arasima said, with a bite in her words.

Cabyl looked up at Snook's face. "I would like to see Berkana and tell her I am well. Besides that, returning to Elom means little to me."

"I have found the answer that all Seekers have sought since the time of Geerna," Snook said. "Hopefully I will someday be able to share that truth with the others of my kind."

"I know I speak for Nutan, Izzy, Dera, and myself," Kalmar said, looking to each one as he said their names. "Our absence will cause our family members to worry. I think we should ask that a message be delivered to them by the draks saying we love them, miss them, and hope to one day see them again."

Dera nodded. "I will miss them too, but think what adventure awaits us. To travel across the galaxy learning other species' thoughts and ideas must be the greatest gift that the First Race . . . Shetow . . . could ever give us."

———

We leave for Pandeelee in two days," Kalmar said as he stood up. "We should go meet our new companions." Everyone stood and walked towards the door with Arasima in the lead.

Kalmar stopped and pulled Dera to him. He looked into her green eyes a moment, then kissed her. When he pulled back, a grin started to cover his face.

"You're not upset that I didn't have the entire blemish removed?" Dera asked.

Kalmar looked at the reddish discoloration that now only covered a thumbnail-sized spot on her cheek. "No, I love you just the same, but why did you leave any of it?"

"After all those cycles of the seasons of feeling sorry for myself, my dream Verna opened my eyes to the importance of the blemish in my life. The blemish shaped how people treated me; that interaction molded my personality. Part of me is the blemish; to remove it would be removing that part of me that constantly reminds me who I am." She reached out and gently touched the smooth skin of his now scarless cheeks. "I would understand if you had kept your scars; they were a testament to your courage."

"My scars were earned on a fool's errand, more a testament to my stupid arrogance than any noble courage. If I had kept them, they would have been a constant reminder of my not accepting your Choosing."

"But don't you see?" Dera looked deep into his eyes. "You did accept me." She leaned over and kissed him on the cheek.

GLOSSARY

Boboi—Largest of the four moons of Elom. Next to Salune, Boboi is the largest object in the Elom sky and makes a complete orbit every 18.38 days.

Cave Lion *(Panthera leo spelaea)*—Also known as the European or Eurasian cave lion. The extinct feline, seen in prehistoric cave art, is the largest feline ever to have lived. In the Pleistocene, the lion was widespread across Europe and stood 25 percent larger than its modern African descendants.

Eeo(Ē-ō)—A brown dwarf star and the binary partner of Salune. Eeo is approximately .0765 the mass of the sun, or 75 of Jupiter.

Elom—Planet. Orbits Salune and its binary partner, the brown dwarf Eeo. Four moons orbit the planet: Boboi, the largest; Menstur, second largest; Quiron, the farthest and the slowest; and Mystery, the nearest, smallest, and fastest.

Elom Year—Approximately 486.66 Elom days; approximately 1.231 earth year.

Elom Month—34 Elom days; 14 months in a year plus 10 days for the Gathering.

Elom Day—18 Elom hours, or approximately 25.05 earth hours.

Elom Hour—approximately 83.5 earth minutes.

Long Tusk—Mammoth.

Menstur—One of Elom's four moons.

Mystery—The smallest and closest of the four moons of Elom; makes a complete orbit of Elom 9.27 times a day.

Salune—A G-class star with a mass 1.124 times that of the sun. With its binary, the brown dwarf Eeo, the star that Elom orbits.

Quiron—Farthest of the four moons of Elom, it makes a complete orbit of Elom every 43.57 days.